Indigo Bend

Books by Alice Walworth Graham

INDIGO BEND

ROMANTIC LADY

NATCHEZ WOMAN

LOST RIVER

ALICE WALWORTH GRAHAM

Indigo Bend

PEOPLES BOOK CLUB, CHICAGO

This is a special edition published exclusively
for the members of THE PEOPLES BOOK CLUB, P. O.
Box 6570A, Chicago 80, Illinois, and 25 Hollinger
Road, Toronto 13, Ontario, Canada. It was
originally published by Doubleday & Company, Inc.

For Roane Fleming Byrnes

Indigo Bend

Chapter One

[1871—] LOUISE opened the shutters so Alan would see the lamp-light when he came back tired from the country and the house would look more cheerful for him. After the long oppressive heat of a summer day, nighttime was welcome, with its depth of shadows and thin starshine. Louise had taken time to pick the roses and sprays of clematis and put them in a wide bowl on the table. Alan would notice. A new copy of his favorite magazine had come today. He would be too tired to read it when he came, but he would to-morrow. Louise planned to make him rest and read after the long ride back and forth. Alan said Louise spoiled him, and she did as much as she could. Her brother was younger than she was, and he had been wounded at Shiloh, and had never been really well or strong since then.

"How'd you ever scare up the money for the subscription?" Alan asked her when the first copy of the magazine had come.

"Here and there. Do you realize how often we've had bone soup?"

"You oughtn't to encourage me to read. You ought to put a hoe in my hands."

"Once in a while we ought to find out what's going on in the world outside of Natchez."

But Alan was right about the hoe. She sighed, wishing she liked the routine of household tasks, and nursing and darning. Her overstuffed workbasket reproached her. She had loved music and pictures and books, and finery and lively conversation. There was none of that in her existence now. Louise spent her time taking care of her little boy, and her father, who had been ill, hopelessly ill, for over a year. He had fallen asleep, and little Tommy was asleep too, clutching a canoe he had made for himself out of a piece of branch, and Louise had come downstairs to the library to wait for her brother Alan.

The library was a stolid sort of room. Its heavy dark furniture, black marble mantelpiece, and big table, topped with black marble too, absorbed daylight and lamplight. But it was more durable than the brighter rooms, and Louise used it, keeping the parlors shut up. The door was open into the unlighted back parlor and a ray of lamplight fell on Louise's piano. She meditated about moving it into the library, since it wasn't possible to warm either of the parlors in winter. But then she had no time for piano playing these days.

Now she went into the parlor and opened the piano, and lit the candles on the brackets and struck a chord softly. Her hand against the keys looked dark and thin. It was a long time since she had heard any good music, or had even touched the piano herself. Once she had played quite well, though her music lessons, like the rest of her education, had been interrupted by the war and never taken up again. And how she loved music! As a child, her violent feelings about it had led her to imagine she had some large talent, some touch of genius. Then she had gone to New Orleans, and had heard a great pianist. At once she had known. Not long hours of work, and she had been willing to work, or her ardor would give it to her. Her closed piano had cost the world nothing, but she had learned not to despise her little hearthside ability. She could play when her sisters and friends and cousins had wanted to sing or dance, and she could make up songs for Tommy. Anything that could have put such a restless, delicate baby to sleep was worth something! And Tom had loved to listen to her music.

She struck only the one chord, but in her mind and heart she heard the rest of the melody. You had to be happy to stand that music, with its stealing rhythm. It was almost as if the room had filled again with people, young people, talking and laughing, and Tom had come to stand beside her, as he had that day, and whisper, "Marry me! Marry me now!" She had jumped up, and flung her arms around him, and kissed him in front of everybody.

Her parents had tried to persuade her to wait, she hadn't been quite sixteen. But she had defied them. "If we can't marry here at home we'll run away!" Her parents had yielded, and there had been a quiet wedding, and a short happy honeymoon, then Tom had gone back to the fighting. There had been letters, and a letter from Vicksburg in the spring of '63. And one day Peter, Tom's body servant had come to the house, and had told Louise that Tom was very ill, and had taken refuge in a wreck of a house across the river, up toward Vicksburg. It sounded almost impossible, but Louise, pregnant at the time, hadn't hesitated. She had set out at once with Peter in a mule-drawn cart he had scavenged.

There had been something dreamlike, divorced from reality, from the context of daily living, about that journey. Yet each detail was vivid, and always would be. Those long, interminable miles, through the day, all through the night. On the way Louise had found out what had happened. Tom knew that part of the country in every detail, and he had been spying on Grant's operations, and sending the information back to the Confederate forces in Vicksburg. Like a shadow, Tom had evaded the Yankees. Not a bullet had touched him, but a sharp branch had scratched his arm. Just a scratch, but blood poisoning had set in, and Peter had half carried, half dragged him to the burned-out shell of a nearby plantation house. One of the slaves had never left the place and was taking care of Tom while Peter set off to Natchez to bring Louise.

Perhaps one reason the trip had seemed so unreal to Louise was her physical wretchedness through it all. Peter had hidden a skiff, and they had left the wagon, and Peter had rowed across the river. There had been dark clouds hanging low over the swampy Louisiana shore; the tangled matted willows had twisted in the wind, and the water had swirled around the skiff, shaking it and threatening it. Afraid, she supposed she had been, but she had been too preoccupied to worry about danger. She didn't remember feeling any fear, not even when the Yankee gunboat had come around the bend and had begun firing, and the Confederate batteries on the heights had answered the fire. For a time, the skiff had been caught in the cross fire, but Peter had swung out of it, into a little cove where a creek met the river. Then she had wanted to scream, because gray, furry spiders had swarmed over the oars and into the skiff. She would have jumped out, if Peter hadn't showed her more spiders in the water.

Once across the river, they had to walk a mile or more, struggling through the mud and tangle of the swamp until they reached the ruin of the house. It was the Burns plantation, and Tom had visited here, on house parties and hunting trips. Peter knew it too, and had known where to hide Tom. They found him lying in an undamaged room in the wing. There had been the shock of seeing him. Then he had opened his eyes and had known her, and she had gone to him.

"Eez," he had managed to whisper. "You shouldn't have come— bad—for you and the baby."

"The baby'll be all right. Don't worry." She had pressed her face against his. Even now she could recall her thrill of terror at the fever's mortal heat.

He had even smiled. "Baby—so grownup of you——" Then he had said "Watch," and had tried to lift his hand, and she had understood what he had meant. His watch was for the baby. That was all they had been able to say to each other.

In a way Louise missed Tom more than she had immediately after his death. Then all of herself had been given over to the baby. She had become a primitive creature in the battle to make the delicate little thing live and thrive. Newly born, Tommy had seemed to be precariously made of little bones like twigs, and on his face there had been such an expression of world weariness it had frightened her. He might not like the world where he found himself, he had threatened her, and might slip from her grasp. He was healthy enough now and the slackening of the terrors and the intensity of those first three years had let her wake up to the life around her.

Louise had never spoken a word about any part of that journey. There was no one alive now who could share it with her. The old servant who had nursed Tom had lingered on in her cabin behind the big house until she had died of a fever. Peter had died during the last year of the war. The past was locked away, to be remembered, to be relived, as Louise had relived it tonight. When he was old enough, she would tell Tommy all of it, and give him his father's watch.

The sound of a horse clumping up to the door roused her. That must be Alan coming back from the plantation. Louise went to the door to meet him. "You must be worn out."

"Sort of tired," he admitted. It was a day's ride from the plantation. That was in good weather. In bad weather the road was almost impassable.

"We missed you." Louise kissed her brother. "Look at you, you're positively gray!"

"It's mostly dust. Is there anything to eat?" Alan came on into the house and followed Louise to the library. When you looked at him like this you would never realize how young he still was.

"Sit down, I'll get your supper." She led him into the dining room and pushed him into a chair. He sat at the table, dumb from fatigue, while Louise moved back and forth from the pantry. When everything was ready, he roused himself to smile at her. "How nice and civilized it looks. Silver and flowers and lamplight! Home's heaven, after being out there!"

"Is it so bad?" It must be, if Alan was moved to such admiration of things here.

"Well——"

"Not now," she interrupted. "Tell me later."

"How's Father?"

"About the same." She didn't enlarge on the hopelessness of their father's illness, or say she had been up with him for hours last night.

"Is there any use my going up to see him now?"

"No, he's asleep."

Alan had been gone from home for five days. The first look at his face had told Louise that he was anything but buoyant about conditions at the plantation, and she wanted him to eat, and to rest a little before he again took on either the problems here at home or embarked on a discussion of the place out there in the country.

"Let's see what happened here. New kittens, for one thing. Five, and Tommy won't let me give any of them away. And there's going to be another baby at the Corwins."

"I don't suppose they can give it away."

The Corwins were their next door neighbors. They lived in a large, rambling house, with galleries and columns, surrounded by a sweep of neglected lawns, gardens, and pastures. Louis Corwin was harassed by the necessity of providing for his mother, and an unmarried sister, and an everincreasing quantity of children. His wife Bella was inefficient, dull, and given to floods of easy tears.

"I've stopped the mousehole by the fireplace so we don't need kittens," Louise said. "Anyway, I don't like cats catching mice. Traps are more humane." She buttered a cold biscuit, put fresh fig preserves on it, and gave it to Alan.

"Aren't you using too much butter when the cow's ailing?"

"The Duels sent us some. And the cow's all right. She ate too many watermelon rinds, that's all."

Whenever Louise was with Alan, or thought of him, and she thought of him nearly always, she forgot about herself. After he had been wounded, the doctors had thought he would lose his left leg below the knee, but they had managed to save it. Now one foot was a little shorter than the other, but he had learned to walk well enough with it, and never complained. Only once he had said he wished they had cut the plagued thing off and had given him a wooden one. "They tell me it hurts after it's gone, so I'd better hang on to it. I'd rather have it aching where it belongs, attached to me, than aching way off buried some place."

He was well again, after a fashion, but he was no longer young, except in years. Neither was Louise. The emotions and violence of the war had caught them up and burned them up and flung them aside, stranded in the wreckage. They would have to pick themselves up and go on.

"What about the place, Alan?" He had finished his supper and seemed to be brooding. Louise thought he wanted to discuss it now.

"It's in bad shape, but I expected that. Very run down. But Indigo's got some fine land, that creek bottom's rich. The house is solid enough. It's just a box of a thing, and the roof needs fixing. It would take money to fix things up."

"Money doesn't exist." The family had never lived on the plantation. It was about twenty-two miles down the river from Natchez, but the road was not straight. It wound in and out, and was dusty in dry weather and deep with mud in bad weather. You could reach it by steamboat and that was an easier trip, though you had to make allowances for the time you spent waiting for the boat to appear. The way down to Indigo by river took about four hours, the way back, pushing against the current, took longer, five or six, depending on the strength of the current and the number of times the boat stopped on its way to Natchez. There had once been a capable overseer on Indigo, but he had gone to war, and after the war had moved to Texas. The house had been deserted ever since, and the land mostly unused since '62. The war and the troubles after the war, had made Louise almost forget about Indigo. Before the war it had been only one of the Hamilton plantations. Most of their land had been across the river. They had lost all of that. Now, except for this house in Natchez, they didn't own anything else except Indigo.

Even the house in the middle of Natchez no longer had its original land attached to it. It had once extended almost to the bluffs, but a good part of it had been sold or had gone to pay taxes. It still kept, like the Corwin place, more lawns and gardens and pastures than one gardener, one horse, and one cow could use or keep in order. The house itself, built in the thirties, was now too big for the people living in it. Across the street was the Duel house, another large, rambling mansion, with only two people, old people at that, huddled in it. The pretty little cottage at the corner, once the gardener's house, was rented now to the Lydells. Then there was the Corwin place. Beyond this block was some rough, unused land, then a huddle of smaller houses began, straggling towards the heart of town.

"Alan, could you get some one to live out at Indigo and work the place?"

"Who?"

"Offhand, I can't imagine."

"Well, I've given it lots of thought, and there isn't anybody. Even if I could find somebody, we would have to pay 'em, and I don't see how. I discussed it all with Mr. Bijah Winsloe. You know the Winsloes."

"I know about them. And I used to know Medora, years ago. She's a cousin of ours."

Mr. Abijah Winsloe lived on a plantation named Avondale. If you went through the woods, Avondale was only about four or five miles from Indigo. Mr. Bijah had never lived in town. He liked the country, and was an experienced cotton planter. He had lived on the land, and had never had an overseer.

"Medora lives at Avondale with her aunt and uncle," Alan said.

"I heard she did. I haven't seen her in years." Louise knew that Medora's mother had died during the first year of the war, and her father had been killed early in '65.

"Mr. Bijah is a practical, sensible man, and he agrees with me," Alan said. "The only thing to do about Indigo is to get the tenants back, if I can. A lot of them have drifted off, but I believe I can get most of them back. Then I can plant a crop and get things going again."

"But how can you, Alan? Indigo's too far from town to go there often."

"It's not so far as the crow flies, but you either go as the river bends or as the road winds. They say the road follows the trail of an Indian dodging arrows. So I would have to go live there."

"How could you live there?"

"I don't want to, but I could, Lou. It's the only way, if we're going to hold on to Indigo at all."

"Then let it go."

"How can we? You know how little money we have. It's the only piece of land we have left. It may be worth a good deal some day."

"It isn't worth your life. Or your health."

"I'm not so sure. What's my life worth?" At the sight of her face, Alan smiled. "I don't mean to put it in such a dramatic way, but what's the use of my sitting here coddling myself, or rather letting you coddle me when I'd much better be out there trying to lick things into shape."

"You've been too ill to do all that hard work." He had had a long slow convalescence.

"I'm as strong now as I'm going to be. And as young."

"We've been letting it slide for years, Alan. Can't we go on being slipshod for a little while longer? Can't you do the way father's been doing? Scare up enough for the taxes and just hang on?"

"No, Lou. We can't afford it." He knew and Louise knew that

their father would never be able to take over the management of anything again.

"I don't suppose we can."

"Besides, things won't stay put. There are complications. We haven't paid enough attention to them, we've been too preoccupied here at home," Alan sighed.

Louise thought of all their troubles, during and after the war. Their mother had died three years ago, and their sister Emma had died a little over a year ago. Their other sister, Caroline, had moved away with her husband and children, and now their father was ill and required most of Louise's strength and time.

"You know Colonel Winsloe owned the property across the creek from Indigo."

"I remember." Colonel Winsloe was Mr. Bijah's brother. Unlike Mr. Bijah who had only been well off, rather than rich, Colonel Winsloe had married a wealthy woman, and had built a fine house on his plantation. Louise had been to Indigo only once in her life when she had been a child, and had never seen Colonel Winsloe's house, but she had heard of its splendors, and had felt a pang when it had burned down shortly before the war. The plantation itself was named Heron's Row, because of the white cranes that nested along the creek bank and waded in the water. Louise knew Medora Winsloe had lost the plantation. Colonel Winsloe, unlike his brother Mr. Bijah, had always been extravagant, and after his death his affairs had been in a tangle. However, it was less his fault, or Medora's fault than the general confusion after the war. Medora, left an orphan, with her Uncle Bijah still away with the army, had not known how to save her property. Heron's Row had been sold for taxes. It was the usual story. Maybe if Mr. Bijah had been on hand, he might have contrived to save it for her, but maybe he could not have saved it.

"Who owns Heron's Row now?" Louise asked.

"That's where the complications come in. A Yankee carpetbagger swooped down and bought it up. There he is, and who's going to dislodge him. That's not all," Alan sighed. "One plantation doesn't satisfy him, he sits across the creek waiting for Indigo to fall into his mouth like a ripe fig."

"But so far we've managed to pay the taxes."

"So far. But there's also a mortgage."

"I know. I heard father talking about it."

"Colonel Winsloe lent father some money, and father put a mortgage on Indigo. Well, when Colonel Winsloe's place went for taxes and the Yankee bought it up, he got hold of the mortgage on Indigo too."

Louise was speechless for a while. "I thought we owed the money to Mr. Bijah or Medora!"

"No. You see there were debts on Heron's Row, too, and when Medora had to let the property go, she didn't understand what she was doing. She didn't keep the mortgage on Indigo. You see, she didn't realize who was buying Heron's Row. The purchaser offered to buy the mortgage on Indigo from her, and as she needed money, she let him have it. Now she's sorry, but it's too late."

"Alan, is there anything we can do?"

"Not a thing. Except meet the interest every year. The mortgage doesn't come due for a long time, and so far we have been able to pay the interest, but the Yankee counts on our not meeting it. So we have to make the place pay for itself, or we'll lose it altogether."

"What sort of creature is this Yankee?"

"One of the hands on Indigo told me a story. It seems the Yankee went out and shot all the cranes on the creek bank. At least as many as he could hit. Now they don't come there any more."

Louise was speechless. She felt she knew the Yankee, knew him and hated him. She looked at her brother. He had been a beautiful child. He was handsome still, in a thin-featured, fine-drawn way, but permanently marked by the long struggle through illness and convalescence. He was no match for the Yankee, either physically, or in any other way. How could Alan, sensitive and honorable, combat that sort of creature?

"Someday Tommy will want that place, Lou. And I intend for him to have it."

"Don't go tangling me up in my maternal feelings, Alan. You want me to say you ought to go out there to live, and I won't say so. You aren't able to stand it!"

"Why not?"

A vision rose before Louise of what life out there would be like. An empty uncomfortable house in disrepair. Fields choked with weeds. Rolling ground, then woods, then the river curving around Indigo Bend. She had a vague memory of two melancholy frazzled cedars in front of the house and a stretch of bare ground, then a cluster of trees, threaded with a road of sorts leading to the main road. The Winsloes were the only neighbors within easy reach. The Yankee, nearer, was much worse than having no neighbor at all. There would be mud, dust, malaria, and loneliness, and back-breaking and heartbreaking work, and isolation like that turned people very queer after a time.

"It's at the ends of the earth, Alan. It's an impossible existence for you."

"I thought about all that, then I rode down to the creek and saw the Yankee standing there."

"What does he look like?"

"He's big. Big and burly, with red and purple veins in his face. He's just waiting for me to give up. Well, I won't. I'm going out there to stay if it kills me. I'm going to fight him, Lou."

One look at Alan told her he meant what he said. It frightened her. It meant change, drastic change, and she had become apprehensive of change. As a child she had longed for it, now any thought of it brought terror. How old and worn out she must be to dread it so! But no change these last years had brought any good. Monotony, an existence crowded with petty duties, repetitious struggles, made her rebel, but she knew she was huddling in the fragile shelter she had built up for herself and had tried to build up for Alan.

Now he was wrenching the pattern of routine with this plan of his. Everything would shift, turn, be different, and be worse! Alan was worn out, and certainly there wasn't anything hopeful about the state of things at Indigo, yet, watching him, she knew she hadn't seen him so alive and determined in years. The hardships she foresaw for him appalled her, but she understood what he was feeling. She had watched Alan battle his way back to some semblance of health only to find himself facing an empty, purposeless future. Love he had, from his family and friends. But not a prospect of any sort of achievement. Now he was going to fling himself into another contest.

Indigo was worth a battle, she admitted that. It had particular and unusual advantages. From Vicksburg to Baton Rouge there were bluffs—an escarpment. The plantations strung along the river, to the south of Natchez, were few. If they were beyond the rise of the bluff, and far enough and high enough to be safe from the river's floods, the land was apt to be poor. If they were situated between the bluffs and the river, the land was good, but in high-water years it was impossible to make a crop because of the floods. The plantation owners were too poor now to keep up adequate levees. But Indigo was different. The creek meandered through it, wandering in and out. Its acres were in the valley of the creek, and the creek had enriched it and built it up too. It was fertile, yet safe from floods, except for a small part of the land nearest the river. Louise saw it in her mind's eye. The curve of the river, Indigo Bend, the landing, and the road, angling up the steep bank, and winding through the fringing trees, through the fields to the house. She forgot about the bleakness of the house and thought about the land, Indigo's choice land, not to be duplicated in any other plantation.

Mr. Bijah's place, Avondale, south, southeast of Indigo was farther from the river, but not as rich. Heron's Row, to the north of Indigo, was rich, but more of its lands was subject to floods. No wonder the Yankee coveted Indigo.

Louise knew that the fight for Indigo on Alan's side would be an unequal struggle, already decided by fate. Yet how could he refuse the challenge? And there was something revivifying about a strong, healthy hate. A righteous hate. Was there such a thing? Probably not. But sometimes a poison, if used the right way, could be an antidote for a mortal illness.

"All right, Alan, we'll fight him." As she spoke, she felt herself taking the first step into the future, and somewhere over the edge of the unknown horizon, they might find some vague glimmer. Hope, maybe.

Chapter Two

"BUT you'll be buried alive!" Lizzie Corwin was helping Louise pack, or rather watching her pack. Lizzie was Louise's age, and they had been neighbors and friends ever since they could remember. Lizzie had been, as a girl, sharp-tongued, but interesting and amusing. Her narrow, meager life as a rather superfluous female in a crowded household was making her bitter. Now she added the weight of her pessimism to Louise's own melancholy.

Louise's father had died early in the summer, and there was nothing to keep Louise from going out to Indigo and trying to help Alan. This was a complete change, and she missed her father, though for his sake she could not want him back. His illness had been too long, too hopeless and full of suffering. Louise dreaded going out in the country. She felt like some shrinking creature drawn out of its shell. Resolutely, she tried to turn her thoughts to all the practical tasks ahead of her, and went on sorting, packing, and discarding.

"This is good tough material," she muttered, folding a wool skirt and putting it in the open trunk. "I wish I had more like it. You remember, Liz, that year we went to New Orleans and bought all those things. Aren't you glad we did?"

"We've been wearing all those clothes ever since. And probably always will."

"Only I wish I hadn't run to barèges, and organdies, and shot taffeta, and bonnets trimmed with blond. I need sturdy things now."

"I suppose it's a very rough life out there. Lou, have you and Alan decided what to do with this house?"

"We're renting it to Miss Ada and Miss Rose Sims." Miss Rose sewed, and Miss Ada would try to run the little school Louise had

23

started, and had abandoned when her father had become ill.

"Those old things won't be any company for me," Lizzie grumbled. "And you'll probably never see so much as a cat out at Indigo."

"Oh, yes I will. People do manage to live on plantations. And Avondale, where the Winsloes live, isn't far from Indigo. Alan sees the Winsloes often. Do you remember Medora Winsloe, Liz? She lives at Avondale too, with her aunt and uncle, and she's about our age."

"I remember her vaguely," Lizzie said. "Wasn't she rather a pretty child with long ringlets?"

"Yes, she was very pretty, and I suppose she still is." Louise examined a ruffled and flowered pink organdy dress, and pushed it back into the armoire, where it swayed a little. It was limp and faded and of no use in the life she was going to live. It could stay shut up with the ghost of the girl who used to wear it. It was a ghost of that other time, so different from now.

Louise had loved beautiful clothes and had known how to make the best possible use of them. Somewhat too tall and slim for current fashion standards, and with plain brown hair and eyes, and a clear skin without much color, Louise had no great opinion of her own good looks, but her eyes were full of brilliance and depth and warmth, she had a great deal of grace, taste, and elegance, a charming smile, and a voice people loved to hear. Her husband had told her her voice sounded the way velvet felt.

Now she was much too thin and pale and tired, and her dull mourning black made her look drab and forlorn. Well it didn't matter. She had other things to think about than her own appearance.

"I wish Alan would let that wretched plantation go," Lizzie complained. "He'll eventually lose it anyway. From what you say, I don't see how he can win. Everything's against him."

"He has to put up a fight for it, Liz."

"I don't see why, if he's bound to lose it. It's just wasting his life to struggle with it."

"I don't think so, Liz. It's better for him to do the best he can for as long as he can. Then at least he won't have to reproach himself with 'if I had onlys.'"

"The whole thing sounds impossible."

"I know it does," Louise agreed, "but since the war all of us are prone to give up and say we can't do any more. All of the silver spoons have been jerked out of our mouths, and we might as well buckle down to it. Besides, it's no use to be too reasonable. You always have to make allowances for the unexpected, the imponderables."

Alan had been living on the plantation for over a year now. "I can't say my head's above water," he told Louise, "but I'm swimming under water." He had collected most of the old tenants, and had planted his cotton, and was getting ready to pick it. He had borrowed enough to buy the necessary mules and was planning ahead, in spite of taxes, and the interest on the mortgage. Visions of his bleak life haunted Louise. She had not even been able to stay out at Indigo long enough to make the stark house a little more comfortable for him. Her father's illness had kept her tied at home. Now she was going out to Indigo to live, though Alan had begged her not to come.

"I still think it is a dreadful idea," he had scribbled. The note had come the day before Louise had planned to leave, and she sat and read it on a box of books she intended to take with her. "You have seen the place, but you do not understand the full horrors of my menage, though since you were here I have acquired the ministrations of the fecund Lillybelle. She and Cornelius live in that cabin near the house. She is always with child, or suckling one. Usually both. Lillybelle is a field hand, not a house servant. At this season she departeth the kitchen, with yard chillun, lap chillun, and the current nursling, to pick cotton, which I encourage, as I need pickers. Then the house is untended, and I eat sweet potatoes. Her spouse Cornelius is useful when sober, and very companionable in his potations, but in them, no longer useful. I would love to have you with me as you know, but I cannot see how you are going to stand it. If you don't change your mind about coming, I will meet the boat. What about Tommy's schooling? There is none."

There was another letter, too, and it was from Louise's young cousin who lived in Europe. Ellen was the daughter of Louise's dead cousin Anna, who had gone to Paris to live immediately after the war. Ellen was very fond of her Natchez relatives, but she preferred living in London and Paris and Florence to living in Natchez or New Orleans. As she was an orphan and in her early teens, she suggested in her letter that it would be just the thing if Louise and Tommy would come to stay with her for a long visit.

Louise had never been to Europe. Ellen's offer was a great temptation, but Louise tore the letter in little pieces. Someday she would set sail and go stay with Ellen in a pink Florentine villa, but now Alan needed her. Ellen would understand her reasons for saying no. The child was conscientious, with a strong sense of duty.

Louise threw the scraps of the letter in the trash basket and was ready to leave the house. She locked the front door behind her and gave the key to Metta. "I'm glad nobody wants to buy the house, Metta, because neither Mr. Alan or I want to sell it."

Metta had been the cook here ever since Louise could remember, and had grumblingly agreed to stay on for Miss Ada and Miss Rose. "You'll be back tereckly, Miss Lou."

"Sometime, anyway," Louise answered. Tommy, a fly-away wisp of a child, had already whirled down to the gate and had flung himself into the waiting hack. He was excited by the air of bustle and change. He jumped up and down, and Louise thought he'd better be more quiet or the hack would collapse. Dust rose from its interior. The driver and horse dozed, and the hack sagged all over. It would, she hoped, get them to the steamboat.

There was an air of climax about the whole proceeding. All the servants and children and neighbors were out to say good-by. Bella Corwin, with the last baby named Margaret, stood silent, shifting the squalling child. Mrs. Duel shouted, "Wait, wait," and darted into her house and came running out again with a large jar of fig preserves and a small glass of dewberry jelly, and pushed them into Louise's overburdened hands. The hack started off. Louise looked back and waved at the group on the sidewalk. Behind the waving people, the house, just visible behind its cluster of trees, looked blank, as lifeless as if it had been deserted for years. Already homesick, Louise yearned after it. These last years had held sorrow and care, yet at this moment she saw the place as a haven of peace and refuge.

"Why wasn't I always happy when there was really nothing to worry about?" she asked herself. She had been a dreamy, rather discontented child, and a restless girl—a fool not to have been perfectly happy then! And it was too late to relive, and to make the most of it. She put her arms around Tommy, and kissed him. She would tell him to be happy when he could, but he couldn't know from any telling of hers, and probably wouldn't listen. Beyond the faded grass, in its trees, the house reproached her, and the China tree at the gate let fall a drift of thin leaves like money carelessly thrown away.

The hack lurched and rocked down the hill. At last Louise and Tommy, boxes and trunks and bundles, were settled on the steamboat, and after a long wait, the boat began to move. Light clung to the Cathedral's spire, then it was only a streak of light until it wavered and melted into the hazy sky. Tommy ran from deck to deck, asking a thousand questions about the machinery and the river, talking to the roustabouts, and finding out more about everything in half an hour than his mother had gathered in a lifetime of traveling up and down the Mississippi.

They went downstream. After the bluffs were passed, nothing varied the monotony of the shores. There was a sheen on the brown water, and near the sand bars there were places where the water was almost currentless, almost limpid, with that spurious placidity the river could assume in dry seasons. Down here, on the Louisiana side, beyond the shore line, there were no deserted plantations or ruined houses. There was only the swamp coming in on all sides, a convergence of swamps, crowded with growth, braided with rivers, little and big, and hung with steady shadow.

First there was Deerpark, then Dead Man's Bend, then Indigo Bend. It was not so many miles to Indigo Bend, but as the river twisted the way seemed endless. Until at last, around another curve, there it was, and the landing, a steep bank, a few planks, and a faint marking of cart tracks. Just those slight traces of human life and human use, set in the midst of more trees and more river.

Tommy came and put his hand in his mother's. "Wasn't it a fine trip?" His eyes were very clear, very dark, but more slate-colored than brown. He, at least, hadn't been tired or bored or apprehensive. "There's Uncle, waiting for us."

A mule-drawn cart was there at the landing. Alan stood beside it, and with him was a small, bandy-legged Negro man. "I bet that's Cornelius," Tommy said. Alan looked thin, and his face was dark from exposure to the summer sun. The boat landed, and the things were unloaded.

"Lou, you shouldn't have come!" They kissed each other. She knew how touched Alan was at her coming, and how glad he was to see her.

"You look pretty well, Alan, but a little frayed. I'll darn you up. How are you, Cornelius?"

Alan turned away and busied himself with the baggage. He was choked with a mixture of feelings, she knew, glad she had come, and yet having a sense of guilt because his needing her had made her come. The wagon was piled high. The steamboat backed off and went its way, shabby, stubby, slow on the darkening curves of water. Alan drove the wagon and Louise sat beside him. Cornelius, agile in spite of his peculiar size and shape, leaped on a trunk, and Tommy insisted on getting in the back of the wagon with him, and struck up an immediate friendship.

They started off along the sandy track under the running-water murmurings of the cottonwoods. "They talk and the river keeps quiet," Tommy said. He looked at everything and noticed everything. It was all newness and adventure, and Louise wished she felt the way he did. If only you could capture childhood's brute joy in the moment, its particular savor! Maybe you could. Maybe it could be relearned.

"Kind of lonesome out here," Alan said, glancing at his sister. "But beautiful, in its own wild way."

In high water the river covered all the bank, but the trees grew tall, and there was grass, rusty now, covered with little seeds, attracting the flittings and feedings of flocks of tiny birds. Then the road wound up into the thick woods, soft and smoky, already gathering the dusk. After a while the trees thinned into open ground, then planted fields. Corn nodded its tassels, and cotton bolls were opening.

"You've done wonders here. It's much better than I expected."

"Indigo used to grow from four hundred and fifty to five hundred bales," Alan said. "I'd like to bring it up to that again. You know, Lou, I haven't done a thing to make the house shipshape."

"The house doesn't matter."

It was bleak, Louise admitted to herself, when she was in it.

"There are mighty few amenities," Alan pointed out.

"Oh, I've seen it before." The walls and floors were rough and there was hardly any furniture. "In time we can fix it up, and it has good big fireplaces and something of a gallery."

Lillybelle came to meet her. She was large and cheerful, and children eddied around her. Clouds of blue smoke and the smell of grease came from the primitive and dismal kitchen, but Lillybelle had fixed an enormous supper. Afterwards, when Tommy had fallen asleep, Louise and Alan discussed the place.

"How are you standing up under all the work, Alan?"

"It hasn't hurt me. On the contrary, I'm better. Walking's tiring, but I ride most of the time."

"What about other things?"

"The crop's good, and most of the hands have come back."

"I thought the Yankee had seized them by offering them all kinds of wild promises."

"A few have moved over there, but most of the ones who belong here feel uneasy with him. Of course I had to go further into debt to get the things I had to have, but I believe I can meet the taxes this year, if all goes well. Mr. Bijah's been a lot of help. He's advised me about everything. Maybe I could swing Indigo, if it wasn't for the mortgage. Or if someone besides the Yankee held it."

"When's the interest due?"

"February."

"We'll scare up the money, somehow."

"Lou, you know how I feel about your coming, I don't have to tell you that. But it's no life for you and that child."

"He'll take to it."

"What about school? He ought to go to school."

"I'll teach him. I brought chalk and books. I was trying to keep a school in Natchez. I can manage well enough, up to fractions."

"This place is grim in winter. When it rains, you're stuck. Nobody comes and nobody goes. I wish you at least had your own horse."

"Maybe I will, someday. I'll find plenty to do. I'll plant first a vegetable garden, then have a flower garden."

Alan smiled. "Remember that fern in a pot you were nursing? It kept shrinking and shriveling."

"Never mind, you'll see what I can do! I'll raise some chickens, too, so we can have eggs."

"There's always plenty to eat out here. You can always go hunt it or fish it if you fall short. Mr. Bijah sent the ducks. He says they'll all ride over Sunday to see you, Mrs. and Medora too."

"Medora's a cousin of ours, on her mother's side. What's she like?"

"I don't really know. The Winsloes are each supposed to be a law unto his or herself. The Colonel built that house, the one that burned. He ran through most of his money, but he married a lot of it. All of it's gone now. He was supposed to be a good officer, a little too headlong maybe, and always calling some other officer out to a duel. Mr. Bijah's very different. He's a calm, plodding sort of man, and a fine planter. He seems to have a natural-born instinct for soil and weather and animals."

"What about his wife?"

"I can't remember a word she's ever said. In fact I don't believe she's ever said anything—not a mumblin' word."

"That doesn't sound scintillating"—and Louise turned the conversation back to Medora—"Is she pretty?"

"Very. She has what lady novelists call large, languishing blue eyes."

That was good. There were ingredients for romance. An orphan, deprived of her property. Of course it would be much better for Alan if she still had it, but her loss would arouse his sympathy. And large blue eyes!

"Curls?"

"Ringlets like Elizabeth Barrett's, falling around her face. Light brown." Alan eyed his sister. He had a way of reading her thoughts, particularly if she was thinking about a suitable wife for him.

"Don't get excited. She doesn't languish for me."

30

"Why not? Why shouldn't she?" Louise admitted she was apt to be rather critical of girls who did seem to be interested in Alan, and, on the other hand, was furious with them if they weren't.

"For one thing, to go on like a lady novelist, her affections are fixed on another."

"Oh!" Louise was disappointed. "Who?"

"Her cousin Jasper Winsloe. Mr. Bijah's son."

"I'd forgotten all about him. You haven't talked about him."

"He wasn't here. He's just come back. He came home right after the war, and then went off. Nobody seems to know exactly where. Now he's back here again."

"For good?"

"They think so. But I'm leery of Jasper. He's got an over-the-hills-and-far-away look in his eye."

"What about his feelings for her?"

"I don't know. He seems fond of her. And his parents want the match."

"I don't see why. I don't like the idea of first cousins marrying. And just because the parents want it is no sign there's anything to it."

"I don't pretend to be a judge of young ladies, but she dotes."

"I'll have to see all this for myself." Louise tried and failed to smother a yawn. The bareness and shabbiness around her, the confusion of just-opened boxes and trunks waiting to be opened and unpacked, blurred before her eyes. She went to her room, and neither forebodings about her life here, or the lumpiness of her mattress could keep her awake. She slept better than she had in months or years, and she was too busy the next few days to think at all.

By Sunday, she had placed the things she had brought from home. The house had one main room. In it Louise put a comfortable rocking chair for Alan, and a desk and a table. Cornelius was going to make her some bookshelves, and her rows of books gave her comfort. She filled a bowl with goldenrod and dusty-purple wild asters, and the bindings of the books, and the flowers gave a touch of color to the general drabness. She put pine branches in the wide fireplace and they had a clean, spicy scent. The delicate tea set had an incongruous air, it was too brilliant and fragile for the rough surfaces.

The sight of it gave her a pang of homesickness, and a yearning for the past, with its grace and luxury, its gay talk, and rustle of silk and stir of plumes and people. Not vanished away, not changed, but as they had been!

Alan came in. "How nice you've made it look!"

Louise forced back her tears, and managed to smile before she turned around to answer him. This, for Alan! When he had been meant to have a Harvard education, and a tour of Europe, then come back to luxury and leisure and a place in the world. This grueling existence! If he could take any pleasure in the efforts she made, so would she.

"I've brought some tea. I'll make it myself."

"I guess you'd better. Lillybelle's sputter and frizzle methods won't be up to it."

"Give her time. She isn't stupid, just raw. Don't I hear wheels and voices?"

The Winsloes had come. The soft dirt road through the trees had muffled the sight and sound of them until their carriage had drawn up at the house and they were getting out. The man standing there, helping the two women, gave Louise a start. With his back to her, his height and build reminded her of Tom. Then he turned and the ghostly resemblance faded, never to come back again, with its taut, hot mingling of pleasure and pain. He was Jasper Winsloe, that was all.

He was a handsome man, with straight features and hazel eyes. He had a pleasant voice and good manners, and as he and Louise spoke to each other, she decided he would do very well as a hero of a romance. Medora was a pretty girl, with an air of gentleness most people would find appealing.

Meeting them, leading them in, Louise was mentally rearranging matters, as easily as she guided Mrs. Winsloe to the best chair and Medora to the next best. Medora might think she loved Jasper, but she would turn to Alan, and he would fall in love with her. Maybe he already was, but hiding it. If so, Medora would have to love Alan.

"I'm glad you've come here," Medora was saying to her. "We can come and go, and be company for each other."

Louise smiled and said she was delighted to have Medora nearby, too.

"It's the best thing in the world for Alan," Mr. Winsloe said, "having you out here." His commendation pleased her. Mr. Bijah was just as she had thought he would be, weather-beaten, square, and sensible.

"Alan says you've been such a help. That makes me very grateful."

"I only wish I could do more. But he's made a good start."

"Yes, a start," Mrs. Winsloe echoed.

Louise turned to her to try to talk to her. She was a plump, fair-skinned woman, rather faded and lined, with neat nondescript features and neat nondescript clothes. Before Mrs. Winsloe had appeared, Louise had forgotten her existence. Now it was almost as easy to forget her, even when she was here in the room. She said very little, and she seemed to subside quickly into being a background for more interesting people. Louise envied her. It would be comfortable to be like that, without too much intelligence or imagination or sharp angles of character. Of course the poor woman must have had her share of suffering too, but she had her husband with her and now her son. Mr. Bijah's sturdy good sense about farming, and his devotion to the land itself had enabled him to escape some of the disasters the war had brought, and Louise felt he must be a stout, protecting bulwark. How wonderful to be able to be just a shadow and an echo! Not to have to think, or decide!

Medora came in for a share of Louise's envy. Jasper had gone to war, but he had come back. Where had he wandered? Alan hadn't said. And why? She thought she knew why. Jasper was of her generation. Luckier than most since there was still a place for him in the scheme of things. All he had to do was to fit himself in to it. Of course there was the gnawing, haunting restlessness they all felt. The peaks and depths of the war were over, thank God, and the present and the future seemed to offer more to Jasper than to Alan or herself, yet he had gone away, driven to seek some rest, some peace, or maybe adventure. He had found what he wanted and was ready to come back, or maybe he hadn't found it, so had come back. Or else his family ties, or Medora, or both, had drawn him.

He sat next to Louise and talked to her about Natchez, and the people he knew there, and her own family. Mr. Bijah and Alan were talking about crops and weather and politics. Every now and then, Jasper threw in a question. He seemed interested. Perhaps he was ready to be contented here. Perhaps love was giving his life its glow and making him happy.

Medora didn't say much. She had less the lures and airs of a coquette than Louise had expected. Only in the fixed quality of her eyes when she looked at Jasper could Louise find signs of doting. He held her attention. His attitude to her was less easy to read.

Louise went out to the kitchen and made the tea and brought it back.

"Pretty." Medora noticed the cup. "We had some china a little like this. It got burnt up."

Jasper looked at her. "I know the set you mean, my uncle brought all kinds of glass and silver and pictures out to that house. Remember those chessmen we used to play with?"

There was a long tie of affection between Medora and Jasper. Mr. Bijah had had a solid, quiet prosperity, but the Colonel had had flamboyant tastes, and the money to indulge them. Medora had been the fairy-tale child in a fantastic palace in the woods. The palace had vanished, but Medora had flowered into beauty for Jasper. There was not enough change in her face, or depth of expression for Louise to grant her absolute beauty, but perhaps she seemed perfect to Jasper.

"It was dreadful for you, having the house burn," Louise said to her.

"I wasn't there. I was off at school." She seemed almost listless, but it had been a long time ago, and so much had happened since.

"And horrible for you to have that Yankee there, worse even than for us!"

"There's not a thing I can do about it now, Uncle says. I wish he'd been here. A Mr. Dane wanted to buy it, and the mortgage too. He sounded nice. He wasn't, he was just buying it for the Yankee, but I didn't know that."

"How could you?" Of course Medora had been sad, and confused, but if only she had understood what she was doing! She seemed resigned, almost as though she was glad there was no chance now

34

to struggle. Didn't she realize how much she had lost? Louise doubted if Medora was very practical. Of course, food, shelter, and clothing was provided by her uncle, but if she didn't care about material things, didn't she feel violence and resentment? Maybe all of her emotions were bound up in Jasper. It was just as well. The plantation was lost, but he had come back.

"Anyway," Louise said, "it's better for the house to have burned to cinders than for that wretch of a Yankee to be in it."

Jasper agreed. "I'd burn it down myself rather than have him there." His hazel eyes had that far-away look Alan had noticed. Louise felt she knew what that expression meant. He was going into memory, looking for the warmth and vividness of that past happiness.

"That's true," Medora murmured. She should have said more. She should have been with him all the way, to point out how she had been part of that happiness and would remake it for him.

"Have you caught a glimpse of the Yankee?" Mr. Bijah asked Louise.

"She won't recognize him when she does," Alan smiled.

"She expects a monster with scales and claws."

"He's got two arms and two legs," Mr. Bijah said, "but some of the worst traits a human can have."

Jasper turned to Louise. "Humans can be a lot worse than dragons with scales."

His look and tone reminded Louise that if he had seen men at their bravest, he had also seen them at their worst, and the horror of what people could become was stamped on him forever. Medora was watching him, intent but frowning in a puzzled way, as if she didn't understand. She ought to—if she had been sheltered from his experiences, at least her imagination should have made her follow him part of the way.

Tommy came in just then, with twigs and leaves in his hair, and scratched and grimy hands. He was building a house on the sprawled branches of a big live oak. He had evidently shinned down, from the looks of his knees. His coming made a diversion. The women asked who he looked like, and the men answered his questions about the horse. By the time he had gone, the others were ready to leave too, promising to come again soon. Mrs. Winsloe invited Louise and Alan to supper the following Sunday, and good-bys were said.

"I believe you're right." Louise watched the carriage lose itself in the hazy trees. "Her affections are fixed."

"Do you like her?"

"Oh, yes, to follow your lady writers, she's a simple, artless girl. By the way, you're hard on lady writers. Think of Emily, and my beloved Jane Austen. I'll read her to you this winter."

"That'll be nice, I love to hear you read. But as a heroine, Medora belongs to the wishy-washy school of lady writers."

"She's too steadily fixed on Jasper to be wishy-washy. I had expected her to be a flirt. She has more depth than you give her credit for——"

"I do give her depth. And she's a Winsloe, and therefore unpredictable."

"I could predict Mr. Bijah as I would the sun's rising."

"He's nature's successful struggle to reassert the norm. But Medora's an unknown quantity to us. Apt to break into 'Winsloeism.'"

"She's very pretty. Don't you want to divert her affections?"

"I couldn't. Besides—— What'd you think of him, Lou?"

"At first I thought everything was fixed and certain. Later, he made me nervous."

"How?"

"There's conflict there, Alan. On one hand duty and affection for his father and mother, and love, I suppose, for Medora. But I think he finds the jog trot of everyday almost unbearable."

"Which it pretty well is."

"But less so for him, than for instance, for us."

"I suppose whether you can stand it or not depends on the effect of what has happened to you on what you, yourself, are in the first place."

"Or what you become." There was always change. In circumstances, in people, in the substance and texture of every living thing. Not only from year to year, but from day to day, and from hour to hour. Perhaps in change there was hope. Far away, but there, waiting. This twilight hour brought its particular tone of loneliness

36

as the gold-dusted purple melted and darkened. A sense of the past overwhelmed her, with its quick and burning joy, unforgotten, and never to be found again. Jasper was looking for the past, and it was no longer on this earth. Tom, if he had been alive and with her now, would not be the vivid boy she had known. That boy would have vanished in life as surely as he had in death.

Chapter Three

LOUISE was too busy in the house to take advantage of the sunny autumn weather. Cornelius and Lillybelle loped away to the fields, the older children following, leaving the baby, the most recent baby, in the precarious custody of an old crone Lillybelle had dredged up from somewhere. Sometimes, Louise, hearing the baby squalling, went over and took care of the poor little thing, and often brought it into the kitchen with her. She was afraid of the cabin catching fire. Why it didn't, with the stovepipe coming out at that crazy angle, she never knew.

Since Alan couldn't spare any of his cotton pickers, Louise found herself confronted with the inadequate pots and skillets, the sulking stove, and her very incomplete knowledge of cooking, and her complete loathing of it. Her mother had prided herself on the perfection of her own housekeeping, and had tried to instill the art into her daughters, but she had supposed her daughters would only have to supervise a staff of well-trained servants, or make a particularly tempting cake or custard, or do fine embroidery. Mrs. Hamilton had never imagined this household or these problems. At home in Natchez, even during and after the war when there was the greatest scarcity, there was still left the skeleton of the usual way of doing. Even when there was hardly anything to eat, there was the efficient Metta to manipulate what did exist. Metta had positively refused to come live in the country.

Here at least there was enough food. Fish and game if nothing else. Alan didn't hunt or fish for pleasure any more, but to bring back some bird or beast they could consume. Panic struck Louise when she found herself alone in the kitchen with six limp partridges. Dead animals! Feet, and feathers, or fur, or scales! Mrs. Winsloe had made her a present of six hens and a rooster and two guineas, but they often turned sulky and refused to lay, and there was a constant battle to preserve them from hawks and rats and owls and possums. The cow, though, thrived, and when Cornelius was drunk and didn't milk her, his eldest boy did. Until the evening when Cornelius was very drunk, and Abe, his eldest boy, had cut his foot with an ax, and Lillybelle had gone off somewhere.

Louise was about to send one of the children for Alan, but she knew Alan was busy. Tommy was with him, and so was Link, Lillybelle's next oldest boy. Louise put a pail over her arm, determined to milk the cow herself. It looked easy. It wasn't, and Alan found her, long after dark, still trying.

He couldn't help laughing. "The cow's asleep and snoring."

Louise laughed too. "If she wasn't so good tempered, she'd have turned and gored me! I'm going to learn. Strictly for emergencies."

Louise did introduce a better and more varied diet. She was proud of her first pudding. "Though I never thought I'd have to escort one from cow or hen to the table."

By trial and error she learned, and Tommy must learn, too, and keep up with his studies. Ruthlessly, she dragged him from his happy ramblings, and made him do his lessons every day. So with her tasks multiplying, it was late in November before Louise had a chance to go and pick up the pecans from the big tree growing in the middle of an untilled field.

From the distance, she had watched the tree's silhouette, seeing, after the leaves had gone, the tight clusters of nuts against the sky. Safe from marauding hands, until last night's gusts of wind. The nuts would be pelting down, and she wanted to be the first to find them. She skirted the ploughed ground behind the house. It would be prettier to have a flower garden here, but that would come later. First, vegetables, and she eyed the dark moist earth to see if the cabbages were coming up. The six hens and their rooster clucked together, and the cow looked bland. Last night, Louise and Alan had gone over the account books and had studied the rows of figures. The crop would pay for the taxes, and if nothing upset their calculations, pay the interest on the mortgage. Of course they would have to borrow for next year's crop. There was no security, not even the narrowest margin, and there was always the political situation, with the carpetbag government of the state in power. It was a corrupt unjust government, and wiser people than Medora had lost everything they had owned by tricks, and sometimes not even tricks, outright seizure. Land fell to the scavengers in power by the simple expedient of raising taxes. Then the owners had to lose their property. For the present, Louise and Alan were hanging on to Indigo.

Once the crop hadn't been cotton, but indigo. Then an insect had come along and devoured the indigo plants. The people here must have seen ruin staring at them, but it hadn't been ruin. They had turned to planting cotton, and had flourished. Maybe this time, too, there was some solution waiting for them. Something to solve their difficulties. Louise doubted if it would be as easy as it had been before, yet somewhere, sometime, there must be an answer, and a way out.

Louise set off on her errand alone, since Tommy had gone with his uncle. She was glad to escape from the house, and the day satisfied her. It had none of October's taunting brilliance to sadden her, to ask her to fill its offered hours with happy adventures to suit its brimming light. Today's mild chill, and the dull sky robbing the world of color, leaving only the simplicity of outlines, made no demands. She glanced back at the house. It was only one room deep, and from this view of it, it had a whittled-down gauntness, and the weathered, unpainted boards were bone bare. In the soggy fields there was a tatter of cornstalks, and rough prickly cotton bolls, empty, except for a trail here and there of dirty cotton.

Louise felt she herself fitted only too well into the general drabness. Spindly as a child, she had been plainer than her sisters. She had watched her cousin Anna, considered "strange looking," bloom into an exotic fascination, and had hoped for such a transformation too. If she lacked the unusualness of Anna's coloring, and was considered too slender, Louise was light-footed, a good dancer, a good rider, and her big dark eyes, full of life, gave change and vivacity to what she considered an average collection of features. It had been a long time now since she had thought about her looks. People had admired her taste, her style and carriage, but she needed the right clothes, and suddenly aware of her appearance, she decided she must have a certain resemblance to the scarecrow in the cornfield. She had become more lank than slim, and she was wearing a thick woolen skirt and cape, still useful, but long past any conceivable fashion. She had become a utilitarian object, but there was satisfaction in knowing Alan and Tommy needed her.

Her destination, the untouched field, had a certain charm of aspect, with the sedge grass rusty under the monotonous sky. Except for her cousin Mary, who loved nature, and her cousin Anna, who seemed to have had a superstitious terror of it, Louise's family, in spite of reading the romantic poets and novelists, and quoting them, had an essential indifference to anything beyond the garden. Scenery, yes, if it was something well known that you paid to go and admire. If there hadn't been a war, Louise would have gone to fashionable resorts, and would have toured Europe, and would have scrutinized famous lakes and peaks. The view from the Natchez bluffs was commended, but the wild roughness of the landscape was left for hunters.

Now, as Louise delved into the deep grass, looking for pecans, she found she liked the space and emptiness. There was the mournfulness of the gray autumn day, but different from the sadness of overgrown plantations and ruined houses. It was an unspoiled loneliness. The grass wasn't as long near the tree, and there were plenty of nuts. They had an almost animal cunning in hiding themselves after they had fallen, but she began to grow skillful in routing them out. She cracked some with her shoe and enjoyed their rich sweetish taste. Someone was calling her, and she looked up to see Medora riding over the fields towards her. There was something almost ghostly about the slight silhouette, and horse and rider had been able to move through the grass without making a sound.

Even when Medora dismounted and was close at hand, speaking and smiling, she seemed, if no longer unreal, at least insignificant, as if the largeness of the sky, the wide undulations of the field, and the drift of woods further away blotted her out.

"I thought I'd ride over before it begins raining again. Lillybelle told me where you'd gone."

"I'm glad to see you. Shall we go back to the house?"

"Let's stay out, if you want your pecans. There's another tree nearer the creek. I can show it to you."

They walked on towards the creek. "I have something to tell you!" Medora pulled off her glove to show the pearl and sapphire ring on her finger. "Jasper and I plan to be married soon after Christmas."

Louise turned and kissed her. "I'm so glad!" Glad her doubts had turned to nothing. They would be married, and at least have that average chance at happiness which was all anyone had a right to expect. "You know I wish you every joy in the world." As she spoke, Louise wondered why she felt no more ardor than she did, since she had become fond of Medora and anxious about her welfare. Maybe she was jealous. That norm of hope had been denied to her for so long. "You've cared for him for a long time haven't you?"

"Ever since I began to grow up."

"And now everything will be all right." If anyone needed love and protection, Medora did.

"And I was so worried after the war, when he went away and didn't seem to want to come back."

"And during it. When you didn't know if he'd ever have a chance to come back."

"Then, of course. Yet somehow I felt sure he would."

For a time, Louise had built up that sureness of Tom's safety, or had tried to, and it had meant nothing at all.

"You're lucky, Medora."

Something in her tone must have struck through Medora's preoccupation. "It was dreadful for you, Louise, losing your husband."

"And is," she sighed. "But still——" And then she didn't say more. She could never bring herself to speak of that time with Tom.

"And hard to bring up a child without a father."

"But where would I be without Tommy! Medora, when do you plan the wedding?"

"I haven't set an exact date. I have to get a few things. I'd like to feel a little like a bride."

"Of course." They had reached the other tree, digging its roots into the creek bank.

Medora sighed a little. "I've waited a long time."

"Where was Jasper, when he was gone?"

"He didn't write much. He was in Cuba, part of the time. He gets letters from there. Sometimes he talks about living there, but I want him to stay here."

"Did he ever tell you why he stayed away?"

"Only that he was restless, and couldn't get used to the way things have become here."

"There isn't much scope for the men who have come back."

"I know, but he'll have Avondale. His mother and father are getting on. We all need him. It's so lonely there without him. I kept wishing I had done as he asked, and married him during the war——"

"He asked you then?"

She flushed a little. "Well, his leave was so short, and I was young, hardly seventeen. I thought things would get better later. He begged me, and I hesitated, and he got furious. Then he wrote, saying to overlook his getting so angry—that he understood how I felt, and we'd wait."

The usual reasons, the usual hesitations. Louise herself hadn't been sixteen, and she was glad of her own violence, and the strength it had given her to defy all caution and all advice. The force of her passion, and passion it was, though ladies were not supposed to use such a word or understand such a sensation, had hurled her into marriage. Passion young and fresh and natural, and how it had flared among them—the soldiers in their teens and twenties, the girls, sheltered until then, but then awake and aware, given a dazzle of beauty, a wild bloom. They had been desirable and desiring. Eagerly they had flung themselves into their hurried marriages. They had known a few nights of ardor. Then the men were gone. Usually forever.

"But suppose Jasper had been killed?"

Medora shivered. "I—I'd have died."

She might have. Louise admitted that, seeing in Medora for the first time a flash of intensity. It set her more firmly into the pattern of the saccharin novels Alan jeered at, but sometimes people did die of broken hearts. There was more to Medora than Louise had supposed. Medora had hesitated where Louise had plunged, and her intensity was not the same as Louise's, but all her feelings were bound up in Jasper, or rather in the idea of Jasper. Did Medora know what he was really like now?

"But he did come back," Louise hurried to console, "and everything ought to be all right for you both."

"I know I'm lucky."

Maybe she was. Maybe the hesitations and cautiousness wouldn't haunt her any more, yet Louise felt that Medora had lost something never to be regained—the first fullness and fieriness of Jasper's love. If she had married him then, in those long ago early days of the war, she might have twined around his nature, able to grow and change with him. Then, she would have married the man she loved. Now she was marrying the man he had become—no longer the same person. Better, much better than no love, but different. Medora didn't seem to see this. Not yet. Louise hoped she never would know what she had missed.

"Let me help you, Medora." Louise warmed to the idea of a festive occasion. "We'll decorate the house with holly and mistletoe, and you'll make a lovely bride."

"Thank you." Medora's eyes filled with tears. "I must go now, it's getting late."

"Come to the house. We'll drink a toast."

Medora shook her head. "I'll just ride on, by the short cut. I told Uncle Bijah I'd meet him." Suddenly her face stiffened and she clutched Louise's arm. "Look!"

Louise turned around, towards the creek, and saw a woman running across the damp sandbar and scrambling up the slippery bank.

"What's she doing over here?" Louise whispered, knowing the strange woman must be the Yankee's wife. A child's chuckle sounded and the bushes were waving where a little boy was pushing through them, trying to hide and coming towards the place where Louise and Medora were standing. The woman caught up with the child and snatched him to her when he was only a few yards away from the pecan tree.

"He ran away," she panted, her voice thin and nasal. She clutched the child defensively. He stared at the two unknown people out of brilliant, jewel-blue eyes. Medora and Louise looked at his mother without a word. They denied her existence for them. Their blank and frozen faces denied her existence for herself. Her reddened hands tightened on the child's shoulders. "Or I wouldn't of come," she added, her tone hoarsening as if she were near tears. Neither Medora or Louise answered her, or seemed to see her. The woman brushed her hand across her face and turned away, leading the child off, down the rough bank, across the sandbar to the other side of the creek.

"I suppose she's lonely," Medora said.

"I hope she is." Though she had not seemed to look at her every detail of the woman's appearance was stamped on Louise's mind, even to the pattern of the ugly calico dress under the coat. It infuriated Louise for the child—he was perhaps three years old—to be so handsome and sturdy. He shouted again from the sheltering trees of the other bank.

Medora shivered. "I'll never get the place back, not an inch of it."

Someday the Winsloe's land would belong to the husky child. The interloper, the enemy. Someday the Winsloes who had hewed the great plantation out of the forest, would be forgotten. "But they won't get Indigo!" Louise promised herself. She hated them. Woman, child, and the man she had never seen.

When Medora rode off, Louise watched her out of sight, and instead of going back to the house herself, she turned towards the woods. The trees, mostly leafless, except the magnolias, had none of the pecan's sharpness of outline. Grouped together, vines and moss blurred them. Like the fields, they had no harshness, but that melancholy softness, that almost caressing dreaminess characteristic of a Southern winter. There wasn't much undergrowth, most of it had died away now and it was easy to walk. There was no sunlight, and no defined shadows. Only a soft gloom. A holly showed bright berries. Louise would remember where it was, and use it to decorate for Medora's wedding.

What risks Medora had taken! And, in a way, how lucky she was, but she would need all the luck she could get, and Louise didn't begrudge it to her. Yet Louise felt almost strangled by her own loneliness. Neither Alan's company or even Tommy could help her now, this minute. Her hand reached for a damp trunk of a tree, and the hushed dimness around her gave her no comfort and no answer.

Perhaps that was the answer—the carelessness, the absolute indifference of nature, nature calm, or nature in a rage, to human woes.

Long before her time, people had had to struggle out of the ruins of toppling civilizations and survive as best they could. Once she had thought that luxury and security and happiness was the usual rule of life. But it wasn't. It was the exception, and always imperiled. Love, that hadn't been safe or easy, or hers for long. Even when it had been hers, it had been full of tension, and mounting danger. But every real emotion carried danger and insecurity.

It was twilight now, and Louise turned to go out of the woods. There was beauty here, somehow faintly sinister, but in the shadowy quiet, no such thing as peace. Every rabbit concealed from her eyes, every squirrel bunched against a branch, represented a hazardous, and brief triumph over a thousand deaths. Even every tree grown tall had burrowed for its nourishment, and had dwarfed and strangled a dozen saplings. Here was the primal pattern of life, growth, struggle, decay, death, and life springing again as impetuous and determined as the seedling bursting up beside the great trunk split by lightning. All of it going on, sometimes in full view, sometimes in loneliness and secrecy. And always the wings of the hawk sweeping over.

There was no reason to go back to Natchez for Christmas. Louise and Alan and Tommy had Christmas dinner at Avondale, and Louise sent word to the hands that there would be a Christmas tree for them on New Year's Eve, and Medora, coming to Indigo one day found Louise laboriously cutting crepe-paper spirals. "I'll help," she offered.

"Never mind, you're busy."

"It's going to be a simple wedding, there's not much to do." With surprising skill she began twisting the paper into elaborate patterns.

"You're much better than I am. We'll haul a cedar from the woods, and set it up in front of the house. If it rains, we'll have to put it up in the barn, and that won't be so nice."

Louise and Alan and Tommy decorated the tree. Carts drove in from the swamp and families meandered across the creek. New Year's Eve was not very cold, and there was a moon, and the scraps of candles burned bright while they lasted, and the children laughed.

Most of them had never seen a Christmas tree, and they were not disappointed in this one. The Winsloes came, and when the tree had been admired, and the meager supply of old mended toys and oranges and apples and little bags of nuts had been distributed, the Winsloes came into the house to sit by the fire and drink the bottle of wine Alan had hoarded. Everybody toasted the New Year and the bride and groom. Medora smiled and turned rosy, but Louise noticed Jasper's face. It was set and strained.

Mr. Bijah said he was going to relax and let Jasper manage the plantation.

Jasper frowned. "I haven't the knack of planting the way you have, sir."

"I hope it isn't only a knack," Alan said, "because I haven't any either. I thought you could learn. That's what I count on."

"Maybe it's something like having a green thumb," Louise sighed. "I don't have it, but I'm urging vegetables out of the ground."

"Do you think you can will them up?" Jasper asked.

Louise laughed, and said she believed that helped them along.

"You and Alan are wasting yourselves out here."

"No! Don't tell them that!" Mr. Bijah was indignant. "What else would they do with themselves? They are right to hold on to the land! Let everything else go, Alan, but hold on to your land."

"If I can."

They talked about the Yankee and his growing influence in the state's carpetbag government.

"I don't think my little efforts are going to offset all the promises he makes the hands," Louise said.

"They like excitement," Jasper said, "and gaiety."

"Bread and circuses," Louise agreed, "and I think they really like the circuses better than the bread. That's one reason they have charm—their liking the circuses best."

"They're very imitative," Mrs. Winsloe contributed. It was the first remark Louise had heard her make since she had come into the house. "Mrs. Winsloe has made me doubt the truth about still waters running deep," Alan had said to Louise. "When she opens her mouth you stop and listen, thinking you're bound to hear something important, and it's always a platitude."

Jasper turned to Louise. "I wonder who does the imitating. Look at us. Haven't we learned to want excitement and color too?"

"We do, and it certainly doesn't come from our Puritan and pioneer ancestry."

"Puritan—why, Lou," Alan smiled. "Aren't we all supposed to be cavaliers?"

"There was a strong flavor of the 'auld kirk' in our religious training," Louise reminded him, "but we softened fast."

"Who was the tall, sulky girl who didn't smile?" Mr. Bijah asked.

"That's Lillybelle's Jessie," Alan told him.

"Uppity." Mr. Bijah growled. "She'll swallow Yankee rantings or I miss my guess."

"She's biggity," Louise admitted, "but she's smart, so I thought I'd teach her to read and write while I was teaching Tommy his lessons."

"Goodness, Louise," Medora said, "you sound like one of those Yankee schoolmarms they send down here."

"But think of wanting to read and not knowing how!"

"I can't see any harm in her learning," Mr. Bijah growled, "but be careful, child, these are bad times. Sometimes I think we're in for worse than war itself."

Louise didn't contradict, and a man might think conditions now were worse than fighting, but she remembered the casualty lists after every battle. Her heart contracted with a physical pang.

"Medora told me you encountered the Yankee's wife," Jasper said.

"She isn't to blame for his goings on," Alan pointed out. "I bet she's pretty miserable down here."

"I hope so!" Louise was vehement. "I hate 'em all!"

Mr. Bijah snorted his agreement.

When the Winsloes were leaving, Louise promised to go over to Avondale soon, and a week later Alan drove her there in the cart.

"I wish you had a riding horse, Lou. Someday I hope to get you one."

"I get around." Alan needed the one horse almost constantly, and she had taken to riding a mule. The one Alan had named Colonel Duel. There was something in the mule's facial contours and general temperament very much like that irascible gentleman's. He was

48

Louise's lifelong neighbor in Natchez, and she and Alan were very fond of him and never openly called him mulish. But when the mule balked, they said he was Colonel Duelish.

The cart was piled with holly and vines, and Louise was trying to guard her precious mistletoe. So far, the jolts of the road had bounced off all of its pale, pearled beads.

All of this land had once belonged to Louise's family. Heron's Row, where the Yankee now lived, was to the north of Indigo, and Avondale was to the south of Indigo. Some of her forefathers had sold off first Avondale, then since the Winsloes wanted more land, they had bought Heron's Row. Indigo was between the two because Louise's family had preferred to keep just those acres, lying level, and enriched by the creek. Indigo's soil never washed away, it just grew deeper as the creek overflowed it.

The house at Avondale was no such mansion as Colonel Winsloe had built on Heron's Row. It was simple and square, but comfortable with wide galleries and well-proportioned rooms. Mrs. Winsloe had colorless tastes. The wallpapers were dark, and the books and furniture nondescript, but the front parlor, when it was vine-wreathed, brightened with firelight and candlelight, and completed by a pretty bride and a handsome groom would look well enough.

"Medora has a lovely wedding dress. She made every stitch of it herself."

"He's given her time to make and unravel several. She's been a regular Penelope."

"I never cared much for Penelope," Louise said. "Those solid dames of antiquity are somehow tedious."

Alan said she was getting radical. "But I guess you always were, though you didn't let on as much as you do now."

In spite of the harshness of the present, Louise realized that her life now had gained a certain freedom. She had always thought as she pleased, now she was free to express just what she thought.

"I guess Penelope was dull"—Alan was allowing his thoughts to ramble—"or he wouldn't, like Jasper, have tarried."

"I remember my wedding dress. Run up in one day. And everyone saying, 'hurry, hurry.'" Louise had never spoken of her wedding, and now Alan didn't look at her.

"Tom wouldn't have tarried."

"No, he would have come straight back to me. But our case was different. We were married. There's Tommy."

"Besides, he was different. He had a fine mind. A complicated, abstract kind of intelligence." Alan paused, groping for words. Tom had been his friend, and Louise waited and listened, realizing she had been missing a great deal in not speaking of Tom to her brother. Alan could tell her things about him that she had never had a chance to learn.

"He loved to analyze, but it was mental analysis. His mind worked apart from his feelings and wasn't confused by them. Emotionally, he was simple and direct. When he married you, love was solved for him, and for keeps. Love was you, and always would have been. Jasper probes and prods his thoughts and feelings too much."

"He's forgotten any Circe he might have met. He's back."

"He's in the grip of worse than Circe. Personal demons. They're still with him."

"I know, but all you soldiers brought them back, Alan. How could you help it?"

"We each of us have different ways of dealing with 'em. He lets his stalk him."

They had reached the house. "Take care of my mistletoe, Alan."

Mrs. Winsloe met them at the door. "Go see Medora, she's in the parlor." Mrs. Winsloe's eyes shifted from their faces and there was something distraught in her tone. In the parlor, Medora and Jasper were standing by the fire, together, and the sight of them reassured Louise. It was only when Medora looked up, her eyes full of tears, that Louise knew something was wrong.

"What's the matter?"

"Oh——" Medora came to her, and put her head on Louise's shoulder and began to cry audibly. Louise patted her. Alan stood in the door. Jasper hadn't moved. He was pale and his eyes looked narrow and dark.

"What's going on?" Alan demanded. His voice was harsh. Louise wondered why Medora had turned to her instead of to Jasper. Even while she murmured to Medora, she wanted to shout, "She's yours! Your responsibility!"

"Is something wrong with Mr. Bijah?" Alan asked

"No—no, he's ridden over to see Dr. Rand," Jasper explained. "The thing is—I've had an urgent letter from a friend of mine in Cuba—a business transaction has come up. If I could be in on it, it will be very profitable! Very! But to share in it, I'll have to go right away."

"Don't cry, Medora," Louise said. We'll have to hurry, but we can——"

Medora looked up, moved away from Louise and wiped her eyes. "Jasper says—there won't be time."

"What's all this, Jasper?" Alan came on into the room.

"I must go at once, I'm afraid." Jasper was glib. "Of course Medora knows it'll only mean a brief postponement of our wedding." He picked up some sheets of paper on the mantelpiece and glanced at them, frowning.

"You mean—you aren't taking her along?"

"Where I'm going, that would be impossible. And there just isn't time to be married. I must leave—right now. The wedding will take place as planned—as soon as I come back. This scheme"—he flicked the letter—"means too much to our future. Medora understands that!"

Medora nodded, and went to stand beside him. He lifted her hand and kissed it. "Medora understands and agrees." It was a graceful gesture. To Louise—and she could see by Alan's face that he too felt as she did—it had a spurious quality. She remembered a story she had read long ago—the bedecked house, the assembled guests, the waiting clergyman, and the bride in lace and satin and pearls being carried out shrieking as the reluctant bridegroom blew out his brains in the garden. That story jumbled in her mind with the *Bride of Lammermoor.*

Dazed, Louise looked around her. The scene here lacked drama, cohesion, reason, and flamboyance. No clergyman, no wedding guests, no decorations except the branches Alan still held, and he was holding them crushed together and the mistletoe beads were falling like pearls from a broken necklace. It didn't matter. But the essential part of this scene was like the story—there was no bridegroom. He said he was coming back!

"We'd better go, Lou, we're in the way here."

Louise squeezed Medora's hand, the engagement ring was still on it. "It won't be long. You aren't staying away long, are you Jasper?"

"No, no indeed! I'll be back just as soon as I can."

When they were out of the house and on the way home, Alan flung the holly and mistletoe out on the road. His face was pinched and black with anger. "I ought to call him out! That fella ought to be shot!"

"If Mr. Bijah can't make him behave, you can't."

"Mr. Bijah must be ashamed of him, that's why he didn't want to face us. He doesn't know what to do."

"You don't think Jasper's coming back?"

"Do you?"

"I don't know. Poor Medora! I feel so empty and let down, what must she feel?"

"She ought to be glad to be rid of him. She's a fool if she isn't. Still, somebody ought to call him out——"

"That wouldn't help. Do you think there's any truth in the business venture?"

"Lord! I don't know. Maybe."

"It may be something profitable, but secret," Louise suggested. "Like selling fire arms to Cuban rebels. You remember Cousin Albert was mixed up in Cuban revolutions a long time ago."

"It's possible, of course. And Jasper may be more adventurous than we know. All the same, I think he wants to bolt."

Maybe he felt himself in a trap, and was clawing to escape. Louise thought he loved Medora in his own fashion. There was probably a conflict in his mind, an affection for her and for his parents and his home, yet at the same time a distaste, a rebellion for the course they mapped out for him. Wife, home, and perhaps children—maybe he saw all those cares looming ahead of him to bind him down.

"I hope if he ever shows up again, Medora'll have sense enough to turn her back on him!"

"She won't, Alan. What else can she do with her life? There's

52

no other man, and except for the old people, who else is there for her to count on?"

"You're alone, Lou. Of course you have Tommy. And plenty of people to love you. But none of us can take Tom's place. You've been through much worse than Medora. And lost a man worth ten thousand times more than Jasper."

"But in a way, her unhappiness is worse, Alan. It's so negative. I've lost more. But I've had—everything. And I have Tommy."

"You're a sturdier character, too."

"Why wouldn't she make Jasper happy? Why doesn't he think so? She's pretty and gentle and dependent. Isn't that what men like best?"

"In easy times, maybe. Though I don't think I'd care for the dead weight of total dependence. But none of this is her fault. It's all his!"

"I suppose he can't altogether help it. He's restless and groping."

"Of course," Alan admitted, "womenfolk set great store by bell, book, and candle."

"Security——" Louise mused. "She wanted it too much, and that's where I blame her, at least a little. She was brought up to a safe, comfortable way, and she wants to get back to it. And it doesn't exist for any of us any more."

"Not in our life time. Maybe things will be better for Tommy."

They talked about Tommy for the rest of the way. The sunset turned the edges of the fields blue and gilded the moss and the trees in the woods, until you felt that just a little beyond where your eyes could see, there was enchantment. Then the light was gone, and there was stillness and dimness, and suddenly, the quick winter dark.

Chapter Four

THAT bad winter, that horrible year, that's what Louise called it after she had lived through it, wondering how they had managed to survive. Perhaps they couldn't have if they had known what was in store for them, but mercifully, ironically it was dealt out to them a little at a time, day by day, and each day's problems were immediate. Nobody had time to peer into the future.

Weeks passed, and Jasper didn't come back. He wrote often to Medora, and his letters must have been affectionate, because she seemed happier when she had just heard from him. Louise learned very little about the contents of the letters, only that Jasper was busy with plans and projects.

"Maybe Jasper'll come back with a fortune," Louise said to Alan.

"Not unless he digs up pirate gold. It would be just like him to delve for it. I can't see him successfully carrying out dangerous plots. But maybe he can." Alan's tone was dry. "You seem to be appointed to comfort Medora."

Louise wished Alan would try to himself. Medora came over as often as she could, and when Louise was busy, helped her. She was apt at domestic tasks, such as making tea and washing fine china. Alan was very kind to her, and as it was the off season, he was sometimes in the house when she came. When they sat together talking, Medora saying very little, but listening intently, Louise wondered what might have happened if Jasper had not been on hand when the first impact of Medora's prettiness and gentleness had struck Alan.

Then the weather turned bad, and she came less often. It grew bitterly cold, with hard freezes and sleet storms. Fires had to be kept going, and lamps had to be filled. The house was full of cracks and drafts. Cornelius got drunk often, and Lillybelle ailed, and

54

when she took to her bed she sent the sulky Jessie to help Louise. The girl was quick, but sullen. One day Louise came in and found Jessie looking at the pictures in one of Tommy's storybooks, poking out her mouth and frowning as she tried to puzzle out the meaning of the letters.

"I'll teach you if you'll work hard at it," Louise promised, and let the girl share Tommy's lessons. After that, she seemed much happier and helped Louise with much more will. The cold lasted, damp and penetrating. At night, Louise, putting her own blankets on Tommy's bed, shook and shivered. The overseer had left a few deerskins hanging on the walls. Louise used them on the beds too, wishing he had killed polar bears with thick fur.

One day Alan went hunting, not because he enjoyed it, but because supplies were low and it took a long time in winter for them to come from Natchez. A freezing rain came up while he was in the woods. Louise paced back and forth, worrying about him. It was dusk before he reached the house, and as soon as Louise saw him she noticed the purplish flush on his face. She jumped up and went to him. "You have a fever!"

His forehead was burning to her hand, and she hurried him off to bed. He needed a doctor, and in that sparsely settled countryside there was only one, Dr. Rand. She sent Cornelius off to find him. On his way to the Rands, Cornelius would have to pass near the Winsloe house. "Go ask Mr. Bijah which is the shortest way to the doctor's. And don't you drink a drop, Cornelius, no matter who offers you any whiskey——"

It might be hours before Dr. Rand came. Alan tossed and shivered and burned. Louise sat beside him, and tried to make him more comfortable. She felt lost and isolated. An hour or so after dark, Mr. Bijah came. "You oughtn't to have come out in this weather!" Louise said, but she was glad to see him.

"Dr. Rand ought to be along. I showed Cornelius the short cut through the woods to his house. I thought you might need some help. I'm no doctor, but I've done some doctoring in my time." He took a look at Alan, and approved the remedies Louise had used. "I see you're a good nurse. I'll stay, though, until the doctor comes."

"What about Mrs. Winsloe and Medora?" Louise knew Mr.

Bijah didn't like to leave them alone after dark, not in times like these.

"Wash is there. I depend on Wash."

Jasper should be at home, taking charge, doing all the things his father had to do. Instead, Mr. Bijah had to depend on Wash, more faithful and steady than his own son.

"You're very good to come. I'm frightened. Alan's not strong. If his lungs get involved——"

The doctor, large and grizzled, came at midnight. He stayed with Alan for forty-eight hours, and when he left Alan's fever had gone down. After that, there was no further danger of pneumonia, but Alan's convalescence was long and slow. The sleet thawed, and changed to weeping, ceaseless rains. The doctor had to come on horseback.

"There's nothing really wrong with him any more," he said, "except he needs building up. Build yourself up too. You must be worn out."

The roads had turned to bogs, and supplies had to come by boat. The boat was slow and uncertain, but at last it was due to come from Natchez, and Louise sent Cornelius to the landing to get the things she had ordered. Wine, and a piece of beef, because the doctor wanted Alan to have beef broth. Louise made the broth herself. She had noticed that Cornelius was a little bleary-eyed when he came into the kitchen. He pottered around, getting more wood, and building up the fire.

At last the broth ought to be ready. Alan said he had smelled it for hours and was getting hungrier every minute. It was the first time he had showed any signs of appetite, and Louise hurried into the kitchen. Cornelius was hunched on the woodbox snoring. When Louise lifted the lid from the kettle, instead of the strong broth there was nothing but water simmering—water lightly filmed with grease. Half an hour ago there had been broth.

"Cornelius!" She whirled on him. "You drank it—you——"

"Miss Lou, I done smelt hit."

Louise picked up a stick of stove wood and whacked him with it as hard as she could. At the moment, she would gladly have killed him, yet she looked with surprise at the broken stick in her hand.

The other half flew across the kitchen and made the saucepans on the table ring and dance.

Cornelius huddled into a tighter knot, and began to cry—whether from repentance or whiskey Louise didn't know. Tommy watched from the door, his mouth open. "Mamma, you hit him!" he whispered.

"I shouldn't have and it didn't do any good." She jerked herself back into her usual self. To fly out like that—a witch on a broomstick—propelled by demons! What a bad example she had set for Tommy! "I was wrong. But there's no broth." Fury seized her again at the sight of the greasy water. Between her teeth she muttered to herself she was glad she'd hit him.

Tommy had scampered off, and she didn't realize he had gone to answer the door until she went into the next room and saw him talking to a strange girl. The girl looked up, smiling at Louise, and even in that first impression, though the girl was muffled in a heavy cloak with a hood, Louise had a sense of brightness and freshness.

"I'm Amanda Rand." Her cheeks were firm and deeply pink. She showed dimples when she smiled and her eyes and teeth were brilliant.

"Oh, the doctor has talked about you!" His daughter was the apple of his eye. "Do sit down near the fire."

Amanda put a big basket down on the table and peeled off her gloves. "I've brought some broth for Mr. Alan. Father said he ought to have it."

"You're an angel!" Louise couldn't say any more, she had to keep herself from bursting into tears.

"I thought you might find it hard to come by, and we've just butchered a cow."

"And you brought it to us in all this weather."

"I'm out in any sort of weather. It isn't far if you know the short cut. I'm used to being out. I hate staying mewed up, don't you? Father's going to meet me. He said he'd be over here in the morning."

"You've saved our lives, literally."

"Then I'm glad I came." There was no shyness about her, only simplicity and directness. And she was beautiful, if a look of health and bloom and vigor made beauty.

"Do come again," Louise urged her, sorry to see her go.

"I will, I'd like to." She pulled her hood over her head, and left as suddenly as she had come. Louise watched her ride off, and then looked in the basket. There was a big bowl of broth, jellied now, a roast chicken, a bottle of blackberry wine, and a pound cake.

"Who's the phantom of delight?" Alan asked, when Louise took him the steaming broth. "I heard her talking, and as the door was half open, I peered at her. I liked what I saw."

"You eat up everything she brought."

He seemed willing to eat for the first time since his illness. Amanda Rand was hardly a phantom. She was large, tall, and strongly made. But Alan, hollow-cheeked from fever, and always combating delicate health, would see the girl as a vision of strength and youth and life.

It was a long time before they saw Amanda again. As the carpet-bag government grew more vicious, people became more than ever tense and uneasy. There had been no unpleasant incidents in this neighborhood, but there were stories about what was going on in other parts of the South, and other counties of Mississippi, and Dr. Rand wouldn't let his daughter ride alone any more. As Alan grew well, the doctor's visits stopped too, unless he was in the vicinity and came in for a few minutes conversation.

As soon as he could crawl on his horse, Alan was out, riding over the place, seeing to the spring plowing and planting. Evening after evening he would come back exhausted, falling into an uneasy doze even before Louise could give him his supper, and his cough hung on.

"You can't keep this up, Alan," Louise told him.

"I have to get the crop in the ground, if we're going to hang on here. And I intend to!"

"It isn't worth it," she grumbled, but she had the same fierce determination to stay, not to be driven off. But she was afraid for Alan. Besides her sharp apprehensions, there were dull, pervading fears clogging her mind by day, haunting her sleep. She was too tired not to sleep, but her nightmares showed her fears in queer monster shapes.

These days Alan always took his pistol with him. "Not that I'm afraid of the people here on Indigo. Or the hands on Avondale, or on the Yankee's place either. They're good, and don't want trouble. But I believe the Yankee wants to stir things up. It's one way to make himself important. So he might import some troublemakers."

Louise kept a loaded pistol in the house too, and if Alan was to be away any length of time, Cornelius stayed in the kitchen, within call. If Tommy strayed off too far, Louise went running after him.

The winter broke at last, gave way to spring, and with warmer weather, Alan stopped coughing and grew stronger. After the hard winter, there were floods. The river rose. Indigo's fields were unaffected by high water except near the creek. It was no longer the sluggish curl of water eddying thinly over the sandbars, but a thick stream spreading beyond its banks. There were windstorms too. One particularly severe. Louise paced the narrow gallery, looking out in hopes of seeing Alan. She clutched Tommy, who wanted to escape. There was a heavy dun-colored cloud in the southwest, and lightning shook all over the sky without a pause.

Cornelius snuffed the heavy air. "Reckon one er dem cooms comin'."

"What's a coom?" Tommy asked.

"Folks call 'em cooms. Hurrycooms."

"Don't be afraid, Tommy. I don't want you to be afraid of storms." Louise's voice was unsteady and she winced at every crackle of thunder. "It's very foolish because there's nothing you can do about them."

"All right, Mother," Tommy strained against her clutches. He wanted to run off and get up in his treehouse and nail the planks down tighter so the wind wouldn't blow them away.

"Come on in the house this minute." Louise dragged him indoors. She wanted to go look for Alan, but she couldn't leave Tommy. "Let's get right in the middle of the bed. I wish I had a good feather bed. Feathers ward off lightning."

She pushed Tommy on the bed and made him stay there, while

the wind swooped with the sound of a freight train, and whistled and moaned through the trees.

"Now don't be afraid," Louise kept saying.

"But I'm not, Mother."

At last it was over, and Tommy scuttled off, flinging open the door and letting in a gust of cool air. He went running to climb to his treehouse and assess the damage to it. Alan came in later. He had taken refuge in one of the cabins. Louise went to get the pots and pans from under the old leaks and the new leaks. Cornelius would have to get on the roof and hammer some more.

With the heat and drought of summer, the floods went down, leaving mud and slime. Louise started her garden over again, and for a while everything grew, until the summer heat scorched it. She was too busy to see Medora often. No women rode alone these days, so Louise only saw Medora when she and Alan could go to Avondale, or when the Winsloes could all come to Indigo. Then there was no chance to find out what Medora really thought about Jasper, or if she had any hope of his coming back again.

Louise hadn't been to Natchez since before Christmas, and one hot day Alan asked her if she didn't want to drive in with him, and take Tommy. "We'll spend the night. I have some things to get, and I don't much like leaving you here."

"The figs are ready for preserving. I don't like to leave them, they'll sour. Go on, Cornelius is perfectly sober. He'll watch out for us." The figs were heaped in a big iron kettle outdoors, with a charcoal fire under them.

"Bring me back some sugar, Alan."

"You've become so capable, Lou." He smiled and kissed her, but his thin face saddened, and Louise knew why. He was thinking of her as she used to be, dreamy, rather idle, except for her interest in books and music, and always beautifully dressed. Someday, she would go back and find that other Louise, at least retrieve whatever traits she had had that were worth keeping. Now she was too busy.

Cornelius hitched up the wagon, and Alan rattled off in it on his way to Natchez, and Louise began her preserving.

Tommy was gathering tomatoes, and eating them. That's the way he liked them, hot and unwashed. Just as he picked and ate dusty dewberries and blackberries, bugs and all. He, at least, had thrived in this life. Maybe it was only because he was a little boy, but Louise thought it was also because he was a creature of the wilds. If only he would grow up happy and contented with things as he would find them, instead of being haunted by the inheritance he should have had, and would never have.

"If only we can keep this for him!" It was hardly a princely estate from her view of it at the moment. There was Lillybelle's slab-sided cabin, with three children quarreling on the steps. Every now and then, Jessie came out to clout them. Two worn quilts hung on the line, and a nod of blue smoke quivered from the crazy stovepipe. Lillybelle was inside, unable to help with the preserving because she was frying sowbelly for her brood. The last baby, born in the spring, wailed unheeded.

Beyond the vegetable garden, Louise had set out a row of peach and pear trees. They were spindly saplings, but they had put out tentative blossoms, immediately shriveled by a late cold snap. But they had struggled, poor things, and now they dangled a spattering of leaves. The cow had calved. The little heifer was named Thomasina, for Tommy, who loved her, and Louise had saved most of the baby chicks from rats, and hawks, and other marauders.

At last the preserves, bubbling and simmering through the day, were done. Lillybelle's oldest boy Abe, a hoe over his shoulder, was coming in, and he took the heavy kettle into the kitchen. Abe was named for the patriarch, but Link, Tommy's contemporary, was, Louise feared, named for the Great Liberator.

Jessie came into the kitchen to help. She looked cross, but Louise's, "Let me show you how to put them up so they won't spoil," worked magic. Jessie liked to learn, and she and Louise worked together in the hot inconvenient kitchen putting the figs in jars.

It was sunset when they had finished. Jessie looked out of the window and gave a shriek, seized the broken broom, and ran out into the chicken yard. Louise looked. The stupid old hen had gone to roost in the top of a fig tree, clucking to her new chicks to follow her. She had done that night after night, and it had taken time and trouble to get her down and in the henhouse with the eleven young ones. Now Jessie had had enough of it. She climbed after the hen, and dislodged her with the broom. The hen tumbled down in a mass of scattered feathers and continuous squawks, and Jessie came after her, whacking at her. "I tech yer ter do yer baby chicks like dat!"

"Don't hurt her," Louise called, then began to laugh. Round and round they went. "Yer ole fool—yer know yer chicks cain't git up in no tree." At last the hen was in the henhouse, and the last chick was in after her, and the feathers drifted then settled. Louise would describe it to Alan when he came back. She always garnered up any incident that would amuse him, and tried to talk as little as she could about the unpleasant ones.

It was hot, and Louise escaped from the house and went out, calling to Tommy, but he was too far away to hear her. His thin bare legs and Cornelius's short crooked legs were vanishing into the dark green cotton rows. Cornelius was usually sober during the busy months. He succumbed during the dreariness of winter, and Louise sometimes envied him his devotion to the noxious brews he managed to get from somewhere. It was an avenue of escape from every day. If Alan wasn't on hand, Tommy attached himself to Cornelius.

Louise went off to the field where the pecan tree grew. Alan intended to plant that field, as the land there was rich. Then it wouldn't belong to her any more. She had fallen into the habit of going there, lured by its emptiness. The mud and sand and slime from the creek's overflow had grown over now, and from a little distance the weeds, almost kneehigh, had a gloss like glass, an undulating smoothness. The big tree outlined its strength of trunk and branches against the sky. The sun had gone, and the elaborate summer clouds glowed and brightened. Above and beyond them, cirrus clouds, a flock of sheep with glittering fleece, seemed to be following the sun below the edge of the horizon. The crickets and katydids never stopped their harsh chorus. There was no other sound, except the cry of a pair of mockingbirds, harsh too, giving their note of fright and anger. Louise tried to ignore it, but towards the creek she could see the gray and white birds swoop and flutter, and she sighed, knowing they would drive her to go and see what was the matter. They had any number of enemies, and built their nests in bushes, or low in small trees, exposing the young ones to constant danger. Louise ran towards a thorny and undecorative sapling, growing near the creek bank. That seemed to be the center of the commotion. The branches were shaking and the birds were louder in their fury. When Louise reached the spot, she stopped, panting, then hurled herself towards the enemy. It was a little boy, the Yankee's child. She recognized him at once. Little devil! He was full of vigor and determination. He clutched a low branch, ignoring thorns, and was trying to pull himself to one higher where the nest was alive with three, no, four, gawping, unwieldy young birds. The child's fat hand reached out, and this time the nest was within his grip, but he ducked to avoid the swoop of one of the parent birds. That gave Louise time to run up to him, grab him, jerk him down and away from the tree. "You horrid little Yankee beast! Poor little birds! Aren't you ashamed of yourself!"

He stared at her, dumb and frozen by her sudden attack. His good looks made her dislike him almost as much as his evil intentions. His cheeks were round and pink and his eyes glowed a deep blue. He had no right to be such a handsome child! "Little wretch!"

He pulled away from her hand. His face puckered, and he began to bawl. His mouth opened, showing perfect little teeth, the brilliant eyes half closed, and tears, round and shining, spilled out and dripped down his cheeks. In spite of herself she was sorry she had frightened him.

"It's bad to take the little birds out of their nest—the poor old birds wouldn't have any children any more."

She didn't expect to make any impression on the boy, he was too little, and anyhow, he was the Yankee's child. But he looked at the nest and began to cry harder. Maybe he was only sorry she had stopped him from grabbing the little birds.

"Never mind," her voice was gentle now. She took his hand and led him away from the tree—let the vociferous parents settle down. The little boy let her take his hand and trotted along beside her. He didn't seem to be a timid child, or easily frightened. Most children would have bolted by now.

"What are you doing over here?" She wiped his eyes with her handkerchief. He snuffled and looked around.

"Runned away," he murmured.

"Your mother will be looking for you. You'd better go back. I'll watch you across the creek." She started to say, "Don't come here any more," but she refrained. "Promise me one thing—no, two things. Don't ever cross the sand bar if there's any water over it, and don't bother the poor little birds any more. Will you promise?"

He nodded, looking down at his scratched, bare toes.

"Run along, then, it's late."

He looked at her, his eyes gleaming, then whirled around, ran down the bank, and went leaping over the sand bar. She watched him scramble up the other bank and disappear into the bushes. A woman's voice was calling. Evidently his mother had missed him and was looking for him. Louise wondered what he would tell his mother, if anything. Somehow Louise was not pleased with herself. Of course her rage had been righteous, in another minute he would have torn the birds from their nest and either killed them or left them to die. She had never been so angry with Tommy in his life as the time when he had gathered all the lightning bugs and had crammed them in an old cigar box. But this time, mixed with her allowable wrath, was the hate she felt for the Yankee and everything and everyone connected with him. Yet she shouldn't have been rough with that child. He'd been frightened, though not for long, and he hadn't seemed too surprised at roughness and anger. Probably he was used to it at home. Little fiend, she needn't feel these pangs of unease and remorse because of her dealings with him. He would grow up soon enough to be brazen and destructive and snatching like his father. A threat to her own child. Yet there was something very appealing in his little face, and something expressive in his eyes—the way he had looked up at the nest, as though he had realized what she was trying to say. Nonsense! He didn't understand. He'd probably come back and finish off the nest.

Louise went back across the field. Waves of violet drenched the trees and dimmed the woods, and all outlines wavered before they were drowned in the still dark. The little birds were quiet now in their fragile, foolish nest, easy to destroy.

Chapter Five

ALAN came back the next evening, unexpectedly. Louise ran out to meet him. "What's the matter?" she asked. Something was wrong. he had that look of strain and anxiety. "What are you doing back so soon?"

"I got out of Natchez as fast as I could. There are several cases of yellow fever in town."

Louise had gathered up her sewing in the corner of her apron, now she knotted and pleated at the stuff, and couldn't seem to stop the useless movements of her hands. When yellow fever struck, there was illness, desperate illness, and often death. She didn't remember a bad epidemic, but she had heard about them.

"Who told you?"

"Louis Corwin. So I knew I had to get away while I could."

"Who has it? Maybe it's just a rumor!"

"I'm afraid it's true. A colored child has already died of it. They'll guard all the roads leading in and out of town. Louis told me the guard will be posted by tonight, so I left."

There would be fires burning in the street during the night and men would be encamped at every road leading to town, to enforce the quarantine. No one would get into Natchez, and no one would be allowed to get out. The town would be beleaguered and besieged in the blazing heat, and the streets would be empty. Louise remembered her uncle telling her about a bad epidemic in New Orleans. Canal Street had been entirely deserted except for a funeral procession coming and a funeral procession drawing out of sight, and the only sound had been the bells tolling for the dead, while the disease had crept from house to house.

"There's nothing we can do." Her voice sounded thin and strange. She felt a bleak isolation, and she knew she must look pale because

65

Tommy was watching her, and for his sake she tried to control her terror. She put her arm around him, then withdrew it. Suppose she already had it, and through her he would get it! It might strike here, or anywhere. There was no sure escape, no real knowledge about it. Where did it come from and why did it come? Nobody knew. They had theories, and had to discard them. There was no certainty, except they knew the fatal symptoms. After the first frost, there was no more yellow fever. While it lasted, and while the hot weather lasted, there was no safety for anybody, in the country, in the town, or for young or old, rich or poor.

"Indigo's far enough away from Natchez to be out of danger," Alan tried to reassure her. If it was contagious, nobody knew that, they were far enough away, but there was no certainty that it might not strike out in the country too.

"I might send Tommy to his Aunt Carrie," Louise meditated. Carrie lived on a plantation beyond Memphis.

"There's been a case reported in Memphis. No, Lou, he'd better stay here."

"I suppose so."

"I'm not scared!" Tommy said.

"Hush, don't talk like that!" Louise was sorry they had discussed it in front of Tommy, but he didn't seem frightened, only interested. He had the resilient nerves of childhood. Fear hadn't yet scored its grooves in his memory. Louise thought how long she had lived with apprehension. It was rooted in her now, and each new worry added its weight. Now all kinds of dark forebodings crowded in her mind. When it was his bedtime, Louise kept Tommy saying his prayers for such a long time he grew impatient.

"We've prayed for everybody we know," he grumbled.

"Say one more prayer for the people we don't know."

She kissed him and tucked the mosquito bar around him and sat beside him until he fell asleep. Involuntarily, the Yankee child's face flashed before her. It was a pity he would grow up to be Tommy's enemy, and the hate and bitterness of one generation would continue on into another.

The relentless summer closed in, dry, blazing with a fierce white light. The news from Natchez didn't reassure Louise. The epidemic

66

was not a bad one, but it was bad enough. Her own friends were well, but there were deaths from the fever. A cousin of the Corwins died, and a niece of the Duels. In their country isolation, Louise and Alan could only wait and hope and live each day as it came, and each day's work had to be done.

Once in a while the Winsloes drove over. Medora looked pale and seemed listless. Jasper still wrote long letters and spoke hopefully of coming back soon. If only Medora had another interest! But what could she do except live on as she was living, helping Mrs. Winsloe in the house, sewing, reading aloud to her aunt and uncle, and waiting.

One evening when the Winsloes came, they brought bad news. Amanda Rand had yellow fever.

"How awful! She looked as if she could never be ill." As she spoke, Louise happened to look at Alan. He hadn't said anything, but even in the yellow lamplight his face had turned ashy.

"It's a terrible thing," Mr. Bijah said. "But she's young and strong, and her father's watching her every minute."

Nobody answered. They all knew yellow fever could kill the young and strong.

"I must at least ride over there and ask about her," Alan spoke at last. "She and her father were so good to me during the winter."

"It'll be running a risk to be near it," Mrs. Winsloe peered at him over the edge of her palmetto fan.

"I can't help that. It's the least I can do."

Louise didn't argue with him. It was no use when Alan had made up his mind and this was one of those times.

The next morning, when he was ready to set out, Louise offered to go with him, but he said he preferred to go by himself. It was a hot, dusty way, but when he came back he was much more cheerful than when he had set out.

"She's had it for over a week but I told Mrs. Rand we didn't know. We've lived so to ourselves. But she's much much better now. She's going to be all right."

Louise was as glad as he was. Amanda was the personification of health and good spirits. Alan had never really seen her, but she had succeeded in touching his imagination.

"Who lives at the Rands?"

"The doctor and his wife, and Amanda, and the two sons, Ben and Jack. They're younger than Amanda. It's a plain country house, bigger and better than this one, but no mansion. They have a nice garden. You would like it, and the view. The ground rises and falls and you can see a blueness in the distance where the swamp begins."

Louise looked up and saw Lillybelle in the doorway.

"Miss Lou, dem folks over yonder is took with de yeller fever."

"Who's got it?"

"Mistah Sanders an' Miss Della."

Louise had never heard the Yankee called by his right name before. She knew it vaguely but he loomed for her clothed in the ugly epithets they gave him. "What about the children?"

"Dey ain't got hit."

"Who's taking care of them?" Against her will, Louise began to worry about them.

"Pershah's dey cook. She'll mind 'em."

"She wouldn't get frightened and leave them, would she?"

"Pershah? Oh, no'm."

Neither Alan or Louise doubted the accuracy of Lillybelle's information. There was a constant shuttling back and forth among the hands, visiting, and churchgoing, and everybody on Indigo knew everything about what happened at the Yankee's place.

"She seems sure the cook'll stay and look after the children," Alan said.

"She'd know about Persia. I think I've seen her over here, calling on Lillybelle. She's a big rawboned woman. There're two children. I've seen the boy, and I think the girl's a little older." Louise told Alan how and where she'd seen the boy. "He impressed me."

"You have a weakness for little boys."

"I know. But I'm unchristian. You know what I'm wishing, don't you?"

"Yes, because I'm wishing it too, thinking how much simpler our lives would be if that man drew his last breath." Alan smiled at her. "But all the same you're worried about those children."

"Children are different. Persia can't do an adequate job of looking after them and taking care of two people ill with yellow fever."

"I know. But even if they were your dearest friends you'd hate to go over there and risk bringing back yellow fever to Tommy."

She sighed. "I wish—— Why are you allowed in war to kill some perfect stranger and yet in peace aren't supposed to want your mortal enemy to die and be out of the way?" Alan grinned. "It's one of the inconsistencies that's made Christian practice so difficult."

"Don't be abstract with me now. I've too much on my mind. Do you think you'll ever get me to feel the South was wrong to defend itself?"

"Not you, or anyone of you 'soft, civilized' Southern gentlewomen. If we occasionally have doubts about some strategic errors on our part, you stouthearted women buoy us up. But since you're so single-minded, what's worrying you? It's wrong for us to wish the Yankee would die, but we do want him to. The only trouble is, he's tough, and I bet he won't."

All the same, Louise wondered if Dr. Rand had gone to see about the Yankee and his wife, and found out from Cornelius that he had. Cornelius had seen the doctor on his way to the Yankee's house. "Do you know how they are getting along, Cornelius?" she asked him.

"Dey ain't daid."

As each day dragged out, Louise felt more and more nervous and restless, and never let Tommy out of her sight. One morning she was watching him from the window. He was playing with Link, the one of Lillybelle's brood nearest Tommy in age. They were busy building fortifications out of mud. Earlier there had been shrieks from Link. He had a horror of snails, and he had said that Tommy had made him swallow one. But Tommy, it turned out, had only told Link to open his mouth and close his eyes, then had slipped a pod of cold boiled okra on his tongue. Now they were too preoccupied with their battle plans to notice her vigilance. It was nearly time for dinner, and Alan came into the house.

"I was down near the gate, and I saw Dr. Rand going to the Yankee's."

"How's Amanda?"

"She's all right, he said."

"What about the Yankee and his wife?"

"They're getting well, but now the children are down with it."
Louise couldn't speak for a minute. "Who's taking care of them?"

"The cook, and the parents are trying to, but they are still weak,
of course."

"Did Dr. Rand say they had a chance?"

"He said it was soon to tell."

"Alan, they'll need better nursing than those people can give
them!"

"The doctor knows that, but who's going to nurse them? Most
of their hands are scared, and stay away from the house."

"I ought to go over there."

"You run a risk if you do, though Lord knows what's a danger
and what isn't. You don't owe those people a thing, Lou."

That little boy's round face and bright eyes flashed before her.
The clash of the plantation bell made her shiver. There was nothing
ominous about it. It was rung every day at this time as a signal for
dinner. Tommy came in and ate two helpings of rice and gumbo,
and an enormous slice of watermelon, but neither Alan or Louise
could eat.

"Alan, I'll have to go over there and try to help them."

"It's dangerous for you. Maybe even for Tommy."

"I've been planning it out, so it at least won't be dangerous for
Tommy. There's an empty cabin not far from the creek. I can have
Cornelius put a big tub of water in it, and a change of clothes, and
I can bathe and dress there before I come back to this house."

"It seems unreasonable for you to risk yourself for those people——"

"It's one of those things. Reason hasn't anything to do with it."

"I know." Alan didn't attempt to argue with her.

Just as he had been impelled to go join the Confederate army,
and to come out here to Indigo, she was now impelled to go to
her neighbors. "If those children should die, and I hadn't tried to
help them, I wouldn't ever forgive myself."

"We'll both go, Lou."

"Not you, not yet. We'd better take turns. When I get tired, then you come." She dreaded Alan's being near yellow fever, but knew he would inevitably help too. "And Tommy, you stay right here and play with Link. Don't wander. Now, mind me."

Jessie had been waiting on the table, and had heard everything. She appeared with the broom. "Ah'm goin' over yonder ter de cabin and sweep hit out fer you, ma'am."

Tommy put his hand in his mother's. She kissed him. "While I'm nursing those other children, I mustn't kiss you. I don't want you to get sick."

She hurried out of the house and took the short cut through the field. In the heat, the brushy weeds with their queer powdery flower had a raw, wild scent. In the afternoon's silence it was easy to feel a waiting deadly quality, as if with every breath you drew in the fever. Where was it, and why did it come? In what you touched, or smelled or ate? As she moved along, she felt a sense of isolation and unreality.

The creek wove in and out, doubling and looping, wandering through its course, to slide at last into the river. It was the dividing line, but a chasm darker and deeper than its shallows separated her from her enemies. War and death and ruin, and greed and hate. Here and there the creek was only a few inches deep, but there was one deep still pool in sight, darkened by the overhanging branches from the trees on the other side. The wrinkled sand bar was free of water and blazed with glare. Walking over it, Louise could feel the heat through her shoes. She made her way easily up the bank to the other side, finding a well-defined path hidden in the willows and briers.

This path she was following suddenly terrified her. It zigzagged its thread towards the danger and hideousness of yellow fever. She knew enough and had heard enough so that her own healthy flesh shuddered. She grasped at a rough-leaved branch to steady herself, pushed on and reached the clearing and saw the house ahead of her. It was a square box without shutters or galleries. In better repair, and newer and stronger than the one at Indigo, it had not the slightest charm, and around it was raw, unplanted ground. Behind it, at a little distance, loomed the ruins of the Winsloe mansion.

Trees and briers had grown up between the wreckage of the walls, but the columns stood, ghostly pale against the wavering density and darkness of the growth behind them.

Louise remembered that other wrecked plantation house in Louisiana, where she had gone to find Tom. She had climbed over broken stones, pushed her way through piles of rubble and through sagging doorways, past the curve of the stairway rising to nothingness, to find him—to speak just those few words. She thought again how it must have been for him, spying on Grant through the ravaged countryside he had known "like the palm of his hand"—known it because he had hunted there so often, had belonged to it, and had gone to brilliant balls and parties in those shells of houses. He must have felt himself a ghost, pitting his shadowy skill against Grant's army.

Hate for the invaders shook her. Why did she come here! Why didn't she let them alone, and let them die. They had come to seize and batten. Let the ghosts destroy them. From the house she heard a faint, weak crying. She put her hands over her ears. The present, the future was calling out to her, and she didn't want to listen. She could turn and go away, but she knew that if she did, she would hear that crying always. Half running, she reached the house and knocked on the closed door.

The door opened and a man loomed up. "What you want?" It was her first glimpse of the Yankee, and at the moment she had no impression of him at all, except to know he was big—a massive bulk of a creature.

"I came to help."

He grunted, hesitated, then said, "We can make do without your help."

"No!" the woman's voice was sharp. She came up and peered from around his arm, her face bleak and pinched, her tow-colored hair hanging in wisps. "If she'll help, let her—the children——"

The man nodded slowly, and moved back out of the doorway, and Louise went in. The woman slumped down in a chair and began to sob.

"Quit that——" the man ordered. "Be of some use, can't you?"

The woman pulled herself up, swaying unsteadily, hardly able to drag herself around. Obviously, she wasn't well enough herself to be a capable nurse. The man leaned against the door, sweat pouring from his face. In the next room, the child began to cry again.

"Will you get some rest if I look after them?" Louise asked her.

"I can't rest with them like they are!" The white, hot light glittered at the windows, the ugly furniture and objects in the room were dim, and the woman's face was a yellowish blur. Her pallid eyes watched Louise. "Jim's got it bad. Francy's not so sick, but Jim's bad off."

Louise went into the bedroom, the woman following her. The little girl was quiet, and didn't seem to be suffering. She was a smaller replica of her mother, with fair faded hair and a thin little face. The boy, in the other bed, tossed restlessly, muttering. His face was flushed and swollen, his half open eyes had a stupid, heavy expression, as if he could no longer really see any more, and his skin was burning hot to Louise's touch.

"Get ice," Louise said. "Plenty of it." The pitcher by the bed had only a few melted pieces in it. She took a spoon and slipped a bit of ice in the child's mouth, and wrapped the rest in a clean handkerchief and put it on his forehead, holding it there.

A long, lank Negro woman got up from a chair at the head of the bed. Louise hadn't noticed her at first. "Ah'll git some mo'." She was very black, with hardly any flesh on her bones.

"Here, Persia, I'll fetch it." The Yankee came in and grasped the pitcher and went off with it. "You stay here and do what she tells you." Louise saw him weaving his way outside, occasionally hesitating as if he was about to fall, then going on to a wooden building, evidently where they stored their ice.

The little boy began to vomit, and Louise and his mother were both busy with him. Louise held him, murmuring to him, and trying to soothe him. She forgot the hot stinking room and the other people in it. After the spell of nausea was over, and the bed changed, and the child seemed more relaxed, she asked for his medicine.

The doctor had ordered morphine. "But he throws it up each time," the boy's mother said.

"We'll have to keep on trying." Louise coaxed the dose down the boy's throat, noticing his tongue, covered with white furriness, and pink and raw around the edges.

"Po' lamb," Persia muttered, fanning him. She must be exhausted, since she had borne the brunt of nursing the Yankee and his wife.

"I've seen you before, Persia," Louise said to her.

"Yes'm. Ah goes ter see Lillybelle onct in er while."

When Jim seemed to doze, Louise went over to the other bed. Francy had much less fever than her brother. Her forehead was damp, and when Louise took her pulse it was almost normal. Except for the lethargic way she was lying, she hardly seemed ill. The children's father, coming back with the ice, went to his son's bed and sat down beside it.

For the first time, Louise was really aware of the Yankee's face. He was large, and normally must be heavy with flesh and muscle, though he was weak and thinned out now. He had a big head, stony light eyes, and thick coarse features. He held his mouth half open as he watched his son. Some of the man's teeth were missing, and the rest were yellow and stained. It was strange to think he was the father of such a beautiful child, yet trying to look at him objectively, Louise could see that once he might have been a handsome man. To think too, that poor little Jim, if he lived, might turn into just such an animal. His mother, though, in spite of the harsh Yankee tone of her voice, was much better than the father, gentler, and more educated.

"Francy ain't much sick, is she?" The woman implored.

"I don't know. I hope not." Louise had heard about cases where the symptoms seemed light at first, and you couldn't be sure. "Is it time for her medicine?"

The afternoon wore on, and the little boy vomited, moaned, tossed, and burned with fever. The nursing was constant and strenuous, and the burden of it fell on Louise and Persia. The others tried to help, but they had been ill themselves too recently. They couldn't move fast or surely. They fumbled, dropped things, and almost fell. Persia bundled up soiled sheets, took them out, let out thin screeches for someone to bring her clean ones. She helped remake beds, fanned the buzzing flies away from the children's faces, held Jim while Louise gave him his medicine, and became cheerful if he didn't immediately throw it up.

"I'd better stay all night," Louise said, "if you can send word to Indigo." She knew she couldn't leave.

"I'll send." The Yankee struggled to his feet. "You stay. Help the boy."

She didn't answer. She was too busy with the moaning, twitching child. He was like someone in the throes of demonic possession. They had thought the Yankee was invulnerable, but he couldn't help feeling the child's helpless suffering. Louise saw he had one weakness. He cared for the boy. Not as much for the girl, but the boy. And, Louise admitted to herself, so did she. Nothing mattered to her now except the lives of these children. She emptied basins and slops, and helped change beds. Persia struggled to keep things clean, but the room reeked with the bitter and bilious vomit and so did Louise's clothes. She didn't notice, she was only thankful it was not the terrifying black vomit, characteristic of the worse form of yellow fever, and nearly always a sign of death.

Just after dark, Dr. Rand came back. He examined the children, and Louise told him everything she had done for them.

He nodded. "So you came, somehow I thought you would. I'll be with them now—I had to go down to the river. A fisherman was choking on a bone, but I won't leave unless I have to, so you'd better go and get some rest."

"I'm needed now. I'll go later, and send Alan over."

Dr. Rand didn't argue with her. During the night, Francy became worse. Minute by minute the almost normal coolness of her skin changed to the dry fire of rising fever. Her mother touched her forehead, and burst into tears.

"Shut up, Della," the man rasped. "None er your caterwaulin'."

His wife cringed, but into the weakness and vagueness and dull wretchedness of her face there came another expression, a kind of malevolence. But she tried to muffle the sound of her sobbing and take care of the child. After midnight, Francy was as ill as Jim. In more danger, Louise felt. While she was sponging the child with cool water, she noticed how thin Francy's arms and legs were already. There seemed no solid foundation of health in her to fight the fever. But the man hardly ever left his vigil beside his son, and managed to follow the doctor's directions with a certain amount of skill in spite of his weakness.

Towards dawn, Dr. Rand told Louise to go get some sleep. "You'll be more use to me if you aren't so tired."

She stumbled from the house, into the freshness and dampness of the early morning air. Exhausted, she dragged herself along the pale ribbon of the path. The familiar places had an air of mystery and strangeness. Mist floated over the creek. The sand bar had patterns of a skeleton—some enormous thing dead for millions of years and now revealing its bones between dark and day, giving a glimpse of some far-off, unknown past the world had once lived. The water in the pool seemed to hold untold depths, and the glow coming toward her was the evasive will-o'-the-wisp, the fox fire of swamps and damp wildernesses.

It was Alan's lantern, and he and Tommy were crossing the sand bar to meet her. "Stay away, stay away," she called. "Wait until I've changed my clothes."

She made her way to the empty cabin, and they followed at a distance. She bathed and changed her clothes, felt better, and was able to walk more steadily through the dew-wet grass. "Don't kiss me, don't touch me," she said to Tommy. He stood away from her, watching her. He must find her unfamiliar.

"How are they?" Alan asked.

"I don't know. It's bad."

"You go to sleep, Lou. I'm going over there." He handed the lantern, no longer needed now, to Tommy, and went the way Louise had come. For a while, at least, the Yankee and his family were no longer enemies, but people. Yet when this crisis was over, they would be enemies again. It was like a truce in the middle of a war, and probably for the same reason—to bury the dead. Her mind jumbled with fatigue, Louise wondered at the strangeness of people's behavior.

She slept for hours, but it was a nightmare haunted sleep, invaded by restlessness and worry. She woke up heavy-headed, wondering with a pang of terror if she were coming down with yellow fever too, but she dressed, and found she was desperately hungry, and ate every scrap of the food Lillybelle brought her. In a kind of panic she set out again, wondering what had happened to Jim and Francy while she had been away from them. When she reached the Yankee's house, she called Alan, and he came out. "I'll go now, and come back later to relieve you. Dr. Rand's staying."

"How's Jim?"

"A little better, the doctor thinks. But that poor little girl!"

Louise and Alan took turns with the nursing. Days and nights merged together. Dr. Rand never left. His other patients were able to spare him now. He fought for the children with all of his knowledge and experience, and Jim began to get better steadily, but Francy grew worse and worse. The doctor gave her sedatives and calomel, but nothing seemed to help her, and her face began to look caved in.

Jim's babyish plump face had become tiny, yellowish gray, and his eyes looked dark and enormous, the iris yellowed too. Dr. Rand carried him to a bed in another room, away from his sister, and in it he stayed quiet and listless, hardly moving a finger, but the fever had broken. "He'll get well," Dr. Rand said.

"Do you hear?" Louise whispered to the child's mother. Della nodded, brushing the tears from her face with the back of her hand. She smiled, and it was the first time Louise had ever seen her smile. It was sad, sadder than her tears. That smile made Louise see that Della had once been a pretty girl. The ghost of an extinct prettiness showed for an instant behind the wreckage made by her illness, and her unhappiness, and the whole tenor of her life.

Louise had seen the Yankee's desperate concern for his son, but as the boy grew better, and the man grew stronger himself, though he still hovered over Jim, he lacked patience and tenderness. "Here, he won't take it," the man would say, giving up the attempt to get a spoonful of nourishment down Jim's throat, and Louise would have to come and coax and wheedle the baby to make him swallow some wine, and a little gruel, and a glass of milk. She noticed too how Jim, inert as he was, seemed to wince away from his father's touch, and yet respond to her arm around him, her tone, and her endearments.

Persia helped her with Jim. The mother was preoccupied with

Francy. Dr. Rand tried everything—enemas, sedatives, cupping—putting heated glass to the small of her back to keep the kidneys from blocking—ice in her parched mouth, ice bags on her forehead. Her gums began to bleed and her tongue became covered with a dark crust. The little girl no longer seemed to be a child at all. It was as though some hideous spell had turned her into a crone a thousand years old, her features pinched and withered, her whole face collapsed. And always the constant, seemingly effortless vomiting went on and on. Louise watched the doctor snatch up the basin and go to the window with it. He tried to check his groan, but she heard. She followed, seeing the pale, greasy stuff permeated with dark threads and patches like coffee grounds. She knew. It was the black vomit, the fatal sign.

Della must have read their faces. A wild terror glazed her eyes. The doctor put his hand on her shoulder. She twitched away from him. "Do something, do something!"

"I've done everything I know how to do."

Della flung herself on her knees by the bed. Louise went to her. "We must both pray for Francy."

"I do! I have—all the time—it's no good!"

Nothing was any use. Francy sank into a coma, and died the next day. Louise was there, in the room when Dr. Rand drew the sheet over the withered face. The glassy sunlight struck at the window. the flies buzzed. The room stank. The Yankee stood in the door, leaning against it. Della stayed on her knees by the bed. "I remember the day she was born," she whispered. "Then—I thought everything was bound to turn out all right——" Her face was rigid, her eyes staring—looking back at some memory of happiness. Persia was rocking herself back and forth in the corner of the room, moaning. Della turned on her. "Get out—get out of here!"

Persia looked up, unfolded her bony height and went out of the room like a black shadow.

"Stop your carryin' on," the man said. "You got no call ter holler at her." He spoke with annoyance.

"No call——" Della began, but he took a step into the room, and she hushed. Louise felt cold. There was no love between the parents to make the hideousness of the child's death less ugly. On the con-

trary, the crisis had only showed up the cleavage and dislike between the mother and father.

Alan had left the house, and Dr. Rand was in the next room, and
Louise wanted to get up and go out, but she found herself numb.
Della's strange attitude to Persia though, Louise thought was the
hysteria of despair. It was ungrateful, but Della was desperate.

"We got Jim left," the man pointed out. It was the kind of thing
you said to comfort, yet he didn't say it in a consoling way.

"I want both my children, I want 'em both!" Della's face began
to twitch. "You—you don't care about her—you never did——"

He took another step into the room. "Quit it, it ain't so."

"It's the truth, the God's truth—you don't care, but I care—she was
mine! All I had that was all mine——" She began to shriek and
laugh and moan. Louise tried to hold her, then Dr. Rand hurried
back to her, mixed some medicine and made Della drink it. The
man didn't help. He muttered something and shambled out of the
house. Between them, Louise and Dr. Rand half led and half
carried Della to the bed in the next room. In a few minutes, the
sedative took effect and she slept.

The doctor packed his bag. "I'll drive you home," he offered
Louise. "That man! What a critter!"

Louise went to the bed where Jim was sleeping, strong enough
and lively enough now to clutch a toy in his hand. Persia hadn't
left the house. She was sitting near him, fanning him.

"You'll keep on taking care of him, won't you Persia?"

"Yes'm I sho will."

"And do everything for him just the way the doctor said—just
the way I showed you?"

"Yes'm. Doan you fret."

"Thank you, Persia, for all you've done." Louise leaned over and
kissed Jim's hand. It was over, finished, except for the funeral. She
had earned her escape from that house and those people. The
Yankee might realize for a while that she had helped his children,
but he would harden again. They would all go back to the old way
of feeling and behaving to each other. But something had changed
for her. She knew she would never feel quite the same sort of
hatred again while Jim was there.

Chapter Six

THE funeral was as harsh and dreary as Louise had felt it would be, and it was nearly a month afterwards before Louise saw Della and Jim again. She came to the house one afternoon, bringing Jim with her. He was still thin, but a tinge of color had come back to his lips and a glint of luster to his eyes. Della sat on the edge of the chair Louise offered her, sat very straight. She was in black and wore a black bonnet. Tommy came and took Jim off with him. "Don't be strenuous with him, son," Louise cautioned.

"I won't." Tommy showed Jim his few battered toys, and even gave him a boat he had carved from a chunk of cedar, then took him to show him the treehouse. They were children in a children's world, but poor Della looking around uneasily at books and pictures, found nothing to say, until at last she managed to whisper, "I came to thank you."

Louise tried to talk to her, but it was no use. Della was too shy, too unhappy and ill at ease. Soon she got up to leave, and called Jimmy away from the delights of the treehouse. He struggled away from her hand, and ran to Louise. His mother jerked him back. "Come on, I tell you! Or your pa 'll fix you!" At the door she turned. "I do thank you." Her red-rimmed eyes filled with tears. An ugly flush stained the muddy pallor of her skin. "He won't."

The epidemic lessened. After the first frost, it was over. It was gone, for this year at least, and the terror lifted. Louise knew she would never forget that summer, or the days and nights of nursing Jim and Francy. After the first early cold snap, there was a spell of warm weather, a somnolent Indian summer, with mild pale skies and gentle slanted sunlight. Only the drift of leaves, and the shortening days, and the honking of wild geese flying over prophesied winter ahead. On such afternoons, Louise hated to stay in

80

the house, and on one such day, looking up from her work, she noticed a spray of cream-colored roses blooming near the window. She went out, scissors in hand. The roses she had planted had drooped during the hot summer, but now they were putting out ruddy stems and buds. Cutting the flowers, she thought how pretty they would look in her pet vase. Then another thought came to her, and she filled an old jelly glass with water and carried it with the roses when she left the house and crossed the fields.

The year's crop had been good and it had been picked but some-one was still lingering to clean out the bolls, because from a distance, Louise heard singing. That meant the singer was happy, though the spiritual itself was full of melancholy. The hands had hard lives, but they knew how to be happy. It was a great gift, and Louise was trying to acquire it. This afternoon, she wouldn't think about the mortgage or the taxes or politics, but see only what was before her eyes.

She followed the creek into the woods before she found a con-venient sand bar and crossed over. Again, she was invading the Yankee's land, and she didn't want to encounter him. It wasn't likely. She didn't feel that he came often to the place where she was going—to Francy's grave in a cluster of pines. Getting near it, she remembered the child's funeral. She had taken a few flowers, all she had, and they had wilted in the heat even before she could put them on the raw mound of earth covering the coffin. From some where, the Yankee had found a wandering preacher, a Yankee too, who had shouted a prayer in a twanging voice. There had been no real compassion in him or in his prayer. There had been nothing to veil the ugliness of the child's death, but today the grave was softened by a weaving of fallen leaves, and a sliding ray of sunlight sifted through the branches. The lavishness and carelessness of the woods had blended the grave into its surroundings, smoothed it over. But it was lonelier than ever.

Standing there, Louise was frightened by the irrevocable solitude of death. Time heals, nature smooths over, but with forgetfulness. When Della died, or stopped thinking about her child, Francy might never have existed, her name would never be thought or said again. Louise knew she was right to cling with all her passion to the shape and color of her memories. They were worth what they cost.

She put the roses on the little mound. They shone pearly against the dark withered leaves. She was turning away when she heard Jim's shout as he came hurtling through the trees. Louise smiled at the sight of him. His legs were sturdy and his cheeks were red again. He remembered her and came to her and let her kiss him, before a squirrel diverted his attention, and he went chasing after it. Della followed Jim, and at first Louise was hardly aware of her, she came so quietly. And for a few minutes she didn't speak, but just stood by the grave looking at the roses. There were flowers in her hands too, early-blooming Narcissus that must have come from the wreckage of the Winsloe gardens, where a few blossoms still struggled through weeds and brambles.

"You thought of Francy," Della said in her timid way.

"I often think about her."

"You brought flowers the day she was buried. So, when I find any, I bring them here too. The roses are real pretty." Della sat down on a fallen log. "Francy was poor and sickly from the day she was born, but I felt like she would change, and get over it and get to be pretty."

"She probably would have."

"I was pretty once," Della said. "You wouldn't believe it now." She showed her ruined teeth in a vague smile. "But folks told me so."

Louise could imagine it. Her faded hair would have had a blond sheen, like Jim's, and her sallowness a young glow. Her features were good enough even now, and it was the wreck of her teeth that spoiled her mouth.

"Here, Jim. Jim, you come back!" Jim looked around, but went on trying to climb the tree in pursuit of the scolding squirrel.

"He's all right. He's within our sight."

"I hate it down here. I'm always scared."

"Of what?"

"All of it! The look of it—and the feel of it. You're used to it."

Louise could understand why Della was afraid, and why the doze of autumn calm couldn't soothe her. It was all strange and terrifying to Della—maybe terrifying to anyone who really noticed. The height of the trees, and the shadows they cast, the flicker and depth of the river, the biting flavor of the wild grapes and the wild plums, the sly little creek, turning fierce overnight. Louise herself was learning to love it, feeling its particular magic. But it was a sinister magic, and called for a heart attuned to some echo of the untrammeled primitive earth. It was not a landscape for the tame or the timid.

"I had a right to be scared," Della muttered. "I knew it—knew something awful would happen to us! If we'd stayed up North where we belonged, I'd of had Francy now!"

"You can't be certain of that."

"I was against coming down here, but Mr. Sanders, he was all for it and made me come too. I was raised strict. I don't hold with your ways down here, but war or no war, I don't believe in ever taking what rightly belongs to other folks. I told Mr. Sanders I didn't want to come down here and live on that land where we are—I told him it wouldn't bring us any good. He shut me up. He won't let me say it. He can't keep me from knowing it." Again, her mouth twisted in that unjoyful smile. "Say it—who'll I say it to—except him? I've lived here over four years. You're the first white person who ever said one word to me. They all hate us!"

"I don't. Not you or Jim."

"I guess you don't. Now."

"And I'll see to it that the people I know won't hate you or Jim either."

"Would you? For Jim. He's friendly. And when he grows up enough, and sees how people around here won't even pass the time of day with him—why, it'll be bound to just break his heart."

"Was he born here?"

"Right here, in that house we built. I—guess I'm talking too much. But how would you like it if not one human soul spoke a word to you for over four years?"

"It's dreary for you. But you can come to my house. Come and bring Jim with you."

"He—Mr. Sanders won't like us to."

"Can't you slip away from time to time?"

"I guess so."

"I couldn't ever promise to be friends with your husband as long as he does the things he does against us."

83

"I know that. He don't want friends. He wants land and money, too. I hope he won't get yours from you folks. It's wrong. And you and your brother been so good——"

"We hope he won't either."

"I'd help if I could. But he don't listen to me now."

"You can bring Jim up to listen to you, and know right from wrong."

The child was swinging on a scuppernong vine, whooping with joy.

"His pa wants to raise Jim to be like he is."

"Let Jim come to see me. I might be able to help him, and Tommy will play with him."

"He takes to you." A sly gleam came into Della's eyes. In the bleakness of her relationship with that man, she was beginning to find the glimmering of a devious and hidden path. She was too afraid of her husband to fight openly, but she was not without perception, and if she found any weapon, Louise thought Della would use it.

Louise got up to go. "You come whenever you can."

"I'll come." Della looked at Francy's grave. "I want a good tombstone. Mr. Sanders says it costs too much."

"One thing we can do ourselves is plant a rosebush."

"That would look nice. I can't talk about her—her pa won't listen. And Jim's too little. He won't remember her."

"You can talk about her to Persia. She cared. She'll remember."

A sick flush covered Della's face and she looked away. "She came. I needed help then. I was low a long time after I had Jim and needed somebody. But I don't trust Persia. I'm scared of her, and I—I don't like her!"

"If you don't want her around any more, why don't you send her away? I'll try to find a place for her at Indigo."

Della still looked off into the distance. "I tried—Mr. Sanders won't let me. It's like having a big black snake come out of the swamp. She—she's wound all over us."

Louise now had some inkling of why Della had spoken so angrily to Persia. She veered at once from the subject. There were things

84

you didn't want to know, but if you knew them, you didn't talk about them.

Louise never spoke of that conversation with Della, but every now and then, Della did come to the house, bringing Jim. When she came, she would sit huddled in her ugly shawl, as nervous as a guinea hen, but much more silent, since she could hardly be induced to speak at all. Louise would amuse Jim with Tommy's old rag picture books and wooden blocks full of tooth marks.

"He's quick." Louise watched him study the letters on the blocks. She took too much pleasure in the sight of him—the rosy round outline of his face, his upcurled lashes, and the shine of his eyes as he grasped first one shabby treasure after another.

"That's one thing his pa likes about him. Francy was kind of slow."

Jim was looking at a picture of Jack and the beanstalk. He put a stub of a finger on the giant. "Pa!" he gleamed. The outthrust head in the illustration, the snarl, and the hamlike hands—Pa! Of course.

"Put it down, Jimmy, put it down." Della took the book. Jim fought and screamed, and Louise thrust another one in his hands. It was not a very good choice either since it showed St. George downing the dragon. "Nice book, nice pictures," Louise soothed him. Wonderful stories, where the hero always got the better of giants and dragons. Maybe things used to turn out like that. Maybe it was still possible, though unlikely.

Just then, Medora came in, and Della, looking terrified, immediately snatched up Jim and went away, Jim howling.

"Let him take the books with him," Louise said. "Tommy doesn't use them any more."

"Oh, no, ma'am." Della was dragging poor Jim along. "His pa might see."

Medora watched them go. "I ran them off."

"Poor Della's afraid of everything and everybody."

"Not of you any more."

"She comes sometimes because she's dreadfully lonely."

"She has no business being here. She ought to go back north where she belongs then she wouldn't be so lonesome."

"That's true." Louise didn't expect Medora to be anything but bitter. The Yankee owned her land now. Once the three plantations —Heron's Row, Indigo, and Avondale—had been one block of land, a Spanish grant, and Louise's grandfather had owned it all. He had acquired other plantations across the river, and these particular acres had not seemed of great importance to him. He had been willing to sell part of it to the north and part of it to the south, to his friends, but had had enough Scotch canniness to keep the best. He had sold Heron's Row to Mr. Dalton, and Avondale to Medora's grandfather, Mr. Winsloe. Mr. Dalton had died, and his heirs had sold Heron's Row to Colonel Winsloe. In those days there had been plenty of land, and plenty of money, but Louise was grateful to her grandfather for keeping Indigo. She would cling to it too.

"Della knows she doesn't belong here, but what can she do about it?"

"Nothing. She's not to blame," Medora admitted.

"And she's lost a child."

"I know, poor thing, but she would have lost both of them most likely if it hadn't been for you and Alan and Dr. Rand. God knows she ought to be grateful."

"She is, that's why she comes here with the boy. But she's afraid her precious spouse will find out, so don't mention it."

"You'd think the Yankee would be grateful too, wouldn't you?"

"No. He probably dislikes us all the more because his wife's made him feel guilty about us."

"That's a handsome child, if he is a wildcat. Probably he'll grow up like his father."

"Not if I can help it." It was the first time Louise had admitted to herself that she was prepared to do battle for the child. It would be an underhanded and dangerous contest, but if that was the only way to fight for Jim, she would have no scruples.

Medora turned from the window where she had been standing and took a chair. "I came to tell you—I had a letter from Jasper. He says he's coming home around the first of the year."

"That's wonderful! We'll have a real Christmas, all together!" Louise tried to be enthusiastic, but she couldn't forget the dreary, low-keyed scene played out in the Winsloe parlor.

"Jasper hasn't been in Cuba all this time."

"You stopped telling me about him."

"You stopped asking. I felt all the tactful silence around me. It's been like living in a vacuum!" She sighed. "Now I can, again. Talk about him, I mean. He's been in Brazil, with a Southern family who've gone there to make a new start."

"It might be a good idea to start life again in another country."

"Not for Jasper, he has a place here. He belongs here." Medora mustered all of her gentle stubbornness.

"He must know that, since he's coming back."

Louise saw how Medora's apathy had already changed to restless hope.

Alan came in and Medora soon left, riding off with old Wash jogging along behind her. Soon she would have Jasper to ride with her again.

"What's gotten into Medora?" Alan asked, "She seems fidgety today."

Louise told him about Jasper's letter. "So that's it. I'm glad for her, but if he can find anything to do with himself in Brazil he'd better stay there, or take her back there. Almost anything would be better than here."

Louise studied Alan's bleak face. He had slaved to make a good crop. "Things can't stay as bad as they are. We won't have carpetbag rule forever."

"I know that, Lou, but then it will be too late to save Indigo. It's the taxes. They have doubled them from last year's."

"From last year? They couldn't do that to us!"

"They have. Doubled."

"Alan, what can we do?"

"Nothing as far as I can see. It's the fate of thousands of planters, with things as they are. But to hand the place over to the Yankee!"

"We can't. There must be some way."

"I've borrowed all I can, you know that."

Louise did know. Neither their sister Carrie or their cousin Mary, who lived in New Orleans, were in any position to help them. She thought of her young cousin Ellen in Europe, but Alan said, "Besides, what's the use of borrowing what we can't pay back, when next year we'd be in the same fix again? No, the Yankee's after us, and he and his kind have all the power."

The darning egg slipped out of Louise's hands and fell on the floor. She noted the little sound of its fall and the fire's hissing, and the lonely sighing of the wind. "If the Yankee had died I suppose somebody like him would have taken his place."

"The only real way to save any of us in the long run is to sweep out the whole lot of 'em, and we aren't strong enough yet. They'd send troops from Washington."

All night, Louise tossed and turned, unable to sleep thinking maybe it would be better for Alan to give up Indigo and go back to Natchez. They would manage some way. No, it would break his spirit and take all the purpose out of his life. And Indigo was Tommy's inheritance.

The next morning she got up early, ate no breakfast, and hurried out of the house so Alan wouldn't see her. She didn't know what she would say but she was determined to find the Yankee and confront him. Almost running, plunging through the long damp sedge grass, she reached the creek. An inch or so of rain water trickled across the sand bar, and deep pools under the opposite bank looked black and cold. As she went across, the sand sucked and tugged, as if it were quicksand and would pull her down. The icy water seeped through her worn shoes and soaked her feet, numbing them so that she could hardly drag herself up the slippery bank, and had to grasp at the first tree she could reach. The tree was thorny, and the sharp spikes cut into her fingers. She hated her errand, and hated her physical discomfort. She wanted to scream, but there was no one to hear, and you learned to keep quiet when there was no sympathy available.

The ruins of the Winsloe house startled her. The pallor of the columns rose among the choking growth of moss-draped saplings and brambles. Everything was ashen as if a touch would make it all flake and powder into the formlessness of ashes. The whole world around her was burned out, life and fire extinguished. Except the Yankee's house, stark, but smug with an air of permanence.

Then she saw the Yankee himself, shambling out of his door, his head thrust out like the giant in the picture. He carried no visible club, but she was aware he had one in his corrupt power over all of them. A stub of a cigar was clenched between the snags of his teeth, and stained spit dribbled from his mouth to his stubbly unshaven chin.

The two of them looked at each other. "What do you want here?" he demanded.

"I came to ask you something."

"What for?"

"I have a right to ask."

"No, you don't. If you think I'm goin' to knuckle under to you and your kind because you came over here last summer, think again. Nobody ast your help."

"You were glad to have me then."

He considered this, chewing on his cigar. Della must have heard his voice, because she came out, Jim running after her, and went up to her husband, cringing when he shoved her aside with his elbow. But she put her hand on his arm. "Oh, Josh—she did! And if it hadn't been for her Jim might of died too!"

"Stop your sniveling." He never even glanced at Della but kept on looking at Louise. Jim trotted over to her and Louise smiled at him.

"Come back, you——"

Jim trotted back, looking up at his father with a scowl, and wandered off towards the house again, calling Persia.

"Where is she?" The man looked around.

"I don't know," Della muttered.

"Find her, go back to the house."

"Josh, please——"

"Shet up! I haven't time to stand here all day."

"I came to ask you to lower the taxes on Indigo."

There! It was said. The graces of tact would be lost on him anyway, she might as well blurt it out and get it over.

"Not asking much are you?" He put his hands on his hips and gave Louise a sour grin.

"No. You can do it. Very easily, if you want to."

"What'd make me want to?"

"Because it would be right."

"Not to my way of thinking."

"Maybe if you think about it for a while, it would."

"Expect to be paid, do you? For coming last summer."

"No."

"Then what made you come last summer?"

"Because I knew it was the right thing to do."

"What good'd it do you if I got the taxes changed this year? Wouldn't help next year."

"Let next year take care of itself. I'm asking for this year."

"And what if I won't?" He was enjoying his power, and Louise's outraged pride burned through every nerve. She had to keep her mind fixed on Tommy and Alan to make herself stand there.

"It's for you to decide. But if you take Indigo from us, we'll get it back. Sooner or later. Things aren't going to stay as they are around here. Other states are freeing themselves. We will too."

"Threaten me, do you?"

"It's true. You know it yourself."

"Oh, Josh," Della pleaded, wiping her dangling hair from her face. "Please be nice, then I'd be happy."

"You, and your whining."

"I wouldn't, if you'd be nice, like you used to be. If anything happened to you what would become of Jim and me down here?"

"Don't be a fool, nothing's going to happen to me. The government 'd fix em if it did."

"The government and the President and nobody else can fix God. If you're mean, God'll punish you. God might take Jim too!"

"Go on to the house." He jerked his thumb at her, and Della went running in the direction Jim had taken.

The man turned to Louise. "Don't know as I care much whether I take over your place now or later. Cotton's low. Might as well let your brother work on it a while longer. Don't much matter. The mortgage 'll come due one of these days, so sooner or later I'll get it anyhow." He turned away and shambled off.

Louise stood still. There was a roaring in her ears—rage beating through her. Frustrated fury clamored for vengeance, with no chance to get revenge. Not yet, not now, but someday she would have it. She started moving, still shaking, when Della came after her, Jim careening in her wake. Just now, Louise hated the sight of Della too. Dodging, rabbity creature! But Jimmy, all smiles and brilliance, she could never hate. "Pa gone," he chuckled, burying his face in a fold of Louise's skirt.

"I'll get around Mr. Sanders," Della panted. "Just wait. I used to be able to manage him real good, but not so much any more. I haven't had any spirit for a thing since Francy—But I'll try. You'll see. He'll fix things better for you."

"Thank you, Della."

"I'll get myself together. We don't want you to go away, do we, Jim boy?"

Louise didn't tell Alan about that encounter. She would wait and see what happened. The next time he went to look at the tax records he came back with such a peculiar expression on his face she knew there had been some change, maybe better, maybe worse, and she hurried out to meet him.

"I'm in a daze," he said. "In fact, I slid right off the horse! The taxes have been changed—back to last year's. How can you account for that?"

Then she told him what she had done.

"Lord! For you to be subjected to his sneers and insults!"

"Don't rage. I can do anything—anything at all for you and Tommy. His sneers and jeers broke no bones. I turned purple with rage and my toes turned purple with cold, but it seems to have done us some good."

"I still wonder why. I can hardly believe he's had a real change of heart towards us."

"He feels sure of his power, and intends to abuse it later. Jim is his weakness, too. And I think he's vaguely superstitious. Not religious, but maybe afraid that God might strike at him. And Della seems to know ways to get at him."

"It didn't seem to me she had the slightest influence over him."

"I think she has some tricks and wiles. She must have. Frightened timid people learn them, because they have to."

"Probably next year he'll quadruple the taxes, so don't let's give him too much credit."

"I don't. But if we can stave off disaster for right now, let's make the most of it. I've learned to make do with bits and pieces of things. The way I'm making this quilt."

As they talked, they had wandered back into the house. The quilt was piled up on a chair. Louise spread it out and showed it to Alan. "Odds and ends, but not calico——" This was being made out of scraps of silk and velvet and brocade, and all the tag ends of cast-off finery. "Just dabs, but one day I'll have a whole quilt, as lively as Joseph's coat."

Alan admired it, and went on pacing around the room. "I hate taking any kind of favor from him. I don't want to seem better off than my neighbors——"

"You aren't. Talk to Mr. Bijah about it, and see what he says." Dr. Rand was a doctor, not a planter, though he cultivated a few acres. Mr. Bijah was much more solidly established at Avondale than Alan was here at Indigo.

"All the same," Alan muttered, "this makes me feel sort of like a scallywag."

Mr. Bijah rode over that afternoon. He listened, and agreed with Louise. "For the Lord's sake, Alan, if you've got a chance to lower the taxes, take it, if ole Scratch himself gave it to you! What we must all aim at is holding on and digging in until we can see our way to sweeping out the whole kit and caboodle of 'em."

"Well, when the time comes I don't want my friends to group me with the scallywags."

"Don't worry. We won't. I've had to sell some land to pay taxes, but I'm going to get it back someday. But I don't see a way in the world of getting that rascal off of Medora's property."

A bleak bitter look came on Alan's face. "When we were in the war we didn't realize it was better than peace was going to be."

"At least you're alive, Alan. And here with me."

"Like a millstone around your neck, Lou."

"Hush." She understood his bitterness only too well, and sometimes admitted, in all her longing to have Tom back, how the dead, safe in their glory, were better off. But she wouldn't admit it often, or long at a time. Being a woman, and a woman with a child, she felt herself obliged to have faith in life.

"Shut up, son." Mr. Bijah filled his pipe, and with Louise's permission, lit it. "We'll use you when the time comes. We'll have to use everybody."

"On the principle that half a loaf is better than no bread."

"Of course it is," Louise said. "We'll scrape up all our crumbs, won't we, Mr. Bijah?"

"Sure. We'll have to. There aren't enough whole men left around here. And to get back to the Yankee—what I believe is that he's smart enough to feel in his bones that carpetbag rule ain't going to last forever. That's the reason, and the only reason, he eased up on your taxes."

"Anyway," Louise said, "I intend to enjoy this Christmas, hard times or no hard times."

"So do I," Mr. Bijah chuckled. "We have to pleasure ourselves once in a while."

Watching him ride off, Alan said he thought Mr. Bijah seemed mighty chipper.

"That's because he believes Jasper's coming back. He won't tell us, but he thinks so. I could just kill Jasper! What he's put those poor people through! And yet, I can see how he is impelled to his wanderings."

"Why aren't you impelled to wander, Louisa? You could. You could leave all this and take Tommy and go visit Ellen in Florence. That's what you ought to do."

"Don't ever call me Louisa! I never could stand Cousin Louisa. She used to rap me over the knuckles and keep handing me a thimble! I wish I hadn't been named for her. I don't want to leave here now, I'm too interested in what's going on."

Alan kissed her. "In spite of all my growlings I do feel better about the taxes. It'll give us a little time, and time's on our side. I owe this breathing spell to you."

Louise prepared for Christmas with more than usual vigor. This year the tree was going to be decorated with whatever scraps of splendor she could muster. "You and Jessie and Medora have made enough paper dangles and doodles to ornament a forest," Alan said. Louise knew that Persia sometimes came to see Lillybelle, and came

93

more often since last summer. Her appearances were mostly around twilight, and Louise looked out for the tall black shadow loping through the other shadows, and one evening, waylaid her.

"Evenin', miss." Persia's teeth flashed. It was a pity Della didn't have teeth like that.

"Persia, are you all going to have a Christmas tree?"

"No'm. Usses doan never have no fixin's."

"Then bring your children to ours. And any of the other children that'll want to come."

"Yes'm. Sho will."

"And maybe you could bring Jimmy too."

"Yes'm, jus' woan say nuthin'."

"You'd better tell Miss Della."

"Yes'm. You jes res easy Miss Lou. I git Jimmy to yo tree."

And he came, marshaled among Persia's dark flock, a skittish little white lamb among the docile black ones.

"Here I'm is," he announced. He didn't have a Yankee voice. He sounded more like Persia than either of his parents.

"I hope you won't get into trouble over this, Persia, or Jimmy either."

"Doan fret yo' self, Miss Lou. Dun got hit fix'." Persia grinned. "His ma know where de Big Minnow at, an' his pa won't know nuthin fer a right smart while. He's ah snorin' an agruntin' lak my ole razorback. Miss Della, poah thing, she amissin' her daid chile."

"I know." Louise thought of poor Della's plight, sitting over there, thinking about Francy, with no company but her drunken husband, and he was probably in Persia's cabin.

Louise had filled a stocking for Jim, and he was in ecstasy over the old mended playthings. It was his first Christmas stocking and his first sight of a Christmas tree. It had only homemade decorations, and stubs of candles hoarded all year, but watching Jim's delight, Louise thought, was beautiful too. She had given the child his first real Christmas.

The candles gave a brief splendor before they sputtered out. For a little while the tree shone with bright magic in the dark, and in the sudden stillness the colored people began to sing. Their voices rose and fell in the starlit night. There was melancholy and longing and hope in their singing. Louise recognized Jessie's true, deep voice among the rest. This year Jessie hadn't been standoffish and sullen. She had worked hard on the tree, and now she sang, leading the choruses, taking the solo parts. Louise watched all the faces turned to the lights. In a little while they would all separate, and each go his way, very much the same as they had been before, but at the moment everyone was united. Not white people or black people, but just human beings, touched by the promise of heaven. Overhead, the Christmas stars, the great winter constellations, ruled the sky. Far away, out of reach, the fields of heaven had a shine and bloom the dark earth lacked.

On New Year's Eve, the Rands had invited Louise and Alan and Tommy to a dance. Everyone in the sparsely settled neighborhood would be there if the weather held. It did. The roads were packed hard, and there was even an icy little slice of moon to light the way. The place chosen was a dilapidated schoolhouse, deserted since the beginning of the war. The Rands came, and the Winsloes. The others—making about forty people, counting the children, and the set of twins, weren't plantation people. Some of them had small farms tucked here and there along the creek banks, or among the soft folds of the slopes. Some of them didn't farm, but roved from one river bend to the next. The men had all fought. Now they suffered less than the plantation owners and former slaveholders. They had less to lose in the overthrow of an elaborate civilization. Inconspicuous, scattered, isolated, they were out of reach of carpetbag greed. Expert trappers, fishermen, and hunters, they could, if they had to, live off of the wilderness. If there was danger in grappling with the primitive earth, there was safety in it too. They could always find the essentials for living. Yet emotionally they were as involved, and as scarred by the war and its aftermath as anyone else. They had given the South all they had, and Louise was aware of the ones not here tonight, the ones who hadn't come back from the battles. And among the ones in this gathering, she saw a man with a scarred face, and another with a black patch over his eye, and someone else with an empty sleeve.

Dr. Rand, standing at the door, welcomed everyone. "We've got all we need. Four walls, a floor, some folks, plenty of vittles, and a fiddle or so."

"It looks like a fine dance," Alan said. There was homemade wine to drink, homemade candles to burn, greenery from the woods hid the cracks in the walls, and the women had brought box suppers—roasted wild ducks and geese, venison, pork loin, sweet potatoes, and peanuts. The fiddles squeaked cheerfully. It promised to be a splendid evening.

Alan found Amanda Rand and went up to speak to her. It was the first time he had really seen her, and Louise felt his idea of her as a vision would be justified tonight.

"We were very worried about you when you had yellow fever," Louise said to her, taking her hands. "It's wonderful to seeing you looking so well and pretty."

Amanda's white calico was sprigged with bright-red cherries, and she had wound cherry-colored ribbons in her glossy brown hair.

"This is my brother, who devoured the broth and chicken you brought."

"And polished the chicken's bones——" Alan's face looked younger and happier than Louise had seen it in a long time, and she remembered how young he still was in years.

"So far, we've only had a basket acquaintance, Miss Amanda."

"We've never really seen each other before, have we? First you were down and out, then I was—Miss Lou, help me get the dancin' started before all the men huddle in a knot and get so wound up in politics you can't budge 'em."

Before Louise could answer, a wizened little man with bright brown eyes came up to her and seized her for a partner. He was half her size and danced like a tornado. "Fine fella—Dr. Rand. He saved my life last summer—I was about to choke on a bone." His name was Davis, and he lived in a houseboat on the river. "And I go and come like I please." Away they flew over the floor. Louise was worried about Alan. He couldn't dance, and one of these young men would whisk off with Amanda. But Amanda was with Alan. They had joined the figures of the square dance, Alan hobbling along. It was too much exertion for him, but Louise quelled an impulse to tell him so. He was enjoying himself. When Louise was near him, he grinned. "That one-armed fella can beat me at the hopping and skipping, but I can clap a lot louder than he can!"

The fiddles were as gay as grasshoppers in summer. A baby wailed, was fed, and fell asleep again. Tommy, instead of going to sleep, had found a gangling little girl, and they were following the music quite well. Everybody was dancing, except the babies. Mr. Bijah was thumping around vigorously, and Mrs. Winsloe was concentrating on every step she took. Medora was light on her feet, and her ringlets swung as she whirled and turned.

Late in the evening, after supper, before the music started up again, Louise saw Amanda and Alan talking together.

"It's New Year, Miss Lou——" Dr. Rand handed her a glass of wine.

"All I can say for the year just over is that I'm glad to see the last of it." She turned to kiss Tommy and wish him Happy New Year. There was a commotion at the door. Louise looked up. Jasper Winsloe had just come in.

Chapter Seven

JASPER was taller and thinner than Louise remembered him, and looked older, but it was hard to know exactly what impression he made on Medora in the confusion of his coming. He spoke to everyone, smiled at everyone, then crossed the room to Medora. Louise couldn't hear what he said, but Medora looked stiff and unresponsive. She hardly seemed to answer him, but a little later, when the party broke up and everybody dispersed, they left the room together.

"His coming made a neat climax to the evening," Alan said on the way home, "but such belated climaxes aren't as effective as the ones that come right on the dot."

"She was furious with him. She didn't want to meet him first in public like that."

"He didn't give her a chance to tell him what she thought of him. He's got all his airs and graces at hand, I noticed."

"Did you have a good time, Alan?"

"Fine. I almost sat on the twins. I thought they were just a bundle of coats, but they were cocooned inside. One of 'em snuffled just in time."

"Did your leg worry you?"

"It did a little, but it capered me around better than I thought it would."

Louise wanted to ask him about Amanda, but she was afraid to venture a word. If Alan had any feeling for her, let it become firmly rooted before anyone put him on his guard against it. Let it take possession of him before he remembered that war had made him much older than Amanda, and poor, and burdened.

All Louise could do was to send a note to the Rands asking them to supper. The Dr. and Mrs. Rand answered they would be delighted to come, but Amanda had just left for the Bellevue Academy for Young Ladies.

"We ought to ask the Winsloes too, since we've killed the pig."

"Go the whole hog."

"Alan! That was awful! And I'm going to hoard every hoof and innard of the pig's. Not that I have much appetite for the pig after listening to its squeals."

The little group gathered the following Sunday. After Mrs. Winsloe had gone to join the others in front of the fire, Louise had a chance to speak to Medora alone. They were in Louise's room, and Medora was looking at her reflection in the dim wavering mirror. Medora was wearing a new dress. No, not new, Louise recognized it as part of the trousseau, unworn until now. Medora's cheeks were flushed and her eyes were shining, but it was not the same sort of bloom she had worn that other time when Jasper had come home. This was excitement and nervous tension.

"Jasper's looking well." That was a safe commonplace.

"He's thinner. I think he looks worn out. It was the climate, I suppose. He says he would have been home much sooner, but he was involved with some people in chartering a ship, and it all took much longer than he had expected. And he felt he had to see the thing through." Medora smoothed her hair. "He made something out of it and gave it to his father."

"That's good. It'll help."

"Having him back is the best help for his father and mother."

"And for you."

"Do I count?"

"You must count a great deal, or he wouldn't be here." Louise was saying what she knew Medora wanted to hear, and she wondered if it was the real truth.

"Wouldn't he? If he got tired of it down there? He talks of us both going down there for a while."

"Then go with him."

"That was just at first. He doesn't talk like that now. He'll stay here."

Jasper was at his best that evening. He wouldn't talk about himself or his experiences, but he seemed to want to know everything that had happened and was happening here at home, down to the last detail, and plunged into a discussion of politics with his father and Alan and Dr. Rand.

"You've certainly managed to keep up with it all," Louise said to him.

"I belong here."

Louise led the way to the table, and told the men to leave their fiery speeches until later. They obeyed. Her guests knew this was meant to be a party, and they put the harshness out of their lives for a moment and spread a mask of social gaiety over the occasion in the same way that the firelight flowing over the room disguised its general shabbiness.

Louise turned to Dr. Rand. "I didn't know Amanda intended to go away to school."

"Her mother and I didn't either, but she took a sudden notion. She says she can read and write and that's all, with the war coming and all she didn't have a chance at much else."

"She seems to be a very capable girl."

"She makes the finest pickles and preserves in this neck of the woods, better even than her mamma's. So why does she want to go pokin' her head into books for?"

"A love of books is a big help on a rainy day."

"Well, I hope school won't give her too many high falutin' notions."

Louise knew Miss Fisk, the head of the small Academy. It had been closed during the war, and had just managed to reopen. Amanda was not likely to become too dazzlingly intellectual, and Louise smiled at most men's horror at the idea of mental attainments in women. Louise wondered why Amanda, all of a sudden, had decided she wanted to go away to school.

"I loved it off at school," Medora said. All evening she had been quiet, but in a taut, unreposeful way. Jasper was lavishing attention on her but she stayed withdrawn, and hardly ate anything. Louise could imagine the conflict going on. Medora was undecided whether to be unrelenting, or whether to admit her love again. Aside from that, there was something different about Medora tonight, unlike herself, or at least unlike the Medora, Louise thought she knew.

100

People did change. You recovered from deep grief, yet you became not the creature you had been, but someone else. Sorrow left an imprint, like the mark the floods left on trees. The river went down, the trees grew on, but there was always left that ghostly shadow.

Jasper was cheerful. He might never have been away so completely did he seem in harmony with most of the people around him. Not Alan, who didn't forgive him. Not Medora, not yet. Louise tried to draw him out. The fate of the Southern exiles interested her. Some had gone to Texas, some to Brazil, some to Europe to live, like her cousin Anna. Had their escape succeeded? Were they reborn and remade? Which was better, to struggle along here, or to change and take your chances in another, unfamiliar country? She said something of this to Jasper.

"I suppose some fail and some succeed. Just as a few will succeed here, as bad as things are. What I'd like to know is it the person or the place that determines it? Will the person who succeeds here be the one who would do well in some other environment too?"

"Or is it just luck? How do we know?" he smiled.

"They seem mysterious to me, the ones who've gone away." As if they had strange and driving secrets in their hearts.

"Is it all in themselves or in their stars? But you mean if Alan, for instance, were to go to Brazil, or to Texas, would he be better off than here?" Jasper considered. "No, not Alan, even if he had every conceivable good luck, because his heart and soul are here. His idea of winning and losing is bound up in what's happening here. What is your personal victory? Yours and his? Keeping Indigo!"

"That's true. It's what he measures by. But what if he wasn't tied up this way?"

"I don't know. Some people simply drift, and no longer care much. Their hearts and souls aren't bound up in anything any more."

He was speaking of himself, and Louise had the sensation some of Blake's poetry gave her—a brush of invisible dark wings—not death, but strangeness. A chill moon madness.

After that evening, the winter rains began, and most of the time, Louise and Alan were hemmed in. Alan saw Mr. Bijah every now and then, and Louise burned to know what was happening at Avondale. If Jasper and Medora were piecing together their worn love affair, or tearing it apart under the fond eyes of the older people. But Alan and Mr. Bijah, when they met, discussed only weather, crops, and politics, and Alan would come in raging at every new instance of outrage and injustice.

Their cousin Mary's letters from New Orleans confirmed all they heard of conditions there. Her husband was a lawyer, and he was working to help his friends in their plans to free the city and all of Louisiana, yet every struggle seemed to tighten the clamp of the carpetbag government. And in Mississippi, with the weak wretch of a governor, the carpetbaggers gorged themselves unchecked on stolen property.

"I want to do something!" Alan said. "Not sit like a bump on a log seeming to take favors from a Yankee."

"Wait," Louise cautioned. "Our own particular pest of a Yankee is in Jackson most of the time, busy entrenching himself in the governor's good graces. I know that from Della."

Della was afraid to come often to the house, but Louise saw her on Indigo's side of the creek bank.

"You know I love to have Jimmy," Louise told her, "but I don't want to make trouble for him." If only there was some way to get the child away from his father, but there was no chance, except for Jim to grow up, and escape.

"It won't make trouble. His pa's off most of the time. Or drinking." That look of distaste crinkled across Della's face. The Yankee probably did most of his guzzling in Persia's cabin.

From what Della said of herself, Louise knew that her upbringing and education had been strict. She had been teaching in a small country town. There she had met her husband. He had probably been handsome, with a masterful air.

"He doesn't pay any mind to what we do these days. Once he did catch Jim coming back from your house, and I was scared, but he said if I wanted to make a fool of myself, go ahead, and Jim was too little for it to matter."

"Then send him over."

"I just believe his pa likes the idea—he thinks you can teach Jim things I can't. I'll say one thing for Mr. Sanders, he wants Jim to have the best."

Louise walked back, savoring the mild winter day. Smoke from the closed cabins spiraled and faded against the silvery sky. Dry bent stalks corrugated the furrows. The tall sedge grass was burnt umber, the veiled depths of the woods were gray and brown, veined with lingering russet and the indestructible green of oaks and magnolias. Already, the woods were weaving shadows for night. In the field, the pecan showed its size and strength. It still held clusters of nuts, looking like opened flowers. Its blossoms were brief and inconspicuous, it kept its real wealth for autumn and winter. It was a peaceful scene here, a peaceful winter, and yet not peaceful. The air of emptiness was suspense, waiting for events to rush in again.

Jim came nearly every day. Gathering the children together, mapping out three different sets of lessons, Louise wondered if any teacher had a more incongruous assortment of pupils. Jim, the enemy's child, busy with Tommy's old books and blocks, and Jessie, the only one of Lillybelle's swarm showing discontent, but with a willingness to learn any kind of new skill she could. And Tommy himself. Maybe this little learning would be dangerous to all of them, making the seeds of unhappiness already implicit in their lives grow into bitter thorns and brambles.

Jessie might never adjust herself to her race and her people. In times like these her better knowledge and her talents might end by making her miserable. No, it was a risk, but Jessie had a right to learn. Jimmy needed love. He was quick and responsive. He would have to have strength—that child—to choose, to channel his feelings the way they should go.

As for Tommy, a time would come when he would see the inadequacies of everything Louise could do for him, and realize the lack of promise in his life. In most ways, it was better for him to be here than in Natchez, where the knell of the past would be constantly sounded in his ears. Here, the present was immediate in its demands. Harsh, often brutal, but giving no time to look back. Indigo was a boy's paradise. Tommy hunted and fished, and escaped into his own adventures in the woods and down by the river. But he wouldn't be a child always, and already adult problems had pressed on his childhood, and the weight of the uneasy grownup world had made him grave and reticent.

In the evenings, Alan would go over the plantation books, sighing and muttering, while Louise listened and asked questions and considered this or that further economy. Tommy listened too. Cabins had to be repaired. It was absolutely necessary to have at least two more mules, all the details accumulated, making a spider web of cares and work. The end of the year had found Alan again without any money. What money the crop had brought in had to go for taxes and the interest on the mortgage. "So we'll have to scrape. And borrow, of course, to plant the crop and furnish the hands." The plantation owners were expected to see to it that the hands had something to eat and something to wear throughout the year. Then, when the crop was in, the hands, if they were able, paid the owner back in cotton. But if the crop failed, the hands couldn't pay for the salt meat and calico and flour and tools that had been "furnished" them.

Tommy was sprawled on the floor in front of the fire. "But it's for Indigo." He was a thin child, showing long on the floor, long like a shadow. His skin and hair were dark, all of a color, a dark tan, but his eyes were much darker. Not exactly brown. "More creek-colored," his mother defined their shade—that clear darkness with a greenish reflection. He looked, and usually moved, like a wisp of smoke, seeming to go nowhere in particular, yet suddenly gone. The love and awe in his voice terrified his mother. She understood all at once the depth of his feeling for Indigo. Different from Alan's. That was a fierce passion born of a sense of duty, and nurtured in an absorbing contest to prove himself and defeat an enemy. Tommy's was a passion for Indigo itself—the ground under his feet, the feel of the cool, thick purplish clods of its earth, the sight of the cotton growing, from its first shoot to the last trembling, straggling stalk, left until plowing started again. Its lights and shadows, and its wild boundaries to the creek, through the woods, down to the Mississippi.

One February day, near dusk, when the rain had stopped but was threatening again, and Louise had gone out to look for a streak of pink in the fish-colored muddle of light in the west, Alan came. "I don't know what you're going to do to me, sister. Something awful, I guess—and I wouldn't blame you."

"What are you up to?"

"Well—I've invited some people—and—er, well—people to spend the night."

"What people? Strange people?"

"Sort of—yes."

"Who on earth?"

"A circus."

"Are you feverish?"

"I've invited them to spend the night here."

"You must be feverish!"

"It's a traveling show—a circus. They're on the road to Natchez. Glued down in the mud. They looked so bedraggled and cold, and the monkey's shivering."

Tommy came out and heard and began to whoop. "Have they an elephant?"

"Monkey—elephant——" Louise found herself murmuring.

"Yes, that's just what they do have," Alan admitted. "Not a very big one, as elephants go. But he, or she, IS an elephant——"

Tommy plunged off in the direction of the circus, and Louise began to laugh.

"I'm glad you take it like that."

"But it's so ludicrous!"

Besides the elephant, there were three monkeys, some horses, and twelve people. The men—there were eight of them—could sleep in the barn, and the four women in the house. There weren't enough beds or covers, but at least they would be more comfortable than spending the night on the road in the cold rain.

"What are they doing in this direction anyway?" Louise wanted to know.

"They had a plan to give performances in the little towns off the rail line between Baton Rouge and Natchez, but the bad weather got 'em."

Louise ran to rouse Cornelius and Lillybelle from their lethargy, and try to find enough food. The news spread, and by the time the circus people came straggling towards the house, all the hands had gathered, even those supposedly bedridden, and the children were swarming. The elephant ambled out of the twilight and was housed in the barn. One of the monkeys chattered on the clown's shoulder, the other two were in a cage. Louise was sorry for them and let them in the house. The drenched, tired people went about caring for the animals in a methodical way, while Louise struggled with enough supper. Fortunately, she didn't have to feed the elephant—his keeper had fed him.

The hands gladly contributed what they had towards supper. Someone produced a string of catfish, somebody else, ducks. There was even an offering of a freshly killed possum. Everybody helped with the cooking, and Tommy helped the men feed the animals. He was delighted with the monkeys and the elephant, but he was disappointed with the circus people. "They aren't in pink and blue shiny stuff," he whispered to Louise. "They've just got on old clothes like you."

"We're travelin'," one of the women explained. "But we've got shiny stuff, honey. It's in the trunks, down in the wagons."

"We're crowding you out," another woman said, "but this is heaven, to be inside, instead of being out there stuck in the mud to the tops of the wheels."

"We're enjoying it," Louise put her guests at their ease. "The children have never seen an elephant, or any sort of circus at all."

Close at hand, the circus people were stripped of their tinsel magic. They were tired, and the women were muscular and weather-beaten. Somehow, everyone was fed, and the animals bunched in the barn, or tethered outside. Then everybody slept.

The next day, all the colored people for miles around gathered at Indigo, to wonder at the elephant, and to laugh at the monkeys. Persia had brought her children, and Jim. Even Della came, standing on the outskirts of the crowd. She looked startled into speechlessness, and she was lugging a paper-wrapped bundle. Louise went over to her and asked her into the house.

"No—no—thank you. I heard about it. I just didn't believe a word of it. A circus!" She handed Louise the bundle. It was a loin of pork. "You'll need it, with all these people!"

"I couldn't believe it either. Thank you for the pork."

The Winsloes came bringing preserves and a baked ham.

"Lou, you must be driven crazy with all this to-do!" Medora shrank from the sight and scent of these unfamiliar people and animals.

"Not quite. We've managed. The men have gone to dig the wagons out of the mud."

The sun came out and warmed and cheered them. The wagons were freed, and after they had passed the deep hole which had bogged them down, they found the road was better. The clown announced that before they left, they would put on the circus for the benefit of their good friends who had been so kind to them. The most muscular woman disappeared and came out again in pink and spangles and paint, and recreated all the fascination of a circus atmosphere. She rode the white horse bareback, and a weedy, tiny man made the placid elephant go through his repertoire, and the clown and his monkey held the children spellbound. Dr. Rand drove up with Mrs. Rand and the patient he had been visiting—a man with a broken ankle.

"He wanted to see what was going on, so I got him in the gig and hauled him over. He can sit and watch."

It turned into a gala occasion, and when all the visitors and all the animals gathered themselves and their paraphernalia and trooped away, the children followed them down the road. Louise followed as far as the gate. Then her legs gave way, and she leaned on the gate, watching the elephant sag into the distance.

The next day she wrote an account of it all to her cousin Mary. "You, of all people, should have been on hand, as you would have flung yourself into the spirit of the thing. I did, but whereas you would have at once, it took me about half an hour. Poor pitiful things, but they don't know they are. The bareback rider talked to me a good deal about her life. The clown was cheerful all the time, contrary to the idea that he should mourn when off stage. For a while, I thought Tommy had run off to join them, as he hated so to part with them. But he came back. The elephant had a great deal of charm. I took to him myself."

One of Louise's sharpest memories of what Tommy called Circus

Day, was the picture of Medora and Jasper standing together, watching the elephant and the clown, and laughing. They looked more united than Louise had ever seen them.

Perhaps the coming of the circus, perhaps a sudden burst of spring brilliance, made Louise restless and a little homesick for Natchez.

"Go for a few days," Alan suggested. "Stay with Cousin Charlotte, she'll be glad to see you."

"It will cost money, and you're too busy to leave."

"Go without me, catch the boat. I have an excuse for you to go. Frank Corwin promised me a mule cheap, and he's offered me a jumper. Of course it's not an elegant equipage, but you might use it."

A jumper consisted of two wheels and a seat and two shafts. "If you attach an animal to it it will take you places. I'd love it. I'll ask Medora to go to Natchez with me."

Alan said it would do Medora good to go somewhere.

Medora accepted the suggestion of the trip, and Jasper drove Medora and Louise to the boat in the Winsloe's old surrey. Tommy went along, as far as Indigo Landing, though he refused to go to Natchez. "Catching the boat always sounds as if you had to run after it," Tommy said, "when you really sit and sit until it gets here."

Today, while they waited, Jasper told them stories of some of the strange characters he'd met on his travels. It was the first time Louise had ever heard him tell about any of his own experiences when he had gone on those journeys, and he talked about other people, rather than about himself. He had brought a picnic lunch and he and Tommy gathered sticks and cooked bacon and eggs over the fire they had made. After they had eaten, Tommy began roving by himself. Medora stood near the water, looking down the sweep of Indigo Bend, and Louise and Jasper remained where they were, sitting on a log of driftwood.

"This is a poky life," Jasper said, "Plantations are a lot of work, then a lot of waiting."

"Here's a nice place to wait." The river rushed past, silent in its power, its darkness and depth veiled in the spangled dance of light on its surface. The cottonwoods on the bank rustled like running water, like silk whispering—a delicious sound. Louise remembered how different this place had seemed the first time she had seen it.

Then a blank loneliness, almost despair had struck her. Now it was familiar and cherished. She had willed herself to endure it, then to enjoy it, but she wouldn't have succeeded so well if it hadn't been for Tommy. He loved it, and because she loved him, she had learned to see it through his eyes and with his feelings.

Medora walked up and down the bank. Today, she had turned silent again, tense and restless.

"I don't seem to have much idle time," Louise said.

"It's just as well. To enjoy leisure you have to have a contented mind. It's no use if your thoughts churn."

"That's true," she admitted.

"Sometimes I don't think the great tribulations drive people crazy. It's the everydayness that does."

"Unless you can find it satisfying." She knew what he meant. She had felt it herself, but little by little, had emerged from that state of mind.

The boat blew from around Indigo Bend, and they didn't finish their conversation, yet Louise remembered what Jasper had said.

In Natchez, at Cousin Charlotte's house, busy with friends who came to see her, Louise hardly had a chance to evaluate Medora's mood, but on the way back the tense quality of Medora's silence was noticeable. To make conversation, Louise asked Medora what she had bought in Natchez.

"Some muslin. It has a green clover leaf in it. It's not very good stuff, but I think I'll make my dress out of it. My wedding dress."

"Oh!" Louise was surprised. "I didn't realize you had set the date again. When will it be?"

"Oh, sometime soon." Medora didn't seem to want to discuss it, and Louise quenched the questions she wanted to ask.

"I have a dress all made, but I won't wear it. Ever! I hate it."

It had been raining and blowing, with the quick moodiness of spring. When the boat stopped at Indigo Landing, the sun was shining again. The roustabouts led the mule down the narrow gangplank, then picked up the jumper and carried it. Then the men cheerfully hitched the mule to the jumper, and helped Louise and Medora into the rudimentary carriage. Then the men went back to the boat, and the boat began to draw away from the landing. The water wasn't high this spring, and the steep bank from the landing was slippery.

"I know the way of our mules but not of this one," Louise urged the unfamiliar animal forward. The mule hesitated, slipped, and began to back.

"Don't scream," Louise muttered, clinging to the reins, knowing that the river was behind them. "Don't look——" Then she was breathless with the effort to get the balky creature up the bank. Back they slipped, down and down—the river was nearer and nearer.

"Jump, Medora——"

Medora didn't jump, she only clung. "Jump!" Louise commanded, knowing she couldn't jump herself until Medora did. But as she spoke, the mule changed his mind, and began to move forward, up the bank. Several times he hesitated, but at last they reached the top and were on level ground.

Sweat poured from Louise's forehead and into her eyes. The reins had galled her hands. When she could speak, she turned to look at Medora, who was green, but quiet.

"You were brave, but you should have jumped."

"I'm going to throw up."

Louise stopped, Medora clambered out, went behind a bush, and reappeared a few minutes later. No wonder Medora felt queasy, she did too. As Medora got back into the jumper, Cornelius came riding to meet them. "Mr. Alan done sent me."

"I wish you'd been here sooner." Louise told him about their adventure as he rode beside them.

"Miss Lou, this heah mule you done brung is ornery. Ah kin tell by his eye. Now Cunnel Dool heah, he got a kin' eye."

Louise wondered why Alan himself hadn't come to meet them, but when they reached the house, the Winsloe surrey was there. "Jasper's here," Louise said. "Why didn't Alan and Jasper come down to meet us?"

When Alan came out of the door it was with Mr. Bijah, not Jasper, and there was such a peculiar expression on both of their faces, Louise forgot to burst out with the story of their peril. Mr. Bijah's head was bent. He was holding something white in his hand. A letter, starkly white in his red bent fingers.

"What's the matter?" Louise asked.

"Jasper's gone," Alan whispered. Medora heard. Mr. Bijah gave her the letter, but she dropped it from her inert fingers. Alan picked it up, but she shook her head and wouldn't touch it, and went over to the surrey and began to get into it. Alan went to her and helped her in. Mr. Bijah nodded to Alan and Louise. "Better get her home." His weathered face was old and puckered. He pocketed the letter, and drove off.

"She's forgotten her package. But it doesn't matter——"

Medora wouldn't need it now.

Chapter Eight

Louise felt Medora wanted to be let alone, so she stayed away from the Winsloes. "What can I say to her?" she asked Alan.

"Nothing, except that he's evidently teched in the head. Plumb crazy. The whole thing's been so long drawn out, I can't see how it could mean much to either of them."

"It does to her."

It was nearly two weeks before Medora came over, with Mr. Bijah, who immediately rambled off with Alan. Louise was counting a recent hatching of baby chicks, and hadn't heard anyone drive up, until she saw Medora, leaning against the crooked wire fence. Her thin pale dress was crisply starched, and a wide-brimmed hat shaded her face. From a little distance, she gave an effect of slender youthfulness, a delicate gaiety, until you saw her face, wretchedly pale and thin.

"Do you still have that package of mine?" she asked without preliminaries.

"Yes, I have it."

"Not that I need it, except I can't waste good material."

"I'll get it for you. Let's go in."

"There's no hurry. Go on with what you're doing."

This time, like the time before, when Jasper had left just before the wedding date, the scene was underplayed. Perhaps if Medora had been more violent and dramatic, Jasper would have felt more challenge. This was scarcely a setting for romantic revelations, with hens clucking and Lillybelle's children swarming.

"Let's go."

Medora was holding a handkerchief to her nose, as if the ordinary odors of a barnyard disgusted her. Louise led her to the house, and was glad to find it empty. "Would you like a little wine?"

Medora made a face, closed her eyes and opened them again. "He's in New Orleans. He gave me his address."

"He intends to come back, I feel sure."

"He says that there's some unfinished business and he can't rest until it's settled. Then he won't give any of us any more trouble." Medora clasped her hands together until the knuckles whitened. "I don't believe that 'unfinished business,' and if there is any, it isn't in New Orleans. It's further on. It isn't real, and it'll always be further on!"

Louise didn't want to look at Medora. She fastened her attention on a sunbeam where a crowd of dust motes danced. Just then, a wild scream made her jump to her feet. It was Lillybelle's voice rising in wild shrieks. At the first sound, Louise thought Medora had begun to scream, but Medora stood still, knotting her hands together. Louise ran out. Tommy—but it had nothing to do with Tommy, he was with his uncle. Lillybelle was yelling, "Miss Lou! Miss Lou!" Persia was with her, babbling wildly, flinging her arms up and down, and every now and then letting out a thin high wail. "Jim!" was Louise's first thought. She seized Lillybelle. "Tell me— tell me!"

"Miss Della—she done took bad. She 'low Pershah done pisen her wid debbil stools!" Lillybelle gulped. "An' Mr. Josh—he in Jackson."

"Hain't done no sech," Persia became coherent. "Ah hain't stewed no pisen ones!"

Louise felt the cold sweat on her face. "Did you give her any? At all? From anywhere?"

"Yes'm. But 'tweren't no harm in 'em."

"Oh, Persia——" Louise began to run. "You might have made a mistake!" She called back to Medora. "Stay here and tell Alan—and send somebody for Dr. Rand."

Then she saved her breath for running. Time enough for questions later. White of egg—no, that was for strychnine poisoning.

"Did Jimmy eat any at all?"

"No'm." Persia loped along beside her, her thin legs covering the ground with an animal's ease. "Ah knows good debbil stools from pisen," she kept muttering.

The sun beat down on Louise's unprotected head. The tall field grass held her back, tangling her skirts. What was the antidote? She couldn't remember. Or was there any real antidote to counteract the effect of the deadliest type of mushroom poisoning? She tried to think, and couldn't, but in the midst of her fear was an undercurrent of relief. It wasn't Jim, it wasn't Jim!

Louise had to hold on to Persia's hand to climb the creek bank. Then Persia ran on ahead, her bare feet flipping up and down, showing pinkish soles. Louise, panting after her, had to pause and catch her breath when the house came into view, and the ruins of the Winsloe mansion. Green laced with gold wavered behind the dauntless grace of the columns, as if even the grand fragments defied the crudity of the new house squatting there. Louise hadn't been near it since last fall. The very sight of it struck her with its emanations of fear and hate and ugliness. She was afraid of it, and afraid of what she would find in it.

She pushed open the door and went in. Jim was sitting cross-legged on the floor by his mother's bed, tears rolling down his cheeks. He scrambled to Louise, and she put her arms around him. "There, baby. Your mother'll be all right. Let me see about her. Don't cry."

Della opened her eyes, and muttered she'd been sick and had cramps in her stomach.

"I sent word to Dr. Rand. He'll come as fast as he can. When did you eat them?"

Della's face on the pillow was startlingly like Francy's had been, and Louise seemed to see the dead child's livid skin and caved-in features. Louise shivered, and her arms tightened around Jim's sturdy warmth.

"I had 'em for dinner," Della said.

"And when did you begin to feel so bad?"

"An hour or so after——"

"Then even if you had the wrong kind, they weren't the worst kind——" Louise began to remember something she must have learned about mushroom poisoning. "Don't be frightened, you won't die." The fatal type was much slower to show its symptoms than the milder poisonous ones.

"Ah tolt Miss Della t'weren't no debbil stools what ailt her. She et her er slab er sowbelly an' it h'aint set so good on er."

Della felt better, she said. Louise took her pulse. It was strong. "All the same——" She mixed mustard and water and made Della swallow it, to make her vomit. Then afterwards, Louise remembered what else to give—sweet oil and whiskey in equal parts. After a while, Della was much better, but Louise sat beside her, her arm around Jim. Time passed, and Della had no more cramps or nausea, her pulse became stronger instead of weaker, and she dozed quietly. Persia, her mouth poked out, fixed Jim his supper, and Louise fed it to him. Della woke up, and said she felt weak, but all right.

"I'm sure you are, but I think I hear Dr. Rand booming outside."

"What's all this hullabaloo?" he demanded, barging in with hair, mustaches, and coattails flying. Louise told him. He examined Della and said there was nothing wrong with her as far as he could see. "But I'll stay a while. Any devil stools left, Persia?"

"Ah et 'em up," Persia sulked.

"Then they must be harmless. Though the North Russians eat the most deadly kind for the effect. They use them for a narcotic, and the things don't seem to hurt 'em. How'd you know what to give her?"

"I just happened to remember."

"That's good. Though it was nothing but an old-fashioned belly-ache, thank the Lord. There just isn't any real antidote for the other thing. It attacks the nervous system, particularly the heart and lungs. You'd better go on home now, Miss Lou. I know you're tired."

He came to the door with her. Outside, he said:

"There's something wrong in this house. I guess it's him."

"I wish I could get the child away from it."

Persia and Jim walked with Louise along the path to the place where it led down the creek bank. "I know you didn't mean any harm, Persia."

"Sho didn't. How come Ah go ter pisen Miss Della? She jes a pore critter. Er pore pitiful los' critter down heah by herself."

"She thought you might have picked the wrong ones."

"Reckon Miss Della tuk a wile noshun," Persia's teeth flashed in the dusk. "Ah knows Ah'm outer de swamp. Black as ribber mud.

Ah knows Ah cain't git me er fine gennmun lak Mr. Winsloe."

"Mr. Winsloe!"

"Him wut built de big house. He done gib Octavy rings fo' her yeahs, an' fine hosses—jes' gran'——"

Louise hadn't known Colonel Winsloe had had such tastes. It was a curious glimpse of his life.

"He wus highbreded. Ah knows Mistah Josh jes' scrub."

"Why do you stay, Persia?"

"Ah doan wanna wuk in no fiel' no mo'. Done gone ter de fiel' onct ter hoe—an lef' two lap-chillun in er cabin wid er ole 'oman. Hit cotch fire an' dey all burnt up."

Hearing about it made Louise feel sick. She put her hand on Persia's shoulder.

"Ain't gonna leave no chillun shet up in no cabin. Anyways, Jimmy an' me gits along. Doan we, Big Minner?"

A lantern flashed on the sand bar, throwing shadows. Alan and Tommy had come. Louise called to them, then turned to hug Jimmy. "Take care of him, Persia, and Miss Della too."

As they walked home, Alan said, "What is all the ruckus over there? Lillybelle sent children scattering in all directions looking for me, but Mr. Bijah and Tommy and I had gone to the woods, so nobody found us. When we got back to the house, Medora told us some garbled story about mushrooms. She and Mr. Bijah went on home, and we came after you."

Louise told them what had happened.

"I'm glad it was all a wild goose chase. I know how you remembered what you did, Lou. A long time ago, one rainy day, you and Mary and Anna and Carrie were reading about mushrooms in the encyclopedia."

"That's it——" Now she remembered. All of them gathered by the fire, a long time ago——

Della sent word that she was all right, and a few days later came herself to the house, more ill at ease than ever. "Run along, Jim." She waited until Jim had trotted off to join Tommy in the tree-house. "I never know how much he catches on to——" She fidgeted with the strings of her sunbonnet. "I reckon you think I was a plumb fool. I don't want Mr. Sanders to get wind of it."

"He won't."

A dark flush stained her face. "You don't think she'll tell him?"

"Persia? Oh, no. No, indeed!"

Della didn't understand Persia at all.

"Maybe not. I—I guess I had some kind of fit. Imagining things. But I was there by myself. With only Jimmy. And her——"

"I had a fit too! I thought she might have made a mistake."

"She gave me that gooey mess—and I started to feel so bad. And there she was moaning out one of those songs of hers, so wild sounding, and thumping her feet."

"You needn't be afraid of her, she doesn't mean you any harm."

"She gets drunk sometimes and goes crazy, yelling and tearing off to the woods."

"That's just to relieve her own feelings. She doesn't want to get rid of you."

"But I want to get rid of her, like I'd want to get rid of a wild animal. And Mr. Sanders, he won't."

"She loves Jim."

"She's good to him, and she was good to Francy. But I don't know what to do. My folks were strict and so were his, but he's changed down here."

"You mustn't blame Persia." Louise didn't pretend not to understand. "It just doesn't look the same to her as it does to you. To her, it's just—nature."

"Then it's his fault!"

"Yes."

"But I can't stand it going on!" There was a hysterical shiver in her voice.

"Can you leave him?" Suppose Della did run away and take Jim back to that Northern town where she had come from!

"I've got nowhere to go. And Mr. Sanders'd kill me before he'd let me take Jim off."

"Do you care about him at all any more?"

"He's mean. But he's my husband."

It was no use pointing out to Della what she had become. She couldn't change herself back. It was too late. And her shrinking and distaste, though the man deserved it, must be obvious to him.

"But you can manage him sometimes. You must have done that on the taxes."

"He put 'em back because you nursed Jimmy. He don't ever say so. But that was why. Sometimes he's mean to Jim, but he loves him."

"I suppose, even though your husband won't admit it, he has a sense of guilt towards you." Maybe he even felt burdened by all of the hate heaped upon him. "Persia's simple and primitive. She takes him as he is, and doesn't expect him to be any better than he chooses to be. She doesn't blame him for anything, and doesn't set any standards."

"But the way he's acting—it's wicked! That's what it is!"

"I know it is. But I'm just telling you why it happens."

Della still seemed puzzled because her husband sought out Persia and clung to her. Louise couldn't point out that Persia offered ease, abandon, freedom, even freedom from himself.

"He said that folks down here for all they give themselves airs and turn up their noses at us, all did the same. Did they, Miss Lou?"

"Not all, of course not. But it happened." Colonel Winsloe, for instance. On a higher level, with a pretty quadroon. "It still does happen, I suppose, but it's wrong." Della was right about the wickedness. Causing endless troubles and heartbreaks and tangles.

"What can I do?" Della asked. "I can't go on this sort of way——"

"You needn't. You can't change the situation but you can change yourself. You can ignore it, and not notice it."

"But I do notice——"

"But pretend you don't know it exists. You don't care for him except from a sense of duty, so that gives you more freedom to do and be what you please."

"Could you do that?"

"I don't know. I've learned to keep quiet about what I'd do or not do in somebody else's shoes."

"All that pretending—it's nothing but humbug!"

"A certain amount of humbug's not a bad thing at times. Or people would tear each other to pieces even more than they do already. And in your case it's the only practical course to follow. It's what you owe to yourself and Jimmy. He's the most important thing in your life. You must make as decent a home for him as you can, no matter how your husband behaves. It's an ugly situation, and you must keep your own dignity. There's a useful proverb that says, 'When an ass kicks you, don't tell.'"

Heavens! Why had she come out with that! But Della didn't seem to care that her husband had been insulted. "I'll see how I can work it out—I'll try," she sighed, and went away.

She might succeed, too. Different as they seemed, there was something faintly alike about Della and Medora, yet of the two, Della had more shrewdness. The Yankee virtue! Della would be more capable of using what meager advantages she had.

One bright, hot day, Medora came riding over. "Come take a ride with me, Lou."

"On what?"

"Oh, something."

"Do you expect me to conjure an animal out of thin air?"

"There must be something around here." Medora's face was thinner than ever, but her eyes had a restless glitter, and her cheeks were flushed, giving her usual gentle prettiness a poignancy it needed.

"Soon—it'll be too hot to ride."

The day had the silkiness of early summer, when the growth was lush, but not too dense. The thin clouds were like lace, and the trees spread like fans.

"I think that black, balky critter's here—the one we brought from Natchez. I'll get Link to saddle him. Though we aren't supposed to sashay through the wilds by ourselves."

"I'm not afraid of any of the colored people around here."

Louise was surprised to hear this, for Medora was usually the timid one.

"Neither am I, but Mr. Bijah'll skin you if you rode over here alone."

"Wash rode through the woods with me."

"Alan can see you home. And I'll bring my pistol with us."

Link saddled the mule, and Louise and Medora rode off together. Near the edge of the woods, there were two big oaks, growing by themselves, not tangled by the other trees, and in the grass nearby there was a magic circle of toadstools, pink and gray and silver, fluted and sculptured.

"Della Sanders didn't eat any of these did she?" Medora asked.

"No, luckily. I don't believe they're the eatable kind. Though they look tempting, don't they? If you make a mistake, you won't get a chance to eat them twice!" Louise shivered, remembering how frightened she had been. "Dr. Rand says he had only one case of mushroom poisoning, and never wants to see another. Yet look at them, popping up like this, so neatly arranged. There's a kind of unexpected charm about them."

Some were smooth, some powdery, some delicately pleated, some capped with brown velvet, making them particularly suitable for gnomes. No wonder legends had it that the symmetrical ring was where elves danced on moonlight nights, where dragons breathed fire and made the toadstools grow, or where the devil himself stole out to churn his butter.

"How do you tell which is which, Louise?"

"Dr. Rand says the ones with the stems set in a socket are bad. After the scare Della gave me, I looked up the subject of mushrooms. The most innocent looking of all, white and satiny with a veil like a bride, is the very worst. Its named the Destroying Angel. That sleek one over there might be one. Pliny said that Nero thought it was such a convenient and amusing poison. He used it to kill off an entire banquet—guests, slaves, and centurions. Let's not try the woods, Medora. We shouldn't. And I'm not too sure of the temper of this beast."

They turned to the left, away from the creek, and towards the open slopes, where the surface of the ground was smoothed with new grass. They were going along quietly, not talking much, when Louise felt the saddle turn with her—so suddenly and unexpectedly she wasn't able to help herself. She knew what had happened. The old saddle, patched and mended too often, had given way—the girth had broken. It would have been all right if it had broken entirely and flung her off, but it had simply pulled apart enough to allow the saddle to turn. When Louise tried to roll off on the grass, clear of the mule's hoofs, she became tangled in the skirt of her riding habit and her foot caught in the stirrup. She found herself hanging, dragged along behind the mule.

Terror made her feel faint and weak, but she knew she mustn't scream or make any move which would frighten her mule. Medora kept her head too, and rode off for help. It was the only thing to do. The mule had stopped. Now he began to move again, nibbling. The sky and trees turned dark before her eyes. She mustn't faint, or do the wrong thing. She would have to try to free her foot, inch by inch, with infinite care, with controlled patience. And avoid arousing the mule's caprices.

The ground had looked smooth, but it felt hard and rough as the mule dragged her along. Worse, the mule was moving steadily towards a gully, and the gully was fringed and lined with prickly pears. The mule found their flat, sharp-thorned green to his liking, and paused to taste them. Louise closed her eyes against their scratches, but her hair caught on the pointed barbs and pulled agonizingly. But her foot was almost free. The mule jerked forwards. Louise flinched in spite of herself, pressing herself against the pears to get away from the flail of the hoof that might strike out. But the mule's next lunge freed her at last. Her bones ached with tension, and her face smarted. There was a taste of grit and dust in her mouth, but she was safe and the mule ambled on.

Louise was just getting to her feet when Medora rode up with Abe.

"I thought he'd kicked you——" Medora gasped. "I saw you lying there—I thought——" Medora's face was gray and her lips were blue.

"I'm all right. I feel like a pincushion."

"Praise de Lawd!" Abe murmured, brushing his hand over his face. He offered his mule for Louise to ride.

"I'd rather walk. You ride Colonel Duel and lead the other one back."

"Take my horse," Medora said.

"I wouldn't ride Pegasus right now." Louise had recovered herself, but Medora still looked ghastly. "You know how you feel if you've been confronted with a bad egg—you don't want to eat even a fresh one for a while. Right now, I'll be happier walking."

As they went towards the house, Alan and Tommy and Cornelius, followed by Lillybelle and whirling children, all eddied towards them, running and exclaiming. Everybody talked at once.

"Do you need Dr. Rand?" Alan kept asking.

"No! I want a tub of water and a comb and brush!"

"Tommy, go get the bottle of antiseptic. Prickly pears hurt." Alan made them come in and poured some wine.

"I've got to go home," Medora said.

"I'll ride back with you later, Medora. You look pretty shaky——"

Medora huddled in a chair, her eyes dazed. Before Alan could hand her a glass of wine, she slipped sideways in the chair, her head lolling. "She's fainted! We'd better get her in bed, Lou——"

They put her on the bed in Louise's room, and Louise bathed Medora's face with cold water. "Find the smelling salts. But she'll come to in a minute."

"She looks bad. Do you think she needs a doctor?"

"Oh, no, she'll be all right."

Alan went for the smelling salts. When Medora did open her eyes, she twisted and bit her lips. Alan was out of the room, and Louise was about to call him, when Lillybelle came in with more cold water. She looked at Medora, then went and closed the door. "This 'omanfolks business!"

"What on earth are you talking about?"

Medora was evidently suffering, she was biting her lips to keep from screaming.

"Ah reckon Miss Medoah done step over er broom."

Somewhere Louise had heard the expression before, but she didn't remember what it meant if she had ever known.

"Yer cain't fool me, Miss Lou—Ah done had 'em myself time an time again. Miss Medoah havin' her er mishap—she gonna lose de baby——"

"Baby——" Louise whispered. "Lilly, stop saying things like that! You're crazy, just crazy."

And yet—Medora was groaning and muttering, sweat beading her forehead and lips. The green-gold light swam in the window, making her look submerged and drowned. Louise caught a glimpse of her own self in the waver of the mirror. Her hair was matted and snarled, there was dirt on her face, and fiery blotches reddened on her cheeks and hands from the prickly pears.

"Don't let my aunt know," Medora muttered. "Or anybody——"

"Ain't gonna let nobody know nuthin', jes' usses," Lillybelle reassured her.

Louise's fingers slid away from the bowl of water she was holding. She watched the bowl break on the floor and the water spill out, and she just stood there. She knew she would have to plan and arrange and take care of Medora, and get Alan and Tommy out of the house, and she felt incapable of moving and thinking. She'd been a fool, to have been so unaware, but she'd never dreamt——

A rending sound made her jump. Lillybelle was tearing up a sheet. "Need mo' sheets, Miss Lou, an' newspapers."

"Lilly, do you think we can manage this without a doctor?"

"Sho us kin." Lillybelle was scornful. "Po' chile, doan bring no doctah alumberin' in heah! An' doan you be oneasy, Miss Lou."

Louise went to find the things Lillybelle asked for and hurried back with them. "We'll fix everything, Medora, don't worry."

Now to get rid of Tommy and Alan. Tommy was outside, and Alan was still rummaging for the smelling salts. "Where'd you put 'em, Lou?"

"Never mind——"

Tommy came in. "What's she groanin' for?"

"That girl needs a doctor!" Alan said, "I should have lit out for Doctor Rand before now!"

"No, she doesn't. It's just nerves. A sort of hysterical fit." Louise tried to choke back her own fears. "But I do think, Alan, you and Tommy'd better ride over to the Winsloes and tell them she's staying here for a few days."

"I guess she's had enough to make her nervous. With all of 'em moping over Jasper! I could wring that fella's neck!"

"So could I!" Fury against Jasper seized her, but she checked herself.

"Shall I tell 'em you want her to stay a while?" Alan asked.

"Yes, and if they ask you to stay to supper—and they will—do."

Louise was glad to be rid of both Alan and Tommy. They would eat supper at Avondale, and Alan would linger talking politics with

Mr. Bijah, and he and Tommy would be out of the house for hours. Louise and Lillybelle took care of Medora.

" 'Tain't gonna be so bad—hit's early." Lillybelle took it all as a matter of course. She had had miscarriages herself and had attended other women through them. As for Louise, she was too busy to think. Alan and Tommy came back late, and took Louise's statement that Medora was getting on all right without any questions. He and Tommy fell into their usual heavy sleep, undisturbed by lights or sounds in the house.

By midnight, it was all over. Before she went to sleep herself, Louise took a look at the room, restored to order. Medora had fallen asleep, and Lillybelle snored in a chair by the bed. Louise tried to tell herself none of it had happened. But it had, and there was no escaping from it.

Louise kept Medora in bed several days longer than was really necessary. "I'm giving you too much trouble," Medora would murmur from time to time. Otherwise, she said nothing, and didn't seem to want anything. She swallowed soup and milk and gruel with docility, and kept her eyes closed. This went on until one evening, when Louise brought Medora her supper. She found Medora up and dressed and sitting by the window.

"I'm all right now, Lou. I must go back tomorrow. I'll get Uncle Bijah to come and take me back."

"Are you strong enough?"

"Oh, yes."

"Then please eat something."

Medora struggled over every mouthful. Louise had put a freshly opened rose on the tray, and Medora picked it up and twirled it in her fingers. "I want to talk to you," she said.

"Let me get my workbasket, and you eat." Louise established herself under the light to tackle her neglected darning, and brushed a moth away from the lamp. "Fool thing!" The moth, pale and thin-winged, reminded her of Medora. Brittle, bruised by a touch, even by a strong gust of air, yet with no gift of self-preservation. Maybe nature found it unnecessary to endow such creatures with any. There were so many of them.

Medora was watching her. "I know you haven't any use for me any more—I haven't any for myself. I—I know it was an awful shock for you."

If shock was a tingling numbness, a wild disbelief, it certainly had been. "I don't stop caring for my friends as easily as that."

"I don't know what I would have done without you—and Lilly-belle." Medora covered her face with her hands.

"Please try not to cry any more, Medora."

"If I hadn't lost the baby—I was going to write to Jasper. I had his address. If I'd told him, he would have come back."

He most certainly would have come, rallying his rather uncertain affection and sense of duty. For that, he would have come. Louise granted him that much. "He shouldn't have gone away, under the circumstances."

"He didn't know. Neither did I."

"I certainly never suspected. But don't keep on blaming yourself, Medora. Things like that just happen."

Jasper and Medora isolated in that lonely place, in the softness and luster of those nights. More than once, wakened by the mock-ingbirds singing and singing, Louise had longed to wander out into the dark, but not alone. If Tom had been waiting for her, would she have cared for anything else? Prudence and convention—nothing would have mattered. And so it must have happened for Medora. "People get carried away. I realize that. I've felt carried away my-self."

"It wasn't exactly that," Medora murmured. "I thought I knew exactly what I was doing. I thought that afterwards, he'd want to stay——"

Louise stared at her. Now she was shocked. For Medora to be overwhelmed by an emotion too strong for her, that Louise could understand. But for her to deliberately try to hold Jasper by such means—— It was pitiful, but tragic. And wrong. Of course, Jasper had been aware of it. He must have seen her motives all too clearly.

"I was terrified when I found he'd gone. And afterwards, I began to suspect"—She started to shiver, and all of Louise's anger against her gave way—"But scared as I was, I felt that Jasper would come back and if there was a real reason to keep him, he'd know he'd have to stay! And once he'd made up his mind, he'd be happy."

"Do you still know where he is?"

"Yes, I do. And he'll be there another week."

"Then why don't you write to him, and tell him? Or go talk to him?"

"No—no—I couldn't do that now. There's no reason to talk to him. It's all over! Everything's over!" Medora picked at the petals of the rose, and Louise violently whisked her needle in and out of a sock, making a puckered chunk out of the darn.

"When I knew I was going to lose the baby, I was glad of it. But now, it's worse. Lots worse. I guess you can't believe that—but it is."

"Yes, I know it must be——" There was a sense of depression after a living child was born, but then the baby claimed your every thought and feeling. But when there was no baby, there was only the sense of loss and waste. Nature, cruel, inexorable in its demands for life, was thwarted, and struck back. And in the place of the new life that should have been, there was a taste of death and nothingness.

"If you wrote to Jasper, and told him everything——"

"No, it's no use! Don't you see? Before, I held on to the thought that if he knew, he'd come. And he would have! That kept me going. But if I wrote now, he'd have no reason to come."

Poor Medora! If she'd tried such devious ways to keep him, why hadn't she tried long ago? She had waited too long to be safe, to be sure, and now she never would be. Why hadn't she tried when he had still been able to feel intensely for her? Then it would have been more than affection and the nag of duty. Now it was too late. Medora saw it dimly, but she saw it through her own mental and physical wretchedness. She didn't see any of it from a real awareness of what Jasper had become.

The air was heavy that night and the storm broke before morning. Louise, awake, listened to the boom of thunder as if the ghosts of past battles sounded again—ghosts of the great charges, exultant with victory, and her memory burned with pride. Then the thunder rolled away. The victories were over and done with. The steady rain clinked and clanked, footsteps in the long retreat.

In the morning, sunlight and heat burst into the house. It showed up stains from the leaks, cracks in the floor, and the shabbiness of the furniture. Outside, Lillybelle's cabin seemed to tilt in a more ramshackle list, and the chickens pecking around it were dull-feathered and scrawny. Louise caught glimpse of her own reflection as she did up her hair. She looked scrawny herself, and her skin was weather-browned. Medora, up, dressed, and moving around the house in an effort to be helpful, seemed to be not only the color but the substance of ashes, as sometimes a burned piece of paper will keep its outline, but will dissolve if you touch it.

But sitting opposite to her in the merciless morning, Louise realized that the structure of Medora's face was an almost perfect oval, with hardly any faults of feature, and she wondered as she had before what made a person beautiful. When she was well and happy, Medora's face contained all the ingredients of beauty, yet somehow she never quite attained it.

It was a brilliant but unstable day. Cumulus clouds rose, melted, and reformed, moving over woods and fields and cabins, until the whole landscape seemed to be slipping and sliding in undulating waves of violet and cobalt shadow. In the afternoon it rained, and stopped at sunset. Thunderheads made glistening peaks about azure lakes of sky. On the ground, puddles shimmered, no longer mud and water, but jeweled.

Louise stopped her work to see what Medora was doing, and saw her wandering through the wet fields towards the edge of the woods. Why should she choose to go ambling about in the wet? And Louise followed her to bring her back. The sky was covered with loops and sweeps of cloud, but as Louise watched, the entire landscape before her was bathed with coppery light. Every color brightened, every outline sharpened. The grass flared to a fiery emerald, and beyond the glisten of the fields, the woods seemed to step forward, no longer blurred, but trunks and branches defined into a massive but detailed pattern. The familiar stretch of ground became invested with an ominous grandeur under the smouldering light, and Medora, moving, then pausing, looked small and lost, like someone all alone in a wild solitude, or like the figure in a classic tragedy, marked and doomed by a baleful fate. She seemed to be looking for something.

Louise shouted at her, and began to run. Medora turned. Closer to her, Louise saw the startled, frightened look on her face. "What are you doing?" Louise's voice was rough with fear. "What have you got there?" Because Medora was holding something in her hands. Louise went up to her. "Let me see——"

Medora turned away, dropping her hands, and the silky caps and stems of the mushrooms she had gathered fell on the gleaming grass.

"Do you realize what you are doing?" Louise managed to whisper. Medora covered her face with her hands and began to sob. Louise put her arms around her. "Did you eat any at all? Even taste any?"

Medora shook her head.

"Promise me you'll never, never——"

After a while, Medora raised her head. "I promise—I swear——"

"You couldn't have realized——" Louise began, her grip tightening around Medora's shoulders. Somehow it was not the moment to point out to Medora how wrong she was to want to do away with herself. Louise couldn't say it now, and so deep was her pity, she felt she never would. Medora would keep her promise.

A mockingbird lighted on a low branch, settling his feathers, giving a few rippling notes, but they were the sad notes of some melancholy bird. The trees darkened and cast a shadow over the two women and the place where they stood and the magic ring of toadstools near them, some of them broken off. Nothing had happened but one thing had become clear. Louise knew it. She would never be free of Medora. She was fated to be Medora's staff and prop, now and always.

Chapter Nine

ALAN was sitting still, but his eyes were restless. He never stopped looking out of the front window, to watch for the first glimpse of Dr. Rand and Mr. Bijah. Any minute now, they would come riding up.

"Have you some coffee made, Lou?"

"I have something stronger. You'll need it." She was turning the pages of a magazine, but the print danced before her eyes.

"Where'd we get the whiskey?"

"Lilly filched some from Cornelius. It seems the Yankee met him on the road and gave him some, and Lilly gave it to me. You know how furious she gets when Cornelius drinks."

"Ole Man Sanders seems to be dispensing gifts around here with right royal grandeur."

"It's good whiskey too. I don't see why he bothers with Cornelius, who isn't going to be turned against us anyway."

"Well, Sanders can afford to deal out whiskey and barrels of flour. He knows he'll get it all back and double in that commissary of his."

The Yankee had opened a store, well stocked with all of the things the hands wanted and needed. Of course it was convenient for the hands to have a place nearby, where they could find thread and molasses and tools and calico. Only a few of the negroes could understand the Yankee's methods of accounting, or realize what enormous rates of interest he was charging, not until he was ready to show them that by the time the cotton was picked they owed him their entire crop.

"I saw him the other day," Alan said. "He was ambling down the road, out to make trouble, and grinning like a mule eating briers."

Louise got up and put some glasses on the table. "You and Mr.

Bijah and Dr. Rand can drink his whiskey while you plot his overthrow."

"We'll have to overthrow him, and all the rest. The fat's in the fire, Lou."

She knew it, everyone knew it, since the trouble at Vicksburg, which had the very worst government of any town in the state. In Vicksburg, there was open corruption and outright confiscation. The black militia tramped the streets day and night. When the time had come for the city election, the white citizens, who had remained quiet so long, had organized to a man. Even in their isolation here at Indigo, Louise and Alan were feeling the breathlessness and tension. It was one of those times of decision when passive waiting isn't enough any more.

"That stupid, blundering fool of a governor," Alan was always muttering.

"It would be much worse for us if he had good sense," Louise pointed out. The governor, uneasy because of the citizens organization, had asked Grant for troops, and Grant had turned down his request. Even in Washington, there must be at last a feeling of guilt. The Democrats had won at the Vicksburg polls, and the determination and courage of the citizens had paid off. After that, the voters had started to clean up the county, marching on the courthouse and demanding the resignation of the thieves who called themselves officials. They had found the courthouse empty and deserted. All the rascals had run, all except Crosby, the sheriff. He was the worst of the lot. He had promptly resigned, then had galloped off to Jackson, to ask Governor Ames for Troops. Ames had denounced the taxpayers as riotous and disorderly persons, and had armed a Negro force to march against Vicksburg.

A hundred armed men on horseback had ridden out to meet them. The commander had calmly asked the Negro army to turn back, pointing out to them that they were the victims of the carpetbaggers. There had been little urge to fight it out, but a few shots were fired. Several Negroes had been killed, and the rest had run away. Another force, coming on Vicksburg by another road, had been scattered just as easily.

Even the Northern newspapers—the just ones—approved of the

citizens' stand, and Louise's old friend, Henry Stacey, wrote flaming articles and editorials, which were quoted all over the country, and all over Europe, too.

"Aren't you proud of Henry?" Louise's cousin Mary had written from New Orleans. "He always likes to get his teeth into a good crusade, and he is doing wonders to justify us to the world. We haven't given up fighting down here, and never will. Alexander slithers off like a shadow nearly every night. When Mississippi is free, it will make it easier for us in Louisiana."

Everyone had watched and waited and the governor had called the legislature. Nervous now, the legislature had fumbled. They had not been able to think of any effective way to curb Vicksburg's defiance, except to petition Grant for troops. The President had instead issued a proclamation ordering the citizens to disperse. The people in Vicksburg had quietly elected a new sheriff, and were going about their own concerns, so the President's decree meant nothing.

Then General Sheridan had taken a hand. He had telegraphed Governor Ames that he was sending troops which were on their way to Vicksburg. And the rascal of a sheriff was immediately reinstalled in office. Now what would happen? Everyone in Mississippi felt that Vicksburg had showed the way to deliverance. The people there had starved during the siege, they had endured the most vicious form of carpetbag rule, yet they had risen with their old spirit and courage. Would it all go for nothing? Was everyone in Mississippi going to sit still and let Vicksburg be crushed again?

Mississippi's General George had confronted Sheridan, and had called on all the taxpayers, and all the citizens in the state to organize. Mr. Bijah had brought that piece of news to Indigo. "If Phil Sheridan thinks we're going to knuckle under, we'll show him different!" And he had gone off to talk to General George. Today, Mr. Bijah and Dr. Rand were coming over to Indigo, to tell Alan what had been planned and what they intended to do.

Looking at Alan's thin, taut face, Louise had an impulse to say, "Whatever has to be done, let other people do it. You stay out of it."

Here at Indigo, they had been living in a state of passive hostility to the Yankee. Busy with his own schemes, he had let them alone. If he felt himself threatened by them the Yankee could drive them away from Indigo. All he had to do was to see that Indigo's taxes were doubled. Years of work and sacrifice would be swept away by scrawling a set of figures in a book. Louise could endure it for herself, and even for Alan. But it was Tommy's despair she felt she could not face. And then there was Jim. The Yankee wouldn't let him come here any more if the people at Indigo declared themselves his open enemies. Louise knew she would lose Jim. Yet Louise didn't say a word. Alan understood it all as well as she did. It was for him to decide. And she watched the grassy track of road through the trees.

They came riding up and Amanda Rand was with them.

"I want to hear everything," she said, as Alan helped her from her horse. She was young enough to enjoy the excitement, and to feel the blaze of courage and decision. But Louise, watching her, understanding her youth, felt old. Old and tired. It seemed a lifetime ago, when she had known such sensations, and had been able to savor the exhilaration of change and excitement. It was a long time ago—the day when war had been declared. Never again would she be able to have any enthusiasm for violence. Loss and defeat had taught her too well.

Tommy had been watching, and came running up to the house, his slate-colored eyes studying every face in turn.

"Come and listen," Louise said to him. She had always wanted to spare him, but his whole future was bound up in what was happening, and in what would happen. "I want you to understand what Mr. Bijah and the doctor have to say."

"I'm a dead shot," Tommy told the men. "You can use me."

"Maybe we will, son." Mr. Bijah put his hand on Tommy's shoulder, and they went into the house together.

"Did you see General George?" Alan asked.

"I did. We made some plans, and came to some decisions." He tilted his chair back. Louise poured whiskey in his glass. He downed it in one gulp. "Two things we've got to hold on to—we've got to win the election this fall, and we've got to keep our heads. There mustn't be any rioting, or any going off half cocked. We mustn't give Grant the shadow of an excuse to interfere."

132

"Mr. Bijah's been named head of the taxpayers league in this county," Dr. Rand told them.

"It's the logical choice," Alan said.

"Look here, Alan," Dr. Rand put in, "we know you're in a ticklish fix. We all got Yankees in Jackson and Washington, but you've got Josh Sanders right on your own doorstep."

"Yeah," Mr. Bijah said. "Watching you like a cat watching a mousehole."

"What are you planning?" Alan wanted to know.

"The latest news is that Ames's gotten authority to organize the Negro militia."

There was a little silence in the room. Amanda leaned forward, her lips parted. Louise grasped the edge of the table. The room and the faces in it looked dark, and beyond the windows, the hot, reddening sunlight dazzled her eyes. There was the ache of tension in the muscles of her arms and neck, like the time when she had tried to urge the mule up the slippery bank. The same feeling—knowing they couldn't stay where they were—and to slip back meant complete ruin. She hadn't realized until this minute how much she had come to love Indigo. Every ramshackle cabin, every clod of earth, every twig and branch. She looked at her son, but Tommy's face was absorbed. He didn't see her, he was watching Alan.

"That's fixed it," Alan said. "Every man in Mississippi'll arm too!"

"We will—we are——" Dr. Rand's voice was hoarse from strain and excitement.

"Revolution—and high time!" Alan's voice was low, but there was not a flicker of hesitation in it, and his eyes were bright. "Count me in on it."

That night, Louise was awake hour after hour, reliving that scene. It kept flashing before her, the men's voices, and their faces and what they had said. Amanda had whispered, "You're a hero!" to Alan as he had put her on her horse.

Ever since Amanda had come back from school, Louise had noticed how she had looked at Alan, and listened to him. If Alan didn't realize how the bits of verse Amanda quoted, the books she tentatively mentioned were as much of an effort to adorn herself for him as the new ribbons in last year's hat, he didn't have eyes at all. And for Alan, with all he was, with all he should have been able to offer, not daring to allow himself to care for a country doctor's daughter! Yet he was right in curbing his personal emotions. This was a crisis. But Amanda's whisper had endeared her to Louise. Amanda had proved how well she understood what Alan was willing to sacrifice, and how much she honored him for it. It proved Amanda wasn't a naïve girl, but a woman, and a woman of heart and perception.

Louise needed all of her self-discipline to force herself to go through with the daily routine in those seething weeks and months. Alan was often away, to attend mass meetings, or to ride with processions of cavalry and marching men. How his health stood it, Louise couldn't imagine, except that the vigor of decision seemed to give him reserves of physical energy. Tommy sometimes went with him, to listen to speeches. The plantation had never seemed so lonely to Louise, who tried to take the burden of running the place from Alan's shoulders.

"You have all of the anxiety and none of the excitement," Alan said.

"It would be too easy to let things slide this summer, and tell ourselves that if the carpetbaggers win all the work will be wasted effort. By the end of the year, we'll need every bale we can raise no matter how it turns out."

"That's what Mr. Bijah says."

"Jasper ought to come back to do his share. Is there any word from him?"

"Not that I know of," Alan answered. "But I tell you who is coming here to be with Mr. Bijah—a young Winsloe cousin of his from South Carolina."

"How old is he?"

"He's just a boy. About fifteen, I think."

"Not old enough to be of much help," Louise meditated.

"Mr. Bijah says he wants to give the boy a home. He's one of a lot of children, and that part of the family's lost everything. So it might work out to be a good thing for the boy, and Mr. Bijah too."

"Yes, if he's the right sort of boy," Louise said.

Every time Louise went out of the house, she took her loaded pistol with her, but there had been no disturbances on Indigo. The hands went on with their work, though Louise knew that the Yankee was trying to incite them. They seemed to show their awareness of the tension by quarreling among themselves. One man was slashed in a game of craps, another had his clothes torn to shreds by his wife, who claimed he was "triflin' on her."

In the midst of all of the tumult, Louise missed Jim. He was evidently no longer allowed to come to her house, and she hadn't seen him for a long time. His absence caused a queer ache in her heart. One afternoon, rather late, she went to the field near the creek, hoping to catch a glimpse of him, or at least to hear his voice somewhere. An air of sleepiness hung over the field in the late sunlight, and the woods nearby were hung with veiling shadows. The long grass had turned brown, and the harshness of the katydids sounded without a pause. There was a sadness in it, as their instinct told them that winter was coming, and they could only keep up a pretense of summer and gladness.

This time next year the field would look different. If Alan managed to keep Indigo, he had decided to plant it in cotton, promising to spare the pecan tree. And if the Yankee owned it— She stopped short. The Yankee was standing there, by the pecan tree. It gave her a strange shock. She waited, and he came forward a little way, surveying her out of his light, stone-colored eyes.

"I know your brother's joined up with that taxpayers league. I know he's riding around the country organizing. Well, tell him from me to go ask what his taxes are this year. And you can git ready to move off here the day they're due."

"I'll tell him." Louise found herself answering.

"But before then, there's an election coming."

The man's eyes stopped focusing on her, and were focusing on something—or someone behind her. She turned. Tommy was standing there, his gun in his hands, his face dark and drawn with such a look of bitter fury all his childhood was suddenly burned away.

"Get off our land!"

"Hush, Tommy—hush——" The gun, and Tommy's rage, made

anything possible. But the Yankee had begun to shamble away. He turned back to say. "You won't see Jim again—I've told him how I'll fix him——"

"Go back to the house, Tommy. He's gone."

"I'll get even with him—I'll get him yet—you'll see!"

"Stop it. Put that gun down. We've got enough trouble on our hands, son."

"Take Indigo! Him!"

"It's possible, child. Even likely. You understood what was going on a while ago, when your uncle decided——"

"Sure."

"I know how you feel about Indigo. And so do I, because you do. But even if it means losing it, your uncle has to help his friends."

"Sure. But we're going to win."

"Then promise me not to do anything wild or foolish. Now go."

She watched him go on back towards the house. His confidence buoyed her up. He saw how everything and everyone had to be sacrificed, if necessary, to Alan's sense of what was honorable and right. Alan had to join in the battle, there was no other way. But for the first time, Louise felt the tingle of coming victory. They would win! And her eyes narrowed. There was a way to get revenge on their own particular enemy. Through his child. And it would be good for the child.

She became conscious of a movement and stir in a biggish tree near the creek bank. Squirrels—but her hand tightened on her pistol, then her fingers went limp as she heard Jim's voice calling her softly, and Jim came slipping and sliding down the trunk, and ran to her. "I got me a treehouse. 'Taint as good as Tommy's."

"Child——" She looked all around. "Where's your father?"

"Gone. I watched til he was. I can see good from my treehouse."

Not a soul was in sight, and the growth on the bank made a thick screen in case the man, or anyone, might be watching from the other side.

"Let me look at you, Jim." She blinked back tears. "Feast my eyes."

"What's feast?"

"Something good to eat. I could eat you."

He smiled, in that beguiling way of his. "I been coming. Most every day."

"If I'd known I'd have been here sooner. We've missed you."

"Me, too, but I'm scairt of Pa. Reckon we could meet here?"

"Yes, sometimes, but I don't want to make trouble for you."

"I can hide good. But I want to be up at your house."

"I want you there. How's your mother?"

"All right, I guess. Sometimes she cries. I want to jes' go to your house like I used to before Pa got so mad."

"Seeing you here is better than nothing."

"Look there's a hollow in this tree. We could have a post office."

"Have you been practicing making your letters the way I showed you?"

"Some. If we have a post office, I will more."

"All right. And Sandy has puppies. Do you want one?"

"Oh, yes—yes—oh—will you bring him tomorrow?"

"I'll try."

"What color?"

"Tan, with white spots."

"I love Sandy."

"Will your father let you keep a puppy?"

"I reckon. It won't be a lie jes' not to say the puppy's Sandy's puppy."

Louise conceded that. Otherwise Josh Sanders might kill the little dog.

"There's one thing I want that your father wants too, Jimmy. I want you to study and learn and so does he."

"By myself?"

"Your mother'll help you if you ask her." Della had taught school once.

"I reckon so. But I like the way you read books better."

"Read them for yourself. You soon can—all of them, if you try."

He looked unhappy then brightened. "I'll write some lettering and words for our post office."

The sun had gone and twilight's blue was stealing over the fields and the woods. "You must go, child. Run home, and I'll come tomorrow." She gave him a kiss.

137

"Shout when you reach the other bank."

He rustled into the bushes, vanished, and after a while she heard his shout. She herself turned toward the house her heart heavy with suspense and hope and a thousand terrors.

She took the puppy to Jim the next day, and promised to put something in the post office at least once a week.

One hot afternoon, when she started to go towards the field, Tommy, who happened to be in the house, insisted on going with her. "You might meet the Yankee."

They didn't see the Yankee. They found Jim's scrawl in the tree's hollow. He had written in block letters, "Pup is well." Louise was turning away, when Tommy whispered. "Look." From where they were standing they could see a bend in the creek where the banks were lower than they were here. The sand bar crossing it at that point blazed white in the glare and a heat haze rippled. A horse and rider were motionless on the sand bar. In that beating light, horse and man were black and featureless, an outline, like some dark spirits— ghost of an Indian brave—ghost of some old violence taking shape here again.

"You reckon it's some of the Yankee's friends?" Tommy whispered.

"No." Louise didn't know why she said no so positively, but the man turned his horse and began to ride towards them and there was something about the way he moved, the way he held himself, unlike anyone the Yankee would be apt to know. Jasper come—no, it wasn't Jasper. The man rode through the shallow water and up the bank. He was as dark as an Indian, but with a smooth, young face, and short, blunt features. When he saw Louise there, he swept off his hat.

"How do, ma'am?"

He was no friend of the Yankee's, he was one of theirs. His gesture, voice, and manner told Louise that. He was not a man, though, he was a boy. "Why, you're Wayne Winsloe!"

"Yes, ma'am. And you must be Mr. Alan's sister."

He had just come a day or two ago, he said, in answer to her questions. She invited him to come to the house, but he said no, he had work to do, if she would just take a message to Mr. Alan.

"About the meeting tonight." He gave her a folded slip of paper, after looking around. He promised to come to the house as soon as he could. He smiled as he said his good-bys, and his smile made him look as young as she knew he was, then his face took on the dark, intense seriousness she had noticed at her first glimpse of him. He turned and rode back into the full sunlight, and again became a black and featureless outline, until he seemed to fade in to the dazzling glare, as if he had never showed his face, never spoken to her and to Tommy—as if she had imagined him, and he hadn't been real, and would never be seen again.

Louise and Tommy went back to the house. Louise handed Alan the folded slip of paper. He glanced at it, and tore it up. Tommy muttered he wished he could go to meetings. "Wayne Winsloe does! He knows everything that's going on!"

"He's considerably older than you are," Louise said, thinking how much older than his years Wayne Winsloe seemed.

After supper, Louise made Alan take a nap, he seemed so tired. "Wake me at nine sharp then," he yawned, and went off to his room. The secret rendezvous must be some place nearby. Even so, Alan would hardly be home again before morning. Louise wondered what other women on lonely plantations were doing. She had an innate dislike for "women's work," and it was no use for people to tell her it wasn't boring. It was. And the reason for that was it didn't take you out of yourself. How could you lose yourself in a piece of knitting? If you were lonely, or worried, or frightened, or in suspense, it didn't hold your interest. Probably Medora was sitting in a dim circle of lamplight too, darning, or embroidering, taking those fine stitches so much more perfect than Louise's own efforts, and thinking. It was more than a year now since that time last summer, and a tumult of events had almost crowded it out of Louise's mind.

Medora rarely came to Indigo these days, and never alone. When she did come, nobody talked of anything except the excitement going on all around them. But tonight, when the other men rode off, Medora would surely think of Jasper and feel that he ought to be among them. No one seemed to know where he was. Mr. Bijah never mentioned his son. Now Medora never did either, and whether Jasper still wrote to her, Louise had no way of knowing.

The house was quiet. Too quiet, and Louise went to Tommy's room to look for him. He wasn't there. He wasn't anywhere in the house. She started to wake Alan, but he was so deeply asleep she hated to disturb him. Tommy must be in Lillybelle's cabin. He often went there. But when she went to look, no one had seen him. She ran out in the dark, calling him. No answer. She was just about to send Cornelius to search, and to go wake Alan herself, when Tommy slipped out of a clump of shadows and joined her. "Ssh! I went down to the woods—and to the clearing, and you know what? The Yankee's down there. He's just carryin' on! You ought to hear!"

"I've been looking all over for you!"

"I thought maybe you were. That's why I came back. Let's wake Uncle and all go."

"You had no business running off. You know your uncle told you to stay put after dark!"

"He told me to take care of you, and I knew he was still in the house. I wanted to know what was going on. I'm going back there and see what's up."

"No, you can't go! And don't wake your uncle, he has to go somewhere else later."

"I know that. But I want to hear what the Yankee's saying. They'll never see me in the dark."

"Then I'm coming too."

"We'd better saddle us a pair of mules then. So we can get away easy if they do see us. Link'll help me."

He called Link, and the three of them went to the barn. Louise got on one of the mules and followed where Tommy led her. He was a born woodsman, and didn't make a sound as they rode into the dark fringes of the wood towards the clearing. "Here," Tommy whispered.

In the shelter of the trees, they could look out over the clearing. A fire was burning in the middle, and near it, the Yankee was shouting and gesticulating. His face was a bursting red and his voice had a grating edge. Grouped in a thin circle, was a ring of colored faces, shiny in the firelight. Skin and eyeballs and teeth shone. The woods around were black, a solid wall of density.

Josh Sanders was ranting on, telling the Negroes to rise up and vote with the carpetbaggers, that Grant wanted them to, and that if they did not, they would be slaves again. Didn't they want land, mules, riches, and happiness? It was the time-honored speech of a demagogue, and Louise hardly listened. What interested her was to see which hands had come from Indigo. A good many of the Yankee's own had stayed away. And there was no one here from Avondale. Wash kept Mr. Bijah's people in order! She noticed only a very few faces from Indigo. There was that stupid boy of Brown Wilson's. Poor thing—did he think the Yankee was going to really give him mules and molasses and shoes? How easy, if you had nothing, to believe anything. Then, with a shock, Louise saw Jessie, her thin arms wrapped around her knees, and her chin resting on her arms. Her eyes were wide open, and she seemed to be taking in every word.

"And I thought she'd grown fond of us," Louise whispered.

"She has," Tommy whispered back. "She's just curious. She told me she wanted to hear——"

So that was how Tommy had known where to go. In a few minutes, Jessie unfolded, stood up, and slid away into the shadows. Hunched forward, Tommy was listening, and as Louise's eyes grew accustomed to the dark, she saw the gleam of the gun he was carrying.

"Careful, careful——"

At that moment the Yankee was shouting, "As Gray says, we'll win this election if we have to kill every white man, woman, and child in this county!"

Before Louise could move or speak, Tommy had raised his gun and fired. In the sharpness of the shot ringing out, its staccato crackling cutting through the nasal voice, and the screaming, the stampede of running and scattering, Louise thought Tommy must have fired straight at Josh Sanders. Then she realized he had only fired well above the heads of the whole group.

The Yankee's mouth hung open as he wheeled in the direction of the shot. "Get out of here, Tommy," Louise urged, "Get out—now——"

"All right," Tommy muttered under his breath, but before he

moved he fired another shot. It sang in the twigs above the Yankee's head and he leaped wildly.

"We can go now, Mother."

Louise kept quiet as they rode off. Shouts behind them, branches brushing their faces, and her own heart pounding in her ears kept her silent. But when they had left the woods and had galloped across the fields, she demanded, "What possessed you?"

"Don't be so scared, Mamma. I wanted to drill him, but I didn't."

In spite of herself she had been impressed by Tommy's sureness and accuracy.

"He was on our land. I already told him to stay off. You think I'm goin' to let him holler those things on our land?" Then Tommy began to laugh. "I sure liked seein' him jump! Just like an ole bull frawg!"

Louise admitted she had enjoyed seeing the Yankee jump. "All the same, son, we've got enough troubles without your making extra. Your uncle will give you what for!"

When they went into the house, Alan was awake and dressed and loading his pistol. "Where have you two been?"

Louise told him, and he lectured Tommy on prudence, and guarding the house and taking care of his mother, but when the boy had left the room, Alan said that Tommy had been too reckless but probably had the right idea. "We've been patient, so the carpetbaggers thought we were scared. We've waited, and let the colored people build up a blind faith in the carpetbaggers instead of in us. We're going to change all that!" Alan's face looked dark and pinched but there was life in his eyes and vigor in his voice. "Lou, are you scared to stay here just with Tommy? Cornelius had better sleep in the kitchen until I get back."

"I'm not a bit scared." She was uneasy for him, draining his strength, going into danger, and yet she knew how the years of inaction had preyed on him.

"As a matter of fact, Tommy did just what we intend to do from now on, all over the state. Whenever there's a gathering like that, we'll break it up."

"I suppose you'll be late getting back."

"Most likely. Mr. Bijah's gone to see General George again, so

I'm in charge around here. Young Wayne Winsloe's going to prove to be a lot of help. He's just come, but he's certainly flung himself into the fight——"

"That's good." Louise could imagine Wayne Winsloe as a fighter. There had been intensity in his face. "And he's from South Carolina, and must have seen the war at its worst." She didn't think he would be likely to forget, even though he had been very young.

"The governor has threatened to arm the Negro militia, but we won't have any of that. We're guarding the state house, day and night. If he does arm 'em, we'll kill him. On the spot. And he knows that."

"We'll win." Louise went with Alan to the door, and Tommy came and joined them. The three of them stood together in the starry dark.

"Take care of your mother," Alan told Tommy.

"I will, sir."

"Then I leave you in charge."

From the blur of the trees, came an owl's cry, its harshness rasping through the quiet. Once, then again. Louise shivered. It was the sound of loneliness, and autumn. It was the voice of the wild places, and the night's wings and eyes and talons. Then she knew it was not an owl's call, but the signal Alan had been waiting to hear. Immediately, he rode off, and the dark folded around him.

Tommy and Louise watched him vanish. Long ago, Alan had fought in a great battle. This was another chance, to lose or win. Louise was remembering a far-off winter twilight, when Tom and Alan, their leave ended, had told her good-by. The winter before Shiloh. And she felt again the same tight, burning constriction in her heart. Tom was beyond all conflicts, but Alan had to struggle on into the uncertain future. Again, she felt she was telling him some fateful good-by. Tommy was beside her, knowing no fears at all. But he was with her in body only. In spirit, she knew Tommy was gone away from her. Gone forever out of his childhood.

Chapter Ten

THE bonfires danced high, and faces moved in and out of the glow. The smell of meat roasting, and the sound of sizzling filled the air. The expert cooks, like Mrs. Rand, were attending to the barbecuing, basting pork and venison with elaborate, and of course, secret sauces, and calling directions to Wash and Lillybelle and Jessie and the other servants.

Louise left them to their intense rivalries with the food. When it was done and ready, it would all be gobbled up, and Louise always felt a little mournful that food, so much trouble to prepare, was eaten in such a short space of time. She was sitting on a log with Medora, ready to help, but glad to be idle. Children laughed and ran about, carts and wagons and horses and mules and old surreys were drawn up in a circle on the outskirts of the firelight—an odd assortment of anything that could move on wheels or legs. A drum began to thump, and Mr. Bijah climbed up on a wagon to make a speech. There were cheers, and the men gathered to listen. The women looked up from their work, but went on setting the long wooden tables, and bustling here and there, armed with forks, bowls, and baskets. Louise saturated with speeches lately, stayed where she was.

The whole scene was like some encampment on the way to the far West, or like gypsies reveling. There was something wild and emotional about it, a little beyond the edges of civilization. She savored its heady, primitive quality. It suited her, it suited them all tonight. She knew everybody felt as she did, dizzy and lightheaded with nerves and sleeplessness, yet buoyed up with exultation. They had been stiff with discipline and resolve. Now they could shout and scream and dance. The carpetbag governor and the carpetbag legislatures were defeated and disgraced. The voters had gone armed to the polls, but General George had promised the terrified governor that he would keep order if no arms were given to the Negro militia and no troops were sent to Yazoo City, where there had been trouble. Washington made no move. The voting had been peaceful, and the carpetbaggers had been swept away. All of them. Louise's eyes were on a banner stretched between two poles. On it was written in crude lettering, "Ames—go back to Minnesota." He would have to go. There was nothing else left for him. There was talk of impeaching him, but Louise didn't care any more. For a while she wouldn't be able to listen to politics, it would all be an anticlimax now. The firelight waved over another banner. "Mississippi—Sovereign State."

She looked for Tommy. He was with the men, listening to Mr. Bijah. She noticed other faces. The wizened, monkeylike face of the fisherman who had danced with her at the New Year's party. He had moored his little houseboat at Indigo Bend, and had come to join the triumph of tonight's celebration. Then there was Mr. Ferris —she'd just met him tonight. He lived on a lonely plantation down near the Buffalo River, but had emerged to do his share at the election, and had lingered for tonight's jubilation. Wayne Winsloe was listening to Mr. Bijah too. Wayne's dark eyes were narrowed against the firelight. His arms were folded, and he was smiling a little.

Link was trailing lengths of firewood to the blaze, Lillybelle was waving a long tin spoon in the air and shooing children, and Jessie was putting plates and cups on the table. "We'd better go help." Louise left the indifferent comfort of the log, and plunged into a group of women, and Medora followed in her wake and began to slice bread.

Dr. Rand's younger son Jack came up to Louise and asked her what she thought Mr. Tiptoe could have put in his famous bottle. "He just laughs and won't tell."

Some weeks ago, before the election, there had been a big carpetbag meeting in Natchez. The druggist, Mr. Tiptoe, had slipped his way into the hall, and had thrown a bottle, or several bottles, and the hall had filled with such choking fumes that the meeting had broken up in wild excitement. The crowd gathered outside had watched the carpetbaggers come running out clutching their throats, and honest Mississippi citizens had taken great pleasure in their enemies' retchings.

"They tell me all of 'em tumbled out like June bugs," Jack Rand recounted, relishing it all over again. "I wish I could have seen 'em skedaddle!"

Louise's own cousin Albert had expressed his feelings in his own way. Cousin Albert, when he had been hardly more than a child, had joined a rebellion in Cuba, had been taken prisoner by the Spaniards, and had been taken to a Spanish prison. Every day, on the ship, one of the prisoners had been executed. It had been Cousin Albert's turn when an order had come putting a stop to the executions. Cousin Albert had stayed in a Spanish prison for several years. When he had been released, he had fought in the Mexican War, then had fought through the War between the States. Afterwards, Louise had lost touch with him. He had withdrawn to the swamps, and was never seen in Natchez. Just before the election, he had made a startling appearance in the town of Waterproof, Louisiana. Without a stitch of clothes on, but painted a lurid blue from head to heel, he had ridden at a wild gallop through Waterproof, firing his pistol and howling he would shoot any carpetbagger on sight. He had seen none, as they thought it more prudent to keep out of his way.

"I can hardly believe all the excitement's over," Medora murmured. Louise guessed she would miss the rallies, the gallopings, the marching crowds, and the incidents. It had given her something to think about besides her own life. Now she would have to go back to its usual routine. "So will I," Louise thought, knowing not all problems were solved. The carpetbaggers in Jackson were on the run, but her own particular Yankee incubus was with them still. "Though some of his snaggly teeth are drawn," she had said to Alan.

The Yankee wouldn't snatch Indigo—not this year. The taxes would be normalized, and the crop, in spite of difficulties and interruptions, was better than usual and would bring a somewhat better price. She thought with gratitude of their own hands on Indigo. In all the tumult, and with so much to incite them, they had been steady and sensible. Her fingers touched a scrap of paper in the bag she was carrying. It was a note she had found in Jim's tree-hole post office. "I am glad you won. I never did want to run you off." It was unsigned, but Della had written it.

Louise wished for Jim, so she could watch him running and playing with the other children. He would have no friends, he would be an outcast always, unless she could help him. Or unless he learned how to help himself. But Della's little note made her feel that she had allies there across the creek, to leaven the bursting hate she knew Josh Sanders must be feeling. Tonight, she wouldn't think about hate, or remember any cares either, but just let herself be carried along, feeling as if her feet were hardly touching the ground, and her head was filled with light, many-colored feathers, and nothing else.

Amanda came up to speak to her. "How pretty you look Miss Lou!"

Louise had taken pains to be at her best. Her dress was only cotton, a plain gingham, but heavy, and the colors were bright, and she had adorned it with an embroidered collar, and had made a bustle out of wads of newspaper. When bustles had first come into fashion, some of the older Natchez ladies had murmured, saying it was strange for a lady to want to accentuate that portion of her anatomy she should do her best to conceal. But now everyone was used to bustles. "You can wear them," Amanda said, admiring the set of Louise's dress. "And I think they have so much dash!"

In the cheerful confusion and clatter of supper, Wayne Winsloe came and sat beside Louise. She found him surprisingly good company. Already he seemed at home here, and he told her little incidents about some of the people gathered around her, and the part they had played in winning the election. "Ole Davis took a harpoon to the polls, or so he says."

"He's my dancing partner—I wouldn't be surprised." Davis was the fisherman who spent all his life on the river in his patched-up houseboat, roving from river bend to river bend. "The meetings and marchings gave you a chance to meet everyone at once. After tonight, they'll fade away to remote plantations or swamps."

"Cousin Medora says you gather people together around Christmas."

"I try to, and this'll have to be a special Christmas."

"Yes, to celebrate some more. That'll be fine."

He seemed different tonight from Louise's first impression of him. He was smiling, and his face was full of gaiety and youth. He asked her questions about the people he didn't yet know, and about how she spent her own days. Louise told him, and invited him to ride over to Indigo. "I'm glad you've come," she said, "to be with Mr. Bijah—and us. My brother says you were a great help before and during the election."

"I wouldn't have missed it." Again, Wayne's face took on that dark intensity she had noticed the first time she had seen it. He had given the signal that summer night, calling from the trees like an owl. It had been a perfect imitation of an owl, yet Louise felt it had had something of Wayne Winsloe himself in its harshness and its violence.

At supper, Louise noticed Amanda and Alan sitting side by side. "Do you think there's something to that?" Medora whispered to Louise.

"Maybe."

Amanda's pink cheeks and smiles looked as though she felt something more than the excitement of political victory.

"It wouldn't be very suitable for a Hamilton," Medora murmured. "The Rands aren't much."

Suitable! Amanda wasn't the idealized vision Louise had once foreseen for her brother. But where was she? That beautiful and brilliant creature, walking in some landscaped Natchez garden, while from the candlelit and brocade-hung mansion music was playing. But now the gardens were weedy, and the brocades were faded, and the great heiresses, fresh from touring Europe, or reigning as belles in fashionable watering places, fluent in foreign languages and all accomplishments, didn't exist either. They were changed into worn women who were glad to take in sewing. Yet Louise knew Medora's remark would be echoed by many Natchez old ladies. How they clung to conventions and attitudes!

"The Rands have been good friends and neighbors. And Amanda is a country girl, she knows how to manage everything." Yet Louise felt a queer little pang. Amanda ruling Indigo, and herself super-fluous. Amanda easily taking over garden and chickens, and cow and calves, doing everything with skill where Louise herself had struggled painfully and at first ineptly. She could picture Amanda's stout, upright vegetables, and the constant glow of her roses.

"Alan's so intelligent. You read together and understand all sorts of things she wouldn't," Medora pointed out, still in a whisper.

Louise quenched her little feeling. If Alan could be happy! If only he could. And if ever he could feel that there was a time when he could ask a girl to marry him, it would be right now, when the fire of victory was running strong in his veins. Later, by tomorrow or next week, all his cares would be staring him in the face again. He would know he was poor and burdened and almost crippled.

"It would be a good thing if he did marry, and she's a fine girl." Louise could put out the smoulder of her jealousy by remembering how Amanda had said to Alan, "You're a hero." By saying it, she had won not only Alan's heart, but his sister's. Then and there, she had showed Louise that she knew Alan for what he was, and had understood how he must put right and honor above everything else, and was ready to sustain him in it.

Alan got up to propose a toast. "Mississippi! Our own again!" Drums thumped. There was clapping, and loud cheers, and the sound of sobbing. Louise turned a little and clinked the edge of her rough mug to the edge of Wayne Winsloe's, with a curious sense that this young boy beside her shared all the depths of her feeling, as if his emotional age was equal to her own. But tonight, you could feel joined in love and understanding with every person here. Tonight you could feel that right did win, that honor and justice could prevail. As if the old, tired, cynical world could show a new face. The fires shimmered, the sparks flew up and lost their brilliance against the dark. Beyond the warm light—red and gold—the shadows were blue—indigo blue and deep purple. There were the fields and the woods and the river. Their own fields and woods and river. Their earth under their feet. Above everything else, Louise wanted Alan to feel that tonight he owned the earth and the stars over their heads.

It was the next evening, after dark, and after supper, before Alan said, "Sister, I want to talk to you." He never called her sister unless it was a solemn occasion. The house was quiet, and Louise felt dull, but pleasantly dull and sleepy and relaxed after last night's celebration.

"I asked Amanda. Do you think I was a great fool? I mean from her point of view."

"Alan, I'm so glad." She went over to him and kissed him.

"How do you know what I asked her and what she answered?" Louise only smiled.

"Seriously, Lou, it's pretty brazen of me to ask any woman to have me. She'll be picking up a crooked stick, and an encumbered stick at that."

"There were some husky young men riding over to see Amanda. She evidently didn't care for them. Amanda's not a child any more. She's a young woman."

"That's it. She is young."

"There're not really so many years difference——"

"Not so much in years, though there are some. But I'm old. You know that."

She understood what he meant. A hiatus in spirit—that tremendous difference between the ones who had lived through the wrenching experiences of the war, and those who had been too young then to be fully aware. Part of Amanda's attraction was just that—Alan felt old and tired, strained almost beyond endurance, and his immediate contemporaries felt old and tired too. Amanda's fresh vigor had drawn him, like an invitation to renew life. But there were pitfalls to that sort of feeling. Alan had sense enough to be aware of them. There was danger of a lack of understanding, of the baffling tensions apt to grow between a complex person and a simpler one.

"I might have thought so once," Louise admitted. "That in a way you are too old. But not now. I feel she understands the essence of you, and appreciates you."

"I tried to be fair. I pointed out all my disadvantages."

"You might just as well have saved your breath. She's in love with you. Sensible girl!"

"You're blind and partial, Lou."

"She's even more so. And that's the way it should be."

"Amanda's a little nervous about the way you'll take it, Lou. I can see plain enough that Medora's prepared to be a little sniffy——"

"Poor Medora!"

"Yes, poor thing, but I suppose some other people will feel that way too. Lord! It's queer with all we've gone through, how some people cling to these tea-party notions!"

Louise laughed but she knew he was right. A great many people, in the total wreckage of the social structure, seized on bits and pieces, propped them up, and tried to take shelter in their flimsiness. "You're both lucky, Alan."

"Will you go over there and say so then? She admires you so much."

"I'll go the first thing in the morning."

They set out for the Rands the next day, and let the work go. They found Amanda busy in her garden at the side of the house. The sun shone on her, the earth she'd turned up with her little hoe was moist and rich, and the rosebushes around her were putting out strong, ruddy shoots.

Louise went up and kissed her, and Alan beamed on them both. Dr. Rand shouted to him, and they went off, leaving the two women together. At first all Amanda could say was, "Oh! Miss Lou——"

"You can't call me Miss Lou any more. It makes me feel old anyhow. Are your mother and father satisfied with all this?"

"They think Alan's handed down. And so do I."

They talked on, then Amanda said, abruptly, as if she had been nerving herself to ask, "What about his sister—his other sister—and his relatives and all—I—I'd sort of counted on you all along."

"We do get along, don't we? And Carrie and his cousins and his friends'll be glad too. We all want Alan to be happy." And if at first they might have their little hesitations, Carrie, and Mary, and Natchez people like Cousin Charlotte and Cousin Sophie, they would soon see what a good thing this marriage was. The Corwins of course would be uppity and scornful, but then Lizzie and her mother always found fault about everything and everybody. As for the men, Carrie's husband, and Mary's, they knew what a decisive part Dr. Rand had played here in the county all summer and fall, and if they came here to the wedding they would see a pretty girl who would cook them a wonderful feast.

"I want Alan to be happy. I hope I can make him happy, he's had an awful time. Of course I don't know all the things you and he know, but I'll try to learn, and read to him the things he likes."

Louise laughed. "You and he are the meekest pair of lovers! Neither you or he think you deserve the other."

Amanda laughed too. "And at Indigo, I'll try to fix things the way you like them. I hope I'm not one of those people who're persnickety about this and that!"

"You do just as you please. I have perfect confidence in your way of managing everything."

"The plain things, I can manage. But long before I knew you, and I'd hear papa talk about what a hard life Alan lived, and the first time I went in the house I saw what you'd made out of it—you turned that shack into a real home. It's downright pretty inside now."

"It'll be a much more satisfactory home for Alan when he has a wife." As for herself, she wouldn't be needed there any more.

"You know, Amanda, I came out here to help Alan. When you two are married I'll go back to Natchez."

"But we want you to stay! Alan wouldn't like it and neither would I if you ran off."

"In a way, I'll hate to leave. It's queer the way things turn out. When I first got out at Indigo Landing and watched the boat pull away, I was as limp and sad as a weeping willow."

"It must have looked awfully lonesome to you."

"I thought it was grisly! And I never expected to see a soul who interested me, and I didn't expect anything interesting to ever happen any more. And so much has happened."

"If you've learned to like it, and me, don't go."

"I have to. Tommy has to go to school. I can't teach him any more. The old house in Natchez needs seeing to—oh, all kinds of things! But we'll visit you, and Tommy'll insist on spending his summers at Indigo, and you can come in to see us. You won't have seen the last of us!"

Her thoughts were not as gay as her tone. It was true Tommy had to have an education. The Natchez house, rented to poor Miss Sims and her sister, who paid only a nominal rent, was vacant now.

Miss Ada Sims had died, and Miss Rose Sims had written to Louise, telling her she could not keep up the house alone. "What'll Tommy and I do, rattling around in it?" Its sad and oppressive atmosphere reached out to her, drawing her, and she resented it. As for money, something would have to be worked out. One thing Louise had learned, confidence in herself. Someway somehow, problems could be unraveled and in a measure, resolved.

When she discussed her plans with Alan, he was indignant at the idea of her leaving Indigo and going back to Natchez.

"I have to go," she insisted. "The house is sitting there, a white elephant."

He muttered and grumbled, then said, "Why don't you go visit our cousin Ellen in Europe? She's always wanted you to spend some time over there with her."

"No, now's not the time to go to Europe. Somehow going to Natchez and tackling the house seems to be the next task ahead. I want to see what I can make of it."

He argued, but she was obstinate. "How'll you exist in Natchez, Lou?"

"I'll take boarders. That's a very 'genteel' occupation for ladies in reduced circumstances."

"You make yourself sound like one of those decayed gentlewomen, and it's a horrible idea."

"But I am a decayed gentlewoman, after a fashion. I've planned it all out. There's Miss Rose Sims. She'd be glad to take a room if I ran the house. Boarder number one."

Alan groaned, and begged her to go to Europe. "You've longed to go to Florence. Go on, before you dodder."

"Europe's just the place to dodder. I'll go when I do, maybe. No, the time isn't now for me. Really, it isn't." She felt it strongly, that sense of how time in its passing, soft and quick, like running water, molded its almost imperceptible yet ineradicable changes in plans and hopes and interests.

Felt it again the day when some of the Natchez cousins and friends, taking advantage of a spell of good weather, drove out to spend the day at the Rands and pay their respects to the bride. Alan had written to his sister Carrie and to his cousin Mary about his marriage, and they had promised to make every effort to be at the wedding. They had both written that if Louise and Alan were satisfied with the young lady, they were prepared to love her too.

Lizzie Corwin was "snippish" and Louise was sure Mrs. Corwin said any number of disagreeable things, but then she always did. Cousin Charlotte, who had come to pay her call on Alan's bride, murmured to Louise, "You seem to like her— Of course Mrs. Rand isn't what I'd call a cultivated woman, but she seems very kindhearted."

"She has plenty of common sense too." Cousin Charlotte's husband, Cousin Louis, reacted just as Louise had expected. He said Amanda was a fine girl, and that he had the greatest respect for the doctor, and that he was glad Alan was showing so much gumption in his choice of a wife.

"That's so, Louis." Cousin Charlotte, blond, handsome, and imposing, but soft-voiced and gentle in manner, always agreed with her husband before she began to argue against what he had said. "Of course Medora Winsloe would have been a more suitable match."

"Oh, no." Louise supposed she must have looked startled. Then she remembered that Cousin Charlotte knew nothing of Medora's real history. No one could seem less like a woman with mysterious secrets than Medora, a little pale, a little pinched now, her manner all conventional propriety. Medora could hide secrets forever. Louise herself had almost come to doubt that there had ever been any.

"Do you think Jasper Winsloe will ever come back?" Cousin Charlotte asked.

"No, I've given him up. And I think they have too. I don't believe they even hear from him any more."

"Peculiar—he must be a very peculiar sort of creature." Cousin Charlotte glanced at Wayne Winsloe who was talking to Alan. "That boy—the cousin from South Carolina—they seem fond of him."

"He fits in very well."

"It's a pity," Cousin Charlotte mused, "that he isn't the age to be a suitable match for Medora. I remember you once thought it would be rather a good thing if Medora and Alan——"

"But not now." And Louise could hardly think back to her own past wishes about Medora and Alan. Yet they had been wishes, and it would have been, perhaps, the best thing for both of them. At the right moment, Medora hadn't seen it or wanted it, and events and time moved along and had implacably carried them away from each other forever.

Louise had planned to leave for Natchez the day after the wedding, set for early spring, and one day Jessie came to her, looking so solemn, Louise knew she was bursting with an idea.

"Us on the place is gettin' up a kin' of speakin' fer you, Miss Louise."

Louise was touched, and said it would be very nice, and she wouldn't ask any questions beforehand, so that everything would be a surprise. It was evidently going to be a complicated performance. Jessie was supervising the building of a wooden platform in front of the house to use as a stage. She had chosen the site with a sense of drama. In front of the house was a cleared space, then the woods began, with the thready little road leading to the gate and the main road. The stage was put up just in front of the trees, so the dark growth would make an effective backdrop, and the audience could gather on the grass. Rough benches were put there, and on a clear, mild night all the neighborhood gathered, white and colored. Lanterns lit the stage, and the performers huddled on one side of it, with Jessie pushing and prodding the children, and putting them in the right order.

In the soft glow, Louise, looking around, saw Persia, and best of all, Jimmy. Della was there too. So she had ventured to come—and in Persia's company! Jessie must have chosen a night when she knew that the Yankee himself would be away. With a kind of wonder, Louise thought how all of these colored people, knowing perfectly well how Jim and Della were forbidden to come to Indigo any more—they always knew every situation down to its finest nuances—would keep Jim and Della's presence here an absolute secret from Josh Sanders. They all knew, and he never would. Louise beckoned to Della to come and sit with her, but Della shook her head. She and Jimmy stood on the outskirts, to themselves. It made Louise sad. They belonged nowhere, those two, and Della never would belong.

Jessie, rustling with starch, came on the platform. She had a bright bandanna around her head and her earrings glittered. They were only brass rings from the old mosquito bar, but they looked as effective as real gold. Miss Louise, Jessie told her audience, had been so nice, had fixed them a Christmas tree every year, and once had even given them a whole circus, with a performing elephant. They were all sorry she was going away, and had fixed a kind of play in her honor. Louise watched Jessie with admiration, she had dignity and grace. She introduced King Cotton—Cornelius swathed in an old quilt, strewn all over with tufts of cotton. He wore a gold paper crown, and held a scepter—a stalk of cotton tipped with three fluffy bolls. Lillybelle was Queen Corn, also robed and crowned. Her scepter was a cornstalk and she wore a necklace made out of ears of corn. Her amplitude suited the role of the abundant Ceres. Children, some fearful, some brazen, spoke "pieces." These were mostly in verse, and Jessie had composed them herself. Then they sang songs. Two very small children, with shining white aprons, and shining round eyes, and stiff pigtails all over their heads, sang, "Rock, Daniel, Sheep, oh, Sheep!" And everyone joined in the chorus.

Louise found herself in tears, and could hardly rally enough to get up and make her own thanks and farewell speeches when the performance was over. But she managed to do what was expected of her, and everyone applauded. Jessie was Louise's great triumph. Jessie had justified all her hopes and teachings. And Jessie's real destiny was to teach her own people.

Afterwards, just before everyone scattered, Louise made her way to speak to Della and Jim. "I wish you weren't going away," Della said. "Now I won't see a soul."

"I'll be back from time to time. How are you getting along, Della?"

"So-so," she sighed. "I'm trying to teach Jimmy."

"Are—things—any better?" Louise glanced over in Persia's direction.

"About the same. But I reckon you were right. I tried like you said to, and I have changed myself some. I don't care as much. I wish you were staying."

Amanda was kind, but she had nothing in common with Della. What Louise had in common was the clinging, terrible memory of the dead child, and their love for the living one.

"Jimmy, I'll be coming back," Louise said to him. She wished she could take him with her, wished he were hers, but she had to leave him. Leave him, and trust him, and someday he wouldn't stand on the edge of things, but would belong, not to his father or his mother, not even to her, but to himself. She would pray for that.

The Winsloes and the Rands were staying on to supper, and Wayne came over to find Louise. They went into the house together. "I'll miss you too, Miss Louise," Wayne said. "I was just getting to know you. But I can see how your going away is going to make an awful gap around here."

"You must come into town to see me." It occurred to her all of a sudden she was going to miss Wayne's company. He was interested in everybody and everything, and noticed everything going on around him. She was glad Mr. Bijah's kindness had reached out to this young cousin of his. Wayne's presence enlivened the dullness of the Winsloe household. It was a pity Wayne wasn't Mr. Bijah's son instead of Jasper. In spite of Wayne's youth, and his superficial gaiety, Louise felt in him a secret current of will and purpose. He would never have run away.

The wedding was simple and quiet. Louise watched Amanda and Alan setting out to take the boat—Dr. Rand's present to them was a trip to New Orleans. The day before Louise was to leave Indigo, she gave Tommy his father's watch, and told him about his father. He was old enough now. He said very little, but he listened, and tied the watch in an old silk handkerchief and put it away reverently. "I'm old enough now, Mother, for you to call me Tom. Everyone called him that, and I'm named for him."

Louise said she would try to remember, and would soon learn. Yes, she thought he was old enough. Tom himself had always called her "Eez" and no one else ever had, and no one else ever would. Not in this world.

Later in the day, Tommy asked her if she would ride over the place with him. "It might be my last chance before summer."

Looking at his face, she put aside her packing and went with him. He didn't want to live in town, but he was resigned to it, and to school, and was waiting and planning for next summer.

"I don't know what I'm going to do without you," Medora had mourned to Louise. But Medora had her duty to her aunt and uncle, and must put up with her life as best she could. Alan, Amanda, Jimmy, Medora, Lillybelle, Jessie, and Wayne, the new friend, and all the others—Louise would miss all of them, and they would miss her.

Tommy's idea of riding over the place was to cover Indigo's entire boundaries, and to push on down to the river. Louise was satisfied to follow him. Let it all be stamped on her mind, the map of it, the whole of it. The way Indigo looked, and what it meant.

They skirted the familiar field, turned away from the creek, and went on into the woods. There was the place where she had stayed and meditated and had tried to draw strength to go on with her existence. She knew just where the old log had been. It had rotted away now, but there were the interlaced saplings, grown bigger. The grassy space near the big oaks, before the woods began, had no phantomlike circle of mushrooms today. They had vanished, and the scene played out with Medora had a ghostly unreality. The details were still vivid in her mind, sharp and clear—the fall of coppery light, Medora's swaying figure, the caps of the mushrooms— yet the whole of it seemed fantastic now, like something dreamt, something read, without any substance.

Further on was where the Yankee had tried to stir the hands to violence. Less than a year ago, yet it seemed far away. Tommy grinned and paused in the clearing. "It's ours now, all ours."

Louise didn't remind him that the mortgage still existed, and that any teetering chance might undermine their fragile hold on Indigo. "Your uncle might have children of his own, and they'll inherit his part of Indigo."

"I've thought of that. But that's different. That's all right. They'll be us."

Louise's love for Alan and his for her, had already made a pattern for the future—a habit of loving to be carried over to their children.

"Last summer was a fine summer, wasn't it, Mother?"

That time of anxiety and strain and danger had been for Tommy the most glowing adventure, the highest point his life had known so far. They rode on, through the deep woods, all muted grays, touched with umber. It was one of those silent, sunless winter days, but already spring was waking up. Here and there, against the faded veilings of vines and dead leaves, the redbud had begun to flower. Louise thought how apt nature was with redbud. Its dark and dusky rose was perfection against the smokiness of bare twigs and pale, moss-hung branches.

At last the woods thinned. The ground, almost imperceptibly, sloped down and down, until, riding on, they reached the river. Louise was riding Alan's horse. She got off, and Tommy tethered the mare, and his own mule, and he and his mother wandered through the cottonwoods to the edge of the river. The ground here was seamed and sandy, sparsely covered with some sort of furry, silvery grass. The trunks of the cottonwoods were pallid, but the water, without a glint, was steely dark, suggesting infinite cold, and infinite depth.

But standing here today with Tommy, watching it sweep around Indigo Bend, Louise didn't feel today that nature was cruel, charged with unending ferocity. The buds were tight and tiny, but they would grow and unfurl. Downstream there was the long curve of Indigo Bend, and upstream another bend. It looked as though the silent power of the water was hemmed in, but it had come from a long way, gathering other rivers to it, and had a long way yet to go, to meet the warm blue of the current circling the world and making the northern shores blossom.

Louise looked at Tommy's face. This unowned earth and sky and water was his home, the place of his soul, and he was feeling a simple, deep, untinged joy in being alive, and being here. A wonderful joy. If only he would never lose it!

Tommy wandered away from her, and she stood there watching him until he was out of her sight. In a little while he came running back to her. "Look what I found! It's an eagle's feather! It's

159

not a buzzard's, or an owl's, or a hawk's. It came from a real eagle!"

She took it from him to look at it. Tommy was always right in that kind of a definition. "It's wonderful! To think of him soaring right over here—where we are!"

"It's from a wing, too. I didn't see him, but he flew over——"

His eagerness and her quick response made them close—one of those times when there is an absolute sympathy and sharing. Louise knew that the place where Tommy had found the feather would have a special stamp and significance for him. Just as she would remember this moment, and the expression on his face, and the sheen of the feather in his hand. They both kept on looking up at the sky, as if the eagle's shadow, and the sweep and beat of his flight still lingered.

Chapter Eleven

[1885—] LOUISE luxuriated in the warm, sunny morning. Thinking back, she realized it was ten years since she had come from Indigo, and taken up her life in the Natchez house again. Had it been ten whole years? It was, to the very day, so this morning was a kind of milestone. It even looked just like the day when she had come in from Indigo, but her own spirit was different, and everything was different. At first it had been a monotonous and grueling existence, then rather a placid and pleasant one, with the changes hardly perceptible, yet the changes had come too.

With the topsy-turvy contrariness of human nature, she had felt as bleak on the day she had come back here from Indigo, as on the day she had first reached Indigo. How she had hated going out to the plantation to stay, and how she had hated leaving it! But she had learned something from living there. She had learned to change, and learned that her own moods changed, and she knew how to adjust, and how to enjoy.

Now, ten years after she had come back here to take charge of her old home, she could look behind her and see what she had accomplished. On the whole, she had done very well with her project of keeping boarders, surprising her friends, particularly Lizzie Corwin, and herself with her success. At first, she had felt moments of despair. She had begun modestly enough by letting Miss Rose Sims keep one of the big corner bedrooms. Miss Rose sewed for a living, ripping, altering, and sometimes making a whole new dress. By day, the bosom of her worn but starched shirtwaist was stuck with serried ranks of pins, but in the afternoons, she changed to another shirtwaist, trimmed with rows of tiny buttons and masses of crochet lace, and her thin, flat little body was rounded out by layers of flannel petticoats. When she talked, she always began with

161

a little squeal. Tommy said it made him jump, he thought one of the pins had stuck her. Fortunately, Miss Rose didn't talk much, since her conversation consisted entirely of reminiscences of past finery, and what a lovely dress so and so had worn to such and such. Her sense of time too was circumscribed by what had been in fashion. "That was the year everybody used worked undersleeves so much," and her little sighs sounded like old silk splitting when you touched it.

Natchez was full of just such semistarving gentlewomen, struggling with ill-paid work, and Louise had wondered how she was going to keep Tommy and Miss Rose and herself adequately fed, or even alive. That was when she had first moved back to Natchez, and then Cap'n Milt came and saved the day. He was a steamboat pilot who wanted a room and board when he was in Natchez, and one day he had rushed in like the river tearing through a crevasse.

He was an enormous man, both in height and bulk, and Louise had wondered how she was going to feed him, and what Metta would say. He had seemed to read her thoughts. "Of course, ma'am, I'll pay full time. And I eat hearty, so I always pay double."

Louise had murmured that it hardly seemed fair, since he wouldn't be in the house all the time.

"I said yes in a hurry," Louise had told Alan afterwards. "Particularly as he had flung himself on that little inlaid chair and I thought any minute he would literally sink through the floor."

Cap'n Milt had moved in, and had proved a great success. Louise had hired Harriet to help Metta, and Metta, always unaccountable had not balked at feeding the Cap'n, but had been pleased to fix "real vittles. Hain't been nuthin' but knickknacks in de house." When he came in, Cap'n Milt mended everything that had fallen to pieces, and told Tommy wonderful stories of river gamblers, steamboat races, floods, and explosions. He had also brought to the house as a boarder a friend of his, Cap'n Luke, a tiny, gnarled silent person, with a vociferous parrot named Lazarus. The parrot loved Tommy, tolerated Louise, but detested Louise's next-door neighbor, old Mrs. Corwin, and shrieked insults at her whenever she came to call. That delighted Tommy and Alan and the whole

162

neighborhood. Everybody wanted to hurl invectives at Mrs. Corwin, but had never dared.

When Lazarus was in residence, his cage hung in Cap'n Luke's sunniest window, and the window overlooked the front yard. If anyone came in the gate with vegetables or kindling or ice to sell, Lazarus shrieked, "Take it around to the back, take it around to the back."

After Louise had been re-established in Natchez for some months, she wrote to Alan about her salon. "It's rather a thin, wizened kind of salon. You know I follow Miss Rose's example and dress myself up in faded finery for the evening. Remember that winter before the war when we went to New Orleans and bought so much? I'm glad we did. I've been making over old silk dresses and pieces of embroidered batiste ever since. So I array myself, put on my diamond earrings and descend." Louise was nearly always at home, and had revived the ritual of afternoon tea. In summer the tea table was set on the shady end of the front gallery, behind a screen of rose and clematis vines. In winter, the silver pot steamed comfortably by the crackle of the library fire. Everybody knew her habits, and her friends began to come regularly. Old Colonel Duel and Mrs. Duel, and Lizzie Corwin from next door, appeared nearly every day, then friends from other parts of town began to come too.

One winter afternoon, when Amanda and Alan had come in from Indigo, they exclaimed at the number of horses and surreys drawn up at the door, and the noise of talk and laughter in the library.

"Why, you made such fun of your salon," Amanda had said, "I didn't think it was much! But you all have a fine time together."

"It seems like the height of polished, civilized society," Alan had smiled.

"It's livelier than it was at first." Colonel Duel was peppery, but everybody gave him the deference due a Confederate veteran. Most of the men and women gathering at Louise's tea table had either wit, or charm, or both, and all of them had the smooth manners and social graces they had been taught in their childhood. "When poor little Mr. Reese started coming I was ready to faint, he's such a bore, but he and Miss Rose whisper in a corner so it's worked out very well."

163

She could allow her thoughts to wander a little this morning, because spring house cleaning was finished, all except for the corner bookcase in the library, and Margaret Corwin had promised to come over and dust the books and rearrange them. The semiannual ordeal behind her gave Louise a comfortable feeling of having some time to herself. It was an illusion, of course, and wouldn't last long, some task was always waiting for her. It was a large house to keep, and when she had first come back to Natchez to live, Louise had missed the smallness, even the starkness, of the house at Indigo. It had never been built for luxury. Even now, when she went out there on visits and praised Amanda's housekeeping, she found herself grumbling, "A few yards of calico and a bucket or two of paint make a difference out here, and you know how the Natchez house is. Every window takes yards of stuff, and new carpets would cost a fortune. Anyhow, I think it grows galleries and steps at night while I'm asleep."

Its faded grandeur had saddened her, with its demands she could not meet, but little by little she grew reconciled to living with the things she couldn't renew, and making it as comfortable and pleasant as possible. She had learned all over again to love the house, and was really fonder of it now than when she had lived her childhood in it.

All the rooms, upstairs and down, smelled of flowers, wax, and freshly starched summer curtains. Standing in the front door, Louise could hear old Peter, the yardman, humming to himself as he chopped and weeded in his desultory fashion. He liked to stay in front, near the street, where he could hail his friends as they passed. The Cherokee rose on the trellis was in full bloom. Bees tumbled in and out of the flat white flowers, and a mockingbird was lugging twigs into the thickest part of the vine's tangle. Trees and bushes hid the street from Louise, but its familiar sounds came to her. The little Italian vegetable gardener was calling out, "sweet potate, moosta' greens," as he came around the corner. His wagon creaked, and his donkey, hardly bigger than a mouse, always had a flower tucked behind one long ear. When the weather grew hotter, the donkey would wear a straw hat. When the little gardener had ended his transactions with cooks and housewives, he wheezed down the street, lamenting, as always, "Giva me ten doll' I leava Natch'."

It was almost time for the fishman. He was large, chocolate, and cheerful. He extolled his catfish by calling, "Dey moufs is red, dey eyes as black as coals!" Louise went out on the gallery to watch for him, and saw Bella Corwin going down the path leading to the Corwin front gate. A line of shrubs separated the Corwin yard from Louise's own, and as both of the yards were large, the houses were far apart, but as the lawns sloped to the street, part of the driveway was in view. Bella, like a featherbed in motion, was languidly waving her parasol at the horsecars ambling down the street. Louise watched Bella's progress with interest, because Alan had made a bet, putting up a quarter, that Bella would never get farther than a block from her house without going back for something. The bet was to last a year, and Louise had put up her quarter in the hope that once, just once, Bella would succeed in getting off without any interruptions, halts, and returns. So far Alan had won. This time Bella was halfway to the gate when her daughter Margaret called, "Mamma, you've forgotten your purse!" and came running down the lawn with it. Bella paused. The horsecars, now at the gate, stopped. Bella examined the contents of the purse, shook her head, then drifted back to the house. The horsecars waited. At last Bella came out again and resumed her progress. This time she made the gate, and the horsecars started towards the heart of town.

The street quieted. The China tree at Louise's gate was a blur of sticky-sweet, faded lavender blossoms, fallen thick on the grass and the narrow brick sidewalk. The sunlight fell on the gallery where Louise was standing, and on the whole front of the house, showing its need of paint, but showing too its solid, yet graceful lines, and the beauty of the front door with its fanlight. It was a shabby house, but now a cheerful one. Louise's "salon" had changed these last years. The older people and Louise's own friends, still came, but Tommy now brought his own friends too. The big, high-ceilinged parlor was no longer shrouded and deserted. The pale gold brocade on the chairs had gently faded, but the big chandelier twinkled with candles at night, and the piano was always open and heaped with old music and new music. Sometimes Louise played while the young people sang or waltzed, sometimes they even made Louise herself dance around the room at least once on some very special occasion. The children were growing up.

Grown up, she admitted, watching Margaret Corwin coming through the gate in the hedge, and along the wandering stepping-stones to the gallery. Margaret had been the current Corwin baby when Louise had left for Indigo, and her howls had echoed as the hack had driven off. When Louise had come back, she had found Maggie a plain, sturdy little thing, her rights as youngest usurped by two more children born in rapid succession, but not old enough to be welcome in the elder children's games. So poor Maggie had been one of those unwanted, middle children in a tumultuous, disorderly household. Maggie had always been in trouble, and had fought for her rights with the pugnacity of a saber-toothed tiger, but Louise had soon realized what a tender heart Maggie had beneath the air of ferocity. She had rescued young birds, nursed sick dogs, and sheltered stray kittens, and had taken care of her two younger brothers. Now at sixteen, Margaret was no longer unwanted. She cajoled her disagreeable grandmother, kept a sisterly eye on the boys, took over most of the management of the house from her silly mother, and soothed her discontented Aunt Liz.

Certainly, she was no longer plain. The square-set pug-nosed child, the gangling girl had changed. She had grown tall and slim, and her tomboyish vigor had turned to grace. "The way she walks and turns her head reminds me of you, Mother," Tom said. "But then she's always imitated you. She still doesn't unfurl a fan, or drape a shawl, or settle her skirts with quite your before-the-war sway and lilt, but give her time."

Maggie was not faultlessly beautiful like Dolly Lydell, but her face had more light and life than Dolly's. Maggie had high cheekbones, her nose still turned up, and there were freckles on the bridge of it. There would be more the way the child was dangling her sunbonnet instead of wearing it. But the strong light brought out the russet gleams and gloss of her brown hair, and the warm healthy red of her mouth. Her brows and lashes were darker than her hair, darker than her clear hazel eyes, and accented her vividness. Her looks were vivid, and so was her nature. Maggie was always charged with some violent emotion, either misery, or excitement, or righteous wrath, or sheer joy.

"Are you ready for me to do the books, Aunt Lou?"

"If you have time."

"Mamma's off, and Grandmother is combed and garnished for the morning."

"How is she?"

"She says she won't trouble us much longer." Maggie's eyes gleamed. "But she ate four biscuits for breakfast." Old Mrs. Corwin always said she was dying. Someday she would, then everyone would be startled, if relieved.

Louise and Maggie went in to the library. "Here's a dust cloth."

Louise went to her desk to do her accounts, and Maggie began to take down rows of books, but soon became absorbed in reading them. Then she began to rearrange the daguerreotypes in the bookcase drawer, and Louise, instead of adding and subtracting, watched her, answered her questions and made comments herself.

Maggie was more often at the house, and more intimate with Louise than any of the group, though all the Corwin boys and girls, and lovely Dolly Lydell, eddied in and out. The young people made their own good times, but they were good times. Lately, they were beginning to flirt. They were not as sudden, or as rashly ardent as Louise's generation had been. There was not the tension and pressure of the time just before the war, and during it, to urge them on. None of them could seriously consider marriage yet, since none of them had any money. But the young bank clerk, Louis Bennet, was gazing at Margaret, and the town's beauty, Dolly Lydell, was certainly showing interest in Tom.

The center of Tom's life, the dead center of his heart was always Indigo. Because of him, and because of Alan, it was the center of Louise's life too. Amanda and Alan had no children of their own, and for a long time Amanda had mourned over it, but now she had become resigned, and gave Alan all of her devotion. Since he had no son of his own, Alan depended on Tom more and more.

There had been good years at Indigo, and bad ones. Alan, like the other planters, was always in debt to the bank for next year's crop. Theoretically, when the crop was picked and sold, he settled his debt with the bank. Sometimes he actually did, but when he had a bad year, the bank carried him on to the next year. So far, Alan had managed to pay the taxes and the interest on the mortgage. He didn't talk about the mortgage often, but they were all aware of the Yankee waiting beyond the creek, biding his time until the day the mortgage would be due.

"And what's going to happen on the day of reckoning?" Alan had asked, the last time he and Louise had discussed their burden. "I'd like to leave Indigo in the clear for Tom."

"I'd like you to be free yourself, too. Don't worry so much about Tom. Let him take care of himself. I somehow feel he can and will."

"That's what you're really afraid of, Lou. You remember that summer when Tom found out how well direct action paid off? Maybe it was a dangerous thing for a boy of his age to find out. Reserved, self-sufficient folks like Tom don't talk much, but they're mighty liable to do something."

What would Tom do if the Yankee could and did take Indigo? The people out there thought of themselves as orderly and law abiding, but they lived by a code of their own. If someone stole someone's wife or even his cow, the aggrieved party took up a shotgun. Out there, civilization fell away, in the looming woods, by the swirl of the river. Dark Indigo, deep Indigo. "I have faith in Tom," and Louise had added, "and in someone else."

"You mean Jim? What can he do? And what will he want to do? You've hardly seen him all these years. You don't know what he's become now."

She hadn't seen Jim for a long time now. During the summers, when she had gone out to visit at Indigo, he had always managed to meet her, and she had known just what was happening to him, including the brief saga of the governess the Yankee had imported to educate the child.

"For all the caterwaulin' Pa set up about my going over to see you, I reckon he misses having somebody to teach me. So he got this lady from somewheres to come down, but you know, Miss Lou, I didn't even lay eyes on her—she took one look and skedaddled like a scalt cat."

168

Alan had given Louise more details. "You're right about the Yankee having grand ideas for Jim, because he got this person from somewhere. I don't know if she belonged to the loftiest range of governesses, but I suppose she must have had some of the virtues of that genteel breed of female. She was the Yankee schoolmarm type, with hair strained back and buck teeth. The boat dumped the poor thing at Indigo Landing on a broiling hot Sunday. The Yankee'd sent a wagon to meet her, but when she reached the house Della was having a weeping fit, the Yankee was sodden drunk on the floor, and Persia was roaring drunk, whooping and brandishing various utensils, among them, I fear, a chamberpot. And Jim was nowhere in sight. The wretched woman took one look at the general Sabbath decor, and fled back to the boat. Luckily, it was still loitering at the landing. I was down there waiting for some things to be unloaded, and so I saw her, and she told me. Oh, and on the way back to the boat, she saw some hands shooting craps in that old cemetery, and another chasing his wife with an open razor. The governess scurried on the boat, and like Ichabod Crane, has been seen no more."

Then one day the following winter, Louise had opened the door and had found Jim standing there, looking thin and tired and muddy. "Why, child, what are you doing in Natchez? Come in, I'm glad to see you, but you know your father won't like your coming to my house."

"He won't know it. I've runned away." He had been carrying a little bundle of clothes and tattered books. He had walked some of the way, he had told her, and had caught a ride in a cart for most of it.

"This is your house," he had whispered, "It's big. And jest grand. Like a house in a story book!"

Louise had warmed him and fed him. He had wanted her to keep him. She'd had to plead with him to make him agree to go back home. She couldn't keep him, she had explained to him. His father would find out, and take him away. "Besides, think of your poor mother. She must be wild, not knowing where you are!"

That had moved him, and he had been willing—not willing—but had said he would go on home. Luckily, one of the hands had come in from Indigo, bringing presents from Amanda and Alan—ducks, and wild geese, and fresh eggs, and Louise had persuaded Jim to go on back with him. The Yankee had never found out, and Della had shielded Jim. It was one of those secrets Della and Louise and Persia managed to keep forever.

Louise had last seen Jim five years ago. After that, the Yankee had sent his son to stay in a small Pennsylvania town with his relatives. At first, Jim had been miserable there, and had poured out his heart to Louise in long letters. "I'm out of whack up here. I just don't talk or act like these folks, and I don't like the sound of their voices. They look at me like I was some wile animul outta the woods, and I think they are just lumps. They eat all the time, then talk about what they are gonna eat. The eats are fine, but that's all that is. But it's a good schoole where I go, and I like one teacher I got. I am tryin to learn like what you always tole me too."

He had changed since that letter, and she knew she must expect more changes in him than his letters were revealing. Their last meeting had been brief, just a glimpse, five years ago this spring, at Mr. Bijah's funeral.

Louise had been the first to notice how Mr. Bijah's health had begun to fail, and had pointed it out to Alan.

"I'm afraid you're right," Alan had admitted. "I see him more than you do, so it hadn't struck me. Or maybe I was just trying to fool myself."

There had been no drastic illness, only a gradual weakening and fading. Little by little, Mr. Bijah had retreated from the fields he loved to the shady corner of the gallery. He had died quite peacefully in his sleep, and had been buried on a windless spring day, with a fine, silvery rain falling. Everyone had gathered at his funeral, all the relatives and friends, throngs of people from Natchez, all the hands, fishermen, and the hunters and trappers from the hidden world of the swamps. Even Jim had come, not to the house, but to the cemetery.

Louise had looked across at Jim. He had stood apart from the others. They were all joined in their grief, but he had been alone. He must have made a great effort to have come. He had put on his best clothes, a good suit, but getting too short in the sleeves, as he was growing fast. Tall and thin, too, with not much of a child's face any more. Only the expression of his eyes had been the same.

Afterwards, when the group had been dispersing, he had come over to speak to Louise. No one else had paid him any attention. Alan would have noticed him, but Alan hadn't really seen anyone or anything on the day they had buried Mr. Bijah.

"I'm going away," Jim had said in a breathless whisper, "but not 'cause I want to. Pa's sending me up North to his kinfolks, so I can go to school up there."

"For long?"

"Sounds turrible long. Years, I reckon. You'll write to me, won't you, Miss Lou? 'Til I can get back home?"

She had promised and had taken his hand. He might have been embarrassed if she had kissed him, because Tom and Margaret Corwin had been standing near her. "It'll seem long to me, Jim. I'm glad you came today."

He had turned back to look at the fresh grave. Mr. Bijah had been buried in his worn uniform, with the Confederate flag on his coffin. Now the earth covered it all, and there was a mound of flowers. Louise had murmured to Mrs. Winsloe, who had walked past her, "He loved our Cause," and Maggie Corwin had begun to cry, and Jim, listening and watching, had said. "Folks sure came today. If I died, I'd like that—for folks to turn out." Then Jim had murmured good-by, and had disappeared into the sheen of the rain-wet trees.

Tom had said, "I don't care if anybody comes to my funeral or not. Just bury me deep in Indigo's mud. That's where my bones belong."

And Louise had thought how little it would matter to her who came to her funeral or where they buried her. She and Tom, dead so long ago, wouldn't find each other on this earth or in it, but somewhere else. What she wanted when her time came to die was to hear her child's voice, and see his face.

At Mr. Bijah's funeral, no one had been missing except the one he must have loved best of all. Nobody knew where Jasper was, no one had heard from him or of him in years, no one had mentioned his name, yet Louise had known that most of the older people gathered at the house and at the cemetery must have thought of him. Mr. Bijah had rounded out a long and useful life. They could all believe his soul had found heaven, and his body had found rest in the earth dear and familiar to him, but Jasper's uneasy ghost had wandered in their midst.

There had been only one reference to him, when Louise had been walking back to the house with Wayne Winsloe.

"I remember when we first came out to Indigo," Louise had said to him. "I don't think we could have existed without Mr. Bijah."

"And think how good he was to me."

"But you repaid him, Wayne. He loved you, and he leaned on you. He told me so himself."

"I'm glad of that. But he had to make do with me. I wasn't the one he really wanted to come and help him. How could I have been? He shouldn't have had to make do. He shouldn't have!"

"Maybe he didn't have to, because in that last long talk I had with him——"

That had been the Christmas before Mr. Bijah died. Louise had gone over to Avondale to see Mr. Bijah, and had found him in front of the fire. "I'm tough as an ole cypress knee in the swamp," he had chuckled, "but you all treat me like one of them fine China gimcracks. Wayne manages everything for me so the ole man can take it easy. He and Alan know how everything's fixed up. They'll 'tend to everything. I don't have to worry no more'n a mosquito. But you kind of keep an eye on Medora, Lou."

"I will, Mr. Bijah," she had promised.

He had fallen into a doze and she had kept quiet, her hand over his. He had opened his eyes. "I guess you met my boy by the gate. He's here for good now. There he is——" Wayne had ridden past the window, and Mr. Bijah had thumped on the glass with his cane. "Lou's come to see us, get on in here, Jasper!"

So, as they had walked back to the house, Louise had told Wayne about that time. "You see how well you filled the empty place." Towards the last, Wayne's presence, and his affection, had mingled with the old man's dream of his son's homecoming.

Medora and Wayne had devoted themselves to Mrs. Winsloe but

she had always been a shadow and an echo of Mr. Bijah, and after he was gone, the shadow had no one to follow. She had slipped easily into death, and two years ago she had been buried beside her husband.

Medora, in tears, had clung to Louise. "Now I'm no use to anybody any more!"

"You are to me," Louise had answered her steadily. "Come to Natchez and live with me and help me."

So it had happened, and now while she was thinking of how it had happened, Medora called down from upstairs. "I think I hear the postman. Will you go, or shall I?"

Louise stirred from her half dream, and came back into the present.

"I'll go," Maggie offered. "Keep on with your sums."

"I haven't even begun."

"You must have been thinking."

"Not thinking, just remembering."

Memory was like the daguerreotypes Margaret was sorting, sometimes flashing into startling clarity, complete with every detail, then fading out of consciousness for a while, until you held the past up to the light of recollection again. As caught and fixed too, as the pose in a picture. You couldn't go back and rearrange. The unhappiness and the joy, the faults and failings and regrets were all changeless.

Margaret came running back, and put a thick letter in Louise's hand. "Good! It's from Jim."

Maggie went back to her work, and Louise read the closely written pages. Jim had never liked his Northern relatives, or the way they lived, or the dull, thrifty town, or the flat farmlands around it. "Stodgy sort of country," he had described it. "Flat and humdrum. Louisiana's flat as a battycake, but it's wild and queer. It has lots of secrets, and this has none."

In her own letters to him, Louise had advised him to adjust himself as well as he could, and to get the most he could out of a different experience. He had followed her advice, and made friends with his younger cousins, and with some of the boys and girls he had met at school. He had worked on farms during the summer and had gone on camping trips. He had learned. His letters had become stiff with acquired knowledge of spelling, grammar, and punctuation. Sometimes Louise wondered if Jim might not decide to go to work up North, and not come back at all. The letter she held reassured her. "I finish with this school in June, and I have made up my mind to come on back home. My father wants me to come back. He could not make me come. My mother wants me to be back with her. So it will not be such a long time now before I will be across the creek from Indigo again. I will tell you about the books I have read when I see you again. It makes me feel better to think I will soon be seeing my mother and you, Miss Lou, and Persia——"

Louise folded the letter and looked up. "Maggie, there's something I want you to do for me. You've heard me talk about Jim Sanders."

"Some. Not much."

"He's coming back here."

"Why does he want to? Wouldn't he like it better up North?"

"He doesn't, evidently. He was born here. He seems to want to belong here. That's what I want you to do for me. Make him feel that he does."

"You mean to try to get our crowd to let him be with us some?"

"That would help. Tom likes him, and you and Tom can influence the others."

"I'll try, Aunt Lou. It's queer."

"What is?"

"For you to like him, when——"

"When he's the Yankee's son?"

Maggie nodded. "I always wondered why."

Louise told her how it had all begun, and Maggie, sitting on the floor, her hazel eyes bright, listened with rapt attention. It was easy to talk to Maggie. In some ways, she was older than her age, and she had so much warmth and quick responsiveness. "You make me see how it all was," she said, "I never knew before how you went and nursed those children."

"It was a bad time. I don't like to think about it." Poor little Francy, it was a long time since Louise had thought of her.

"I guess you had to go, Aunt Lou. I guess I would have felt that way too."

"Jim was such a little thing. And an appealing little thing. He seemed to need coddling."

"He was lucky you had some feelings left over from what you gave Tom." She sighed a little. "I was lucky too, you had some to spare for me."

Louise knew Maggie was thinking of her own family, and she understood how someone with Maggie's lavish emotions had suffered in that arid atmosphere. "I think I care about Jim, and you, partly because of the way I feel about Tom. When Jim had yellow fever, one thing that made me go there was imagining it might have been my own child, needing help."

"Some people would have gone for duty. And when Jim was well, it would have all stopped. You went on."

"Caring? Once I started to, I kept on caring."

"Lots of people have just a little smidgin of love, and it doesn't go around very far."

"Oh, if Jim hadn't been what he is, I would have stopped." And Tom had always been independent. As Lillybelle said, "He ack so mannish." Early, Tom had found a world of his own and a life of his own at Indigo. It was just as well. He wouldn't have an easy time, and Louise was glad he was self-reliant. Tom felt things deeply, but he didn't seem to need to express his feelings often, or to have other people express theirs.

Maggie said, "Tell me more about Jim."

Louise described the Yankee, and Persia, and Della, and the kind of life they lived.

"Ugh!" Maggie shuddered. "Poor boy." She meditated, then said, "And the grisly way they live isn't because they're dirt poor."

"They really have a great deal more money than the rest of us."

"You know how it is at home. Grandma and Aunt Liz are always moping because we haven't any——"

The Corwins did make lack of money an excuse for everything they did or didn't do.

"They make me boil!" Maggie said. "But look at you—you

haven't any either, but this house is fine, and you make wonderful times for us over here."

"Stop boiling, Maggie. Your grandmother's too old to change. Take her lightly."

"I will. I feel for Jim, though. I was a miserable sort of brat too. Until you came back here."

"Well, your poor mother——"

"Oh, I don't mind. Not now, I'm grown up." Once when Maggie had run over in a rage against her mother, Louise had told her that her mother had no time, and Maggie had answered, "But you always have, Aunt Lou." Bella Corwin had spoiled and scolded her boys, but had utterly neglected her daughters. Three of them were married and out of her way, and now she found Maggie useful. But both Louise and Maggie knew that it had been Louise who had wiped Maggie's nose and mended her apron and her dolls, and had read to her and listened to her, and convinced her that she wasn't hopelessly bad or ugly. Above all, that she was not completely unwanted.

"What'll happen? When Jim comes?"

"I don't know. It worries me. That's why I want your help."

"You've made me want to," Maggie said. "It won't be too easy. Stuffing him down Dolly's throat. Or Milly's. But Dolly'll do anything Tom wants——"

"Will she?"

"Oh, Aunt Lou! You must have noticed!" Louise had, but she didn't admit it now.

"Milly'll follow the herd. She's a sheep."

"What about Wayne?" Louise asked.

"He isn't around us much. I don't know. You'll have to manage him, Aunt Lou."

Wayne had an easy-going manner and high spirits, but Louise remembered the day she had first seen him, down by the creek bank. She didn't think Wayne would find it easy to forgive Jim for being who he was. She had recognized a quality in him she knew well. Wayne was implacable.

Maggie got up from the floor. "We've talked so much I've only dusted one shelf, and now I've got to go see to dinner."

"It doesn't matter, do them another time."

"I think I'll like Jim. I liked his looks."

"When did you ever see him?"

"He came up to speak to you at Mr. Bijah's funeral."

"Oh, yes."

"I liked his eyes. And he's fond of you."

"I don't know that I've been good for him, in the long run. I loathe his father."

"Well, we all do." Maggie took hatred for Yankees in general and that one in particular as a matter of course.

"I've tried to strike at the Yankee through Jim. That makes me less than perfect."

Maggie didn't like her idols to be less than perfect, and her eyes turned gray with her clouding thoughts. "But you really do like Jim though?"

"Oh, I don't pretend about that."

"Then that makes everything all right."

Did it? Louise wondered. She had meddled as much as she could, and for reasons of her own, and stirred up the ready discontent in Jim. But where was her blame? Since Jim was the kind of person he was, he would dislike his father in any case. Did she want Jim to admire the creature, or be like him? Jim would have to feel strongly, and be strong to move, break out, get away, and find his real place. If he resigned himself to being a lump, a brute, a clod it would be such a waste. He wouldn't, but he would come back to a difficult situation.

Maggie heard the clock strike, and rushed off, forgetting her sunbonnet. Louise watched her running through the sun and shadow.

Chapter Twelve

THAT afternoon, evening, Louise called it, since it was after tea time, when she was sitting on the front gallery, she saw Wayne Winsloe turn in the gate and come walking up the lawn. Her callers had just left, and Medora and Miss Rose had gone in the house. Louise went to the steps to meet Wayne, and told him she was glad to see him. "Where is your horse? You couldn't have walked in from Avondale."

Wayne had been living on at Avondale, running the plantation. Since Mrs. Winsloe's death, Medora had been with Louise, and Wayne was in the country alone.

"I came in style—in the buggy," he said, "but I lent it to Hank Corwin, so he could go calling."

"Then you'll spend the night. It's much too late to start back." She stopped his protests about giving her trouble. "The spare room's ready, and I haven't seen you in quite a while."

"I know, I want to talk to you too, and see Cousin Medora. Did I barge in on the tag end of a party? I saw a lady-loaded surrey ambling out of the gate."

"Just some cousins. Come and have tea. It's still hot."

"This looks nice." He took the chair she offered him.

The lawn was in shadow, but the tree tops still gleamed, and moved a little in a south breeze. There was a chorus of birds, and a spatter of sunlight glinted on the silver teapot and the bowl of red and pink roses. The cloth on the table was darned in places, but Medora had darned it and her work was so fine it hardly marred the texture of the material.

Wayne admired Louise's dress. "It's very becoming."

"I always thought it was pretty stuff, and Miss Rose refurbished it." The fine lace at the neckline, and the velvety rose Louise had tucked in her breastpin made it rather festive. Louise herself looked younger than she had ten years ago, less thin and worn. The coils of her brown hair were thick and shining, her skin, if it lacked brilliant color, was clear and smooth, and her eyes were full of warmth and brilliance. As a child and as a girl, Louise had been drilled in the art of holding herself well—she claimed she had walked miles with books balanced on her head—and the art of managing her hoops. She had learned how to come into a room, and how to leave it, how to dance, and how to be still. She could wear an old dress with an air of elegance, and if it was not in the latest fashion, give it a style of her own. If she had no actual beauty, except her eyes, she had all those subtle accessories to beauty that can add up to an effect of it. There was grace in the way her head was set on her shoulders, in the way she walked, or folded a shawl around her. Her voice was pleasant to listen to, and her smile had a particular charm.

She poured Wayne's tea, and put in just the amount of sugar and cream she knew he liked.

"Good tea." He looked out over the grass, where the shadows were growing longer, and seemed in no hurry to say anything. He did his work well, and was always busy, but he had an air of leisure, and an enjoyment of leisure. It made him a comfortable companion. Louise had sometimes walked over the fields with him, and had noticed how quickly he covered the ground, yet watching him, he never seemed to be moving fast. Somehow he gave the impression of not talking much, perhaps because his voice was low and quiet, yet when she reviewed in her mind any conversation she had had with him, she realized he must have said a good deal. One reason she liked his company was his ability to savor, as she did, a moment of golden idleness.

He reached for another cookie. "You know you have a knack of making a creature feel coddled and pampered and flattered. Yet I can't remember you actually saying anything flattering to anybody."

"I'm much more likely to growl at them than cajole them. But I like to pamper all of you. Amanda's taken over spoiling Alan——"

Wayne laughed. "She sure does."

"Well, all of you need a little. And I worry about you, Wayne, all by yourself. The way Alan was when he first went to Indigo."

"He wasn't very strong, physically, for one thing. And I am. Then I haven't had to put up with such a grueling situation. The Yankee won't get his clutches on Avondale. Or on Indigo either, when the chips are down!"

Louise wished she could feel sure of it, but she didn't want to think about the Yankee now. "I can't think about Indigo in the evening. If I do, I can't sleep all night."

"Then don't let's. As for my being lonely, it doesn't seem as isolated out there as when you all first went to Indigo."

"It doesn't, does it? The weather's as bad, the distances are the same, but the atmosphere isn't as tense as when the carpetbaggers had everything in their grip. Then too, there seem to be more people, or else what people there are manages to see each other more."

"Remember that summer when we fought the carpetbaggers? I'm glad I was in on some of it."

"You were in on most of it."

"We all drew together then, and we've kept together ever since. You know how it was, men you didn't realize existed popped out of the Homochitto swamp, and wandering fishermen from some God-forsaken sand bar or bunch of willows gathered with us to help run 'em off. I got to know all those folks. Now I go down in the swamp to hunt with them, or just swap yarns, and they drop in to see me from time to time."

"They're very good company too. Do you ever see Old Davis? He's my favorite. He's so dire. He always predicts we're going to have a 'turrble' high water, and then we do."

"He prowls up and down the river, you know, but when he's anchored off Indigo Bend in that boat of his he always sends me word."

"Amanda seems to inaugurate a good many fish fries and barbecues," Louise said.

"She told me you were the one who started things going in the neighborhood when you went out to Indigo, and now she tries to keep up what you began. So we have you to thank, Miss Lou, for what we have in rural amusements."

Wayne's suit was worn shabby and it was dusty from the long ride, and he lived buried in the country, yet no one could seem less rural. On the contrary he had a gloss of worldliness, Louise couldn't decide how to define it, unless it came, partly, from his ease of manner. He could and did hobnob with tramps, trappers and fishermen, and he could talk weather, woods, dogs, pigs, cotton crops, and politics. The hands were fond of him, and Wayne sometimes went to the little Negro church, not only for funerals and baptizings and weddings, part of the duty of every planter, but went on other occasions too, to hear the singing. He had even composed a hymn himself, and they sang it often. But Wayne enjoyed the company of women too, and noticed their clothes, and like Alan, relished the tidbits of news from Natchez. Sometimes Louise didn't see Wayne for two or three months, but he always remembered what she had told him the last time they had met, and wanted her to continue some unfinished episode. "Has your Cousin Charlotte started organizing that play she wanted to put on?" Or he wanted to know more about what progress Miss Cora Fane was making in her pursuit of the young minister. They liked Browning, and enjoyed the novels of William Dean Howells.

Wayne and Louise discussed the faults and merits of the latest books. They had both read the books and the articles they argued over, but neither of them had seen any plays or heard any music for years. That didn't stop them. They admired or tore to shreds actors and actresses and musicians as if they went regularly to concerts and opening nights.

"You'd think you both practically lived in an opera box," Tom said, "and you've never heard a note that Melba ever warbled!"

"There was an article about her trills in the last Harper," Louise would rebuke him. "Wayne and I can imagine perfectly well how she sounds."

Wayne didn't have a subtle face. His eyes and hair were almost black, and his skin, naturally dark, was burned darker still by sun and weather. He had Jasper's long, graceful eyebrows, but not Jasper's eyes. Jasper's had been dreamy, rather narrow, and Wayne's blazed with life, and Wayne didn't have Jasper's finely cut features either. Wayne's face, particularly the upper part of it was broad, his nose was short and blunt, and his mouth full. Louise supposed you could call Wayne's face "frank and open." There seemed to be nothing secretive about him, nothing hidden, though sometimes there was a startling intensity in his expression. But under his gaiety and good humor, Louise guessed he had a complicated nature. She might not have guessed if she had not caught glimpses of it that first summer he had come. She felt he only seemed easy to know, and that he was more likely than most people to let his feelings drive him.

"I want to talk over something with you," Wayne was saying, "This is a pretty little teacup, I like the gold lining."

"I like this set too. Medora always washes it herself." Medora was particularly good at little delicate tasks, like fine darning and washing the best china, just the sort of thing to arouse Louise to a violent exasperation and impatience.

"When I come to Natchez I'm always startled."

"Why, Wayne?"

"Because houses like this are still standing in it and around it." Wayne's own house had been in Sherman's path.

"It's like a kind of miracle."

"They're rather shabby shells of houses now. And that's rather sad too. Though I'm glad they are left standing."

"It's a lot better than having them wiped out of existence, even if they are shabby. I don't believe houses like this will ever be built anywhere any more. Not ever."

"Someday, Wayne, we'll pick ourselves up, and prosper."

"I'm sure we will. I believe in the South. But of course it'll be different from the way it was."

"Very different."

"Beauty is a queer sort of thing," he meditated. "It has a tendency to run away."

"It certainly has." A face changing, growing older, or lost forever; not to see or be seen, hear or be heard, not to speak to or be answered, ever any more. "But it reasserts itself."

"Yet not in the same form. Lose, destroy one form of it, in a house, or a picture, you don't get just that same thing back again."

"Like time. You get other times, but not this one, not this minute."

"You know how to get the good out of now. I've watched you

182

and tried to do it too. I believe most people are really afraid of every day."

"I've learned to be grateful for a little monotony. But I think you're right, Wayne. All of us have been storm-tossed, and we've formed a habit of looking far back, before the storm, or else almost regret the storm itself, horrible as it was. Some people find drabness harder to endure."

"I guess we miss the excitement. Or why do Tom and I talk so much about that summer when we banded against the carpet-baggers? I guess I'm one of the kind that's afraid of everydayness too."

"Don't say that! I used to tell Alan, Jasper was afraid of everyday-ness!"

"I reckon he was, when you boil it down. Though I've always thought he must have been crazy. Be—have been—we don't even know if he exists or not! Which brings me to my object. I came to talk to you about Cousin Bijah's will."

"What about it? And don't you want Medora to come down and hear?"

"Later. Now, if you don't mind, I'd rather talk it over with you. You see, not knowing if Jasper's alive or not, complicates every-thing——"

Jasper, whatever had happened to him, whatever his real motives, had certainly tangled other people's lives.

Wayne frowned. "I feel I can't speak my mind about Jasper in front of Cousin Medora. In fact I never mention him to her at all."

"I'm glad you don't. But how did you know not to?"

"It was the silence eddying around the subject of Jasper, I guess. When too little is said, you wonder. Wasn't there a romance?"

None of the younger ones, not even Tom, had guessed Medora had loved Jasper, or anyone. They saw her as she appeared to them, gentle, with little finicky ways. "It was very unhappy for her. He kept going, and coming back, and she thought everything would be all right. Then he left that last time——" Louise lowered her voice, and she shivered a little, recalling that time. "And as far as we know, that's the end of him."

"I wish I could plop a nice, plump tombstone on top of him."

"Wayne—you shock me."

"I do, though. He's left a lot of complications in his wake. A solid tombstone, with the certainty he was under it—every time I see Jasper's name written I have an irresistible yearning to shoot him." Wayne was not joking, he meant it.

Louise knew how Mr. Bijah's will read, because Alan and Wayne had been named executors, and they had discussed it with her. Half of everything went to Medora outright, the other half was left to Jasper, and Alan, Wayne, and Medora were guardians of Jasper's interest.

"You know how it goes," Wayne said, "And you know Cousin Medora wants to sell Avondale. And can, without Jasper's consent. There's a clause in the will covering that. Of course, if she sells, she'll put half the money in Jasper's name."

Ever since Mrs. Winsloe's death, Medora had been obsessed with the idea of selling Avondale, but no one wanted to buy it, except the Yankee. He hadn't dared make his offers openly, but he had made them through other people, but Alan and Wayne had traced them back to him, and they agreed with Medora—selling to the Yankee was impossible.

"What I want to talk to you about is that there's another offer for the place. Not the Yankee this time. Ben Rand."

"Ben—that would be wonderful!" The Rands had very little acreage, and Ben, like Tom, had always wanted to plant cotton, and had a particular affection for Avondale. Neither Medora, or Mr. Bijah, if he could know, would object to Ben. Dr. Rand's oldest son would be a suitable owner for Avondale.

"But what about you, Wayne?" Louise asked. "Medora wouldn't want you to have to leave Avondale. Neither would Ben."

"Don't worry about me. You know Cousin Bijah had some investments. Alan and I talked everything over with the bank, and we decided to let them alone. They aren't worth much now, but some-day they might be. But to get back to the place——" He explained how Ben, with his father's help, intended to finance it. "Of course the doctor is really buying it for him. I don't know if it's wise to sink your all in a cotton plantation, but Ben's a good farmer, and if they want to——"

"Medora would want it, I know. But what will you do, Wayne? Stay on and help Ben?" Louise knew Mr. Bijah had left Wayne some money, but Wayne had used it all on necessary improvements for the plantation.

"Oh, no, I won't stay."

"Do you intend to go home?" The idea of Wayne's going back to Carolina frightened her. She realized she would miss him.

"Not that. My parents have the other children. And I have to stand on my own feet. The truth is, I don't want to stay on at Avondale. I could, but I don't want to. I don't like land. I don't like planting cotton. I never did."

"Why, Wayne! You mean all this time you've wanted to get away?"

"Not exactly that. I had a good reason for being there. Now, if Ben buys it, I'm free."

"And you want to be free?"

"Yes."

"You didn't give us any inkling."

"I didn't want any of you to guess. After all, Cousin Bijah gave me a home, gave me everything. I saw he needed me. What could I do but stay, and make the best of it? And afterwards, Medora's needed me there. She couldn't run the place."

"I never dreamed you didn't like being there," Louise murmured.

"I didn't hate it. But it wouldn't have been my choice. And you would have done just as I did, Louise——"

She noticed he called her Louise, instead of Miss Louise as he usually did.

"You did the same thing," he said. "You made the best of living at Indigo."

"But I grew to love it. And you told me once you loved cotton."

"I do. It fascinates me. But not the dreary round of putting the seed in the earth and coaxing the cotton out of the ground. After somebody else grows it, I want to gamble with it."

"Gamble——"

"On the market. Shares, futures." He smiled at her. "I've studied a lot about it. Didn't you ever hear the Winsloes were gamblers?"

She thought even Medora had been. "One dead and gone Winsloe is supposed to have gambled away two fortunes, and won a third. But it's a dangerous vice."

"I know. I have the instinct. It's in my bones. Down in the marrow of my bones. But I intend to harness it. After all, playing the market's no worse than planting. What's a worse gamble than that?"

"Nothing. But I'm still dumbfounded at what you've told me about yourself. You were fifteen when you came, weren't you? And all this time——"

"The time's gone pretty fast."

"And you never told a soul what you really wanted. Not even me." Louise wondered why she had said that. Why should he have told her? Instead of Alan or Tom? Yet she felt she would have been the one.

"I didn't want any of you to think I wasn't satisfied when all of you had been so good to me. Cousin Bijah had enough to put up with, his own son had gone. Besides, I got a lot out of it, living there. But if I can settle things the way Cousin Medora wants, I'll be free. Twenty-five and free! That's not so bad." He looked at her.

"You must have had a hard time between fifteen and twenty-five."

"Yes. With the war, and after."

"You never say much about it."

"Everybody around me had their own troubles."

"I remember the war. I don't talk about it much. I can't. It's like a scar that makes you wince when you touch it. The ones who re-member belong in one generation, and the ones who don't—who were too young to remember—are different."

"They hear about it, and feel about it, but it isn't the same." She wished they, the younger ones, could be entirely free of it, but they wouldn't be. "Wayne, have you made any definite plans?"

"Mr. Clements'll take me in his office. I'll live in Natchez. Could you—would you take me in? Or do you have room? Metta told me you'd squoze lots of folks in."

"They aren't 'squozed.' There's plenty of room. We rattle. You can have the spare room."

Tom came in while they were talking, and listened without saying much. Then Louise called Medora, and they all sat on the gallery in the dusk, discussing every detail connected with selling Avondale.

"I'm glad Ben wants it. Uncle Bijah was fond of him."

Medora had hardly changed in ten years. She was still slim and delicately pretty. Mr. Bijah's death, then Mrs. Winsloe's, seemed to have been the last major alterations in the course of her existence. Now she seemed to have taken herself out of any struggle and had become an onlooker. She hardly seemed to want any life of her own, and she preferred to let other people manage everything for her.

"The Rands are getting up in the world, aren't they? Amanda married to Alan, and now Ben will own Avondale!" There was no resentment in her tone, only a vague sadness, as if she contemplated the closing in of her own obscurity.

After supper, Wayne walked down the street to see Mr. Clements, and Medora went upstairs. Louise said to Tom, "Did you ever know Wayne wanted to come to town instead of living at Avondale?"

"It surprised me. I wonder how he's managed so well with the place if his heart wasn't in it. Except I guess his heart was in doing the best he could for Mr. Bijah, and Cousin Medora. Mother, if he's coming here to stay, could you make out without me if I went out to Indigo for good?"

"You've wanted to go for a long time, haven't you?"

"Not really, because I wouldn't have felt right about leaving you here to manage everything by yourself. But with Wayne in the house, you'll have somebody to turn to, and I'll feel better satisfied."

"I'll miss you. But your uncle needs you." Alan had been rheumatic during the winter and early spring.

"And I guess I need Indigo."

Louise looked at Tom, sitting there with the light from the library table shining on him. He had pale tan hair, and a darker tan skin, and his eyes were darker yet. Maggie said Tom drifted in and out like a curl of smoke. "He's here, and when you look up, he's dissolved and disappeared." Perhaps there was something of the same elusive quality in his nature.

"It worries me, Tom, for you to set your heart on anything as precarious as Indigo. But I know if you give your heart to anything, or anybody, you are in danger."

"I don't mind risks. If the game's worth the candle, and Indigo is, to me."

So far, the peak of Tom's life had been the summer when he had grown up, grown away from her, and found himself. What she feared for Tom, and for Jim and Maggie and Wayne, was a dwindling of experience, until their maturer years would find them poor and timid and tired, instead of bringing them the richness of life their hope and their capacities promised. It could happen, and often did happen. It would be particularly easy for it to happen to them. They could excuse themselves for their failures by saying they had inherited ruin. They could blame their mistakes on conditions not of their making. They were young, and the glitter and freshness they saw was not in the weary old world, but in their eyes. Youth itself is a kind of talent. The ardor of their courage would have to last. If it did, it could carry them, not without danger, not without unhappiness, but it could take them into a fulfillment of themselves, and make them the people they were intended to be.

In hoping for them, loving them, and watching them, Louise realized something had happened to her. She had not thought of it before, but she knew it now, this minute, sitting here with the lamp's globe a round gold disc, and outside a thin moon glittering through the trees, and the perfume of locusts in flower, and honeysuckle drifting in the window. She no longer lived in the past, and not altogether in the present. She was looking at the future. It called her, and she was going towards it.

Chapter Thirteen

IN JUNE, Louise went out to Indigo for a few days visit. Since Tom was living there, she was drawn to the plantation more than ever. Tom met her at the boat, and drove her back to the house. The woods had a soft brilliance, and the fields an early summer richness. In a week or so, all the leaves would darken, the glare would swim in waves to the horizon, and the earth would bake hard under the relentless sun.

Tom talked more than usual, pointing out the repairs he had made to certain cabins and fences, and admitted the weather had been good and that the crop was coming along.

"By the way, mother, Jessie's come on back. She looks like a scarecrow."

"No wonder, with the life that man led her."

Jessie had married one of the hands on Avondale, and Lillybelle had been right when she'd said Jessie's husband was the laziest man ever born. It was ironic that Jessie, quicker and brighter than the rest of her family, and ambitious too, would make such a choice. Louise and Tom and Amanda and Alan had given her a fine wedding, but had attended it with forebodings, soon justified. Then a month ago, Jessie's husband had drawn a knife on another man, during a dice game, and the man had shot him dead.

"Of course she's much better off without him," Tom said. "He was always in some kind of fracas. Now she'll be able to settle down."

"I'll go see her right off, poor thing. I brought her a dress. Is that biggish cabin by the creek still vacant?"

"Yes, because you can't get any of the hands to live in it. They say it has 'hants.'"

"If we fixed it up for a little schoolhouse, Jessie might teach the children, hers and the others on the place, when they weren't busy in the fields. It's a waste for her to work in the fields."

"Yet, it is," Tom agreed. "Why not talk to her. I think she'd like it. I remember when you used to go to that cabin to change your clothes when you were nursing Jim through the yellow fever."

"Have you seen Jim yet?"

"I saw him the other day, when I was fishing at the mouth of the creek."

"Has he changed much?"

"Well, he's grown up. But not really changed. He asked all about you. I told him you were coming, and he told me he'd ride over late today. After the first strangeness wore off, we took up where we'd left off."

"Did you like him still?"

"Yes, I did. I had to adjust myself to his being a grown man. I'd always felt so much older. I told him to come on over."

"I'm glad you did. I want to see him."

Amanda and Alan were waiting for Louise on the gallery. Alan looked better than he had during the winter, and Amanda, though she was rather too plump these days, still had her fresh color and bright eyes. The house needed paint as much as ever, but Tom had widened the gallery, and the rose Louise had planted had grown and climbed and was blooming now.

Amanda led Louise to her old room to wash her face and comb her hair, and stayed talking.

"Alan says his rheumatism's much better," Louise said.

"Having Tom here helps him. Tom takes so much off of his shoulders. You were good, Lou, to let him come out here to live."

"It's where he wants to be, you know."

"All the same, you could have said you needed him, and made a fuss."

"What's the use of keeping him that way?"

"Not a bit of use, but I bet I would have grumbled more than you did. How's Wayne getting on?"

"He seems glad he came to town."

"Wayne's good company."

"Very." Louise was standing in front of the wavering mirror, recoiling her hair.

"I like the way you do your hair. You're looking so well, Lou, and so young and pretty."

"Am I?" Louise laughed. "I'm glad to have you say so, this mirror is always so discouraging."

"Isn't it awful?" They went out on the gallery together, and Louise went off to Lillybelle's cabin to talk to Jessie, who was living there now with her three children. Lillybelle's enormous brood had grown up and scattered to cabins of their own. Link had married, but he was as devoted to Tom as ever, and now that Cornelius was getting old, Link was taking his place.

Jessie's husband had spent every penny gambling, and Jessie and her children had come back home in rags. Louise comforted and consoled, and gave the children stick candy and unrolled the black dress for Jessie, who had longed for something suitable to wear for mourning. The dress, and Louise's suggestion about starting a school, made Jessie much more cheerful.

"Set out to Chuch in de good dress Miss Lou brung you," Lillybelle counseled, "an' hole yo' haid high. Folks respecs' a well-actin' widder 'oman."

Her call of condolence over, Louise went back on the gallery, and settled down to talk. Tom was mending a chair, and Amanda was sewing. Alan and Louise enjoyed their idleness.

"I knew that man was no good," Alan said, as they discussed the misdeeds of Jessie's late husband. "Yet when he talked to me, he beguiled me. As a rule, worthy souls don't have such thick molasses manners, whereas beguilement is a rascal's stock in trade."

"The Yankee isn't at all molasses dripping," Amanda said.

"He isn't born lazy. If you have an absolute, rooted aversion to any form of work, you try to learn ways and means of keeping from doing any."

"How's Wayne getting on?" Tom asked. "He must be working hard. He hasn't even come out to fish."

"He seems to like what he's doing."

"Like everybody else I was surprised when he wanted to go to town," Tom said, "yet looking back, it seems natural enough. He doesn't care about money in any greedy kind of way. Yet he wants a sort of large existence."

"What do you mean by large?" Amanda wanted to know.

"Maybe I mean civilized. Now I'm not civilized. A shack on the river bank'd suit me. But Wayne would like to fix up a big Natchez house the way it used to be, and live in it, and have a wife who'd always be all dressed up."

Louise agreed with Tom's picture of Wayne. "And one reason he'd like money is to help his family."

Tom wanted to know how Wayne and Maggie were getting along.

"The arguments they have! About everything under the sun!"

Tom and Maggie had teased each other, and Maggie, when she had been younger, had tagged after Tom, giving him a kind of hero worship. They were fond of each other, and Louise hoped their affection would grow into something stronger. Maggie would be an ideal wife for him, and Tom fascinated most women, perhaps because he was elusive and preoccupied by his own masculine interests. Yet now that Tom was grown up, he showed no signs of falling in love with Maggie, or anyone, though Dolly Lydell showed definite signs of caring more for Tom than any of the young men who thronged around her. On the other hand, Maggie seemed to be able to analyze him with a coolness indicating detachment.

Amanda looked up from her sewing. "Wayne and Maggie. How would that do for a match?"

"No!" Louise didn't know why she answered with such promptness and violence. "They wouldn't do for each other at all!"

"Mother's right. Maggie's too—well she sees everything in black or white. Wayne would like more arts and snares. He'd recognize that they were just arts and snares, but he'd like 'em all the same."

"Tell me about your garden party, Lou," Amanda said. "I wish I could have come in for it, but I was preserving and couldn't let my berries spoil. I bet everyone had a good time."

Twice a year, Louise gave a party, one during the winter, and one in early summer, held in the garden if the weather was fair. Everybody came, not only Louise's usual callers, but everyone who was anyone. Some of them lived in moldy mansions deep in the woods, and hardly ever appeared, but they came to Louise's parties, wearing their best clothes and their best manners. Louise described her own dress to Amanda. She had come across some bands of black and white embroidery in her armoire, and Miss Rose had used it to trim a thin white dress. "With a guimpe made of beading, run through with narrow black velvet ribbon. It turned out very well."

"Everybody in Natchez lives out of attics and old trunks," Tom smiled, "but at least your armoire smells of that nice stuff—vetivert —instead of mothballs."

"Several rained down from Mrs. Corwin's shawl—you know her cashmere."

"I know it well," Alan said.

Cousin Sophie had trailed her lengths of yellowed lace, and Mrs. Duel her moulting plumes. "But there were a few birds of paradise, Tom. Dolly always has new dresses, and Kate Lennerd came wearing the latest Paris fashions. The garden was in bloom, and the girls helped me pass the tea and cookies."

Alan asked if Mrs. Corwin had said anything outrageous.

"Oh, yes, she was talking to Cousin Sophie, and she was saying how dreadful it was to be old, and to have lost her beauty. 'We're both old women, Sophie, but you can't imagine how sad it is for me, because I was beautiful, and you don't know anything about that sort of loss.'"

"Mother's parties always have a decided flavor, all their own," Tom said. "I suppose because all the freakish people, or the ones somewhat tainted by the breath of scandal, come and mingle with the staid well-behaved people, and everybody behaves as if nothing untoward had ever happened, and usually something untoward does happen, and that always lends zest."

"Oh, I almost forgot!" Louise said. "Something untoward did happen this time. Your Cousin Albert appeared out of the depths of the swamp! Up he drove in an oxcart with six towheaded children."

"Lawd!" Tom sighed. "Did he bring his wife?"

"No, he never does."

"How'd you manage, Lou?" Amanda said.

"Oh, everybody rose to the occasion. And Wayne came in and talked to him for hours about Cuban rebellions. We put him and the six children up for the night, and he left again the next morning."

Cousin Albert's life was one of those tragedies Louise knew only too well. He had been a born adventurer, and his exploit at Waterproof had been the last flare-up of his restlessness and rebelliousness. That election had given him his last chance at daring. Now he had sunk below the surface of normal living, and would drag out the rest of his existence in a sodden stupor. He had outlived all of his adventures. He had lived, as people often did, too long. He was a ghost, as Jasper, if he were still on earth, was a ghost, and their ghostliness haunted her.

"Look." Tom got up from the gallery railing where he had been lounging. "Here comes Jim. On that horse I wish I had."

Louise watched Jim come riding up, and went to meet him. He got off his horse, said good evening to everybody, then went up to Louise. "It's been five years, Miss Lou."

"You still talk like a Southerner," she smiled, holding out her hand. He had grown tall and broad-shouldered. Except for a certain heaviness of bony structure, he was not in the least like his father. She was tense at this meeting with him, and knew he was too. They were like teacher and pupil. She was anxious for him to show himself to the best possible advantage, and he wanted to acquit himself well. Fair-haired, tanned, his face flushed now at the effort to say the right things to everyone, Louise felt he was still the same Jim, though with a new maturity and seriousness. His manners were good, and his dark blue eyes shone with joy at being with her again.

"You look fine, Miss Lou. Tell me everything that's been happening to you. The things you left out of your letters."

"I didn't leave much out, and you're the traveler."

"I'd rather forget that, and just sink down into being back."

"I think your going did you good, though."

He admitted it had, and said it was hard to believe anybody could know as little as he'd known, and though there was still plenty to learn, he felt he'd taken in something. He had always been quick to see and grasp new impressions and new ideas. He took the chair Amanda offered him, and they all talked together. In a little while, Alan and Tom, knowing Louise wanted to have a conversation with

194

Jim, found duties needing their attention before sundown, and Amanda said she had to see to supper. "You stay, Jim." Since her father and Louise and Alan and Tom liked Jim, Amanda was ready to accept him too.

"Thank you." His blue eyes darkened, and the flush in his face deepened. "But——"

"Do stay," Louise urged, and he said he would be glad to, if it wouldn't be any trouble. When the others had gone, Louise asked him what had made him decide to come back. "At first I was sorry for you, you hated it there. Then you grew to like it, so I was afraid you might decide to stay for good."

"I had a fight with myself. I thought about looking for work up there—in some ways it'd be easier."

"Yes, if you'd learned to feel at home there."

"I didn't. I missed—being here. Up there, they called me a Rebel." He smiled a little. "I had plenty of fights because I took up for the South."

"Did you take up for us?"

"I did so, Miss Lou. They don't understand about how things are down here. Sometimes I got licked, but mostly I licked them. I liked it."

"What? Fighting, or winning?"

"Their thinking I belonged down here. I—let 'em think so."

Louise understood how passionately Jim had longed to be part of the place he thought of as his home and his world. Here he had been born, and here were his roots and his heart. Really, he belonged nowhere. Not in the North, not here. But the people he had been with hadn't understood how isolated his carpetbagger family was in the community around them, and Jim, boasting of "home," had pretended that loneliness didn't exist.

"If you feel you belong down here, Jim, and want to, you will." More and more she felt how grown up he was, and how much he had changed, yet at heart, he was the same Jim. His way of talking had changed. Before, it had been a mixture of Persia's phrases, and his parents', and a smattering of words he had learned from his visits to Indigo. Now he spoke correctly, and every now and then paused to find the precise word he wanted.

"That's what I hope, ma'am. But—Miss Lou, I can't blame you, and everybody, for the way you feel—about my father."

"I don't think the way we feel matters to him."

"It does, Miss Lou. In a way. It makes him more set on getting—rich." He hesitated, then plunged on. "He wants me to go his way."

"How are you getting on with him?"

"He wanted me to come back. So it's all right. For now. I told him I was grown, and I was going to come and go as I pleased. If he didn't like it, I'd clear out, for good and all. He can't keep me from coming here, if you all will have me."

"We'll have you."

"I hope. I guess he sees there's no use in his raising a ruckus, either. I don't like the way he runs things. One of these days we'll come to grips about that store of his, but right now——"

"Settle down awhile, Jim, before you make issues."

"I hope I can. Miss Lou, while you're out here this time, would you see my mother? She misses you a lot."

"Of course I will."

"You won't have to go down by the creek bank, either." A tense look came to his face. "If it's all right with you and Miss Amanda, I'll bring her over here tomorrow about this time."

"Do. It'll be perfectly convenient."

"She's a big reason why I came back."

"I thought so."

"I'd like to make up to her some. For the kind of life she's had."

"Having you back will help."

"If my father and I could get along——" he sighed. "Miss Lou, when I was a little boy, I knew there was plenty wrong between your family and my father, but I took it for granted, I guess, that you'd go ahead and like me. Now I see it takes a special effort on your part—to like me.

"Not such an effort, Jim."

"A lot of people won't bother to make any effort, though. But I expect that. I expect to earn my way here."

Amanda came out and said supper was ready, and the talk became casual. Tom asked Jim about his horse. He'd bought it, he said, with money he'd saved by working during the summers. When he left that night, Jim said, "This evening's the sort of thing I've been looking forward to for five years."

Late the next afternoon, Jim brought his mother over in the surrey. Della had made great efforts for this call. She wore a black silk dress, badly made, and much too hot for the day. Its folds swallowed her up, accentuating her pinched sallowness, and she was more nervous and ill at ease than ever. Tom took Jim off, to look at a mule he had bought, and Amanda, with the tact of a really kind heart, saw how her presence made Della speechless, and said she would fix something cool to drink.

"Now I'm giving her trouble," Della murmured.

"She's never satisfied unless she's fixing something to eat or drink," and Louise hurried on to admire the new surrey which had brought Jim and Della.

"Jim gave it to me. He'd saved his money." Her mouth quivered. "He's a good boy." After that, Della lapsed into silence, shrinking into the folds of her dress, and peering around for Jim to come and take her away, but Louise talked on resolutely, about the weather, about raising guineas, and about Jim, until Della lost her reserve, and began to talk too. "Things are better with Jim back." She bit her lips, and added, not looking at Louise. "I don't know if you remember, but a long while ago, I told you something, and you told me how I oughtta act."

"I don't know if my telling you was any help."

"Not at first. But later, I guess what you said was handy to me, because I tried to act right, for Jim. It was worth it. Jim's worth anything. Then, I reckon most a year ago, Persia told me she was quitting. It's a queer kind of thing, but you know what happened? I was scared she would quit. I quess you won't be able to take that in."

"Oh, yes, I understand. You were lonesome, and she's a good thing, good really, in spite of—her drinking and all."

"I guess she is. And I begged her not to go off, just to stay. She was the only company I had, month in and month out. I reckon it was weakness in me, asking her."

"Well, so often, time, just going along, makes changes in things and people."

197

Della fumbled her hands together. "She's there. She just said she wasn't quitting *me*. That's all she did say. But I reckon I knew what she meant. I wanted you to know how things turned out about it all. But I don't want Jim ever to know anything at all."

"He won't, Della."

Jim and Tom wandered back, and Amanda brought out a delightful drink she called Blackberry Shrub. Della sipped at hers, then drank it, and even had the courage to ask Amanda about Dr. Rand. Then Jim and Della said good-by and drove off in the new surrey.

"I used to wonder why you bothered with her, Lou, but I guess you couldn't help it," Amanda said, before turning back into the house. "She gives me a sad sort of feeling like a poor mouse caught in a trap."

Louise and Tom stood at the foot of the steps, watching the little cloud of dust sift and settle among the trees. "A new surrey," Tom meditated. "She won't have much use for it, but I guess it makes her feel good to have it. Particularly since Jim gave it to her. He makes no bones about coming over here, does he? And that ole rascal has to put up with it now. I guess maybe too, in his mean, lopsided way the Yankee's proud Jim's got some git up and git."

"Very likely. Tom, I didn't know you remembered my nursing Jim."

Tom's slate-colored, shadowy eyes looked out at the darkening trees. "Sure. I remember. I went across the fields before morning, and there was that smell of dew and dust and creek, I swung a lantern, and you called out 'don't come near me.' I remember that, and lots of other things when I was a child, just as plain. And the way you fixed things, like Christmases and birthdays. And the day we went and found the eagle's feather." He turned and smiled at her, with that smile like her own. "I don't say much, but I don't forget."

Between them was that harmony and accord, that sense of nearness making words unnecessary. Tom never delved into his feelings long, and when he spoke again he said he thought he liked this time of day best of all. He was young, and didn't yet feel the stealing melancholy of darkness coming. He and Louise watched how

Indigo, cupped in the rolling country around it, gathered the twilight first.

"Right now, Indigo deserves its name, not just because we once planted Indigo, but because—well, it looks as if it ought to be called Indigo. The fields and the treetops are hazy blue, and the ground and the tree trunks are ink blue, and beyond the trees here in front, if you go on to the road you can look way over and see where the swamp begins, and the streak on the horizon's a bright dark blue, turning violet."

When Louise left the plantation to go back to Natchez, Amanda told her to bring Wayne and the girls out for a picnic, but Wayne was busy that summer, and Dolly went off to visit her aunt and go to the Springs, and Maggie was helping nurse one of her sister's children in Jackson, so the summer was almost over before Louise really thought of the picnic plans again.

One morning, she was writing in her diary, putting down hot, clear day. Ever since she had come back to Natchez, Louise had been keeping a diary, not at all like the one she had owned in her girlhood. That one had been bound in rose-colored velvet, with mother-of-pearl clasps, and a tiny gold lock and key. Intermittently, she had written out some of her thoughts and feelings, and even a verse or two, then years later had found it in the attic, had laughed at her effusions, and had torn out the pages. The diary she kept now was a stiff little black notebook, and the entries were all prosaic. She wrote, in a hurry, "Few eggs. Hens moulting. Cow got into front yard and ate Maréchal Niel to quick." She closed the book and looked out of the window at the wreck of her favorite rosebush. It was early, but the sun already seared. At night, though, the sun would yield to a brightening moon. It was a pity to waste such moonlight, so she began a letter to Amanda, suggesting a picnic.

Amanda answered at once. Her brothers and Tom wanted a picnic too. The men could sleep at Avondale, and the girls at Indigo. There were plenty of chickens ready for frying, and ears of corn for roasting. The group from Natchez could take the boat, and after a day or two, Ben would drive them all back to town.

"I can get away," Wayne said, "if we make it Saturday. I was thinking how sweet the moonlight must be sleeping on yonder bank, so we can go eat on it and in it." Everyone else was enthusiastic too, except Medora, who preferred to stay in Natchez.

"Cousin Medora has a true Southern gentlewoman's abhorrence for moving about in hot weather," Wayne said, when he and Louise were standing on the boat's deck, waiting for the girls to come.

"She never cared much for jaunts in the woods."

"Did you always?" he asked.

"No, but I learned to."

"I don't think Cousin Medora learns new ways much, but then she's getting older."

Louise smiled. "Stop harping on her age. We're contemporaries."

"Are you?" Wayne looked surprised. "You don't seem at all of her vintage, Louise."

He had fallen into the habit of calling her Louise, and she liked it, because it seemed to bridge that gap of years between them. She didn't look as old as Medora, or even much older than Wayne, standing there, smiling, with the breeze blowing the skirts of her thin pale dress, and her yellow straw hat framing her face. Under its shadowy brim her brown eyes were full of light, and there was grace in the poise of her figure, and the pose of her head.

"Do you ever miss Avondale, Wayne, or do you like being in town as much as you expected?"

"No, I don't miss it, and I think the work I chose was right for me. When I'm dabbling with cotton I hear the roar of all the markets of the world in my ears. I like that feeling, of being part of the tumult of all the rest of humankind, instead of being shunted off. And I particularly like being in your house. Best of all, I enjoy our long, meandering talks."

"I enjoy them too."

Wayne often worked late, and he usually lingered with Louise after the other boarders had gone upstairs. Louise consulted him about her daily problems, and he told her about his work, then they went on to discuss everybody and all kinds of subjects, books, poetry, history, and general ideas.

"Oh, one thing, Wayne, before the others come. I want you to do me a favor. I asked Jim Sanders to meet us on the river bank. Be nice to him, please."

Wayne's face turned somber, and took on a shadow of that look she had seen the first time she had ever met him, down by the creek, when, motionless in the glare, and turned towards the place of his enemies, he had been to her a symbol of implacability.

"I won't promise to like him, but I won't insult him." He turned to face her. "Look here, do you think your friendship with Jim will have any good effect on Indigo's future?"

"I doubt it. He's much more likely to break completely with his father than to exert any influence. And his father controls everything."

"And even nice people are queer about things like property and money. It takes mighty fine-drawn scruples to make Quixotic gestures with money. I thought, though, if you had some subtle scheme in this weird friendship with Jim, I'd be glad to fall in with it."

She told him something of the same thing she had told Maggie. "Revenge in a petty sense is stupid. If we were free of the Yankee, and out of his clutches, I wouldn't have to think about him any more. But we aren't, and as he causes me sleepless nights, I think I would rather he would hate me than just be able to ignore me."

"Yes, I understand that. And I'm glad you aren't altogether angelic."

He smiled. "Angelic beings are rather one-dimensional. They're just head and wings. I like people to be in layers. It makes them more interesting."

A hack was slowly making its way down the hill to the boat. "There're the girls now." Louise waved to the faces peeping out of the hack's windows.

"I'd better go help them on board. There's Dolly Lydell. Where's she been all summer?"

"Visiting. Then her aunt took her to the Springs."

Wayne had met Dolly, but didn't know her well. Louise watched him while he went and escorted the girls to the boat. There was a flurry of laughter and a whirl of skirts and a flapping of hat brims. Maggie ran sure-footed and independent. Camilla Dale, plump, fair and sleepy-eyed, trundled cautiously after her. Dolly Lydell, holding up her parasol, clung to Wayne's arm, shuddering at the narrow strip of water.

Dolly was one of those rare creatures, a redhaired beauty. She was tall, almost as tall as Maggie, but she had a tiny little face, small hands and feet, and delicate features. Louise thought Dolly's face, if you analyzed it, was too even, too changeless, and her light blue eyes, with their innocent stare, lacked expressiveness, but then nobody, or hardly anybody, ever did analyze Dolly's looks. Her wonderful hair and skin startled and dazed. She would have been just another pretty girl, if it hadn't been for the drama of her coloring. Her skin was petal white, and her hair was rust-gold, red-gold, gold-gold as the light shone on it. No one had ever yelled carrottop at Dolly. She had always been the beautiful princess in the fairy story, and the shining angel in the Christmas pageants.

Dolly's father and Maggie's were law partners. The firm of Corwin and Lydell didn't make much money, but Dolly was an only child, whereas Maggie was one of a horde. Dolly's parents had given all their thoughts and time to their daughter. Mrs. Lydell had almost put her eyes out sewing and scalloping and embroidering Dolly's dresses. There had been music lessons and dancing lessons, and two years at a finishing school. Dolly was older than Maggie, eighteen, nearly nineteen, Louise remembered, but she seemed younger. Everyone had coddled and protected her, while Maggie had fended for herself.

"Dolly spends nine-tenths of her life guarding her complexion," Maggie said, and now, as soon as she was on board, Dolly chose the shadiest corner and muffled herself in yards of green veiling.

Wayne asked her if she'd had a good time at Cooper's Wells.

"Wonderful. The band played every night and there were lots of people and we danced and danced."

"Everywhere water bubbles up and tastes bad, hotels mushroom and people flock," Wayne mused. "Do you suppose that stuff ever cures anybody of anything?"

"We used to go to various places like that," Louise said, remembering past trips to fashionable watering places. "We went loaded with trunks and everybody dressed up. I don't know if it helped anyone's health, but resorts help romances along."

Wayne laughed. "Miss Dolly, we know your present bloom isn't due to water you drank, but comes from the aura of your triumphs."

"I declare, Mr. Wayne, I don't see why you laugh at me about my beaus. A girl's got to have beaus."

"Regiments?"

"At least a good many," Maggie explained. "A girl has only one privilege—she can say no."

"I bet you find it more exciting, Mag, to refuse hordes than just one or two."

Louise smiled. "The discarded seem to console themselves."

"That's tame of 'em. In the good old days, they fought duels, or at least had the grace to blow their brains out in the garden."

"You know, Wayne, I believe they fought more duels over horses and cards than love affairs." Maggie prided herself on being modern, and tried to defend herself against her strong sentimental attachment to the past.

"But I don't have regiments." Dolly had to bring things back to herself. "Last Sunday, there were only nine, no, ten." She turned to Louise. "I do wish Tom wouldn't bury himself out in those ole woods." Her light little voice was plaintive. "Can't you make him come back home?"

"To him, Indigo is home." Poor Dolly might as well know what she faced with Tom. She couldn't draw him back to the cozy, neat little house she undoubtedly visualized, where she could give card parties and serve little cakes and sandwiches, with painted place cards for everybody.

"Well, I'm just dying to see Indigo. I've heard so much about it."

Tom was waiting for them when the boat landed. Dolly smiled at him and waved her parasol. She had even gone so far as to lift her veil, though the sun was still in the sky. Louise noticed her eagerness, and when they all piled into the wagon, Louise took pity on Dolly, and told her to sit next to Tom. Most people found the woods around Indigo, and the plantation itself rather frightening at first, and the sight of its wildness might check Dolly's feelings for Tom. The woods were rank and dark with growth. In the fields the cotton stalks were drying, and here and there opening to show gleams of whiteness. Dolly murmured admiration over the woods, and later over the corn and cotton, though Louise felt that poor little Dolly must find one clump of woods very much like another.

203

There was the house, and Amanda and Alan.

"Well, here we are." Louise kissed them both. "A horde of locusts."

"I made a dormitory out of your room, Lou. You come in with me, and Alan has a cot on the gallery. Girls, I know you want to primp before we set out." She led them in. Two dozen guests wouldn't have disturbed Amanda. Louise went in the kitchen to speak to Lillybelle and Jessie, who looked much stronger than when Louise had last seen her.

"Put those tin forks in the basket, Lou. Is that very pretty girl the one you think likes Tom?" Amanda asked.

"She seems to."

"Goodness, what would she do out here?"

"I'm sure I don't know. Maybe they'll both realize she wouldn't like it long."

"Just so they realize it soon enough. Don't let me forget the coffeepot."

They went out to find that Jack and Ben Rand had come in wagons piled with hay. The girls exclaimed over it. Nothing was better than a hay ride.

"Jim says he'll meet us," Alan told Louise.

"Now, girls, be pleasant to him," she cautioned.

"I would be pleasant to almost anybody today," Maggie said.

The baskets were packed, and everybody scrambled into the wagons. Ben drove one, and Tom the other, and Dolly sat next to Tom. Ben had asked her to come with him, and she had told him she had already promised Tom. Louise hadn't heard Tom ask her. Off they went. Lillybelle and Jessie getting the clothes from the line, waved to them. A brightness washed the sere fields. The hands were coming in from their work, singing as they came. Their voices sounded far off, and echoing, then nearer and nearer. The edges of the woods gleamed, then the wagons plunged into the shadows. When they left the woods, the blinding glitter of the river and the sky almost dazed them. The usually dull sand at the water's edge, flashed with radiant particles, the tall pale weeds waved gilt feathers, and the soft south breeze made the cottonwoods sing. In a few minutes, the sun set, and the light mellowed.

"We'd better eat before it gets dark," Amanda advised, "or we'll put strange insects in our mouth."

"Red ants taste like pepper," Wayne said. "I've swallowed a many a one." He looked up. Jim Sanders was riding out of the woods.

"Is that Jim Sanders?" Wayne asked. "Good horse he's got." He frowned as he watched Jim dismount and tether his horse, but by the time Jim had reached the group Wayne's face had smoothed. As Louise introduced Jim to the girls and to Wayne, she thought it ought to be easy for them to treat him well. He soon went off to help build the fire, and talked easily to Tom and the Rands. If Wayne didn't feel any cordiality for Jim, he at least didn't show any lack of it, and the girls admitted he was very good looking. The women unpacked the baskets under Amanda's directions and spread the checked tablecloth not too near the fire. Everybody gathered and everybody ate fried chicken, and roasting ears, and salad, and cake, and preserves, and Amanda's good bread, and drank coffee. After the sun had gone, the woods turned from blue to a soft impenetrable color. Here on the river bank, they couldn't see the moon yet, though it must have come up, and was shining on Indigo's fields. The woods hid it, but the dark treetops defined their undulations against the swimming honey glow in the eastern sky, then caught a luminous sheen.

Louise noticed Jim. He didn't talk much, but he seemed more at ease and mingled better than she had expected. In an undertone, she asked him if he was getting along well.

"If you mean with my father, just so-so. But it's a busy time, and that helps. I walk on eggs. I guess, in his way, my father does too." By the flicker of the firelight, Louise could see his face. He looked tense, and she changed the subject, and he relaxed, then began to smile at something Maggie said. She hoped he would have a chance to be happy, he had a capacity for it.

Wayne stirred the light, idle talk to liveliness by asking Maggie what she'd said at the Averys' party.

"I said I believed in women's rights and I do."

Everybody began to talk at once, and Wayne was pleased because he had started a violent discussion.

"Votes," Dolly shivered. "It sounds so bold and horrid."

"If women ever do vote, Maggie, just don't expect politics to take on a dazzling purity," Louise said. "Women are human and not all angels by any means."

"Goodness," Amanda gave everybody more coffee, "I'd hate to waste as much time mulling over politics as you men do."

"Bloomers," Dolly challenged. "I'd like to see Maggie in old ugly, baggy bloomers."

"Don't carry your rebellious spirit that far," Wayne begged, "when just a glimpse of ankle is so enticing."

"That reminds me of another rebellious spirit," Alan said. "I remember our cousin Anna getting into a carriage, and my sister Emma told her she was showing her ankles, and that there was a man coming along the sidewalk, and she said, 'Let him look, then, he never saw a finer pair.' I don't suppose he ever did, either."

"I tell you one thing." Tom reached for the coffeepot again. "I wish all you ladies would ride astride."

"Oh, Tom," Dolly gave her little shriek.

"I mean it. You look very graceful on a sidesaddle with your skirts sweeping the ground, but it's dangerous."

"It surely is," Alan agreed. "Do you remember the time when your mother was dragged by the mule?"

"That's what I was thinking about. And Cousin Medora was so scared she fainted and had hysterics."

Louise felt herself turn pale, but Tom had no idea of what had happened that night, and it came to her again how little anybody knew about anyone else, particularly how little the young knew about the generation ahead of them. Even to herself, the sudden memory of that time seemed violently implausible.

Wayne turned to Louise. "Did you ever want to vote?"

"Once. And you know when."

"But you did your part, you backed us up." He was serious now, thinking about that summer, that autumn, when they had flung the carpetbaggers out of office. That time made a bond between them. She knew a side of Wayne's heart and mind these girls would never know.

Milly Dale said she didn't want to work, and the only right she wanted was the right to have some man take care of her. The others laughed, but Maggie was in earnest. "There! Just waiting for some man to marry you! I'd rather work than be a dependent female, and a millstone around some poor man's neck."

Maggie was always violent, and not always logical but Louise knew how the child felt. She saw her own father burdened with the support of a bevy of women, and part of her zeal for her cause came from her own sense of being trapped. She was like an oak tree planted in a flower pot. She would shrivel away if she couldn't break out to grow.

"I think you're right, Miss Margaret," Jim hadn't entered the argument until now. "The way things are may be fine for women who are protected and sheltered and happy, but plenty of 'em aren't. They have a miserable time, and there doesn't seem to be any way for them to get out."

He was thinking, Louise knew, of his own mother's life, realizing that none of these others here, whatever their poverty or their problems, had any idea of the grimness of his own household, or the grinding drabness of his mother's life. Not dully drab, but sordidly drab.

Maggie didn't answer, but she looked at him, and he looked at her. In the moonlight, their faces were grave, but their eyes were shining. It was as if they were asking each other unspoken questions, and waiting for the answers.

Louise found herself saying, "For the millenium, everybody's love story would have to come out right."

Tom got up and wandered to the river's edge, and Dolly followed him with her eyes. And Wayne, Louise saw, was watching Dolly, and there was an expression on his face Louise had never seen before, his eyes a little narrowed, a smile curving his mouth. The moon was high now. The dusty track of the road had changed to a pearl-paved way, leading into the woods, and the woods had become strange. The Louisiana shore was no longer mud and willows. It was a rootless vision, and the river, no describable color, dreamed in its deep silences.

Dolly's face was in the moonlight, and had a flower's secret luster, and her eyes, usually shallow and light, looked dark with mystery, and a flicker from the fire touched her hair, making an aureole flame around her head.

Louise didn't understand, why, as she took in Dolly's beauty, and Wayne's drugged, bemused study of it, her own heart began to beat wildly, or why all at once she felt completely alone, and all the magic the moon had made turned bone bleached, bone bare. From the woods, an owl called. Instinct was awake, and hungry, and seeking. Louise shivered at the sad, harsh, cry. It reminded her of that other summer, with its tensions and violence. She hadn't known Wayne then. He had been the outline of a stranger, and a shadow among the shadows of the trees, striking her nerves with his owl's call.

Chapter Fourteen

Two weeks after the picnic, on a hot afternoon, Louise was reading aloud to Maggie and Dolly and Milly. The library was dim, and at least seemed cool. The half-closed shutters held the tawny fierceness of the sunlight at bay. Milly was putting new sleeves in a dress, struggling with her stitches. Dolly was zealously working tiny scallops on a flounce for a petticoat. Dolly was particular about her petticoats. Each flounce had to have beading run through with pale pink or blue ribbon, and a border of hand embroidery. Maggie was darning socks. Her needle flashed in and out, but she tangled her thread, because she was hurrying too much and her fingers were unsteady.

Louise read well. The tone and quality of her voice, never monotonous, gave the right emphasis and inflection to the words, and made the descriptions and dialogue spring to warmth and life, but today she felt she was droning along, not much aware of the sense of what she was reading, and not much interested in Romola's moral struggles. Her racing thoughts intruded, making sharp little pictures, and echoing with words spoken. She told herself the heat had affected her, yet the sense of loneliness, striking her at the picnic had persisted, and with it a dismal awareness of relationships subtly shifted. Her reason might contradict this, but stronger than any rational denials was the lightning flash of intuitive knowledge.

Why shouldn't Wayne look at Dolly and think she was beautiful? Everybody thought so. Then, on the Saturday after the picnic, Dolly had given an evening party. Louise had made Tom put in an appearance. Before they had left Indigo, she had taken him aside. "Dolly's feelings will be hurt if you don't come."

Tom, lounging in the door, his long legs tangled together, had said it was his busy time.

"I don't care! You've got to come to town once in a while. You're getting to be a complete—vegetable!"

"All right, since you're so set on it. To please you——"

"Why not to please Dolly? That would be more natural."

"Why do you take up cudgels for her?"

"I'm not. It's just——"

"She's a feast for the eye. But after I've listened to her for a while, I want to take to the tall timber."

He had appeared at the party, and had danced dutifully with Dolly and the other girls, and had asked his mother to dance. "Why not?" he'd said when she had refused. "You still waltz better than anybody." Then he had retreated, and had spent too much of his time talking crops and politics with the older men. Wayne had asked Louise to dance too, but she had said no, and had watched him waltz with Dolly. In her pale ruffles, Dolly was as lovely by candlelight as she had been by moonlight.

"With her looks," Lizzie had remarked, "Dolly ought to catch a rich husband." Lizzie had been sitting next to Louise, on the sidelines, with the dowagers, the old maids, and the wallflowers, and had made her acid-tinged comments.

"Where'll she find one?" How the Corwins always stressed the importance of money! Louise had watched Wayne with Dolly, and again, he had worn that drugged, bemused look. Louise had envied them both, because they were young. Though why should anyone want to be young? It meant dangers, treacheries, disappointments, yet somehow all of her hard-won content had slipped away from her and faded with the heady feverishness stealing over her.

If her own mood was strange and uncertain, so was Wayne's. He had been silent, and when he did talk, he had been abstracted, as if he hardly knew or cared what he said, and between him and Louise there was no longer the old sense of intimacy. She knew now how much she had cherished it, since she missed it.

Pausing to turn over a page, Louise glanced at Dolly, busy with her perfect little scallops. With Wayne, Dolly had the pretty flirtatiousness of manner she used with every male creature, nothing more. It was Wayne—oh, what did it matter? What concern was it of hers after all? Besides, Wayne would surely become aware, if anyone would, of Dolly's triviality. Yet again, Louise felt that pang of envy, for Dolly's eighteen years, and her glittering hair, giving her such conspicuousness, and even for Dolly's shallowness. Her meagerness of mental and emotional equipment. It could protect her from the suffering deep thoughts and deep feelings usually bring.

Dolly said she had run out of embroidery floss, and would have to get some more. She declined what Louise could offer from her own workbox, saying it wouldn't match.

"It's all white anyway, and won't be noticed," Louise tried to tell her, but Dolly shook her head. She lived only three doors down the street, but she armed herself with hat and parasol for the walk. "Now don't read a line until I get back."

As soon as she was out of the door Maggie said. "Shucks! For a petticoat! Go on, Aunt Lou, she'll never know the difference."

Louise read on, stopping when she heard Dolly at the door again. Maggie was right. Though Louise had read four pages while Dolly was gone, Dolly never knew the difference, and Milly, Maggie, and Louise exchanged glances over her unconscious head. Louise finished the chapter, and closed the book. "That's enough for today." Dolly thanked her and said she was due at home anyway. She had gone, but Milly and Maggie were still on hand when Wayne came in, earlier than usual. "Am I interrupting?" He looked around, then the eagerness of his face faded.

"We've finished. Come in and sit down."

"I'm sorry, but I'd better go on up. I have some work."

"Didn't Dolly have a nice party?" Milly said. "And she told me she thought you were the handsomest and most distinguished man there."

Louise had never seen Wayne blush before, but he blushed now. "Did she?" He smiled—a foolish, drunken kind of smile.

Louise was violently angry with him. What crass stupidity! For him to be taken in! "I don't want to disparage your looks or distinction," she found herself saying, "but I'm afraid Dolly scatters her flatteries wholesale." Now why had she said that? And for perhaps the first time in her life she found herself blurting out the wrong thing, knowing it was wrong, but compelled to say it. It sounded malicious!

"Very likely," Wayne said, and went on upstairs. Milly folded up her work and said she had to go too, but Maggie lingered, still restless.

"I could finish the bottom part of the bookcase now."

"If you want," Louise was listless. "It's hot."

"It doesn't matter." Maggie sat down on the floor, opened the bookcase and took out the box of miniatures. She was too preoccupied with thoughts of her own to have noticed the tingle in the air. Louise glanced at her. Maggie had unwrapped one of the miniatures, and looked at it for some time before she held it up. "Who is she?"

"My cousin Anna. Ellen's mother. You've heard me talk about Ellen."

"Quite a lot." Maggie studied the black hair and pale face, with its full mouth, the lips deeply indented at the corners, and the light, clear green eyes.

"You and Aunt Liz talk about her too. She sounds interesting. But somehow, I don't think I'd like her."

"You would. We all adored her."

"Not Aunt Liz."

"No——" Lizzie had always been too jealous. "But the rest of us."

"I wouldn't have——"

"You should, because she was a rebel. So are you." Yet Louise realized Maggie's rebellions and her dead cousin's would be of different kinds and probably for different reasons Maggie had violent impulses, though.

"She was a sort of enchantress, wasn't she?"

"Very much so."

"I guess I just don't like them much." Maggie had that obscure but natural distrust of the responsible, unselfish woman who realizes she must earn her way to any happiness she might get, for the Circes of the world. Besides, Maggie wanted, or thought she wanted, in her youth and inexperience, new and shining rights for her sex, rather than the eternal and subtle victories of charm and enchantment. After one of Maggie's flaming assertions, Medora had murmured, "I suppose Maggie's very intelligent, but she feels things in a very strange way."

212

"Oh, no," Louise had contradicted, but mildly, because if you contradicted Medora she became as stubborn as cold molasses. "No, I think Maggie's head's in the clouds and her brains whirl with many-colored vapors, but she can feel straight. That's her strength. Not in her head. In her heart."

Maggie gave one more glance at the miniature and then put it away. The glimpse of it had aroused Louise's memories of her own young days, full of turmoil and violent love. Often, as she knew, love, obsession, passion, came from a worship of beauty and warmth, of form and color. Wayne and that girl! There was no force in Dolly. But love, once taking fire, could feel itself for a long time in its own flame. Sometimes a fatally long illusion.

"Aunt Lou," Maggie looked up frowning. "Give me some advice——"

"About what?"

"Jim Sanders wrote me a note—he wants to come and see me. Next Sunday."

So this was what was making Maggie so restless! "What do you want to do?"

"I'd like to see him, but——"

Louise remembered the night after the picnic, when they had been on the way to the Rands for supper, and Maggie had asked if Jim had been invited. He hadn't been, and Louise, preoccupied, had forgotten Maggie's interest.

"Well, then—I suppose you'll let him come."

"My family mightn't like it. You know——"

"Very likely they won't."

"You know how Grandma can be——"

"Oh, yes——"

"And Aunt Liz. It'd be bad if they hurt his feelings. I thought if you'd talk to them—tell them——"

"No, Margaret," Louise spoke with a sharpness she had acquired since the night of the picnic, and Maggie had never heard from her before. "I won't meddle in this. I won't try to persuade your family to approve of him."

"But Aunt Lou—it's only an afternoon call!"

"Then if it's that casual, and seems to bother you—give it up."

213

"I don't want to——" Maggie picked up a palmetto fan from the chair near her and ran her fingers along its ridges.

"Goodness, Maggie, stop that! It sets my nerves on edge——" Lizzie had little fidgety movements and mannerisms, and Louise had taught Maggie that the fewer mannerisms any one had the longer their company seemed pleasant. She herself never made little useless gestures, never indulged in any waste motion at all.

Maggie put the fan down. "I want to see him."

"Look here, child," Louise spoke more gently. "I suppose it was a mistake, your meeting him. Since he is who he is."

"But you wanted me to—you wanted us to like him, and be nice to him. Now you won't do anything!"

"Now I've let you down?"

"Well, sort of——"

"Yes, I have. I made a mistake introducing you. But if you think— you might come to feel anything for Jim, it'll all be very tangled, and difficult——"

"Aunt Lou, you're jumping ahead——"

"I know, but still—I'm just saying if you insist on letting him come, let him. But you'll have to work it out your own way."

"I suppose I must," Maggie gloomed. Then she smiled, rather wickedly. "Isn't he well off?"

"Who? Jim? The Yankee must be. Very."

"If I tell Grandma and Aunt Liz he's rich—you'll see—they won't be snippish to him!" She got up from the floor. "I'll handle it myself! You needn't bother. And—and I'll tell him to come on!" She blew a kiss to Louise and went flying off, forgetting her work-basket and her sunbonnet.

Maggie and Jim! Louise had never dreamt of such a thing. Or had she? Perhaps it was nothing, but for Jim to venture all that way, to risk rebuffs—— Louise wondered if she really regretted bringing Jim and Maggie together, or if she only realized she might have good reason to regret it later.

That following Sunday, Jim, dressed in his best, came to see Louise before he went next door to the Corwins. Louise was sitting on the gallery having her tea, and as Jim came up the lawn

214

his height and his good looks impressed her. Maggie wouldn't have to apologize for what Jim was himself!

"Miss Maggie told me to drop in over there," he explained, turning red as he mentioned Maggie's name.

Louise gave him tea, and his cup chattered on its saucer, but that was the only outward sign of his nervousness, except his deepening color.

"Why did you come by boat?"

"Because I didn't want to get all dusty," he smiled. "I'll pick up a boat tonight—there's one. It'll stop at Indigo Landing."

"When? About dawn? You'd better spend the night here."

"Oh, no, ma'am, thank you."

Louise didn't urge him, guessing that Medora's presence in the house, and Wayne's, would make him uneasy. Wayne wasn't here at the moment. He had gone out after dinner. Louise hadn't asked him where he was going. Already, in these last two weeks, he had taken to frequenting the group of young people. Not long ago, he had preferred to stay and talk to her.

"There seem to be a lot of folks next door."

"Mostly family. It's a big family."

"I'm scared of 'em," Jim sighed. "But Miss Margaret—I'm scared of her too, but she's so—nice."

Cousin Sophie and Cousin Charlotte had turned in the gate and were coming slowly up the path by the driveway, parasols aloft, and gloved hands holding up their skirts. Lazarus the parrot was in residence, and from an upper window he muttered down at them, "Good-by. Well, good-by. Good-by now."

Jim looked at the two ladies, and got up at once, and fled, clawing off his hat as he passed them.

Wayne came back for supper. "Jim Sanders showed up at the Corwins—— At first everybody acted like chickens when a possum sidles into a hen roost. You know, all bunched together."

"All afternoon?"

"Just at first. I must say he held his own. He didn't say much, but after a while, it worked out all right. I'll gratify you this much, Louise. I'll admit he's nobody's fool."

"Who was over there?"

"The family. Louis Bennett, and Miss Milly Dale, and Miss Dolly."

So Dolly had been on hand! Wayne must have gone looking for her at her own house, found out she thad gone to the Corwins, so he had gone there too. Louise's fingers tightened on the palmetto fan she was holding.

"Louis Bennett can make music on his banjo. Jim Sanders up and played on it too. Not as well as the Bennett boy, but well enough."

"Was there any applause for him?"

"Miss Liz said she hadn't supposed he'd know anything but Yankee tunes——"

"She will jab——"

"He didn't let on, he said he always played Southern tunes. Particularly when he'd been staying up North." Wayne gave Louise a sidelong look. "Louis Bennett outplayed him on the banjo, but Jim Sanders outstayed him. In the daytime, Bennett can't pretend he's coming up on horseback. He does, after dark. He claps his hands all the way from the gate and hollers, 'Whoa! There.' It's to impress Maggie."

Louise laughed. "How absurd you are!" She had missed Wayne's nonsensical moods.

"He does. I've heard him. I believe he half persuades himself he comes galloping up on horseback, even if the rest of us know better. You think Jim Sanders is setting up to Maggie?"

"He said he just wanted to drop in."

"It seems like a long way to come."

After supper, Lizzie Corwin, carrying a small lantern and the enormous key to the Corwin front door, came across the stepping-stones to talk to Louise.

"You know that boy—that Jim Sanders came to see Maggie to-day."

"Didn't she tell you beforehand?"

"She mentioned it."

"Did you tell her not to let him come?"

"Her father wouldn't let us. He said if you thought the boy was good enough to have around, it was all right for Maggie to see him. Be that as it may be, we don't think so! It's a very different thing,

Lou, for you to have your peculiar tastes in people, at your age, than for a young girl like Maggie! You shouldn't have introduced them."

"Maybe not," Louise conceded. "But I like him. I wanted him to know people of his own age."

"Let him know po' white trash."

"He wouldn't want to."

"Well, it was imprudent of you, Lou."

"Is there any real harm in it?"

"When he looks at Maggie in that moonstruck way! Ha!" Lizzie snorted. "Think of who he is! Who his father is!"

"I often do."

"I suppose they're rich." Lizzie pronounced the word "rich" with awe.

"Certainly very well off. There's the Winsloe property, and that store. And Alan says the Yankee has his fingers in a good many profitable pies."

"Uum. Well, that boy's nice looking. And I wouldn't say his manners are bad—— My brother was pretty spineless, letting Maggie have him at the house. But I wash my hands of it!"

Louise knew she wouldn't. Lizzie picked everything to shreds, but through all her fretting she was sniffing at the aroma of money. Maggie's father was a simple soul who drudged without complaint, and had always been cowed by his mother. Louise had never heard him harp on the subject of money, but the women of the family, except Maggie, constantly referred to it, or rather to the lack of it.

After Lizzie had gone, Louise picked up a book, but she couldn't read. The house quieted. Formerly, she had prized her few moments of solitude, but tonight she felt lonely. The bleak mood, striking her the night of the picnic, had persisted. That night had changed them all. Dolly had been more open in her pursuit of Tom, and Tom had showed himself more elusive. Wayne, most of the time, had been lost in some dream of his own. Wayne, Dolly, Jim, Maggie, Tom, and herself—the cobwebby moonlight had tangled them all in its invisible strands. "Ill-met by moonlight."

Some days later Louise was sorting out Tom's winter clothes to send to Indigo. They were badly worn, and she stitched and mended as well as she could, thankful he had stopped outgrowing his things. Medora came in with some shirts.

"He can get some wear out of them. Mercy, it's hot. You're beforehand, Lou, to be thinking of winter."

"It's just around the corner. Look at the yard, full of leaves. They look as if they'd been fried."

Medora went off to set her room in order. She was very neat, and complained if anybody moved any article an inch out of its place. Louise went on folding and wrapping. As a child, she had loved this season best of all, exulting in autumn's coming, but now the sunlight slanting and the leaves in their slow drifting seemed intolerably sad.

Paper rattled in one of Tom's pockets. Louise reached down and brought a thin packet of letters, and recognized Dolly's pretty, curly handwriting. One of them was out of its envelope, and folded wrong, and before she could stop herself Louise saw it began "Oh, Tom." She didn't read any more, but tucked them away again. Dolly had been writing to Tom, as long ago as last winter. Why write when he had been living in Natchez where she could see him? Because she never saw him alone, but only in a group, and there were not enough times when she could tell him what she wanted to say without making herself too conspicuous. The poor child must have stored up everything she wanted to say, and written to him when he had been out at Indigo. Nobody out there, except Tom, would know her handwriting. Dolly's secrecy amazed Louise. She must have written this summer too, but those letters would be at Indigo.

It was clear enough what had happened. Dolly was used to having men in love with her, and had the assurance her beauty gave her. She had expected immediate response from Tom, and when there was none, she had done her best to hide her feelings from her friends. They knew, but it would be important not to seem rejected. Tom had slipped more and more out of reach since he had gone to live at Indigo, and the letters didn't seem to move him either. Dolly had showed her preference plainly at the picnic because there were so few times now when she was with Tom.

Louise had hardly supposed Dolly would think of writing, but

218

then, as she had seen, Dolly was quick enough with little tricks and stratagems and small feminine arts, obvious to every other woman. Obvious to men too, but since they were flattering tricks, men liked them, or else the glow of Dolly's hair blinded them. For Dolly to write "Oh, Tom," instead of "Dear Tom" showed how far her feelings had carried her. That was real desperation. Louise felt a pang of sympathy for the girl, and a throb of anger at Wayne. He was a fool to gaze at her and mope over her. She wasn't thinking of him! He had plunged into his work, and lately on all social occasions he had seemed a shell of himself, unless Dolly was on hand. Then he watched her and listened to her. Louise had hoped that common daylight would dissolve the trick the moonlight had played, and show him all the strings and props and papier maché quality of the magic he had seen, but he hadn't recovered, or come to himself.

"Wayne doesn't show much gumption hanging on Dolly's every word," Maggie whispered to Louise when the group, all except Tom, were gathered around the piano in Louise's parlor one chilly night. Dolly was playing a waltz, and Wayne was standing near her, watching her. How young she was, and how her hair gleamed and glistened in the firelight!

"They're dull words," Louise whispered back. There was no danger of being overheard, they could have shouted, because Cap'n Milt was one of the cluster around the piano, and he was roaring out the words to the waltz and making a chantey of it, his gusto enough to make you tote bales of cotton on board his boat. Cap'n Luke was smiling and silent by the fire, with Lazarus perched on his shoulder. Lazarus sang too, not at all like a bird, but like an old lady, in a high-pitched, quavering, cracked voice.

"Remember the time," Maggie said, "when Cap'n Luke and Lazarus first came, and Miss Sophie was singing, and he joined her from upstairs? She got so mad! You had to go get Lazarus to show her it wasn't us making fun of her."

Louise smiled. "I remember." It seemed to her that the years just passed, with all the difficulties, had been full of content, and little pleasures. Now the sweetness had burned away, leaving her in some dry blaze of feeling, like a glaring day when all outlines and colors fade in the pale quiver of incandescence.

"Aunt Lou," Maggie ventured, "it's getting near Christmas——"

"Is it? Yes, it isn't far off——" Louise hadn't been thinking about Christmas.

"You'll go to the plantation, won't you?"

"Tom'll want to stay there." All Tom's ideas of Christmas centered on Indigo.

"Ben Rand wrote Dolly. He wants us to come out the day after Christmas——"

"Who's us?"

"Why, Dolly and myself. And Wayne, if he wants to come. He can stay at Avondale, and Aunt Amanda said she'd put us up. You know we've never seen the Christmas tree for the hands——"

Louise knew the Christmas tree was only incidental. Dolly would want to see Tom, and Maggie wanted to see Jim. This would be her chance to be with him away from the critical eyes of her family.

"Where's your gumption, Maggie? You let Jim come to see you all the time. Where's it going to lead to?"

Maggie flushed and turned pale. "I don't know."

"Why don't you stop?"

"It—it's—well, it's too late," Maggie whispered. She was making a great effort to confide this much to Louise, and in Maggie's changing color and trembling mouth, Louise read the confusion and wretchedness and ardor of a first love affair.

"You're so young."

"But—you told me you weren't any older—when——"

"That was different. And times were different."

"People weren't. Not our kind of people." Louise knew what Maggie was trying to say. She had ranged herself with Louise, feeling that she, like Louise, was one of those people destined to plunge into life. Louise had encouraged her. Now Maggie saw a likeness in her love for Jim with Louise's love for Tom Delavain. But there had been no real obstacle there! Only Louise's age, and the fact that the war had begun. Tom had been suitable for her and right in every way.

"I blame myself, Margaret, about all this. And like most self-blame, it comes after the harm's done."

"Is it harm, Aunt Lou? To love somebody!" There was a baffled reproach in Maggie's tone. Hadn't Louise been the one to abet Maggie in throwing off the burdensome allegiance to the past? At least those backward yearnings in Maggie's family, the constant whining and moping for money and prosperity and material ease. Louise knew Maggie had expected more sympathy from her.

"Can't you care about somebody because he's worth it? Why do you have to think about anything but that?"

"Because other things come into it."

"Why? Why let 'em? Jim—well, he's Jim." She seemed ready to cry.

"All the same, his family, his surroundings will matter in every-day life." Louise's voice was weary. Maggie was so young and brash!

"Those—are outside things. We won't let 'em make any differ-ence. We just won't!"

"You'd better go out to Indigo, Margaret, and get Jim to take you over to his house. You'll have to see for yourself." Louise's touch of ferocity didn't daunt Maggie.

"I will!" She got up and joined the others at the piano. The light music whirled around her. Her face was flushed and her eyes were shining with the blaze of her defiance.

Medora announced her distaste of going to the country. "You go, let me stay and take care of things here. I'd rather."

Louise didn't urge her, she could understand how Medora wanted to end all connection with both Indigo and Avondale.

"Wayne said he'd go sort the books and furniture. He knows what I want to keep and what Ben can buy."

It never occurred to Medora to go and do the work herself, and no one expected her to do it. Even if she had gone, she would only have been in the way, and it would have been hard on her to see Ben Rand established in the house she had lived in so long. Medora had given Wayne a multitude of confused instructions, and a dozen neatly written lists, all contradicting each other.

It rained all Christmas day, but Ben and Wayne rode over from Avondale to have dinner at Indigo.

"I don't think I'll ever make head or tail of what she wants and what she doesn't want."

"Doesn't matter," Ben said. "If she changes her mind about any-thing, and decides she wants it, she can have it. I won't hang on to it." Ben had Amanda's amiability. He helped himself to more turkey. "This is a mighty good dinner, sister." He paused, looking out at the rain. "Whatever happened to Mr. Bijah's son? Does any-body have an inkling?"

"No," Dr. Rand said, "unless Louise knows."

"I don't, the lawyer doesn't. Medora doesn't." Louise wondered if Dr. Rand had ever had the slightest suspicion about Medora's hysterical attack. But then she hadn't let him come. Just before Louise had left for Indigo, Medora had said, "There's a book of Shelley's poems, bound in green. I want it. Jasper gave it to me."

Louise hadn't made any answer, except to murmur she would tell Wayne.

"I didn't want it," Medora had added. "But now—I think he's dead."

"What makes you think so?"

"No reason. I just do."

Now a little silence fell, and no one at the table spoke of Jasper any more, but Louise felt all of them thought of him. It was almost as if he had come back to their midst again, with one of those sudden and troubling appearances of his. The mention of his name seemed to have touched everyone here with melancholy, bringing to the older people an echo of past sorrow and lost love, and to the younger ones perhaps a foreboding of how tangled and unhappy love could be.

The rain stopped the next day, and Tom went to meet the boat, and came back with the two girls. Now the group had gathered, and the surface was smooth enough, but they were together only on the surface. Each one of them lived in his or her preoccupation. Watch-ing them that night, when the Christmas tree for the hands was lighted, and the presents given out, Louise thought about how little any of them guessed her own involvement. They supposed she was above and beyond any personal interest, and was watching them with benevolence, wishing them well. Yet she felt all their separate currents of feeling converging within her, and the shock of turmoil rocked her, like one of those eddies on the river where only the smoothness of the water gives a warning of the whirlpool.

It started raining again the next day, but Jim came over in the surrey to drive Maggie to his own house. It would have been easier and quicker to walk across the creek—the sandbar was still passable in spite of the rain, but Jim would be as formal as he could with this visit. Maggie was watching for him. "I'm glad nobody's here but you to see me go over there," she tied her bonnet strings with shaking fingers. Tom and Wayne and the Rand boys were out hunting. Alan, who hunted no more, had taken Amanda over to see Dr. and Mrs. Rand. Dolly had crept away to take a nap.

Maggie ran to the door before Jim could open it, and Louise watched the two of them get in the surrey and drive off. Lillybelle had gone to her cabin, and Louise was left alone. The fire hissed, and the wheezy clock struck. All the dogs had gone with the hunters, and only the cat, a battle-scarred tom, inadvertently named Daisy, slept by the hearth.

It was not an auspicious day to visit the Yankee's house. The rain came down, and the sodden earth looked blue-black. The trees, mostly bare, or clinging to draggled dun-colored leaves, were agloom with moss. Louise could imagine that other house, bare and cheerless outside and inside, not from lack of money, but from lack of any love or happiness or any standards of taste. The Yankee would probably be drinking, and undoubtedly mannerless, and poor Della —— And as a backdrop, the ruins of the Winsloe splendor.

Dolly crept into the quiet room. "Miss Lou, you all by yourself?"

"Everybody's gone off in different directions."

"Then can I talk to you?"

"Of course. What's the matter?" Louise turned from the window. Dolly's eyes were red. She dabbed at them with a small violet-scented handkerchief. "About—Tom."

"What about him?"

Dolly flung herself on the old sofa, and all the broken springs screamed. She buried her face in her hands, and her shoulders heaved. Louise came over and stroked the brilliant hair, then lifted her hand as if the glow of it had burned her. She could make out Dolly's muffled words "love" and "Tom." But she knew what Dolly meant to say.

"I'm sorry, child. I wish I could help you, but what can I do?"

Dolly shook her head, fumbled with her handkerchief and at last sat up. She was young enough and lovely enough to stand a crying fit, even if her eyes and nose were red.

"I oughtn't to have——" she gulped.

"Don't worry about anything you say to me." Louise was sorry for the girl, and Dolly's confidence in her touched her.

"I couldn't bear it if anybody——"

"Nobody'll know. I won't ever say a word," Louise assured her, hoping Wayne wouldn't know. Let him think Dolly had some chance with Tom. It might give Wayne time to wake up!

"What happened, Dolly? But don't say, if you'd rather not."

"Nothing." Dolly plaited her fingers together. "That's it, Miss Lou. Not a thing! And I'd counted so on this!"

"You mean this visit?"

Dolly nodded. "And now, I know it isn't any use."

"You know, child, you'd really be very unhappy stuck way out here. It isn't the sort of life you'd like. Someday you'll see that."

"I guess so—I guess maybe I will," she sighed, "But it isn't going to be a bit of fun."

"What isn't?"

"Getting through to it. To that someday or other."

It was a mistake, as Louise had found out, to dismiss a stupid person as an entire entity of stupidity. There were areas of sharpness even in the stupid, just as there were blind obtuse islands in the intelligent, and Dolly was aware of her own interests. She knew, for instance, how there was no hope of Tom. As a long acknowledged belle, she had learned a certain understanding of men, and felt, if she couldn't define it, how her beauty drew men to her at once, or not at all. It had not drawn Tom, and now she realized it never would. She sighed, got up, and murmured, "Thank you."

That "thank you," faint as a kitten's mew, and as pathetic, even if the kitten wants cream it can't have, moved Louise. "You don't owe me any thanks, Dolly."

"It sort of helped, saying it." Dolly trailed out of the room. She didn't want to confide in the other girls, and couldn't in her own mother, who would only point out the disadvantages of marrying

Tom anyway. Part of Dolly's sorrow came from the rebuff to her complacent vanity, but not all of it. Some of it was real, and Louise paid homage to it. How secretive they all were! Medora, Dolly, her own self! All except Maggie, who was simple, impulsive, and direct about her feelings. As Louise too had been at that age. Maggie had some likeness to that Louise of a long time ago, and Louise would have liked to be that girl again, honest, able to defy, but she never could be, or at least, she could never behave like her. She was trapped in her years and her dignity. She had imposed a surface on herself, but beneath it, her real nature woke and struggled.

It was dusk before Maggie came back. Jim didn't come in with her. Louise watched him turn from the door, his head bent. Maggie looked pale even in the firelight, but her face, with its strongly marked eyebrows and high cheekbones, showed all its strength. There was no time to talk to her, the others came trooping in, but without Wayne, who had gone on back to Avondale.

At supper, only Amanda and Alan seemed normal. Tom didn't talk much. Neither did Dolly. She was composed, but she didn't look at Tom, or say one word directly to him. Maggie talked too much, but disjointedly, and didn't listen to anyone else.

"You girls look tired," Alan said kindly. "Get a good night's rest."

After supper, Dolly went to bed. Maggie sat on a stool in front of the fire. Amanda sewed, and Tom and Alan sat at the chessboard. Louise slipped out of the house and started for Lillybelle's cabin. A visit to Lilly was soothing. Cornelius would be gently snoring in his corner by the fire, Jessie would be struggling with some schoolwork, and her children would be playing on the floor, or else already asleep, all together, in the bed piled high with faded patchwork quilts. Lillybelle would be "jes' a settin' "—her vast bulk overflowing the unsturdy old rocking chair she loved. In her soft voice, she would tell Louise all kinds of anecdotes, and stories about Indigo, and her ripe good humor and sweetness always had a tang to it, like the taste of wild honey.

Louise had only stepped into the yard when Maggie came rushing after her, panting, and clutched her arm. Maggie's face, wild and pale, swam out of the dark like a drowning face emerging from deep water.

"Oh, Aunt Lou," she gasped. "It was awful there. Just awful."

"I know." Louise put her arm around Maggie. "You could never live there." It was one thing for Maggie to put up with the shabbiness, even the hatefulness, of her own family life, the ill tempers, the grayed walls, the faded curtains and tarnished silver, but the Yankee's house had another sort of grimness.

"I couldn't stand it! I told Jim. But he knew anyhow. He won't be able to either, for long." She shook her loosened hair back from her face. "What can we do?"

"Wait."

"Women seem to spend all their time waiting. That's just what I don't like about being one—wait, wait——"

"But you'll have to, if you care——"

"I do. A lot. But those ruins—they reminded me—of all sorts of things. Of your saying about Mr. Bijah, 'He loved our Cause!' "

That had been at Mr. Bijah's funeral, and child as she had been, it had impressed Maggie. Louise remembered how Maggie's eyes had filled with tears. She tried to escape from the past but there were times when it held her. Louise wanted it to hold her, if it meant the honor and loyalty of the past.

"And those people," Maggie sighed, "they're on the other side. But not Jim, Aunt Lou."

"No, and it isn't fair to lump him with them. But you can't be part of them ever. So he'll have to work his way into belonging with you."

Maggie stood up straight. "He will. I just know he will." But her eyes searched the dark, as if she saw there all the dangers crowding to menace her. She shivered. "That other house—it loomed at me."

Thrust through with briers and saplings, the ghost glimmer of those long columns haunted Maggie. No matter how hard she tried to escape into the future, there were times when the past she had inherited would confront her with its ashes and its pride.

Dr. Rand was going to Natchez the next day, and he took the girls with him. Both Dolly and Maggie left in a mood different from the happy one they had brought with them. Wayne stayed on at Avondale, sorting and packing, and Louise kept to her habit of staying at Indigo until after New Year.

In the middle of the day, the rain stopped, and after dinner, Louise left the house to wander outdoors. The sky lowered, and mist clung to the ground and folded around the trees. No one was in sight. She walked on, taking the soggy path running along the fields, until she came to the field by the creek. Tom had cleared and planted it, and there were empty dark cotton stalks now instead of the waves of russet-rose sedge grass, but the big pecan tree still spread in its pride. At some distance was the cabin where Jessie held school. She didn't believe in long Christmas holidays, since school had to stop early in the spring so the children could work in the fields. Now the drone of voices made a buzzing like distant bees.

Louise looked towards the creek, and saw Jim wading across the sand bar. He waved to her, and came sloshing through the mud to her. "I had a notion you'd be out—I was looking for you." He smiled at her, though there was a look of strain on his face. "When other folks hole in—you wander."

"Will you come up to the house?"

"No, ma'am, I'd rather not. Could we—just talk?" He sighed, then said abruptly, "Did she—say anything?"

"Maggie? A little."

"But you knew. About us."

"I think everybody does."

"I guess so. Well, why not?" He sighed again, "Only——"

"What did your father say?"

"Nothing much." Jim kicked a clod of mud out of the path. "He's no help! He said, 'bring her here—we'll push over.' He knew just what I know. I couldn't take her there."

"That's out of the question." Louise could imagine the Yankee's saying it, with that leer of his when he thought people had no hope.

"We don't want anything he could give us. I told him that."

The whole situation seemed insoluble. Jim worked hard for what his father gave him, and where else could he work? He would have to go away, or stay where he was. In either choice, there seemed no way of his being able to marry Margaret Corwin.

"I reckon he sort of took things two ways. He said I was like the folks down here——" Jim glanced at Louise, and flushed.

"How?"

"A lot of big notions and no money."

It was characteristic of the Yankee. "There's a grain of truth there."

Jim gave a twisted grin. "Margaret kind of scared him, though. The way you do. You know—he's got a sneakin' respect for her. And for me, ever to get a girl like that to look at me."

He would be proud of Jim, but in a rage because his son had the taste to love her. It meant his son had gone over to the enemy, not for a little while, but forever.

"What about your mother?"

"Well, she just doesn't take to it. Margaret put herself out to be nice and all, but Mother—well, she mopes, and acts like I'd turned against her. It isn't so, but——"

"Because she felt you'd just come back to her, and now——"

Jim's blue eyes, warmly blue, had a haunted look. "There's a lot of things to face up to. On Margaret's side too. Her family won't like it."

They had tolerated Jim, but the Corwins wouldn't like it, since if he broke with his father his prospects of having money would fade.

Jim looked over the creek to the boundaries of his father's land. "Did it have a name—our—his place?"

"Yes, Heron's Row."

"I never heard it."

"Nobody calls it that any more. There used to be a lot of white and blue cranes on the creek. They nested near here. We used to call them fly-up-the-creek." The white ones shone silver against the matted green growth. The blue ones were shy, rarely seen.

"I don't see 'em around much—a white one, now and then."

"Your father shot them. The rest left."

Anger flashed over Jim's face, and blue lightning was in his eyes. At last he said, "Maybe they'll come back—one of these days. Right out here—everything sort of began for me——"

"Jim, do you remember a story I used to read to you? You made me read it over and over."

"Which one? I wanted you to read 'em all over and over."

"This was your favorite. About a child who wandered in the woods, and the queen of the Little People stole him."

"That one! I remember. She was dressed in green. I know pages of it still." He looked at her. "What made you think about it?"

"He stayed away a long time, and when at last he went back home, he was different."

"Because he couldn't forget that other place he'd seen." Jim smiled. "I guess I know what you're driving at—you think I'm that child."

"Aren't you?"

"And you acted like the queen of the Little People, taking me off and showing it to me."

"Maybe it was wrong for the child. There was some wickedness and mischief-making in the Little People."

"No! No, Miss Lou, it wasn't. He was a lot better off, seeing something and learning—and you know how it ended? With him setting off to find that other place again——"

"I wonder did he?"

"I think so, it was where he belonged. He knew it, and so do I. Think of it!" His face burned with joy and eagerness. "She cares. So I can lick the whole world!"

That night, Alan and Tom took up their chess game. They sat silent, without moving, throwing still shadows on the wall. The chessmen were carved ivory, and their elegance asked for tapestries as a background, and a marble fireplace, rather than the cracked plaster and uneven brick hearth of this room. But the logs burned high, lapping everyone and everything in a blend of flamelight. The big spotted dog snored comfortably, and wagged his tail if anyone moved or spoke. He was rather a stupid dog, but had an amiable naïveté. Daisy the cat slept too, his scarred face emphasizing his inherent cynicism. Amanda's begonias and geraniums and flowering cactus flourished in the windows, and Amanda was busy with a pile of mending. Louise was helping her with it, but Amanda worked quickly, intent on what she was doing, and every now and then Louise put down her work, and listened to the wind swooping around the corner of the house.

"Tom, I wish you'd get at that window," Amanda said. "It rattles so."

"Um——" Tom crouched low over the chessboard and didn't

look up. Louise envied him his concentrated interest. The dullness of what she was doing, and the silence in the room made her want to scream. She would have liked to be able to sail off on a broomstick, or on Daisy's arched back—that cat would make a good devil's familiar—and ride the wind, off to some wild, black revel. No wonder lonely old women, tired of meager lives, had tried to imagine they could escape from their lives and weave spells and gain evil power. Maybe the sense of freedom, and the reputation of wicked supernatural wisdom gave them an exhilaration worth what it cost.

The clock struck half past ten, and Amanda folded up her work and told Alan he was tired and ought to go to bed.

"One more move, and I'll come."

"You won't be ready to make one until some time next week. Come on."

He muttered she was bossy, and a she-dragon, and that he couldn't call his soul his own.

"I don't care about your ole soul, but I'm going to look after your health." Amanda wouldn't let Alan eat what he pleased. He had to eat what was good for him, and she had broken up his owlish habit of staying up half of the night. He was all Amanda's now, and Louise knew the old brother and sister relationship of herself and Alan had changed forever. But Amanda was good for him, and he needed her.

When Amanda had steered Alan out of the room, Louise opened a book, and Tom came and stood in front of the fire. He was watching her and she tried to make her face smooth and serene, and forced her eyes to travel down the page. She saw the letters clear and distinct, but not the words or what they meant.

"Mother——"

Louise put down the book. Tom stood there, balancing one of the chess pieces, a queen, on the palm of his hand. The queen was a rigid, intricate little figure, part of a long and complicated game. Tom had been a wisp of a child, a tanned string of a boy, and now he was all leanness, length, and muscle. He was not as handsome as Jim Sanders, or as defined in features and coloring as Wayne, yet he didn't seem to need any particular good looks or decided coloring. His eyes were not like his mother's in shape or setting, but like hers, they were expressive, and he had too, her attractive smile, and her distinction, that grace in movement, or in stillness.

"Mother," he began again, "why on earth did you get Dolly out here?"

"I didn't. It wasn't my scheme. Her heart was set on it."

"I just don't understand——"

"Understand what?"

"What you're up to——"

"What do you mean?"

"It was awkward, having her on my hands."

"On your hands! You got out of the way! You were anything but the perfect host."

"I was scared to be. That doesn't sound well, I know, but at least I can be frank with you, I hope. You'd have been the first to give me what for if I'd raised any false expectations."

"I feel sorry for Dolly."

"What makes you so softhearted about her? You ought to be on my side!"

"You know I always am."

"This time you seem to think I'm somehow to blame. You act like I ought to love her. And I can't if I don't, can I?"

"Don't then."

Tom had known Dolly too long, and no longer felt the impact of her beauty. A bare tree, a crinkled sand bar, an opening cotton boll could wake his admiration year after year, but Dolly bored him.

"That's what I want you to say, Mother. Back me up. It gave me a funny feeling, your seeming to want—because in the first place, you don't like her all that well, and another thing can you see her fitting in out here?"

"No, but I suppose I respected her for being willing to try——"

"I must say she isn't mercenary. A girl that pretty could do much better, and I hope she will. But you needn't worry, Mother. I would more, except she'll get over it. And soon, I bet. Dolly's no willow wearer."

Tom was right. Dolly would let herself find consolation. All a girl like her could do was to marry, and she would marry all the sooner since her vanity had been hurt.

231

"You won't have to worry about her long, Mother. Let her marry Wayne."

"Oh, no!" Louise spoke before she thought. The words were wrenched out of her. Then she realized Tom was studying her with a puzzled look. "She doesn't suit him any more than she does you!" She tried to make her voice steady."

"I wouldn't think so. But he does, and as long as he does——"

"Does he?" She leaned forward, feeling her face stiffen with strain.

"He seems to." Tom yawned, kissed his mother, and took the queen back to the table, then went out of the room before Louise knew he had gone. What had he seen or guessed? She got up, and paced back and forth. A force she hadn't been able to control had impelled her. She picked up the queen Tom had been holding. Stiff, fretted little figure, carved all over, part of a game, and put aside when the game was finished. This particular queen was on the sidelines now. Someone had made her move, and the move had been wrong, and she had played her part, and was out of the game.

On New Year's Eve, Wayne and Ben Rand came over to Indigo, and they all walked over to the little Negro church to hear the singing. The church was on a tree-covered knoll. Its narrow-pointed windows glowed through the branches, and the chorus of voices, led by Jessie, brought out all the depth and meaning of the old spirituals, with their solemn awareness of evil and their acknowledgment of the world's illusions.

Wayne was very quiet on the way over. Once, Louise thought, he would have had a thousand things he wanted to say to her. On the way back, he walked with her. The velvety night fell around them. They were ahead of the others and the lantern Tom was carrying sent its beam in front of them, and there their two shadows stalked, long and lean.

Jim loved music, but he hadn't been at the church, and Louise guessed he had gone to Natchez to see Maggie. Wayne was thinking about Jim and Maggie too, because he said, "You were wrong, Louise, to let Jim and Maggie meet."

"Wrong!" Her smoldering anger against Wayne, kept in leash for months, blazed out. "I didn't plan for——"

"What happened to happen? You should have guessed it might."

"Why?"

"Well, two people, at an inflammable age. I always thought it was a bad idea, having him around."

They were quarreling in such low voices that the others, some little distance behind them, and talking cheerfully together, couldn't hear.

"Stop being so wise after the event."

"I was before," Wayne pointed out.

"All right, all right, so something's come of it!"

"It surely has."

"Suppose it has? It's probably the best thing for them both!"

"Now, Louise——"

"Why not?" She was perfectly conscious that she was talking in direct contradiction to all her arguments with Maggie. Poor Maggie ought to hear her now!

"Jim Sanders and Margaret Corwin. Lord!"

"If there was something wrong about Jim himself I'd hate it. But there isn't. Not a thing!"

"He's all right, I guess. In himself. But a whole lot of things are wrong with the rest of it."

Family and background and pride and hate, the whole network of the past, to say nothing of practical considerations, such as what they would live on, or where they would live.

"Theorize all you want to, Louise, about two fine young people, when you get down to brass tacks——"

"I tell you, I mean to help and encourage them all I can!"

"You're being stubborn. I thought you'd be more realistic. But you have a blind spot about Jim."

She withdrew her arm from his, and started walking ahead. He caught her arm back again. "I'm sorry, Louise, I had no business saying that. I apologize."

"You should. Particularly as you are blind yourself these days." Oh, why had she said that? When for months she had never said a word! It sounded immature, and worse. They thought she was serene and above their problems, wise and dispassionate. They didn't know!

233

They must never know. "I'm sorry, Wayne. I shouldn't have said that."

"You needn't be sorry. Only I'm not blind. I know Dolly's head over ears in love with Tom."

There was a relief in having the long silence ended. This was like the moment when the poised storm breaks, or when the drawn battle lines sound the signal for the attack. It would be worse, but for a moment at least there was a lessening of tension.

"It isn't only that," she tried to choose her words carefully, and weigh each one, but the constricting anger she felt made them take fire. "You're blind about her! Can't you see she's a shallow, trivial little thing? All she really cares about is her looks—and her clothes!"

"Why, I thought you were fond of her!" Wayne's voice was blank with amazement.

"I am," Louise struggled to sound calm, "but I know what she's like!"

Couldn't Wayne see it for himself? He thought her stupidity un-worldliness, and her little vanities youth and innocence.

"Then if that's what you think, why would you want her to marry Tom?"

"What makes you think I do?" She stopped and tried to read his face, but it was only a blur in the dark.

"It looks like it. You invited her here. You threw them together."

She had. Tom had seen it. Wayne saw it.

"I was sorry for her." And she had been, for a moment, when she had found Dolly's letters to Tom. But not now.

"Well, I am too," Wayne sighed. "And for myself."

They neither of them spoke any more for the rest of the way back. Everything had been said. He was in the grip of an obsession, and so was she! It was like a snake, coiling its folds around her. A mottled, hidden snake, huddled up invisible, then striking. She hated Wayne and she hated Dolly. Most of all she hated herself, and the snake's fangs struck sharp in her heart. The lantern light threw her shadow and Wayne's clear and unblended, black and hollow.

Chapter Fifteen

"DEARLY Beloved, we are joined——" The young minister's full voice rolled through the crowded church. The younger ladies sighed, and looked not only at the bride and groom but at him. It was the last day of June, scintillating with heat and light. Candles glowed, and so did flowers, the real ones, and the ones trimming hats and bonnets. Louise thought Dolly looked rather like a candle, all white, crowned with ruddy gold.

From her place in one of the front pews, Louise looked at the bride, then looked around the church. Outwardly, nothing could be more conventional or correct than the wedding. Dolly and her mother had planned every detail with the greatest care, and no one could find any fault with the music, the decorations of the church, the beauty of the bride and the precision of the bridesmaids, and the becomingness of their hats and dresses. Louise felt no fault could be found with her own outward composure.

Her cousin Ellen had sent her a Paris dress. It was thin and soft, a misty gray, banded with lace, and when Louise had taken her place, her friends and neighbors had murmured their admiration. Louise had let Miss Annie Curtis inveigle her into buying a hat to match the art and subtlety of the dress. Feeling guilty because the hat was too expensive, and reckless because she had thrown prudence to the winds, Louise was wearing it. It was a pale gray straw, trimmed with green velvet ribbons and ears of pale green wheat, and though it didn't make her happier, it stiffened her spine to know she was looking her best.

No one must think, no one must guess—the people gathered here must see her as the devoted older friend of the young couple, doing honor to their wedding. If a hectic rose color burned in her cheeks, and her eyes sparkled with a dark brilliance, everyone aware of

235

her would think she was pleased and excited, and never suspect what a fierce fever had been darting and twisting through her very bones.

Sometimes, during these last months, Louise had wondered why her bones and nerves didn't turn into charred ashes, and let her drop into a powdery heap, but nothing happened to her, nothing at all, and here she was, with an air of friend and spectator, watching Wayne Winsloe take Dorothea Lydell for his wedded wife. For a long time Louise had schooled herself, careful of her every word, look and inflection. She had prepared herself for the inevitability of the wedding, and the actual event, taking place before her eyes, was an emotional anticlimax. Perhaps she had felt too much too long, and was no longer able to feel any more. And she knew she was not the only person here with something to hide.

Less, considerably less than a year ago, the bride had been in love with the best man. Maybe Dolly had forgotten that. Louise hoped so. Dolly had accepted Wayne. Louise wondered if Dolly felt any regrets, or if she was wishing now that it was Tom slipping the ring on her finger instead of Wayne. Dolly must never admit it, never even feel it.

Milly Dale was probably wondering if she would ever marry, or if she was destined to be an old maid. Maggie, adjusting the bride's train, would certainly be thinking about the thorny wanderings of her own love affair. Poor Maggie looked thin and pale, and had lost her old high spirits. She seemed much older than she was as she tried to adjust herself to waiting.

One day in the spring, when Louise had gone to Indigo, Jim had come to see her. Her first look at him had told her a crisis was at hand.

"I'm clearing out," he had told her, without preliminaries.

"Do you mean you are going away?"

"Not too far away, Miss Lou."

"But why? What's happened?"

"I tried to talk to—my father again. About getting married. I told him I'd have to go somewhere to make a living. He couldn't see why I couldn't stay where I was."

"You had trouble with him last fall, about the store."

"And he gave in, at least part of the way. And let me have some say-so."

That in itself had showed how much the Yankee wanted to keep Jim.

"I told him Maggie and I didn't want to live in the same house—all together. So, he even went so far as to say he'd build a house for us——"

"Would that work?"

"How could it, Miss Lou? With us right there, under his thumb. I thanked him, though—but I told him that wasn't the wedding present I wanted—I told him I wanted him to do something about your mortgage."

Louise must have turned pale because Jim had said quickly, "Don't think he would!"

"Oh, I know that. But your asking——"

"I reckon it did more harm than good, Miss Lou. He went off on a rare——" Jim had run his hand across his eyes, as if he were trying to erase the scene from his mind. "The upshot of it all is I've got to get out of there."

"But where can you go?"

"Oh, I'll hang around. I wouldn't go way off from Margaret—I couldn't. You know Elsinore?"

"I've heard of it. It just about beyond everywhere."

"Across the Buffalo, and back. Jack Rand told me Mr. Ferris fell off his horse and broke his hip, and he doesn't know how long he'll be laid up. Maybe years. Even maybe always. He's all by himself out there, so he'll need an overseer. I told Jack to tell him I was looking."

Jim had gone and buried himself at Elsinore. He worked hard, never came to town, and could only see Maggie at long intervals, when she could make her way out to Indigo and he could struggle through the woods and swamps and meet her there. Not only that, the Corwins had turned against Jim. In vain, Louise had tried to placate them, pointing out to them that Jim had only tried to do what he felt was right.

"It's impossible, Lou," Lizzie Corwin had screeched. "That boy hasn't a picayune now, and no prospects at all! Overseer in that mud-hole!" She had added, "And all of us are furious with Alan and Amanda for letting Maggie meet him at Indigo. It's disgraceful!"

"You mustn't say that, Lizzie. I won't put up with it. As if Alan, or Amanda either, would abet anything disgraceful!"

Maggie's father had come over and apologized, and Lizzie had said she didn't quite mean that, but a coolness had grown up between Louise and the older Corwin women. So now Maggie, here at Dolly's wedding, had to put up with waiting and waiting for her own. Louise could guess Maggie's feelings, but not Wayne's. He looked solemn. Did he have any apprehensions about Dolly's rather placid acceptance and wonder if she still cared for Tom? Did he have any faint hesitations on his own account? If he did, no one must know that, either.

It was done now, and bride and groom went down the aisle. Dolly's lace and illusion brushed Louise's arm, and Louise caught the faint scent of her flowers. Tom glanced at his mother as he came by, and Louise smiled at him. He must never think—— But she was able to disguise herself and keep up adequate pretenses. But not hide from herself, not any more. At first, she had, and that was one reason why she had hated herself. She had not wanted to admit the nature of her feeling for Wayne and her hatred of Dolly as a rival. It was beneath her dignity. What had she wanted? She hardly knew. Wayne was ten, almost eleven years younger than she was, and love, or marriage between them would be unsuitable. Love, she told herself, was over for her when Tom had died. Yet unexpected, unbidden, stealing her content, love had come. Without reason, and without hope. She had hated Wayne because he didn't respond, and didn't see.

All hatred was over now. It was right and natural for Dolly's youth to draw him. As for hating her, a child Louise had watched grow up, who didn't suspect, who trusted her, Louise could not hate her any more. As her hate ebbed away, so did the bitterness of her self-contempt, and all its shame and anger. She no longer despised her own folly, or even called it folly, knowing how love is seldom harnessed by suitability or convention. She admitted her feeling for Wayne was natural too. He was not of her generation, but he was not of Tom and Dolly's and Maggie's generation either.

238

Even in that very first glimpse she had had of him, when she had said to Tom, "This isn't one of the Yankee's friends, this is one of ours," there had been a kind of shock or recognition. What she had seen, from the first, was that Wayne belonged to the pattern of the men of her young days. In his spirit, in his love of largeness and lavishness, in his eagerness, he was like the young men before and during the early days of the war. Her heart held an image, and he filled it.

Now she was left to her loneliness again, and Louise saw herself like some piece of land submerged for a long time under the dark current of the river at flood height. When the flood recedes, there is blankness and bleakness, and a bedraggled dishevelment. Yet the river has brought the gift of a new and richer layer of soil. So there was something left to cherish in this unruly emotion of hers. It had given her, in her mature years, a resurgence of youth and the sensations of youth. It was better to struggle with a tumult of feeling, better to be caught into life again, than not to be able to feel anything more at all. She had paid for it, was paying for it, but it had brought with it a capacity for new growth.

That renewal of life must have showed in her face, though perhaps it was the Paris dress and the too expensive hat, because Colonel Duel, coming down the aisle, muttering with fury over his stubbed toe, and blaming his wife, paused, ceased groaning, and seized Louise's hand. He actually began to smile. "How you bloom, Miss Lou." Other people noticed too. At the reception, Mrs. Corwin, greedily eating cakes and reaching for more, shrilled, "I must say, Lou, people with plain dull coloring like yours do wear well. Everybody goes on so about Dolly's hair and complexion. Won't last. I could have showed you a complexion—why, talk about brilliance——" And she went on to the triumphs of her youth. Nobody listened. The triumphs sounded implausible. Wayne had rather aptly described Mrs. Corwin as having eye of newt and hair of bat.

"That family," somebody was muttering. "Why the Don Miguel they're so proud of was nothing but a slave trader!"

"Oh, no, Charlotte, not a slave trader. A pirate, but NOT a slave trader."

Louise found herself able to kiss Dolly and wish her well, and mean what she was saying. Wayne took both of Louise's hands. "How elegant you are!"

"To do you honor," she smiled. He kissed her. The only time she had ever kissed him was on his wedding day. At last the reception was over, and people began to eddy away from the Lydells' house. Cousin Sophie drove Louise and Medora home. "Wayne must be doing very well to afford a wife."

"He's had a lucky streak lately," Louise said, not going into any details.

"Then, too"—Medora pursed up her mouth a little—"he has a reckless streak."

Louise glanced at her. Medora was very neat, extremely precise in all her ways. The house had been in an uproar as Medora had dressed for the wedding because one of her long bone hairpins was missing, and she was convinced she couldn't fix her hair without the requisite number. At last the missing hairpin had been found behind the back leg of the bureau, and had been placed in Medora's smooth knot. Louise wanted to say to her, "You were once reckless too."

The house was quiet in the twilight. Medora went upstairs to take off her best dress and hat, but Louise, careless of hers, sank down in a chair on the gallery, and flung the too expensive hat on another chair. Her clothes had played their part and so had she. Lazarus was walking up and down the gallery railing, croaking to himself. Then he became vociferous, in Spanish. Cap'n Luke had told Louise how he had bought Lazarus from a sailor in Panama, and Lazarus was no doubt uttering foul oaths picked up in some dive in a tropic seaport. Perhaps the quick-falling dark, the heat, and the tangle of vines around him gave the parrot some obscure sense of other homes.

Cap'n Luke came out. "He botherin' you, ma'am?"

"Oh, no. If he's swearing, let him swear."

The burst of violence from Lazarus was somehow a relief to her own pent-up feelings.

After supper, Maggie came over. "I feel let down," she said, "but it's a relief to get out of all those frills."

"Dolly does run to fluff. Plainer lines suit you better, but you looked very pretty."

"I was feeling sorry for myself, Aunt Lou. And still am."

"What do you hear from Jim?"

"He's still stuck out there in the swamp. And there he'll stay I suppose until Mr. Ferris dies or gets well. Or until something happens. And maybe nothing ever will." Maggie sighed and ran her fingers through her hair. "He wrote he'd a touch of malaria, and I know he's yellow and skinny and run down. I wish I was out there with him."

"Do you think you could stand it?"

"You stood Indigo, Aunt Lou."

"But Elsinore is swampier and further away. There're no near neighbors at all. Good or bad."

"All the same, I'd marry him and go there tomorrow. Only I don't want to be another burden for him."

Jim was not really making a living, and could hardly support a wife. "But I'm glad Jim broke with his father."

"It was bound to happen."

"I wasn't the only cause. There're lot of bones of contention between them. But now his mother hates me——"

"She doesn't like me either any more."

"Why? Why you?"

"Because you met Jim, because she thinks I was the original cause of your meeting him." Louise, on her last stay at Indigo, had been wandering near the creek, and Della, knowing her habits, had waited for her there. Della had blamed Louise, or at least blame had been lurking in what she said. "Just when Jim came back, he met up with that young lady."

The unfriendliness in Della's tone, the note of sharpness amazed Louise. She felt as if a rabbit had turned and bitten her. "Now he's gone off. I ought to of seen it from way back."

Louise could understand Della's resentment, almost sympathize with it. Della had turned and gone off, and Louise had watched her out of sight. Where Louise had been standing, the new leaves and branches of willow, the tangle of briers had flared in a glaze of green fire. A shy crane, with the sheen and elusiveness of quicksilver, had been wading in the creek. Spring itself had been responsible for Jim's almost ruthless decision to seek a place of his own. Like the crane, he wanted to build a nest.

Maggie sat in the lamplight, her changeable eyes searching the shadows beyond the circle of light. "Families are just horrid."

"Not all families."

"Well, not yours. But Jim's. And mine too. Do you think my grandmother and my Aunt Liz ever let up harping on how that man would be my children's grandfather? They know how I hate that idea!"

"But it's something you have to take into your calculations, Margaret. A fact. And you have to decide whether you can stand it or not."

"Oh, I see it, all right! Aunt Lou, how much do you think blood and family matter?"

"How can anybody tell exactly? There are lots of new things being found out about the laws of inheritance. But that's science, and doesn't have anything much to do with family in the sense your aunt and grandmother mean. In a generation or so, the Sanders clan will be 'family' here in Natchez. Less, if you marry Jim and his father ups and dies."

There would be whispers, and mutterings, as there were about the source of Don Miguel de Saldes' fortune, ancestor of the family-proud Massingales.

"Suppose my children turned out like the Yankee!"

"It isn't likely. Jim comes of sound enough stock, I should think. And his mother's nice. She's never had a chance. And his father would have been better if he had stayed where he belonged. People's sins don't stay static. You either weed them out, or they grow and take you over. He gathered up the spoils of war, and grew greedier. We hated him for grabbing. He hated us for hating him. Any number of great names have begun by battening off of the carcass of the enemy."

"He could have a coat of arms with a buzzard on it," Maggie said. "Today I couldn't help envying Dolly and Wayne. Everything's so smooth for them."

"It hasn't been particularly smooth for Dolly."

"You mean that fancy she had for Tom? She's over it. She has those, they don't last."

"She has to be over it now."

"The wedding looked so right and usual and snug! And everybody showered blessings. They won't on Jim and me."

"Maybe someday you and Jim will be happier than Dolly and Wayne."

"Are you encouraging me, Aunt Lou?"

"I couldn't at first. You had to go your own way."

"But since I'm going it—going, going, gone——"

"You still have to go it alone, child."

"But having you back me up is something. Someone to talk to——"

"You don't need anybody. Headstrong as you are."

"Am I? Just because I think loving someone is the most important thing there is?"

"I think it's the most important thing, too. But it isn't meant for wishy-washy people, only for strong people."

Maggie sighed. "If only I could make a nice shiny new world, without past and families and all the old tangles to get in the way!"

Louise looked at Maggie's face, thinner than it had been, sharpened by the conflict within her, yet unlined and unmarred, vivid in coloring, interesting in its irregularities. The rush and vigor of youth, faded soon enough. You had to seize happiness, if you could, when you were young, and felt the blind, relentless push to grab life. It not only whirled by, but you lost the sharp ruthlessness, you faltered and wavered, and all the old tangle caught up with you and smothered you.

When Dolly and Wayne came back from their honeymoon, they lived with Dolly's parents in the pretty, neat little house at the corner, not a block away from Louise. She went to see Dolly, and admired all the presents, and listened to Mrs. Lydell saying how nice it was to have Wayne and Dolly under her roof. "I don't want to lose my little girl."

Louise doubted if Wayne liked the arrangement. She didn't mention her doubts, though when she went out to Indigo early in September, Tom reinforced them.

"I'd think Wayne would feel mighty cooped up there with all of them."

Louise and Tom and Alan and Amanda were sitting on the gallery, and Louise thought it was just such an evening as it had been a year ago when they had all gone on the moonlight picnic. Tom was coiled on the gallery railing, and lounging against one of the gallery posts in that seemingly boneless way he had of disposing himself.

"If you had the face of a snake, you'd look like one," Louise told him. "I saw Dolly the other day. I think she has an eye on that new house they're building two blocks down the street."

Tom said he'd noticed it going up when he was last in town, and that an ugly new thing was more glaringly ugly than an ugly old thing.

"What's it like?" Amanda asked. She hadn't been in town for a long time.

"It's fretted with fretwork, and it has a pointed gable, with a glass window in it, and the window gives the effect of one eye walling down at you," Louise described it, "but Dolly's taken with it."

Amanda wanted to know if Wayne could afford to buy it.

"He's doing well. Then he doesn't have to help his family any more. His father has a position, and so does his brother, and his two sisters are married, and to rather prosperous men."

"That's good," Alan said. "Wayne was always worrying about them. And helping them out. Of course it was only right for him to——"

"When are you going to find a wife, Tom?" Amanda wanted to know.

"We'll have to get the mortgage off of all our necks before I go drape a wife around mine. Mother, you must go look at the cotton in the field by the creek. It's a good stand."

Tom and Alan worked and struggled, and from across the creek the hostility beat stronger than ever. Time was creeping on, closer and closer to the day when the mortgage would be due. They tried to put it out of their minds, but they all thought about it. It shadowed all their hours, and darkened all their plans.

One afternoon, when Louise was back in Natchez, and on her own gallery, armed with a watering can to sprinkle her ferns and begonias, Wayne came up the lawn. She didn't see him come, she only heard him say, "You're a jealous critter, Louise."

She started and turned, but he was smiling. "For years you've been carrying on a grim, undeclared contest with Amanda, trying to outshine her in the matter of potted plants."

"Of course I have, and whenever I come back from Indigo, I struggle wildly with mine. Sit down, and tell me things."

"I have a hack waiting at the gate. I want you to come with me. I have something to show you."

"What is it?"

"A house."

'What house?"

"One I've bought."

"Good heavens, Wayne! Where is it? What's it like?"

"Come along, you know it. But come look at it again."

Louise, full of questions and curiosity, and some uneasiness, put down the watering can, and went with him.

"It's the Fennell place," Wayne told her, putting her in the hack. "Don't you like it?"

"I've always loved it. You mean you've already bought it?"

"It's a bargain, and I've wanted it ever since I first saw it."

It was like Wayne to keep his longing for that particular house a secret. "Does Dolly like it?"

"I hope she will."

"Haven't you told her you've bought it?"

"I haven't had a chance. I've just come from the office."

"But——" Louise didn't finish her thoughts aloud. Dolly didn't know, and he should have told her first, taken her through it before he took anyone else.

Wayne gave Louise a quick look. "I'll tell her right off. But I wanted you to come gloat with me. It'll give me confidence, and make me sure I did the right thing."

"But aren't you sure?"

"Certain."

"Then you don't need bolstering. You never do when you pounce on your canaries and swallow them. Because your pouncings are the outwards result of some long silent processes within your head."

He laughed and admitted it. "But this is a rather large canary, and I want to show it off to you and have you tell me how beautiful it is."

"Won't Dolly?"

"She's bound to, because it is. And I know she wants a house, so when I had some luck, I made up my mind."

"Shouldn't you have consulted her first?"

"I was afraid someone might see what I see and snatch it first."

"Oh, Wayne, it's been on sale for years!"

"To tell the truth, Louise, Dolly rather had an eye on the house they're building down the street. It's for sale too."

"I think it's ugly." Louise could understand how Wayne would loathe it as much as she did. "But it's in style."

"What a style! So, if I whisk Dolly into the Fennell place, quick, and show her——"

Wayne might convince Dolly how much more beautiful an old Natchez mansion was, but Louise wondered if Dolly would be reconciled to the loss of the other's shiny newness. The Fennell house was on the edge of town.

"It isn't really far," Wayne argued, as they turned in the gate. It was not as convenient, though, and it was shabby.

It had been raining and the late sun glittered on wet leaves. Live oaks arched their branches, and there was a tangle of a garden on one side. Louise and Wayne got out of the hack, and as Wayne unlocked the door, they could catch the scent of the boxwood hedges, neglected and grown wild, but high and flourishing.

"I'd forgotten how lovely it all was," Louise murmured. "You could make something out of this!" She forgot Dolly, carried away as she was by the charm of the place. The neglected garden was full of richness, only waiting to be pruned and cared for again. The little summerhouse was tottery, but it had an enchanting peaked roof, and there was a sundial.

Wayne opened the door. "Look at the staircase. Look at the moldings. Look at the proportions of the rooms."

Louise looked. "Oh, I'm as bad as you are. To restore it, to bring it to life the way it ought to be——"

"Instead of letting it fall to pieces and go to waste, that's what I think."

Dolly's interests receded as they wandered upstairs and down, talking, planning, until almost dusk. Then Wayne drove Louise home, and went to break the news to Dolly.

Dolly came to see Louise the next day at teatime, the very fringes of her trousseau parasol quivering with her indignation. She refused the tea Louise offered her, but took one cookie, nibbling on it with quick, angry little bites. "Wayne bought a house! That old Fennell place, and I wanted a nice new one, not that falling down thing!"

Maggie was on hand too, listening, and glancing first at Dolly, then at Louise. "It won't fall down, Dolly. It'll last forever."

"That's worse, then!"

"It's a beautiful place," Louise tried to soothe her. "It needs some fixing up, but your pretty things will really show off in it."

"I wanted a nice modern house, not an old-timey one."

"The one you liked is a monster," Maggie said.

"Yes, Dolly," Louise hurried on, "when it gets old and styles change you wouldn't like it a bit. This place will always be worth having. As time goes on it'll be all the more rare and valuable."

"I don't care," Dolly pouted. "Wayne makes me so mad, buying it without telling me!"

"He should have told you, but men just don't know how women feel about things like that, and he counted on your taste." Dolly didn't have any taste, but she didn't know that. Just as nobody ever thought he or she lacked a sense of humor.

"Mamma says I ought to give in and be nice now it's done, but I'm not going to pretend to like it when I don't."

"But you will like it, I believe. And everybody will be so glad for you and Wayne to be living in it." Dolly liked to be admired, to feel herself an integral part of a group.

"You're lucky to have it," Maggie said briskly. "Stop fuming and fussing."

"Wayne's just got a lot of foolish notions about old-times and old things." But when Dolly left in a whirl of her elaborate petticoats,

247

her anger was somewhat appeased. When she had gone, Maggie gave Louise a knowing smile.

"Wayne told you about it first, didn't he?"

"Ssh! Don't you ever breathe——"

"Oh, I know better! And he's smart enough and you're smart enough to keep her from figuring that out." Maggie's eyes followed the blob of Dolly's parasol out of sight. "It won't be so smooth for them, Aunt Lou. They'll never see eye to eye about anything."

"Oh, I don't know. Wayne just had one of his quiet emotional frenzies."

"Then he gets his way. Like he had his way about marrying Dolly. The house'll wear better."

"Don't say things like that, Margaret."

"I won't. Except to you. You would have thought he would have seen how she was going to get on his nerves."

"Now, Margaret."

Wayne had known, must have known that the gap between Dolly's nature and his own could never be crossed, but now Louise could understand his craving for Dolly's youth, and how the particular quality of her beauty had lured him, with its combination of a crystalline, almost ethereal freshness and its suggestion of fire and ardor. That came from the color of her hair, and not from the color of her soul. Dolly was the most conventional of creatures.

Dolly and Wayne moved into the house he had bought, and Dolly, if she still grumbled, at least did her best to keep the place in order, and took pride in her housekeeping and in her pretty things. After they had moved, Louise did not see them so often, and she would not let Wayne lure her into discussing this piece of furniture, or that color scheme. When he asked her advice, she always told him to consult Dolly, and tried not to express her own opinions. Wayne and Dolly had gone a little out of the orbit of her every day life, and she found it a relief not to be tempted to sympathize with Wayne's tastes, and not to listen and have to soothe Dolly's dissatisfactions.

That winter, Louise was taken up with Maggie's emotional turmoil. One cold rainy day, Maggie came flying in, without her coat. Her cheeks were stinging with color, her eyes were wildly shining with tears and excitement. Jim had written to her, Mr. Ferris had written to her, but she was too breathless to say any more at first. She wandered around restlessly, clutching the letters.

"What did they say, child? Is Jim all right?"

Maggie nodded, and Louise had to wait until Maggie could talk with coherence. "Jim's all right—only I don't know what to do! I do know what to do. Marry Jim. The only question is, when?"

"I should think when he can take care of you."

"When'll that be?"

"What did Mr. Ferris say?"

"Here, read it, Aunt Lou. He says if Jim and I want to get married, he'd be glad to have me out there."

Louise read the letter. "He seems very nice, and kind."

"I could keep house, and be some help."

"You'd find it hard work. It's very primitive."

"Oh, Jim doesn't mince matters. He says it is. And he says he has nothing to offer."

"It's an existence, I suppose. But if Mr. Ferris gets well, he wouldn't need Jim, then what?" Louise doubted if Mr. Ferris would get well, he was an old man, but it was a possibility to be considered.

"We'd go somewhere. Do something. At least we'd be together, not wasting our lives away from each other."

"What are you going to do, Margaret?"

"Get married. As soon as we can get things fixed up!"

Louise had never seen Elsinore. She had met Mr. Ferris once. When? At the barbecue, the one after the election. Everybody had been there.

"After all, Aunt Lou. You went to Indigo to live."

"Getting married's more irrevocable."

"Aunt Lou, could we be married at Indigo? You know what it would be like at home! They'll be so mad at me. But if you don't want us to be married at Indigo, we'll just go off and get married——"

Louise didn't argue with Maggie any more. It was no use, and then in all of Maggie's headlong impatience she heard the echoes of her own youth.

When Maggie told her family she was going to marry Jim and go live at Elsinore, the Corwins raged. Her three sisters, married and living away, wrote her angry letters. Her Aunt Lydia who had married prosperously, was cold, but sent her an elaborate punch bowl. Maggie laughed and said it was just the thing for the elegant parties she would be giving at Elsinore. Her brothers were too young to do anything but gawp. Bella Corwin wept and moaned, her Aunt Liz snapped and scolded, and Ole Mrs. Corwin, with her adder's fork of a tongue, stirred up a witches brew of maledictions and prognostications of ill. Her father was passively sad about it all, but agreed to come to the wedding at Indigo.

Louise, with Alan's and Amanda's agreement, had decided to have the wedding there. Since they couldn't stop Maggie, they might as well make what cheer for her they could. The ceremony took place on a gusty March day, harsh with spatterings of rain and rattlings of branches. There was nothing auspicious about it, in spite of Louise's attempts to decorate the house and Amanda's fine wedding cake. There were only a few people, and there were great gaps in the ranks of the families involved. Maggie's father came, looking doleful, and glancing around nervously, as if he feared the reproaches of his womenfolk. They stayed away. The Yankee of course would never show his face at Indigo, but Della came, and Persia grinned from the doorway. Louise was glad to see Persia and made her welcome. Jim must have persuaded Della to come. She wore the black silk dress Jim had given her. Louise knew Della probably had nothing else to wear, but its funereal blackness was like an ill omen. So were Della's tears. She felt she had lost Jim, but she very evidently wanted to be friends with Louise, and Louise, understanding her timidity, met her more than half way, and took her back under her wing.

"This is all so bleak," Louise whispered to Tom, but when she looked at Maggie and Jim, she took heart. The earnestness of Jim's love showed in his face, and in his glowing, brilliantly blue eyes. Louise hadn't seen him lately, and his good looks impressed her more than ever. He was no longer a boy, he had become a man. He had a new assurance, but in the depths of his eyes was that haunting expression, haunting, appealing, asking, that had always melted her heart. He had, she felt, more to give Maggie than the warmth of an affection-hungry nature. He would be grateful to her for loving him. More than that, he would fight for her, and not only to win her, but after. He was able enough and young enough to feel he could conquer the world for her. Maybe he could.

Since Ole Mrs. Corwin had declared that the family's stored array of rotting lace and yellowed satin would be desecrated by Maggie's wearing any scrap of it at the sort of marriage she was making, Maggie was using Louise's wedding dress and veil.

"I won't change or alter anything at all," Maggie had said. Her eyes had filled with tears. "I can't get over your offering it to me. It means a lot to me, Aunt Lou, your letting me wear it."

There Maggie stood in the wide-skirted, tight-waisted fashion of nearly thirty years ago. A lovely fashion, Louise thought, giving a pretty woman the look of a many-petaled flower. Watching Maggie pledging herself to uncertainties and difficulties, Louise saw herself as a bride, and her own reckless ardor as she had plunged into her own marriage. Her memory of Tom as he had been was as clear as if he was standing where Jim was standing now. The others, too, thronged before her, her sisters, and her cousins, as they had been, young and vivid and daring. They were dead or scattered. Louise looked at Alan, and wondered if he remembered too. He was the only person here who could recall her wedding day, and how for a little moment they had been gathered together in the thunderous sunset of the brilliant morning they had known, and with sorrows and hazards crowding ahead of them.

Later, Louise watched Jim and Maggie drive off into the bluster of rain. Her mind was full of forebodings, and she wondered if she had been to blame in drawing Jim into their midst. As she thought of Maggie's wedding, she thought too of one that had never taken place. Medora's. No, Maggie, in her rashness, was right, as she herself had been right. Maggie, like herself, was strong enough to abide by her impulses, and feel no regrets. As for Jim, the changeling child, a dream, a spell was imprinted on him forever. He had to go and find the "other place" his soul craved, and love was the gateway to its magic.

Chapter Sixteen

The Natchez house was large and lonely and silent without the young people. "I'm glad when Cap'n Luke brings Lazarus back, to chuckle and swear and sing," Louise told Medora. The place was too quiet.

Louise kept to her usual habits and gathered her old friends around her, but she missed Tom, and Maggie, and perhaps she missed Wayne most of all. Sometimes she caught herself about to tell some everyday incident with a queer or amusing angle, then had to keep it to herself, or wait until she wrote to Alan, or saw him. There was no one to listen or to find it as funny as she did. She and Alan and Wayne laughed at the same things. Or else she found herself needing advice about some business detail, something not important enough to write out to Tom or Alan. She had always discussed things like that with Wayne. She didn't go to his house often. Dolly loved card parties, and had a younger group of friends.

Louise saw Wayne at church, and he always lingered on the church steps with her, where they had a brief and interrupted talk about what they had been reading.

"Those were the days," he said to her once. "When I stayed at your house, and you and I toasted our toes or fanned our brows and talked and talked and talked."

What could he say to Dolly? He wasn't interested in her fancy work or her card parties, and she couldn't undertand the intricacies of the cotton market. But Wayne worked hard, took an interest in refurbishing his house and his garden, and by all accounts was a good husband. By July, he had a new interest. He became the father of a daughter. Louise gave little Dorothea a silver mug and six silver coffee spoons, said all the right things to her and about her,

252

and went to church to the christening, and afterward the house, where Wayne and Dolly offered wine and cake to their friends, and the nurse took charge of the squirming scrap of a baby, lost in a cascade of featherstitching, insertion, tucking, beading, and ribbons.

Wayne had accomplished wonders already with the old house. The garden was clipped and pruned and showed its graceful plan. Inside, there was not much furniture, but Wayne had found a mirrored pier table for the double parlors, and there were a few good chairs and tables and a perfect little sofa. There was space and dignity without austerity, and Louise felt the house was living up to all its promise.

"It's one of my favorite houses," Louise said to Dolly.

"It's a barn," Dolly said.

"You'll collect things little by little. Would you like one of my love seats for that corner?"

"That would be nice, Miss Lou." Dolly thanked her without any real enthusiasm. "None of the furniture Wayne buys is a bit in style."

"It's old Natchez style, it suits the house."

Wayne had gone across the room to speak to some of the other guests, and Dolly looked after him frowning. "Wayne's doing well, but everything's so uncertain. He'll buy things and then say now we've got to go easy. I just never know where I stand."

"So it must be hard sometimes for you to know just how to manage."

"Oh, it is, Miss Lou. I wish Wayne had some kind of more steady sort of work. Not this seesaw kind of thing. It's like being married to a gambling man!"

Louise didn't say, "You are." She murmured she was sure Wayne would do well in the long run.

"How can I tell? And now we have a child."

Wayne wandered back to Louise, and someone engaged Dolly's attention. He asked Louise how Maggie was getting on.

"We write long letters to each other. She says it's wild and lonely, and that the hands are fresh out of the heart of Africa, but she rides

253

a good deal, and she and Jim read and study at night. She's always asking me to send her books and magazines."

"I met Mr. Ferris," Wayne said, "the summer before the election. He seems a nice kind of fella."

"He's been very kind to Jim and Maggie. And she isn't in the way, because having her to run the house makes him more comfortable."

"I should think so, laid up as he is. Maggie's efficient."

"And never spoiled at home. Wayne, I know you think her marrying Jim was a bad thing——"

"And I'm not as sure as I was about it being so bad. Anyway, I admire them both for going ahead——"

"I believe they have a very good chance of being happy."

"Maybe," Wayne conceded. "I despise the Corwin women for the way they've acted. They didn't put their foot down when Jim first started coming, because they thought he was well off. For all their big talk about old values and old traditions being violated, they'd swallow the Yankee himself if they could, for his money!"

"So you caught on to that! Is that why I don't see any of them here today?"

"I told Dolly I wouldn't have any of 'em in my house."

Louise said she wished she could keep them out of hers. "There's a great coolth between us now, but soon Lizzie'll come fidgeting across the steppingstones, and I can't turn her out." There was an old tie there, of long friendship, and a family connection. Besides, as Louise knew, Lizzie depended on her companionship, whereas she could do without Lizzie's. "But I'll speak my mind."

"Plenty of people can speak their minds, Louise, but you are able to act out your thoughts."

"So do you. Only I don't think either of us act out our thoughts as much as we act out our feelings."

"But your feelings are right." He said it a little sadly. He had pursued his madness for Dolly to its ultimate conclusion.

"Not always."

"Mostly." He smiled at her, and took her hand and kissed it with one of those flourishing gestures men had used when she had been young. It became him. "And I'll make a great concession. I believe you are right about Jim Sanders being worth something. He had the git up and git to cut loose."

As she was driving away from their house, Louise thought about Wayne and Dolly. Dolly had her side, Louise granted her that. The shadow of the lost war fell on Dolly too, though she didn't know it. It had given her a longing for security. She wanted life to unroll before her like a piece of cloth, or a certain dimension. On it, she would set her neat pattern, and cut it out, according to the pattern, and sew it up.

For Wayne, life was a shimmer, and a beckoning, and an unfolding. Early in his life, he had lost all faith in security. He didn't expect anything settled, or fixed, or bounded. He could make clean-cut decisions and hold on to them, in silence and determination, but they were usually based on emotions. He had moods, Louise knew, though he kept them secret. Memories sometimes caught him, and black hates. Dolly wouldn't know anything about that side of his nature. She saw him as lighthearted, careless, and prodigal. His stubbornness about the house must have surprised her. Louise understood why he had bought it. He was trying to recreate for himself a little corner to bring back to life the space and brilliance he remembered from his early childhood, then had lost. That was why he shut himself in his little office. When he was there, he could touch the roar and excitement of London and New York and Paris. Louise felt that Wayne would be rich someday, not so much because he wanted money, but because the game of winning it would more and more fascinate him and absorb him, with its chances and its challenges.

Louise was restless that autumn and winter. A load of responsibilities, and the tension of emotional problems had kept her chained to Indigo and to Natchez. Through the years, she had kept up a steady correspondence with her sister who lived on a plantation beyond Memphis, and with her cousin Mary who lived in New Orleans, but it had been a long time since she had seen either of them. In the fall, she went to visit Carrie for a month, and after Christmas, took the boat to New Orleans. When she came back, she could tell Alan all the accumulated family news.

There was news awaiting her at home. Maggie wrote, saying she was expecting a baby sometime towards the end of June. Medora shivered when Louise told her about it.

"That's dreadful!" she sighed. "What will Maggie do with a baby way out there?"

Soon Lizzie Corwin came over to add her note of pessimism. "We gave all the baby clothes to Camilla and Frances when they had their children, so they are worn out. And how can Maggie afford new ones?"

"That's easily fixed." Louise thought of how Tom, born during the war, had managed to grow up in spite of a lack of baby finery. "I've already talked to Dolly. She'll send some of Dotty's things."

"She'd better keep them. She may need them again." Louise rather thought little Dotty would be the only child, cherished, pampered, and beautifully dressed as Dolly had been. "And Medora's already set to work making sacks."

"Well, I don't see how either her mother or I can possibly get out to that Godforsaken place to be with Maggie."

"Did she ask you to come?"

"Oh, you know Maggie has no family feelings! She prides herself on not having any!"

The Corwins didn't want to give Maggie anything, yet they resented her independence. "How'll she get a doctor?"

"Young Dr. Jack'll go, I'm sure. Dr. Rand doesn't go so far from home any more." Louise didn't say so, but she planned to go herself and be with Maggie. She would write and ask Mr. Ferris if it would be convenient for him to have her in the house.

As Louise had thought, Mr. Ferris had the easy hospitality of country people. He wrote to Louise himself in a crabbed tight hand. He said he would be glad to have her come as a lady needed other lady folks with her at such a time, and he himself would be honored to renew her acquaintance.

The Ferris family was an old one. They were good people, but they had never emerged from their isolation until they had gone to war. Three of the brothers had been killed. This Mr. Ferris, a childless widower, had played his part in freeing Mississippi from carpetbag rule, then had retired to his plantation, losing all contact with the outside world. He was old now, and the fall from his horse had made him too helpless to run his plantation alone, or to live by himself. His hands would do the best they could for him, but they were hardly able to give him the care he needed now.

Louise went to Indigo in the middle of June. It had been a rainy spring, and nearly every day there were thunderstorms. The river was high, and the creeks spilled over their banks, and Tom was unhappy because he had had to replant his cotton.

"Lord knows, Mother, I hope some of this water'll go down before you have to set out for Elsinore, or I don't see how you'll get there. The Homochitto is way out of bounds and so's the Buffalo."

The rainy spell was over by the time Jack Rand and Louise started on their way, but the road was still bad, and they rode horseback. Louise took Jessie along. Maggie would welcome her efficiency. Taking a backward glance at Indigo's house, plain and shabby in the sun, but homelike, Louise asked Jack Rand what the place they were going to was like.

"Mighty wild, Miss Lou. Though it's a right nice old house. I just hope there're no complications with this baby, that's all."

They plunged into the steaming woods, and rode on and on. Louise wished the baby was already safely born, but the journey itself interested her. She liked going to a place she had never seen before. Mile after mile the horses sloughed through the sticky mud, until they reached the flats where the Buffalo River ran. It was usually a shallow, torpid little nothing of a river but now it filled the lowland on either side of the road. Water rippled through the willows and snakes hung idly from the branches or slithered through the current. "If you think you see a stick floating," Louise murmured, "it turns out to be a snake. And if you think you see a snake, you do."

"I hope the bridge is there," Jack peered ahead. "Because I wouldn't like to have you try fording the Buffalo right now."

Indigo seemed the heart of civilization. It was in the Mississippi where boats came, and Avondale was within easy distance. Louise remembered how at first it had seemed such an undertaking to get to and from Indigo. Now she made the trip so often she thought nothing of its length or its difficulties. She wondered how anyone had found Elsinore in the first place. Evidently for the same reason someone had chosen Indigo. Because the land was rich.

Jim met them before they reached the Buffalo.

"Look at him," Jack said. "Scared to death."

Jim's eyes were dark with worry. He was too sunburned to look pale, though there was a tint of greenishness beneath the brown of his skin and a white line around his mouth. Maggie seemed fine, he said. "All the same, you all'll never know how glad I am to see you! And Jessie too."

In an undertone, Jim told Louise the hands were good people. "Mr. Ferris has a man named Zed who takes good care of him, but I'd never leave a baby with 'em after I've seen what they give their own children."

Louise remembered how, early in her stay at Indigo, she had at last dissuaded Lillybelle from feeding Link a little piece of fried rat meat, supposed to be a sure cure for bed-wetting.

"It's not far now," Jim said when they had crossed the river, and at last they came to fields wrenched out of the surrounding wilds, and finally to a dark, long, low house huddled in the shadow of some big and splendid oaks. The slant of the roof, the gallery, narrow, running along the front of the house, and the steps going up from a flat brick pavement under the gallery, had an unexpected charm. Louise felt she was allowed to walk back into some past era. Here, you could either feel as lost and as gloomy as one of Poe's semispectral characters, divorced from reality, or you could feel yourself in some secluded Eden all your own.

Maggie came out and flung her arms around Louise and then around Jessie. "I'm almost as glad to see Jessie as I am to see you."

Mr. Ferris was on the gallery. He couldn't get out of his chair. He was a dark, thin man, and when Louise shook his bony, trembling hand she felt he would never be well. He made them welcome, and a very black woman scuttled out of the house with a tray of steaming, sharp-tasting coffee, and rushed away again. Louise drank her coffee out of an old shaving mug. It was in better condition than the pieces of crockery the others had.

"What a beautiful place," Louise said, "and I love these old houses that look a little Spanish."

His eyes brightened. She guessed he loved his house and his land, and that at night, when his hip hurt, he had been afraid he would become too helpless to stay here alone, and here was where he wanted to die, and not in some strange surroundings.

Jim had been watching Maggie. Now he turned to Louise. "I always liked the looks of this house too." Jim was not yet quite sure of his esthetic judgments, yet he had more natural taste than Dolly. Maggie took Louise inside, and Jim followed them. "I just wanted to tell you if it's all right with you and the baby's a girl, Maggie and I want to name her Louise."

Louise said she would be delighted, but the incongruity of it struck her. The idea of the Yankee's grandchild being named for her! Inside, the house was not as bare and comfortless as Louise had expected. There was a lack of china and silver, and of any comfort or convenience developed since the war. The Ferris family had lived here a long time, but they had never been big planters, they had lived in back-country austerity. The furniture had the hand-hewn and handmade sturdiness and simplicity of early days. There was a low bookcase, holding the Bible, and Shakespeare, and Pilgrim's Progress, and a few other volumes. There was a spinning wheel by the hearth and faded hooked rugs on the floor, and Maggie showed Louise a little hand-carved cradle, already fixed in readiness for the baby. "Mr. Ferris wants me to use it. His father made it for his oldest brother. The one killed at the second battle of Manassas."

"It's like pioneer days." Maggie's touches showed in the bowl of flowers on the table, the workbasket and books she had brought, and the cushions she had made for Mr. Ferris's chair. "You know, Maggie, the old ladies wouldn't like me to say so, they prefer to meditate on ancestral splendors, but Natchez was new rich in the forties and fifties." People went to Europe and imported mirrors and china and heavy furniture and brocade draperies. "Not that there's anything wrong in being new rich. It would be delightful!"

The baby didn't start to be born until the following night. Once, during the long hours, Jim turned to Louise and with a groan said he should never have brought Maggie way out here."

Louise was severe with him. "Don't sentimentalize things. You were never happy in your own house, and she was never happy with her family. You're both much better off as you are."

Mr. Ferris sat up too. When Louise gently suggested he ought to try to get some rest he said he didn't sleep much anyway. She learned that after he had fallen from his horse, no one had found him for hours. Then, it was a whole day before Jack Rand could reach him. Anyway, he said, this night wasn't like other nights. "This is the first baby born in this house since I was born, near seventy years ago. I never had chick or child myself, ma'am." He told Jim to get the box he would find on the shelf. Jim brought it and Mr. Ferris opened it. Inside were a few handmade toys, a skiff, a little wagon, a tiny wooden doll with a faded painted face, representing an Indian brave. These things had been his and his brother's. Louise thought of the children who had played with them and cherished them. Three of them were dead, and one was ill and old, and she wondered what would be the fate and the life and the world of the baby soon to be born.

The sun was just rising when Dr. Rand came to say, "Well, it isn't little Louise. He's little what you may call him, but he's mighty fine."

When Maggie woke up, Louise was sitting beside her holding the baby. "How are you? I've deserted you. And Jim and Tom. This is my new child, and his fate is settled. He's going to marry Dotty Winsloe."

"James. He's James. That's not Jim's father's name." Maggie studied her son's face.

"He doesn't look like Jim's father either," Louise reassured her. "He looks like a nice little pink mouse."

Maggie regained her strength quickly. Louise stayed for the rest of the week, and planned to leave Jessie for a month or more, until Maggie was completely well again. Two days after the baby was born, Maggie's father appeared, to see his daughter and his grandchild. Della sent a package of baby clothes, and Persia sent jars of preserves.

"I'll miss you and James and Jim and Mr. Ferris," Louise said to Maggie on the last evening of her sojourn at Elsinore.

"You've won Mr. Ferris's heart, Aunt Lou."

"We talk about old times and the war."

"You know, Aunt Lou, when I'm lying here, watching James and gurgling at him, I laugh at myself. I had such fancy ideas of changing the world, and here I am doing the same old things. I'll get up and take care of James, and mend Jim's clothes, and maybe try to fix something to tempt Mr. Ferris to eat a little more, and let the world wag on the same old way."

"You've got time. You may change the world a little bit yet. And it's just as well to have the usual experiences. It keeps your feet on the ground."

"Well, I'm happier now than I've ever been in my life."

Maybe happier than she ever would be again, with the first delight of being married to the person she loved, and the excitement of the first baby. Louise put James in the cradle and rocked him. There were plenty of baby beds at the Corwins, and at her own house, but let James use this one. The sight of him asleep in it gave Louise a sense of the freshness and hope and courage of the time when this part of the country had first been settled. It was not so many years ago. It had flourished, then crashed. Now they must all start over again, and people needed the same strong spirit their grandparents had brought here. Maggie and Jim were in their way pioneers too. In their marriage and in their children, there would be a healing of discord and a rebuilding.

When Louise reached her own house in Natchez again, in the early part of a hot afternoon, its faded stateliness and its silence made her feel a little sad. It was much cooler in the wide hall than outside, the long mirror glimmered dimly, and the dark furniture had vague outlines in the greenish shadow. Cap'n Milt was on the river, and this was the hour when Medora and Miss Rose napped, or stayed in their rooms and read the Bible. Old ladies, they were all getting to be old ladies. Cap'n Luke was in town, but there was no sound from Lazarus. He must be napping too, hanging upside

261

down on his perch. Louise went upstairs very quietly, so as not to wake any one. She was tired, but after she had bathed, and changed her clothes, she felt better, and quenched her mood of vague melancholy, and prepared to go have her tea and take up her usual routine. As she left her room, she heard Lazarus calling, "Well, good-by," so she knew someone had come. As she went downstairs she saw Wayne standing in the hall.

"I dropped in, Louise. Hoping you were back."

"I'm just back."

"Tell me about Maggie and the baby."

"They're both flourishing. Let's go have some tea."

Harriet had set the tea table in the usual shady corner of the gallery. Miss Rose and Medora came out, trailing scent of lavender and scent of cologne, and armed with the largest of their palmetto fans against heat and mosquitoes, and their thinnest scarves against the possible though improbable coming of too much breeze. They talked about Maggie and the baby. They had their tea, and Louise poured Wayne's in the flowered, gilt-lined cup he had admired the day when he had asked her if she would take him as a boarder.

After the subject of Maggie had been thoroughly discussed, and Louise had described Elsinore and Mr. Ferris, Louise and Wayne fell into one of their long rambling talks. Miss Rose and Medora sometimes entered a word or a comment now and then but mostly they listened, though Medora complained about the clasp of her mosaic brooch. Wayne took it, adjusted the clasp, and gave it back to her. The mosaic showed a scene of three broken columns, a Roman ruin, but after Miss Rose and Medora had wandered into the house again, Wayne said, "That pin of hers always reminds me of the ruins of the Winsloe mansion."

Louise said she had always thought the same thing. Wayne showed no signs of getting up and going home. He lingered on. The sun set, and for a little while the curled cloud above the pine tree, and the grass and the blooming roses and verbena shone with a clear definition, a still hot intensity of color and luster before the dusk came.

After that day, Wayne stopped by the house two or three times a week, then, little by little, he began to come almost every day. At first, Louise felt a little guilty. The second time he appeared, she asked him if Dolly wouldn't be expecting him.

"No, she's at her mother's. She likes to stay there late. I'll pick her up there."

Mrs. Lydell loved to have the baby with her, and she and Dolly would be happily discussing dress patterns for little Dotty. The next time Louise asked Wayne if Dolly knew where he was, he said Dolly was giving a card party and he'd only be in the way.

"You used to come and make yourself agreeable at tea parties."

"These are such young people. Of course Dolly is young."

"So are you."

"Lord no, Louise. People her age seem like another generation from mine. I was old when I was a child."

His sense of the difference between Dolly and himself worried Louise. It was not her fault he was discovering it, but perhaps her company made him more aware of it, so when she saw Dolly, she said to her, "Wayne nearly always stops at the house on his way home, and stays a while. Do you want me to hurry him along to you?"

Dolly had laughed. "No indeed. He likes to talk about business and books. You understand all that, Miss Lou. Let him tell you, then I won't have to listen to him."

Louise was more than ever glad to have him come because every day and particularly every night, her gloom deepened when she thought about Indigo. Now she was thinking about it nearly all the time. The mortgage was due in the fall of ninety-three, and the date loomed in black letters, getting larger and larger. Turn and twist it in her mind as she did, she could find no real answer to the insoluble problem. Every time she saw Tom, she noticed his silence, his struggle to seem cheerful, and she knew he was dwelling on it as much as she was, though she tried to keep herself from talking about it to him or to Alan.

She wouldn't have discussed it with Wayne, but he brought up the subject one day when he found her alone.

"You don't look well," he said abruptly. "You're worried about Indigo, aren't you?"

She admitted she was.

"You're getting thin over it."

"It's Tom. If the worst comes to the worst, Alan and Amanda can come live here with me. But Tom——"

"I know. I've been thinking about it a lot too. You get along here. They eke out at Indigo. But finding a lump of money— Whew! Haven't you any wealthy kindred?"

"My cousin Ellen in Europe is well off, but though I'm very fond of her, I have no claim on her. I wouldn't like to ask her to lend me that much money. She's not that rich, not so rich that it might not disturb her investments. Besides, to ask——"

"I know how you feel about asking. There ought to be some other way." He looked around, "Where's my cousin Medora?"

"Cousin Charlotte took her off to pay a round of calls."

"I don't want her to hear me. Lump of money reminds me. Jasper's share is quite a lump now."

"Is it? Medora has half of what Mr. Bijah left. Half of the money from the sale of Avondale, and she gets some dividends from stocks. She has more than she used to, but not that much more."

"Jasper's stocks have done better than hers. And as Ben pays on Avondale, I invest Jasper's part of it. Medora keeps hers in the savings bank. The stocks I've bought for Jasper have soared."

"And nothing's been spent."

"Not a penny. It's all been lying there, building up. Besides, Mr. Bijah had a cousin who went to live in New York. He died, and in his will he left a piece of property in New York City to Jasper. Its value has tripled, sell it and you have a good sized fortune right there."

"But it's all Jasper's. What good does it do us?"

"No good, now. Though it isn't doing him any good either. If it was Medora's, you could borrow some of it and pay the mortgage."

"How could I pay her back?"

"Would it matter? Who's she got in the world besides you and Tom?"

"I wouldn't mind Medora's owning Indigo. She wouldn't be the kind of creditor the Yankee is. But as things are, she can't touch that money. It's Jasper's."

"I knew you'd feel that way, Louise. I suppose you're bound to. But there it sits, not doing anybody any good."

"Least of all, Jasper himself."

"Louise, has any serious effort been made to find Jasper?"

"Not since Mr. Bijah died."

"He wrote to Medora for quite a while didn't he?"

"A long time, I believe. Oh, I don't really know! I stopped asking." Any reference to Jasper and Medora always made Louise uneasy.

"I wish I could read those letters."

"I don't know if they even exist any more, and besides——"

"She'd never let me. But I bet she still has 'em."

Wayne sat looking out at the sun and shadow streaked lawn. It was October, and still warm enough to sit on the gallery. Wayne's eyes were half closed, and only a dark gleam shone under his lids, but he didn't look somnolent, but intense, as his features hardened and sharpened with a fierce concentration. "I tell you what I wish you'd do, Louise. Get Medora to go through those letters, and write down all names, all dates, all references to places, and all postmarks in the proper sequence."

"I'll ask her."

"See that she does it. Are you going to Indigo soon?"

"Before too long, though maybe I won't get there before Christmas."

"Then ask Alan to try to remember what he can. Cousin Bijah might have told him something about what luck he'd had trying to trace Jasper. Get it all written down."

"Jasper was in Cuba, and in Brazil. I'll try to remember. There was a Southern family he knew well. They went to Brazil. I'll write to Alan and ask him what their name was. What are you trying to do?"

"I'd like to know what became of Jasper. Whether he's still alive. Or dead."

Wayne was frowning. "Did you know that there's no record of the mortgage?"

"I didn't know there ever was——"

"Oh, of course there was. All mortgages are recorded at the court-house."

"I didn't know."

"Alan must know the record's gone. I suppose he didn't say anything because it does you no particular good. The Yankee has the original, and I bet he sleeps with it under his pillow."

"Then would the record matter?"

"Not as long as he has the original document. But if that didn't exist either, then he'd have no legal claim on Indigo."

"What happened to the record in the courthouse?"

"It mysteriously disappeared. The Yankee must have scanned that empty space many a time." Wayne's eyes were dark and bright.

"Wayne! You know!"

"Don't say that out loud. Right after the election when we cleared out the carpetbag officials, Cousin Bijah and I went to the courthouse to look around. We'd put old Jonathan Baynes in office. Cousin Bijah said, 'Jon, remember that bottle of wine I got off the Yankee supply train? You drank over half of it. You take a look out of the window at that tree over yonder. Mighty interesting tree.' Mr. Jon laughed and said he'd do better than that. He had an errand down the street. Off he went. When he came back the page with the Indigo mortgage had gone."

"Does Alan know?"

"Sure he does. It won't do any good, but I think we were right to eliminate the record. Might as well."

"Don't tell Tom."

"He knows already, I bet. What's the matter? Why shouldn't he know?"

Louise didn't answer.

"I can guess. You're afraid it might tempt him to do something forceful about the original."

"I don't want Tom to be—violent about this."

"He won't, don't worry about it. Though I can see what you mean—it would be a temptation." Wayne got up to go. "Let me see if I can find some traces of my baffling Cousin Jasper."

"All the trails are cold."

"I haven't much hope."

266

Louise sighed. "I wonder what he made of his life."

"He wrecked Medora's pretty thoroughly. Or maybe nobody can wreck your life for you except you yourself."

A little chill had crept into the air. Louise shivered and drew her shawl around her shoulders. Soon they would be sitting by the library fire. How short the days were! All days, all time seemed short now.

When Louise next went down to the plantation, she hated the hours she spent on the boat. Usually she found the long slow boat trip restful, her melancholy oppressed her too much for her to find it soothing this time. She needed a constant restless activity now, and leisure had become hateful. The town on the bluffs faded away, and the boat followed the curves of the river, and civilization with all of its patterns seemed smudged out of existence.

The sky had the empty luster of glass. There was no wind. Light polished the dull water, and made the Louisiana shores vague and undefined. The river was low and the sand bars stretched out, like the backs of sleeping beasts, monsters rising from the cold depths below the surface. Her own thoughts took the shapes of monsters too. Out here, force became the usual, the natural law, and there was no other. The river was passive in this season, but when it needed freedom from its bounds, it took its own ways of escape. It flooded the land, sloshed over the levees or tore through them. Impatient, from time to time, the Mississippi changed its channel, cutting through impeding points of land.

Louise thought of Wayne and herself. Why should she be so scrupulous of Dolly's rights and feelings? Why did she watch her every word and look? Why not play on Dolly's dissatisfactions, and Wayne's, for her own use?

As for Tom and Indigo, why did he too have to lose what he loved? Why couldn't he seize what was morally his? The letter of the law gave the Yankee the power to seize Indigo. In this case, the letter of the law was wrong. Tom could only get back what was his by force, and the only effective force he could use was to get rid of his enemy. The only way he could get rid of the Yankee was to contrive his death. If Tom did, would he be so guilty?

Louise became afraid of the violence of her thoughts and struggled to banish them. They made her shiver. The boat blew for a landing, and she left her place and went to look for Indigo Bend. There it was, the long curve just before Indigo Landing came in sight. At this point you could imagine the river itself ended here. She remembered how she had felt the day she had come to take up existence at Indigo, a kind of hopelessness, as though this was the end of everything for her, as if she was forever condemned to stagnate. It hadn't been an ending, only a course set in a new direction, just as the river was not walled in by Indigo Bend, but turned south.

She told herself there was no reason for despair now. It would be another year before the mortgage was due. In that year there was hope.

Since the weather was dry, Maggie and Jim and the baby were able to come from Elsinore and spend a day and a night at Indigo. By cutting himself off from his father, Jim had won complete acceptance from Tom and Alan and Amanda. Before, they had been fond of him, but in spite of his name. Now he seemed to exist for them as a separate entity. Now they had forgotten who he was. He had become one of themselves. Louise thought he deserved this acceptance, he had paid a price for it. He had kept on learning since his marriage, and he seemed to have assimilated Maggie's tastes, standards, and code of manners with perfect ease, but Louise guessed what constant ambition to improve himself must underlie that seemingly effortless equality with the others. He was ambitious, as ambitious as his father, but in such a different way it was not apparent.

Jim had gone ahead on the way he had set for himself, but Maggie, Louise felt, had changed, though it was hard to define in what way. At first, Louise thought it was only the different kind of life Maggie was living, and a deeper experience, yet—no—there was a subtle alteration. Maggie's dress was a plain calico, clean, but faded, and she looked thin and sunburnt, but then her clothes and her complexion had never mattered much to Maggie. Louise herself had learned to do without luscious materials, plumed hats, and

French gloves, yet she always missed them, and seized on them with delight when they came her way. Maggie simply didn't care. However, simplicity had always suited Maggie better than elaboration, and the sun-browned tint of her skin suited her too, bringing out the bright-greenish hazel of her eyes and the tinge of russet in her hair. Her young prettiness had changed into a kind of beauty without softness, but full of vigor and strength.

"Jim wants his mother to see the baby," Maggie told Louise, "and I dread going over there."

"But you'll have to take little James."

"I guess so. Jim worries about his mother." She was going in concession to Jim's feelings, rather than because she felt Jim had any obligation to his mother.

When Jim and Maggie came back from their brief call on Della, Jim was silent and brooding, and Louise could see that Maggie was bursting with anger. While Maggie was putting the rosy lump that was little James to bed and tucking the mosquito bar around him, Louise came in to talk to her.

"What happened, Maggie?"

Maggie tugged at the mosquito bar until the rings at the top jingled. "One reason Jim wanted to go over there was to talk to his father, and try to make some agreement with him about the mortgage."

"I'm sure he couldn't."

"Jim, of course, knew that. But I suppose he finds it's hard to believe anybody's as awful as he knows his father is! That man—that creature—you know what he said? That maybe little James wouldn't be the plumb fool Jim was—maybe he'd know which side his bread was buttered on and would be glad his granddad knew how to make money!"

"I'm not surprised. I didn't have any hope he'd changed. Don't worry about it, Maggie."

"I had to get away from there—quick! One good thing, it showed Jim he'd been right to leave. Another good thing, it makes him hate his father harder than ever!"

"You oughtn't to feel that's a good thing, it's a kind of tragedy, Margaret."

"Well you wouldn't want Jim to like him, would you?"

"I'm sorry for Della in all of this."

"She shed floods of tears over little James. But she sags so!"

"Her springs are broken. Life can do that to people." Louise had seen before the misery of a woman caught between the enmity of her husband for her son.

"She hasn't put up much of a fight! Oh, if we could only cut ourselves off completely from his people and mine too!"

"You're fond of your father, Margaret."

"But I can't respect him much. Mamma's tears, and Aunt Liz's scoldings and Grandma's complaints and mock sinking spells have turned him into a quaking jelly."

"Watch out, Margaret, you have dominating tendencies yourself." Maggie laughed. "Jim can stand up to me!"

He could, since he could be steady when necessary, and was also practiced in ways of evading and escaping. Of the two, he was the more subtle and complex nature. But Louise understood now why she had thought Maggie had changed. It was because she had always rather discounted Maggie's cloudy theories, but now she saw that Maggie's impulses had crystallized into a certain ruthlessness of behavior. She not only thought her family ties were a burden, she was ready to act and to cut herself away. Louise herself had sometimes felt a disunity between herself and her own parents, and though she had been ruthless too about marrying Tom when they had cautioned prudence, she would never have admitted out loud that she found close-knit family life itself unreasonable and ready to be discarded. Perhaps she envied Maggie's capacity for honesty. It shocked her, but when she thought of the Corwins, she could understand Maggie's point of view. Jim's family might be the exception, though there were plenty of sordid family situations, but Maggie's family was almost usual. Her father was rather like a male insect devoured by female insects, but Maggie's mother was a victim too, swamped by the brood of children she had produced. Natural or not, it was a pattern Maggie didn't want for herself. Perhaps she was of a new generation, new in ideas as well as in years, and would tear down, then rebuild something else. Maybe something better.

Maggie grit her teeth. "It makes me so mad—when I see you and Uncle Alan and Tom so depressed over Indigo!" Her eyes glittered with tears. Maggie's headlong will to have her own way would always be tempered by the strength of her love.

Tom was depressed. He tried to hide it, but Louise felt it in his silences and his abstraction. One afternoon he asked her to ride over the place with him. They set off and circled the fields until they came to the one nearest the creek. Tom reined his horse and Louise stopped hers too. "The crop did pretty well in spite of the bad weather last spring." Tom's slate-dark eyes watched the line of growth, thinning now, that marked the creek bank. "But I couldn't help thinking what on earth's the use——"

"Something might happen."

"I don't know." If she had to, Louise would write to her cousin Ellen, and explain everything and ask for a loan. She hated the idea of asking a cousin she hadn't seen for years to lend her the money. It might mean, for Ellen, even if she was able to lend such a sum, to take it out of some good investment to put it in a very precarious investment. Louise thought how Wayne's face had looked when he had been talking about Jasper, and in spite of what her own common sense told her, in spite of his warning, she felt a vague hope.

"Uncle's worn himself out all these years fighting to keep Indigo," Tom said, almost in a whisper. "I ought to do something!"

"Tom! Promise me you won't."

He turned to look at her. "You seem scared when I say that."

"I am."

"I know there's no record of the mortgage in the courthouse. I looked." Tom smiled, not a pleasant smile. "I know where he keeps the original. I crept up to his house one night. There's a safe and I'm sure he keeps it in the safe. That night, I'd have set the house afire, if I hadn't known the safe wouldn't burn."

"Tom! Stop——"

"Don't you think I'm tempted? Don't you think it would be easy to have something happen to him—as easy as shooting a sitting duck!"

Everywhere around them there was peace, in the dark field picked clean of cotton and ready for sleep, in the clear sky, in the rust-tinged light, with the only sound the leaves' dry whisper. But there was no peace within themselves, or in Tom's voice, at last speaking his thoughts aloud. "Accidentally shot when he was out hunting, though he doesn't hunt much any more. Drowned on the river— almost anything. Who'd care? Not his son. Not his wife. Not the people on his place. Who'd ask too many questions?"

Nobody. Tom could contrive something with hardly any risk. No one would know exactly what happened, down in the woods, or near the river, or even right here, on the creek bank. The Yankee might very well have his fears, and take what precautions he could, but he was no match for Tom. The Yankee was growing old, and he was heavy and often drunk. Tom had an unerring aim, a steely strength, and could slither through the woods like an Indian. Tom, if he chose, could kill the Yankee in half a dozen different ways. It needn't happen in some remote spot. Tom could manage to quarrel with the Yankee in the open, and kill him in front of half a dozen witnesses. No one would bring Tom to trial, or testify against him. Tom would be free, all of them would be free.

"You could do it, Tom, but you won't."

"How do you know I won't?"

"Because you are what you are. Every night I read my Bible, and nothing impresses me more than the passage about gaining the whole world and losing your own soul. You have a soul. You won't lose it for a piece of property, even if its Indigo."

"No, I wouldn't. Even though Mississippi river water runs in my veins and the rest of me is made of Indigo mud——"

"Dust——" Louise smiled. "Dust we are——"

"Indigo dust, then. I thought it all out long ago, Mother. I could get rid of him, but I won't." He smiled, his own smile this time, like her own, and was suddenly more cheerful. "It wouldn't be much sport in it, would it? It would be too easy. I wouldn't even be risking my neck. Anyway, I promise you——"

"You don't have to. You aren't only my child, you're your father's child. I know you'll remember that."

"I do. Always."

Louise looked at him, trying to see in his face some likeness to his father. There was nothing obvious. Sometimes a glance or a gesture brought back to her the image of the other Tom. But Louise didn't need any outward likeness. What Tom had been survived in his son.

Chapter Seventeen

[1893—] "Louise." Medora put down her work. Louise, just finishing her accounts, closed her ledger and looked up. She and Medora were sitting at the library table. It was a hot summer night, and the lamp near them made them hotter still. Louise pressed her hands against her head. Arithmetic always gave her a headache, but then she had headaches often now. Yet she was almost sorry she had finished adding and subtracting. As much as she disliked doing sums, at least she had to give the figures her whole attention. Once she no longer had to concentrate, her worries took up their fixed positions in her mind again, and there was no escape from them.

Certainly not in the dull trickle of talk she heard from Miss Rose and Medora. Miss Rose, thank heavens, had gone on upstairs. Cap'n Luke and Cap'n Milt were both out of town. Their talk was much more interesting than the women's. The river they knew had a life of its own, and sometimes listening to Cap'n Milt—Cap'n Luke seldom spoke—Louise could lose herself in his stories of shoals and currents and spectacular floods. Now she tried to give her attention to what Medora wanted to say.

"I was thinking," Medora continued. "I know you've been worrying yourself sick over Indigo——"

"You mustn't worry about it, Medora."

"But I do."

"It's no use, there's nothing you can do."

"But I can," Medora said. "I want you to take my money and give it to Alan and Tom to pay the mortgage."

Louise's eyes filled with tears. She was nervous these days and tears came easily, but Medora's offer touched her, and brought to her with painful sharpness, yet with a certain sweetness too, the memory of that past they had shared.

Louise got up and kissed her, then went back to her own chair. "It's out of the question, Medora. The idea! For you to give up everything! Times are bad——" And Medora was getting old. "You have to keep your little security. Tom and Alan would never dream of such a thing!"

"I was afraid you'd say that. But you've done everything for me, and this means everything to you. With Indigo gone, what would Tom do?"

That was what haunted Louise. What could he do? Ben Rand had offered to let him come to Avondale, but Tom had refused. "Ben doesn't really need me, besides, it's too near Indigo."

In the course of time, Jim, if his father didn't disinherit him, would own Indigo, and Jim and Maggie would almost certainly give it back. But time had to run its course, and until then, what would happen to Tom? Louise was afraid of what he might become. It would be easy for him to slip in the dull listless routine of some ill-paid work in town. He would never have his heart in it. Louise saw too many hopeless, useless men around her, drinking too much, or secluding themselves from companionship, and getting strange as they grew older.

"Well, if you won't take anything from me as a present, Lou, let me at least lend it——"

"No, that wouldn't do either. A plantation is too uncertain. Times are so bad we might lose Indigo even without the mortgage. Oh, no, you can't tie up your little money out there. No!"

Medora sighed. "There's Jasper's money. But Uncle Bijah expected me to keep it for him."

"And you must. It's his."

"I wish I could feel right about using it."

"You never would, and neither would I. We wouldn't feel honest."

Medora said, "Why did Wayne want to know everything he could about Jasper? Is he trying to find him?"

"He was, I don't think he's had any luck."

For a long time, Wayne hadn't mentioned his struggle to find Jasper. Louise supposed he had given up hope, as she had. Wayne had seemed tired this summer, and preoccupied with the fluctuations of the market. "This panic won't last," he kept prophesying. "The thing to do is to keep clear of it, buy up the good stuff when its low and hang on."

"Don't gamble too wildly," Louise had cautioned.

"Think how well you've done, and dedicate yourself to prudence."

"Now's the time when a really wild gamble might pay off, eventually."

Medora sat still, her hands folded. She was slender, and her light brown hair hardly showed any touches of gray, and there were not many lines in her face. The warmth of her sympathy, her emotion for Louise had given her a glow of color and liveliness of expression and made her look young again for a little while. Her age didn't show in her face or figure, really, but in her attitudes and her mannerisms.

"I hope Wayne finds out about Jasper, Lou. Because then we might do something about the money. And if I felt free to do what I pleased with it, you couldn't keep me from helping you. I'd get Wayne to make you take it."

Louise wondered what Medora thought about Wayne's visits. She had never said. Medora began to gather her things together in preparation for going upstairs. Medora never moved from one part of the house to the other without a number of accessories, what Lillybelle called "cutterments." She put her thimble in its special place in her workbox, stuck her needles in the strawberry-shaped emery, closed the workbox, picked up the novel she was reading—*Molly Bawn,* by "The Duchess"—and retrieved her fan. She never liked anyone else to use her fan. There was a search for the little crochet bag she always carried.

"Medora, do you think Wayne comes here too much?"

"Dolly doesn't care. This house is Wayne's real home. He's used to it." Once something became a habit, Medora was inclined to accept it. If Wayne had come once in a long time, she might have raised her eyebrows, but as he came every day, Medora catalogued his visits as part of the evening's routine.

"Does anybody say anything about his coming?"

"Only old Mrs. Corwin. Nobody pays any attention to her. If only he finds Jasper," Medora sighed. "Not that it would matter to me any more."

276

"Wouldn't you be glad to know what really happened to him?"

Medora thought a few minutes. "I wanted to know. But now I don't care." Looking over her possessions to be sure she hadn't left anything, she went out, and Louise sat alone thinking about Jasper and about Wayne.

Not long after that night, Louise was getting up from the dinner table as the clock struck three. Miss Rose and Medora began their slow amble upstairs to sequester themselves in their own rooms, where they would take off their heavy petticoats, layer after layer, except the last layer, and unlace themselves out of their stiff whale-boned corsets, and put on dressing sacks made of dotted swiss or China silk. Both ladies would read the Bible, a verse and sometimes a whole chapter, though in hot weather they were apt to skimp and read only a verse. Wayne said once he wondered what the very strict and proper ladies he knew made of some parts of the Bible. "You know Holy Writ does call a spade a spade." The Bible reading over, the ladies would then lie down and rest. Their shutters were tightly drawn against the glare, and Miss Rose—her life was easier since she had inherited a legacy—and Medora would stay cocooned in the dimness until five o'clock. Then they would rise up, open the shutters, wash, and put on corsets and fresh layers of petticoats and clean dresses, and come down and sit on the gallery. In summer, Harriet brought tea at half past five. Louise didn't allow herself a nap. At half past four she hurried upstairs, and bathed and changed from her neat house dress to something more suitable for evening, some thin material in summer, and a heavy silk in winter. She refused to wear the high-boned collars in style. Bustles were no more. How strange the first person without a bustle had looked, deflated, sheered off in the back! Louise didn't follow all the ways of changing fashion any more, unless she particularly liked them. Little by little she had developed a style of her own and clung to the low necklines and softening lace fichus of her younger days. She was aware it was a sign of age to prefer the modes of the past, but she couldn't help thinking they were prettier and more becoming.

After the others had gone, Louise lingered in the dining room, giving Metta some directions for tomorrow, and trying to think up something far more cooling than gumbo, when there was a clatter of a carriage coming up the drive. Nobody came calling at such an hour. Something must have happened, and she rushed to see who it was. The sun gleamed on the carriage Wayne had bought for Dolly, and Dolly flung herself out of the carriage, her veil fluttering back.

"What on earth——" Louise felt her heart pound, until she couldn't speak. Dolly's cheeks were tear-stained and her eyes were wild.

"Is anything the matter with Wayne? Or Dotty?" Louise gasped.

Dolly shook her head. "They're all right." She groped her way blindly into the house. She didn't get further than the hall, but sank down on the nearest chair and covered her face with her hands.

"What is it, child?"

Dolly lifted her head. "Wayne's lost everything!"

Louise felt a wave of coldness wash over her, but part of it was relief. She had been afraid—afraid of all kinds of things. She went in the dining room and brought a decanter half full of wine, and a glass, then found some smelling salts in her desk, and held the salts under Dolly's nose and made her drink a little wine. In a few minutes Dolly would tell her what she wanted to know. The clatter of the carriage had brought Medora out of her room. Louise was aware of her standing on the steps watching and not speaking, very much like some ghost of the house.

Dolly's huddled position and bowed head indicated grief less than the details of her appearance. She had brought no gloves and no handbag. She was in her everyday morning dress, and hadn't even drawn her veil over her face.

"I haven't even had—courage—to tell Papa and Mamma. They'll be heartbroken!"

Louise kept herself from saying little Dotty might have been taken seriously ill, or that something might have happened to Wayne himself, instead of to his money. She thought of him, and what sort of mood he must be in, or how deep in despair he might be over this sudden ruin. Not despair. Wayne was like herself. The loss of money, even of a large amount of money, wouldn't make him despair.

"Where is Wayne?" she asked.

"Back at the office."

"Come in the library, Dolly, and tell me." Louise led Dolly to the library sofa and made her lie down.

"What'll we do?" Dolly moaned.

"Start again."

"That's what Wayne said. But think of it, Miss Lou! Everything gone! I'll have to give up my carriage. We'll be dir-rt po-or, and it was so-o nice not being!"

"Just for a while, Dolly. Wayne'll get on his feet soon. You'll see."

"He was too—headlong—I told him, and he just would be!" Dolly gulped and sat up, angry now. She was less lovely than she had been. Her lips were narrower. When she grew old, she would have one of those thin, tight little mouths, and the freshness of her skin had somewhat faded in spite of all of her care.

"What happened, Dolly?"

"I don't know, I don't know about business. He came home and told me. Then went off. He shouldn't have gambled everything we had. It was wrong of him!"

"I wonder why he did."

"I asked him why. He said it just seemed like a good thing. He ought to have thought of me, and Dotty. Our house and our furniture!"

Dolly hadn't cared for the house, but lately she had grown proud of it, enjoyed being a hostess, and was pleased with the place because all her friends admired it and an architect from New Orleans had told her it was a gem.

"You'll get it back, Dolly."

Dolly stayed for over an hour, groaning and talking and repeating herself. Louise comforted her as well as she could, while she thought about Wayne and wished he would tell her what had happened. She felt swept away herself, realizing how she had been clinging to Wayne, buoyed up by his air of sureness. Now he had sunk with the pressure of his own misfortune. He would begin swimming again, but for a while she must try to forget her own problem and be as much help to him as she could.

At last Dolly left, mournfully remarking that it was her last ride in her new carriage.

After she had gone, Medora came down. She had heard part of

what Dolly had said. "It was wrong of Wayne," she sighed. "Gambling's in his blood. He's a Winsloe." It was if she felt some inescapable fate doomed the Winsloes to risk everything and lose it. Medora didn't see this crash as a temporary fluctuation of a panicky market, but as a foreordained family curse.

"He'll pick himself up."

"But I don't blame Dolly for the way she feels."

"He's feeling pretty badly himself just now."

"But he did it."

"But if he'd won, you and Dolly and everybody else would be delighted with him, instead of blaming him for taking risks."

"The Winsloes aren't lucky."

"He's been lucky, or brilliant, or both. Up to now."

"The Winsloes have streaks of bad luck. His luck's run out."

"Everybody's does, from time to time. Up to the war, your family either had a great deal of luck with money, or else a knack of making it."

Medora had already delegated Wayne to a dreary resignation, so much a part of her own nature. Medora didn't see people as they were. Now she couldn't quite understand that this ruin, total as it seemed at the moment, would probably be only an episode in Wayne's adventures. She saw it only as it seemed to her, the end of everything.

Louise waited for Wayne through the rest of the afternoon. Her tea tasted bitter, and she couldn't swallow a mouthful of supper. She had kept up as well as she could, through newspapers and articles and Wayne's conversation, with the upheavals in the rest of the country. Industrial plants in the big cities had closed, people were out of work, and the market was behaving wildly. She realized these quakes and tremors reflected themselves in low cotton prices, and added to her own troubles. The crop was beautiful, but who would buy it this fall?

"At least I'm going to gather it in and sell it before the Yankee can get it," Tom had told her the last time she had been at Indigo, and they had watched the ripple of the clustered dark leaves. The mortgage could hardly have fallen due in a worse year than this one, and she wondered if Ellen would be able to lend her any money. It had become impossible to borrow money.

Louise had tried to understand something of the complexities of free silver as against the principle of sound money, and had listened to the men argue over it by the hour. She had great confidence in President Cleveland, the only Democrat in the White House since before the war. He would do something about the tariff and that might help the South. Yet, because she lived in a small town away from centers of industry, or in the primitive simplicities of the country, the panic of industry and the roar of railroads falling into receivership came more or less filtered to her. Wayne lived in the isolation of Natchez too, but his real life was spent in the complications of finance. He had skillfully used the panic. Now he had fallen a victim to it.

After everyone else in the house was upstairs, Louise waited for him. She felt sure he would come, and at last she heard his step on the gallery. It was after ten o'clock. She went to meet him, holding the hall lamp in her hand. The light showed his face dark and tired and haggard, but he managed to smile at her. He followed her into the house without saying anything.

"Cap'n Luke brought me some good whiskey. Let me give you some."

"No, thank you, I don't like it when I'm tired. How peaceful it seems in here!"

A tall vase held butterfly lilies. The lamp flung a luminous circle, banishing the uproar and clatter of the rest of the world and drawing Louise and Wayne close together in the harmony they felt in each other's presence.

He closed his eyes, then opened them. "Has Dolly been here?"

Louise said she had, but didn't tell him all Dolly's lamentations.

"Poor Dolly," he sighed. "It's hard on her. It makes me feel like a brute to tell her the house and carriage must go."

"I feel very sorry for her, but I was worried about you."

"It's bad, Louise, but not as hopeless as it looks."

"Tell me about it, if you aren't too tired."

"You know what state the country's in. Mr. Clements and I deal in cotton futures, but for myself, I branch out once in a while. I had some cash, and when stocks fell thirty and forty per cent, I bought all I could. Outright."

"How did that ruin you?"

"That didn't. It was another speculation, too long to tell in detail. I lost, but I don't owe anybody anything."

Louise smiled. "If we didn't owe anything I would only have a sensation of delicious freedom. But this puzzles me. If you don't owe, why will you have to give up house and furniture and Dolly's carriage?"

"Because I have a few stocks left. My shoestring. I'd rather hold on to them, and sacrifice other things."

"Is that fair to Dolly?"

"Um. She might not think so, but it is. When I get on my feet again I can buy another old mansion."

"Maybe that one. They don't sell fast."

"That's what I think. And I'll never get those stocks at a bargain. They'll go lower, but someday they'll come back. The panic won't last forever. Look what happened today. Twelve hundred shares of Evansville and Terre Haute were sold for seventy-five. Yesterday you couldn't buy them for one hundred and twenty-five. No sellers, and nothing's happened to depress them that much. A lot of this is just wild fright!"

"Aren't you frightened?"

"Not really. When I see a good chance——"

"Not again!"

"Next time, it'll work. I'll double my money."

"There speaks the Winsloe gambling instinct."

"They often doubled theirs."

Louise sighed. "This hasn't taught you a bit of prudence!"

"I won't take such a long chance, but I don't intend to be too prudent. Look at Medora, she's prudent or——" He might have wanted to say, "Or is she?" He didn't, he said, "About her money. I could have doubled and tripled her money then she would have had enough to——"

"Aren't you glad you weren't trying to double it today?"

He said he didn't speculate with other people's money, only his own. "Jasper's investments are as sound as gold nuggets. A little depressed, but they'll come back. Jasper—well, never mind."

"Wayne, you must have known you were taking a long chance. With all your wild talk, I know very well you do look before you leap. Why didn't you this time?"

There was only one other time when he had leaped without looking, when he had insisted on marrying Dolly. Maybe this time too he had been in the grip of an obsession. Though it was not like him to have an obsession about money. The game of chance itself must have lured him too far.

"If it had worked out it would have meant a lot of money."

"Why did you want it so much?"

"I got—carried away." He evaded her eyes. "It happens every day."

His answer didn't satisfy her, but he was looking discouraged again, and she didn't want to prod and insist.

"I must go. Thank you for listening to all this."

He went to the vase and picked one of the lilies from its stalk. "I like these things. Can you give me some bulbs?"

"Plenty of them." She stopped remembering the garden wouldn't be his. He guessed what she was thinking.

"I'll plant 'em anyway. Before we leave the house."

"By the time you get the place back they'll be ready to bloom for you."

"Don't you blame me for my rashness, Louise?"

"No. You're the same person as you would be if you had won." Her words were rational, but her voice quivered a little with her feeling for him.

"It's nice to have you to come to in my defeat."

She had tried to console the victims of great defeats and irreparable losses. Compared to them, this was a minor overthrow. Wayne was looking at her and his tired face took on warmth and eagerness again. "Good night, Louise." He went out and the darkness swallowed him up.

On a hot August morning, Louise, with a parasol over her head and gardening gloves on her hands, walked down the lawn to the mailbox at the gate. The morning papers were full of Bryan's long

283

oratorical speech advocating free silver. It had impressed numbers of people, but not the President. In the mailbox Louise found a letter from her sister and one from her cousin Mary. Carrie wrote that everyone was well, but that she knew Louise was worried about the plantation, and she wished she could help.

Louise had been careful not to say too much to Carrie who had burdens enough of her own. Mary, living in New Orleans, had an easier and less isolated existence, but she had had a great many anxious years and personal sorrows, and lately she hadn't been in good health. Louise didn't want to intrude her own turmoil into her cousin's mind. She leaned against the mailbox and read Mary's letter, while the thin fading leaves of the China tree floated down and the round, sour-smelling China berries came plopping around her.

Mary was better, that was the first thing Louise saw, then, assured of that, she read the rest of the page twice.

"Alexander and I have been worrying over that wretched mortgage. You must ask Ellen to lend you the money. I know nothing about the present state of her finances, but ask. I wish we could give you some substantial help. Alexander is sending you a thousand dollars, and wishes it were more."

Louise hadn't seen her young cousin Ellen in years, since Ellen preferred to go on living in Europe, but there was that fondness between them, and if Ellen could not lend the money, then Ellen would have to say so with all frankness.

"But I'll write, I'll ask," Louise resolved.

It would not be easy to write such a letter to Ellen, but Louise went back to the house and began it. She thought of Tom and Alan and what it would mean to them to free Indigo. Not free it, but at least change creditors. She thought of Jasper, and wished she could bring herself to take his money. Mr. Bijah was no longer alive to protect his son.

How many hours the old man must have spent, devising, consulting lawyers, how sad and tired he must have been, trying to think out all details to be sure Jasper would always have what was rightfully his. He had been fond of her, and of Alan too, but his fondness for them was not to be compared to his love for Jasper. That was a love stronger than death.

She finished her letter and waited for Wayne. She wanted to talk to him about it. First came Cap'n Luke, with Lazarus's cage in his hand, and Lazarus perched on his shoulder, nibbling at Cap'n Luke's ear. Cap'n Luke only offered a "Good evenin', ma'am," and Lazarus only gave a hoarse cackle, very much like Mrs. Corwin's laughter, then both of them went in the house. Colonel Duel and Mrs. Duel were less easily disposed of, and Louise watched their slow progress towards her with a sinking heart. She managed to smile, and prepared to listen to Colonel Duel's oration on Bryan's oration. Medora deserted, saying she had a bad headache and had to go lie down. The tension in the house was telling on Medora. She hadn't seemed well lately, and Louise resolved to try to be more cheerful for her sake.

The Colonel prosed on, and at last Wayne came and joined them on the gallery. Wayne, like Louise, listened politely. Nobody deferred to the Colonel's opinions, which were usually absurd, they deferred to his years with the Confederate armies. Wayne said some of Bryan's ideas were good but he was a sound money man himself. While the Colonel rambled on, Louise thought about Wayne's own predicament. He and Dolly and the little girl had moved in with the Lydells again, who seemed glad to have them. Dolly complained of her poverty, and Louise told her the story of a friend of her own. "Before the war one of her plantations alone was worth a million dollars. After the war she had two dresses. She gave one to a beggar woman, and said after that she always knew what to wear."

Wayne himself didn't seem disheartened. They wouldn't starve, and he told Louise he had irons in the fire. Louise could hardly get him to speak of his own affairs, he seemed preoccupied with hers. At last the Colonel and Mrs. Duel left.

"Tillman's election in South Carolina worries him. It's the passing of the old order. People like him, like Cousin Bijah was, like all of us, won't have their political power any more. Change is in the air."

Louise told him she had written to Ellen.

"It's high time. You should have cabled."

285

"No, I wanted to explain everything." She told him about Mary's letter, and her loan. "She knows everything in such detail, and I didn't tell her much."

"They know. Take what they can lend, and be thankful." Wayne got up and began to pace the gallery. "One thousand from your cousin Mary, and four thousand five hundred from your cousin Ellen, if you can get it. It's a good thing your family's so fond of you and Tom."

"I hate trading on their fondness."

"Don't be squeamish, Louise. Remember you are doing it for Tom. You won't be free, but get it out of the clutches of the Yankee. Why four from Ellen? My arithmetic says four thousand five hundred."

"I have the five hundred."

"Where'd you get it?"

"I mortgaged this house."

"Lord, Louise!" he groaned. "When?"

"Last winter."

"If you had to do it, it was just as well you did it then. From the bank?"

"Yes, that's all they would lend on it. Nobody wants houses like this. If Ellen sends the money, how'll we ever pay her back?"

"It'll be worth more some day than it is now."

Lately, Louise had tried her best to think objectively about the Yankee. Admitting he was a coarse, greedy, drunken creature, admitting he had used a legal trick to take the Winsloe plantation, there had been a time when she and Alan might have come to some agreement with him. Just after she had nursed Jim through yellow fever. Then had come the struggle to get rid of carpetbag rule, and that had been the end of any peace. If, when Jim had come back home, he had been able to work on his father, he might, in time, have gained some influence. Instead he had fallen in love, and to prove himself, to prove his right to Maggie, he had cut himself off from all ties with his father. He been right, yet Louise could see how the Yankee would feel he had to prove his own power. Angry, stubborn, convinced that the only way to conquer these proud and hostile people was to take what they wanted, as they had taken from him the thing he wanted most, his son. He was immovable

286

now. There was no hope of him. The only hope was to have the money ready.

Wayne studied Louise's face. "Remember you told me once there were always imponderables in a situation. Something might change, something might happen so you could pay your cousins. The thing is, you can't wait to pay the Yankee. Get the money. In the bank, in your hands. After you have it, you can take a deep breath and hope for something to turn up." He snatched up his hat and went off in a great hurry.

After Louise had mailed the letter, she felt she had done all she could. She didn't mention she had written to Ellen. It was no use to raise her family's hopes until she learned if there would be any fulfillment of them. Hard as it was to leave them to their gloom, it was better not to speak until after she had heard from Ellen.

Tom asked her to come out to Indigo. It would take longer for Ellen's answer to reach her there, but not much longer, and if Tom wanted her company, she would go to him. As the boat slipped down the river she felt in better spirits than on that other trip when she had felt lost as she had struggled with the violence of her thoughts. The bitter quality of her loneliness was gone too. Her inner world had safety and warmth. Tom and Alan and Amanda, Medora and Jim and Maggie, Wayne and her cousins who were trying to help her were drawn together, giving each other comfort and protection.

Tom was waiting for her at the landing. He smiled at her but his smile didn't reach his eyes. His eyes were dull, as if he had a fever. They rode in the old wagon under the rustling cottonwoods, and beyond into the soft silence of that stretch of deep growth before they came to Indigo's fields.

"I want to get the crop in before October the fifteenth," Tom said. "The Yankee might get next year's but not this year's."

Louise couldn't answer, she leaned over and kissed him and could feel the throb of the vein in his temple. He said nothing more about the mortgage, and no one else mentioned it either. Yet every subject seemed tangled up with it. That night at supper when Louise asked about Link's new baby, she wondered what Link would do. He would follow Tom, yet he wouldn't follow Tom to town. Link belonged to the country. Maybe Ben could find some nook for him on Avondale. What would Lillybelle do? She was now able to take her ease in her bed piled with quilts, within her walls pasted with old newspapers. Mary had sent Louise a New Orleans paper with a tinted section of Carnival floats. Lillybelle had seized on it with delight, and loved to watch the firelight play on the wall bright with Mardi gras fantasy. Lillybelle would never stay in her cabin if the Yankee took over. And Jessie's school—the upheaval, if it came, would affect more than Tom and Alan and Amanda and herself. Louise was glad she had written to Ellen. Her pride mustn't be allowed to stand in the way of any help she could get. Too many people were involved. She knew Tom and Alan were thinking of those others as well as of themselves. Link and Lillybelle and Cornelius, and all the ones who could not or would not put themselves under the Yankee's sway, would look to Tom and Alan to settle their problems, and Tom and Alan would accept the responsibility of their loyalty.

Every question Louise could ask would lead inevitably back to the main problem. Even the ferns on the gallery were part of it. If she moved, Amanda would have to find a place for them. After this visit Louise knew she might never be in this room again. Its starkness had repelled her the first time she had come here, but time and use and the patient contrivance of the people who had lived in it had given it a homely comfort. Louise had made Cornelius build the shelves to hold the books she had brought from Natchez. Alan's old leather armchair had a freshly covered cushion in it, and Amanda had made the red and white curtains for the windows, and the windows framed Indigo's deep-blue twilight. The dusk Tom loved would not seem the same to him anywhere else. He liked to watch it steal across the cupped flats of Indigo's fields and blur the feathery outlines of his own woods. Louise wanted to share the hope she felt, but she dared not. She made herself talk about Natchez, and Wayne, and Jim and Maggie.

Maggie had written that little James had had a bad attack of stomach trouble. It made her anxious, and no wonder, since numbers of children died of "summer complaint." But James was all right now.

288

"Maggie wanted to set the world on fire," Tom said, "and now she's living buried in a swamp."

"She makes the best of it," Amanda said.

"All the same, she's trapped down there."

Jim and Maggie couldn't leave Elsinore, as they had no other place to go. Even if they had a chance to go somewhere else, they wouldn't leave Mr. Ferris alone. He would not get better, only worse. If Maggie and Jim were trapped, so were most people. Wayne and Dolly were trapped, Louise herself was, and Tom. Yet Tom, more than any of them, seemed able to hold on to an inner freedom, to possess his own soul. Perhaps he loved his freedom too well and would hold on to it too long, and might end by being lonely. Louise wondered if he would have been better off if he had married Maggie. No, he was too elusive for her, and she too strenuous for him. And Dolly, no, she was a luxury object. Or was she? She had loved Tom, and might have been a consolation to him now. He wouldn't think so! Outside, the dusk had turned to night, and the squares of the windows were black. Across the creek, the Yankee waited, but he wouldn't get Indigo.

Newspapers and letters came three times a week. The postman rode out in a jumper and delivered it at strategic points, mostly at little crossroad stores where he also picked up letters and packages to be mailed. There was no store near Indigo, and the mail was not brought to the house, but left at a cabin on the road to Natchez. During this visit, Louise didn't wait for Cornelius to go for the mail in his poking way. She herself left the house, much too early for the postman, but she was impatient, and walked through the trees to Indigo's gate and down the road to the cabin.

Trees arched over the road, and shadows splashed its dusty windings. At last the white dust began to whirl far away, and the postman's jumper came wheeling along. Louise went out to meet him. There was nothing for her. She watched him out of sight then turned back to Indigo, telling herself she had asked for the impossible, and wishing she had cabled Ellen. But a cable was too short and stark for the demand she was making. It was much too soon to hear from Ellen. She envied Tom his feverish activity, this idle waiting for news was more than she could bear.

Goldenrod was beginning to open on either side of the road's high banks. In a field, cornstalks were tattered brown ribbons, and farther back there was a stand of cotton, and the cotton was fuzzing out of the bolls. The stalks were a darker brown than the corn's burnt umber, and everything was held in a trance of honey-colored sunlight.

Louise thought how seldom nature's moods coincided with her own. The country around here could be and often was violent, but the romantic novelists she had loved as a girl had suitably provided thunderclaps for the mental tumult of their characters, and this scene only offered her its dreamy calm to put against her wild impatience.

Useless, useless as she felt it was, Louise went for the mail whenever the postman was due. On a Monday morning, the postman put a cablegram in her hands. "Brought it out," he said cheerfully. "Might be important." Only the postman's saying it was there and real, made it less impossible. She opened it. Ellen said the money was waiting for her in a New Orleans bank.

There was a letter from Mary's husband Alexander, too. "When Mary and I learned the details of your problem, Mary wrote to Ellen, who immediately made all the arrangements to let you have what you needed——" There was more but Louise couldn't read it then and there. At first she couldn't move, and a jaybird hopped from a branch and took a dust bath in the road near her feet, watching her with his bright black eyes. All of a sudden she moved, and the jaybird, with a wild jeer and a whirl of disordered feathers, flew off. She could move and she could run. Running without stopping, she reached the house hot and breathless.

"Amanda——" she gasped, "Call Tom, call Alan."

Louise saw Amanda's mouth open in a round "o" of surprise, and when Amanda kept asking, "What's the matter? What's the matter?" Louise handed her the cable.

Amanda read it and reread it, muttering over it.

"Oh, Lou, you did manage to fix things!"

"Well, not completely——"

"Let's go find Tom and Alan, and tell them"—Amanda hesitated— "Or are you able?"

"I'm able, I feel years younger." They trudged out to find the others. Louise couldn't run any more, as she talked to Amanda and explained it all to her, her first exhilaration faded. "But still, it's better, much better. Tom and Alan are going to have all kinds of scruples, but make Alan take the money."

"Don't worry, I will."

Following the vague directions of first one cotton picker then another, they found Alan. Then Tom, seeing the three of them grouped together, came riding over to read the cable and the letter, and exclaim and ponder.

"Do get in the shade, Mother," Tom ordered, and they found the sparse shadow of a prickly little plum tree.

"The thought of Ellen did cross my mind," Tom said, "but I didn't dare ask her for that much. How did you bring yourself to do it?"

"How'll we ever pay her back?" Alan said as Louise had known he would. "But if the worst comes to the worst, Ellen can have Indigo. It's at least worth the mortgage."

"I'd rather she'd have it, than the Yankee," Tom smiled. "Mother, you must have hated the Yankee a lot to do this."

"You're an idiot, Tom," Amanda said. "She didn't do it for that. She wanted you to be happy."

They went back to the house, and Tom set out for town to make arrangements with the bank. Louise flung herself down on the old sofa, listening to Amanda and Alan talking. She felt dry and parched from rushing about in the heat and glare. The room, the voices, and her thoughts blurred, and she fell asleep. Dreams came, but not of her own people. Instead she dreamed she was in the woods where Francy's grave was, and there were white roses on it, and Francy came walking through the trees and pointed to the grave and said, "This is mine."

When Louise woke up the room was dark and no one was in it except herself. Amanda had put a pillow under her head. No one was with her, but the sharp image of her dream was still clear to her. She hadn't thought of the dead child for years, or so vaguely it was hardly a thought. The dream had reproached her as if the little girl had wanted to say, "You promised to think of me." She saw the little face, pinched and wasted, and the pang she had felt the moment when she had known the child was going to die came back to touch her heart again.

Tom came back the next afternoon, late. The others were waiting for him. When the jumper came through the trees, they saw Tom was not alone. Wayne was with him. Louise stood up to watch them come. "Is anything wrong in town?" Louise asked. Medora might have been taken ill, or the house might have burned down, but, no, Wayne looked triumphant. His face was grave but there was something brilliant about it.

Tom said, "Wayne has something important to tell you."

Wayne spoke to them all but he looked at Louise.

"Jasper is dead."

Louise knew she must have lived too long on her nerves. She felt nothing at all, only blankness.

Wayne stepped up to her and took her arm and gave her warmth again. "Here, you'd better sit down." He led her to a chair. Tom, solicitous, said, "Mother, do you feel faint?"

"Nonsense, of course not." She drank the wine he brought her. "It's a little too sweet this year, Amanda." She felt she might ramble on forever, saying nothing that mattered, but Alan was asking Wayne how he knew about Jasper.

"I've been trying to find out what had happened to him for a long time."

The others were quiet while he told them what he had learned. He had taken all the names and dates Louise and Alan and Medora had given him, and all scraps of information, and had written to each name Jasper had ever mentioned. "Some of the people were dead, some were gone from the addresses I knew, and some, who answered, couldn't tell me anything." The last address, the New Orleans one, proved the most fruitful. Wayne had written to Mary's husband Alexander, who had gone to the house in New Orleans where Jasper had stayed before he had disappeared forever. The old gentleman still living there remembered Jasper. Better still, recently he had heard from one of the members of that Southern family who had gone to Brazil. That family—the Danvers—had been friends of Jasper's. Alexander had telegraphed at once to John Danvers, and John Danvers had searched for and found the letters

Jasper had written to his father. In them, more recent than anything Jasper had written to his own family, was the final clue. After all kinds of wanderings, Jasper had settled on a sugar plantation in Cuba. There he had died of yellow fever five years ago.

"The last stretch of waiting was the worst. But finally I heard from the plantation owner, and he sent me proof of Jasper's death."

"You didn't tell me how much you were learning," Louise said.

"I wanted to, but didn't want to raise any false hopes."

"Now I know why Alexander and Mary knew so much I didn't tell them."

"Yes, through me. I told Medora all this today."

"Did it upset her?" Alan's voice was low and hesitant. Louise knew he was thinking of Jasper and Medora as they once had been.

"No, she was perfectly calm."

There had been a time when the news of Jasper's death would have plunged her into despair. Her calm now seemed to Louise one of the saddest things about all the old tangle.

"Medora only said she wished she had known long ago and could have spared you all so much worry. She's giving you enough to pay the mortgage."

"Not a gift," Alan said. "A loan."

Wayne smiled, "The papers can be drawn up any way you please. It won't matter in the long run."

Medora could own Indigo outright and it would be a nominal thing. Not long ago she had said to Louise, "Everything will be yours when I die."

"Stop talking about dying," Louise had scolded her, "you sound just like ole Mrs. Corwin."

"Say it'll be Tom's, then, when we're both dead."

Louise gave a long sigh. "It's much better than borrowing from Ellen."

"You'd always be worried about how you were going to pay her back. And I don't blame you for refusing Medora's little money when it was all she had. But Jasper's share is a lot. Take some of it and be thankful."

"I am. We are."

Tom hadn't spoken. He got up, "I'm going to ring the plantation bell, and tell them all." He went out and the others followed. It was strange to hear the clang of the bell at this hour. It was dusk and the pickers had all gone home. The bell brought them out, in ones and twos and threes, their lanterns swaying like large fireflies. When they had all gathered, Tom made them a short speech. He told them he knew they had wondered about the place changing ownership, and knew some of them hadn't liked the idea. Now everything was settled. Indigo would belong to Mr. Alan and Miss Lou. When he had finished there were loud murmurs and shouts of thanksgiving. Link's white teeth gleamed, but Jessie didn't smile. There were tears in her eyes and her lips trembled. "After the crop's in, you can fix your school the way you want," Louise told her. "I'll help you."

Going back to the house, Louise found Lillybelle walking beside her. "Ah knowed you'd fix hit, Miss Lou."

"I didn't. It was something else." In a day or so she would tell Lillybelle all about it, but not now.

"Lilly, do you remember Mr. Jasper?"

"Yes'm." She gave a wheezy sigh and whispered, "Lawd!" Even to each other, Louise and Lillybelle would never mention the secret they both shared. Jasper hadn't really disappeared. From now on his ghost would always haunt Indigo, vague and chilly. A horse and rider glimpsed through the trees in the dusk, or flitting past the windows in a winter rain. But he had a right to be here.

After supper, Alan wrote a cable for Ellen. Wayne would take it to town. Then they spread papers on the table and began to discuss business matters. Amanda, calm and happy again, was prodding at the roots of a big fern with an old tin fork. Louise had seen how Amanda had tried to seem cheerful through all the suspense but had lost interest in the minor details connected with the house and garden. Revived by good news, she was picking up the little threads, reweaving all the fabric of her household in that meticulous way she enjoyed.

Louise listened to the men while she wrote a long letter to Ellen, then she drew her shawl around her and went on the gallery. She heard Tom say he had to go talk to Link, and watched him go off. He didn't even take a lantern with him. Tom could see in the dark, like a cat or an owl, but this was not a dark night, not after you were in it. There was no moon, but the sky had a silvery sheen. Tom would go talk to Link, and then would go on, farther. No four walls could hold Tom tonight. He would wander, savoring the feel of the dry, crumbly earth, and sniffing the dew-touched scents around him. As well as if she were with him, Louise could map his way. He would go to the woods and into the woods. Maybe he would find his way to the clearing where the Yankee had once harangued the hands. Then he would wander on, even to the river's edge, to catch the voice of the south wind in the cottonwoods and watch the luminous arch of the sky and the pale glimmer of the sand bar and the smoke-dark silence of the water. He would feel, as anyone who knew it well did feel, the force and wildness underlying the gentleness of this night. Tom's eyes would follow the long, rounded sweep of the Mississippi's southward curve, and Indigo Bend, and beyond, and he would feel he owned it all, and could give himself up to being owned by it.

There was a little chill springing beneath the night's warmth. Tom, if he went to the river bank, would see Arcturus and the Scorpion dip below the southern horizon. Here, facing the southeast, if she stayed out long enough, Louise could see Aldebaran and Orion swing over the trees. It always made her a little sad now when she first saw their familiar glitter. They were certain heralds of winter, and of another year's ending. But this year, she might feel as she had once, not a year ending, but one beginning.

A ray of lantern light was glinting on the trees and on the ground. One of the hands coming to the house, or maybe even Ben Rand, if he had heard the good news. The hands communicated any tidings to each other through distances as effectively as their ancestors in Africa had done with drumbeats. The lantern was near and she saw it was a man on a horse. When he reached the clearing he held up the lantern. It was Jim. The light cut his face out of the dark with a particular drama. His blond hair glittered, his deep-set eyes gleamed, and his sun-browned skin was suffused with a flush of color. All of his features had a defined clarity. That glimpse told Louise something had happened and she ran to meet him. He swung himself out of the saddle and whispered, "Don't say anything, Miss Lou."

"Is anything wrong?"

"James and Maggie are all right. It's——" He glanced at the open, lit window. "Can we talk here?" He put out the lantern, and for a minute he faded out of her sight, until his face emerged again, colorless in the dark, yet still impressing her with its definition.

"What's the matter, Jim?"

"I don't want to see anybody but you, just now. I went to see my father. To make one more try——"

"It's all settled, Jim. We don't have to worry——"

He was so deep in his own tumult he didn't grasp her meaning.

"I guess it is—settled. I went there, I saw him, and when he wouldn't listen, I lost my head. No, it wasn't that. I didn't. I've wanted to since I was three years old, so it happened. I hit him and knocked him down."

"Oh, Jim, you——"

"Don't tell me I was wrong, Miss Lou. I don't feel wrong." He looked out at the dark, still deep in the scene. Louise could paint it for herself, and even see the room. Was it just the same as it had been years ago? Jim told her, sometimes pausing for breath. Sometimes his words rushed along, jumbled together. He had tried to reason with his father about the mortgage. His father was just getting up from the supper table. He'd had a bottle of whiskey on the table and he had taken a good pull out of the bottle. "Nothing I said could budge him, but this time he got worse than usual, and started swearing at me, and at Maggie too. I told him to shut up, and he threw the bottle at me. All right, I told him. You've had your chance. Now I'll take what I want. So I hit him."

"Where was your mother?"

"Right there. She didn't scream, or burst out crying. When he crashed down, and dragged a dish and a plate off the table, and they crashed too, she just looked at him. She said he had it coming to him."

"Jim——" Louise knew she would have to explain how everything was settled, and how he could have spared himself. The scene rose before her, thick with the heat of smudgy lamp light, and the reek of whiskey and greasy food, and the big man falling, shaking the whole room, shaking the whole nature of things for its occupants. And Della, watching. At the beginning of the quarrel she must have been quivering with terror. Then after the man had fallen, she must have felt a sudden calm, even satisfaction.

"And Persia—she came running, and when she saw him there, she let out a screech. Then she began to laugh."

"Jim, I must tell you——" Louise told him about the proof of Jasper's death, and how it had changed everything. He listened quietly, his face a blur except for his eyes. She could not see their color, only shadowness.

He drew a long breath. "Miss Lou, you don't have to pay anything at all. I'm glad he acted like he did. Because I would have knocked him down anyway. I knew he kept the mortgage in the safe. I knew he always kept the key on him. I found it. I almost forgot how to work the safe, then I remembered. It was there, the mortgage I mean. I found it. I burnt it up. He watched me."

Louise thought of the Yankee in his total defeat. She felt no particular exultation. It had all gone on too long. "I admire your courage, Jim. But in a way I feel guilty."

"You needn't, Miss Lou. I wanted you and Mr. Alan and Tom to have a little peace and quiet about the place. But what I did, I would have done anyway, sooner or later. When I hauled off and hit him, I felt like—well, like a bolt of lightning had hit me. A kind of sizzling streak going through me. Like it wasn't me doing it. Yet it was more me than anything I ever did."

The accumulated anger had been building up ever since his early childhood. "I'm sorry. Not for hitting him. For everything. For the kind of life my mother's had——"

"What about her, Jim? After this?"

"It'll be better for her. It's got to be. Or—well, he knows I can and will look out for her."

Jim was right. The Yankee respected force.

"None of it need have been like it is. Now it's too late."

She invited him to spend the night, but he said he'd rather get back. He relit the lantern, and the light flared on his face, his features clear-cut and hard, his eyes a jeweled blue.

"Thank you, Jim, for caring about what happened to us."

He smiled at her, and his face softened, and looked young again, and his eyes had the appeal that had haunted her when he had been a child. "Good night, Miss Lou."

He rode off and the trees swallowed him up. All night he would ride, and Maggie would be waiting for him. Louise evaluated her sense of shock at what he had done. It came from her training and environment. She had been taught there was something sacred in the relationship between father and son, and perhaps little James would learn it too. It would have been easy to have taught it to Jim, but too long ago any sacredness had been torn away in brutality. In his dealings with his father, Jim had reverted to a simple tribal code, a natural one, since you saw it in animals, how the young, grown to strength, fight it out with the old leader and decide the long contest by force. The Yankee could endure the loss of Indigo. This other defeat would eat into his soul. It was, in its way, a tragedy, since it needn't have happened to him.

The next morning, Wayne rode over to Avondale, and Tom was out in the fields. Louise had slept late, and she went to find Alan, to tell him about Jim. Alan was at his desk. From the kitchen came sounds of stirring.

Amanda was making a cake, in spite of the scarcity of eggs. All at once the sound made Louise remember tastes and tangs she had forgotten for years, like the deliciousness of raw dough on the cake spoon, or the vapid pulp of snake strawberries, delightful because forbidden, and she found herself yearning for a piece of sugar cane to chew.

Louise and Alan discussed Jim's encounter with his father. "But I'll pay the man anyway," Alan said, "and be quit of him."

"I was thinking, Alan, of the night you came back from Indigo and told me you were going to fight for it." He had survived, and somehow she wondered how he had survived. He was younger than she but he looked older.

"I can hardly take it in, Lou, what it's like to be free."

She went to him and put her hand on his shoulder. His hand closed over hers, and his face wore a look she hadn't seen for years but had not forgotten. For a minute he was her young brother, a boy not yet sixteen, handsome and full of pride, showing himself in his new uniform. Whole and sound, unmarred by the battle waiting for him or the long struggles afterward.

When the shadows from the woods began to move across the fields, Louise left the house. Her destination was the little church on the knoll. No one would be in it at this hour, but the door was never locked, and she wanted to go there and say her thankful prayers. She skirted a cotton field picked clean, and rows of empty cornstalks. First the Indians had planted corn, then the first white people to come here had planted indigo. It had dark leaves, she had read, and a bright red berry. Then all the planters had turned to cotton. It no longer made them rich, but that didn't mean it never would again. They had been right to battle for Indigo all these years, its level acres held the soil, and its goodness would always hold some promise.

In the shade of the woods, the well-trodden path led to the church. She met no one. The hands were proud of their church. They had built it themselves, adding the steeple and the bits of glass for the windows. They had no glass windows in their own cabins, but like the people of the Middle Ages, they gave their best to the church.

Louise climbed the little knoll. Pine branches gave a pleasant scent, and pine cones made her think of Christmas and how she gathered baskets of pine cones to crackle on the fire. This year she would try to give Indigo's people the finest Christmas they had ever had. She went in the church, and by the flicker of the sun seeping in she read the Bible she had brought with her. She knew she didn't hate the Yankee any more, and that gave her freedom too. In the quiet she could hear the echo of the old spirituals echoing around her.

When she came out, she saw Wayne leaning against a tree trunk waiting for her. "I came to escort you home. Dark comes early these days."

As they walked along together she thought about the last time they had both followed this path. Her heart had been hot and heavy with her bitter jealousy. She had conquered it, and if she had not conquered her feelings for Wayne, she had controlled, tempered, and mellowed them.

He asked if she had been singing a "Te Deum" for victory.

"In a way, I suppose I was. I have a feeling of trumpets and banners."

"The way we felt after that election."

"Exactly. And I hadn't felt it since, until now. It won't last——"

"Peaks never do."

"No, there'll be other troubles and problems. But right now I intend to enjoy myself."

She asked him to take a letter to Medora. "I'll be going back in a few days to really thank her."

"It's good for her, being able to do this. She feels a sense of achievement."

Louise agreed. She paused as a squirrel, a nut in his mouth, streaked down a tree trunk and sat up in the path to watch, then flickered away.

"On a day like this," Wayne said, "I feel the attraction of Indigo. Tom's ears stay tuned to its ways and rhythms. It's too much out of the world for me."

"The world comes creeping in."

"Yes, and makes you a victim. Of course I was one this summer, but that was my own fault."

"How are you getting on now?"

"Better."

"No one's bought your house."

"Maybe after Christmas we can move back in it. There's no security in my business, but I feel I have more of a finger on the world's pulse than I would out here." He smiled at her. "Maybe someday I'll corner the cotton market."

"Maybe you will. The Winsloes get money."

"It comes to them. Look at Medora. Lucky with money. Unlucky with love." Louise suspected he might be thinking of himself too. "Jasper kept running away. And never really could, because he was running away from himself."

Then death had come and he couldn't run away any more. Maybe he was relieved to be caught. "The door of Death I open found——"

Wayne hesitated. "I've always felt there was some sort of secret between them—Medora and Jasper."

Louise didn't speak, and he added, "Oh, I don't want to know it."

Louise didn't think he could possibly suspect, he simply sensed there was more than was said or known. She knew that secret but there was another she wanted to know. Wayne had never told her the real truth about why he had been so rash. He had not caught some frenzy, he hadn't let a vision of great wealth sweep him away. There was always the steadiness of a fixed purpose behind the seeming wildness of his ideas and decisions. Why had he taken such a chance?

Suddenly, strolling along this path with him, she knew. He had wanted money so he could give it to her to pay the mortgage. He had run that risk, staked his hard-won security because he cared so much for her happiness and her peace of mind. He had put her above everything else. He cared more about her than anyone or anything. The shock of her knowledge, the rush of feelings it brought, made Louise weak. She stumbled and caught at a branch. He drew her arm within his as he had that New Year's night. "Careful."

Careful, she didn't dare say a word! That other time, in her anger, she had flashed out at him. Now, with the warmth of his touch and her own sureness, she could only keep silent. It was wrong, wrong, and yet—she cherished her sureness. She couldn't trust herself now, but someday she would tell him—not that she knew he cared—never that, but some time, far from now, she would tell him she knew what he had done for her. He had lost it cheerfully, and kept on trying to find some other way to help her. That's what convinced her beyond any doubt, his cheerfulness, his air of hope. He had allowed himself no regrets, because he had done it for her, just as she would have had no regrets for whatever she had risked for him.

Chapter Eighteen

LOUISE was packing, getting ready to take the boat back to Natchez when she heard Lillybelle calling her with that extra note in her voice always indicating excitement or alarm, usually both. Lilly was trundling from her cabin to the kitchen as fast as her bulk would allow, with a small black boy behind her, taking refuge in her voluminous shadow.

"Miss Lou," Lillybelle panted, "dis chile say Mr. Sanders done been took. He brung word from Miss Della."

"Took?" Louise reached for the folded scrap of paper grubby from the child's hand. "Is he dead?"

"No'm, doan reckon."

Louise suppressed a feeling of disappointment. "Took" could mean anything from the violence the Yankee sometimes showed when he was coming out of a spell of heavy drinking, to a minor illness, to a serious one. Della was easily alarmed. Louise read the note. It was only a few lines. In a wavering and uneven scrawl Della said her husband had fallen on the floor unconscious, and she had sent for the doctor. It sounded like a stroke. Louise was wondering what she ought to do when Amanda came back from the chicken yard, a basket of eggs in her hand. Louise showed her the note.

"Do you want me to get hold of Tom or Alan and ask them what to do? Do you think either of them ought to go over there?"

"Not yet, do you think? It may be nothing much. Then their being there would be awkward."

"It'll be a while before they can locate Jack," Amanda said, "and get him over there. Father's likely to be at home. If it's bad, he'll go."

"I'd better go look after Della," Louise said, "in case it is serious."

"Maybe. It's funny, Lou, with all that's happened, for you to be the one to have to go——"

"I know, but that's the way it seems to work out. If I'm not back when Tom comes to take me to the boat, tell him."

She was sorry for Della, always alone except for Persia. The more capable hands had found out the truth about the Yankee's dealing with them, and whenever they could, had deserted him for other plantations. He preferred the simple and stupid ones he could cajole and deceive. In an emergency, he had no reliable help near at hand. No one like Wash had been to Mr. Bijah, or Link was to Tom.

Louise started along the familiar way with the silent child. She had put on her good dress, a dark silk, for the boat ride, and holding it up as well as she could from the dust and rough grass, she wished she had taken time to change it before she had set out. She bitterly resented any harm's coming to it, and for the Yankee's sake! Of course it wasn't for him. It was for Della. Really, for herself, as it had been that other time.

This time she wouldn't have to take up her hate again. The ugly house was there ahead of her. She could go into it and come out of it, free. Persia poked her head out of the door. "Miss Lou, Ahse glad ter see you."

"What's the matter with Mr. Sanders?"

"Usses doan rightly know."

Della came into view behind Persia, her face flushed when she saw Louise, then broke into tremors of lips and eyelids. "You were good to come."

She told Louise what had happened. The Yankee had come in from the fields and had asked for coffee, then whiskey. He had been sitting at the table and had fallen on the floor unconscious and very red in the face. Della and Persia, with the help of one of the hands, had managed to get him in bed. He was still unconscious, and Louise could hear his heavy breathing all through the house. She went to the door of the room where he was lying then came away.

"You think he's bad off?" Della pleated at the edges of her apron.

"The doctor'll have to say."

"What do I do for him?"

"I don't know. Maybe there's nothing we can do." Della sat down. "I—sent for Jim."

"Remember it'll be a long time before he gets here. It's far away."

Della pleated her apron faster than ever. "He came—Jim did. The other day. He and his pa——"

"I know. He came and told me."

"It was about your place."

"That's all settled. It needn't worry us any more."

Della dropped her hands. "If I'd of had my say-so, it wouldn't of happened like it did."

"We know that. But about Jim and his father. It wasn't only our place, he did what he did on your account."

Della's face brightened. "I reckon it was, at that."

Louise waited until the doctor came, not Dr. Jack but his father, and when she saw Dr. Rand getting out of his battered surrey, his bag in his hand, memory took her back to that other time when she had waited for him, and again she thought of that dead child Francy.

Dr. Rand examined the sick man and came out to where Della and Persia and Louise were waiting. It was a stroke, a bad one. He might recover consciousness, he might not. He might die, he might live. Nobody could tell.

Louise left the house and found Tom waiting for her on the other side of the creek, and she told him what had happened.

"Things have taken a queer turn. But thank the Lord, whatever happens to him doesn't have anything to do with us. We don't have to want him to die."

Della, waiting for Jim to come, seemed to cling to Louise, and Louise instead of going on to Natchez, went back the next day to the Yankee's house. The man regained consciousness, but his side was paralyzed and he couldn't speak. Louise was there, sitting outside on the steps, when Jim rode up. She told him about his father's condition.

"Was it—could it have been—anything I did to him?"

"It couldn't possibly. It would have happened if you hadn't been here."

Jim gave a sigh, and his darkened eyes brightened.

"Go in," she said.

He hesitated. "The trouble is, I'm not sorry for what I did. Even now." He bit his dry lips. "Maybe I'd better just see my mother."

"He'll want you. Go in. If you don't, later you'll regret it." Death gave no second chances.

Louise and Jim went in the house together. Della fell on Jim's neck. Louise went close to the bed. The man's eyes were open. She said, "Here's Jim," and left them. When she was out of the room it occurred to her that if the Yankee could still think and feel it would seem to him that she had brought Jim to him. For years she had wanted revenge, and now in this strange, unplanned, inadvertent fashion, she had it. It didn't matter, it had no significance for her.

Della's tears were not for her husband, but because she was glad to have her son back with her. Perhaps she was glad to have a reason to draw him back and hold him to her. Louise went on down the path. At the edge of the creek bank she turned and looked back. The house stood on bare ground and a few of Persia's skinny chickens scratched in the dust. There had never been a garden around it, or curtains in any of the windows, or books, except the ones Louise had given Jim, and there had never been any happiness in the walls. Persia's cabin with its slanting roof and crooked chimney seemed much more of a home. Perhaps Louise's shudder at the ugliness of the house came from association too. She had never seen it except on occasions of crisis, or illness, or death. The fates stood near it. The one who wove the threads, and the one waiting to cut them.

Beyond it, were the ruins of the Winsloe house, more than broken stones. It was a reminder that civilized grace could flower in the wilds. Louise felt that it had affected all of them more than they had realized. Perhaps if it had not been there the Yankee might have adapted himself better to his surroundings. It confronted him in all of his comings and goings, a symbol of the defeated, but telling him of their pride and the riches they had owned, and the power they had used. He had wanted all of that for himself and had tried to seize it, but some essence of it had always escaped him. Now he

305

was finished, and though he would never know why he had failed, he would know he had failed.

Jim too had been moved by that suggestion of sweep and stateliness. As a child, he had scrambled around in the ruins, and once he had told Louise he had "played like" it was all whole with things in all the rooms and fine toys and a big family there with children his size. Jasper had remembered the whole and happy place of his childhood. It had been part of a past he could not forget and couldn't find again, so he had tried to escape. Louise thought of the time when she had first seen Wayne. He had been down by the creek because he had been to spy on the enemy's stronghold, and had seen, too, a glimpse of the Winsloe's former splendor, a phantom of all of his destroyed world. He had not run away. He had stayed. He had hated and defied, and he had planned to rebuild for himself some part of it.

Before, whenever Louise had seen that broken wreck of a house, a pang of melancholy had struck her, but not now. Whatever human beings had planned and made, they could, in some form, make again. Waves of growth crowded through and around the columns. Waves of greenish light washed over them, until they seemed to be rising out of the tremblings of deep water. Their pale lost grandeur had the air of a legend, and legends and visions have a queer life of their own.

Louise went back to Natchez, and one day in October Jim came to see her. When she saw him standing there, she remembered what day it was. "It's the date!" It had burdened her for years. It had taken her sleep and her appetite, and had turned her nerves into thin tingling wires. The date the mortgage was due, and now she had forgotten! "I've relaxed so much," she told Jim, "it had slipped out of my mind."

"That's good. You look a lot better too."

He went with her into the library. "Miss Lou, I guess you know my father is still paralyzed. Jack says he won't get over it. He might last a year, two years. More or less. He had another stroke after you left."

"They wrote me about it."

"So I have to manage everything. You all aren't going to pay a cent. I've already talked to Tom and Mr. Alan and Wayne. As far as I'm concerned, there just isn't any debt. It was never really right, and do you think I'd feel right, or Maggie either?"

"But Jim, you have problems——"

"Plenty. So let's wash this one off the slate. Margaret and I feel we can't walk out on Mr. Ferris, good as he's been to us. He wants to die in his own house, and we feel he has a right to——"

"Yes, I suppose you must stay with him. But what about Heron's Row?" The name the Winsloes had given their plantation was still on the maps, but no one had used the old name as long as the Yankee had been ruling it. Now it was in Jim's hands and Louise could give it back the old name. Jim must have understood, because his eyes began to shine.

"I've hired a good nurse to help Mother. The place can rock along pretty well until planting time. Then I'll have to find an overseer. I hate to leave my mother in that fix but she understands about how I feel about Mr. Ferris."

"Tom and the others will keep an eye on her. If there's an emergency she can get word to them."

Jim smiled. "She always does, doesn't she?"

"There's a—a bond between your mother and me."

"I know. She spoke about it. About her. My sister."

"I don't suppose you remember Francy at all."

"Sometimes I think I do, a little. But maybe I only dreamed about her. I think I used to miss her, or can you miss someone you can't remember?"

"I suppose you feel a blankness where that someone should be." She hesitated, then said, "Jim, your father didn't show it in any way you wanted him to, but he always cared about you."

"I guess he did. I've learned something. How to make things very different with James." At the door he turned. "Miss Lou, when we go back to Heron's Row to live, we'll try to coax the cranes to come back. I like the way they look."

Not all of Jim's and Maggie's problems were solved, and never would be. Louise didn't see them again, either of them, until after Christmas. In spite of falling cotton prices and taxes coming due, everyone said it was the best Christmas Indigo had known since the one after the election, or even better. The great celebration, though, came not for Christmas, but for Louise's birthday, a week after New Year. Indigo, Wayne said, was turned upside down and inside out. Nobody knew how Amanda was going to manage with all the people she had invited, yet they were sure she would manage. She baked hams and chickens and turkeys. Tom shot ducks and quail. Fruit cakes sat soaking in whiskey, and layer cakes rose to new heights. Packages tied with ribbons began to heap up. On the evening before the birthday, Jessie composed and directed the finest pageant of her career, and Louise said she felt like Queen Victoria at her Jubilee. Everybody came for the birthday dinner. Even Carrie had made a special effort to leave home and be on hand. The Rands came, Medora came, and several Corwins, and the Duels, and Cousin Charlotte, and Cousin Sophie. Wayne and Dolly were on hand, and Maggie and Jim, and Della, wearing a new dress, a Christmas present from Jim and Maggie.

"It's nicer than the other one," Della said. "This time I tried to make it like the one you had on when you came over."

So Della, at the bedside of her stricken husband had taken time to notice what Louise had been wearing. Louise whispered that to Wayne, who remarked that the clinging vine doesn't always fondly twine around the fallen log but sometimes pushes tendrils in other directions. Lonely for so long, Della was glad to bask in a sense of being part of a friendly circle, and no longer an alien and an outsider.

At the dinner table, everyone drank toasts to Louise.

"I remember how glad I was to hear you were coming to Indigo," Medora said, "to be company for me. I didn't know how much company! Or that you still would be!"

Maggie told about one of her first encounters with Louise. "Not long after you came back to Natchez. I was yowling because the moths had eaten my doll's eyelashes. You melted her eyelids a little and fixed the most beautiful eyelashes for her out of fringed mohair silk."

"When I first saw Amanda," Louise said, "she came through the woods like Red Riding Hood, with a basket."

Wayne smiled. "That was symbolical. She's been feeding us all

308

ever since." He looked at Louise. "You and I first met down by the creek——"

He didn't know how often she had thought of it since. Sometimes one moment can be like a seed holding the unknown future.

After the festive dinner, most of the guests left. The Rands drove home, and the Natchez people set off. Dolly went with Cousin Sophie and Cousin Charlotte, but Wayne said he was going to spend the night at Avondale, and Jim and Maggie, and Carrie and Medora were staying at Indigo.

Maggie and Louise stood together, watching the sortie of people and vehicles and waving good-by.

"I hadn't noticed what a sad, glumpish-looking day it's been outside."

Louise looked around, and said the sky was just the color of a catfish's stomach, and the trees looked all jumbled together like a child's scrabblings. "We can go inside to the fire." They found themselves alone in the room. Wayne was lingering outside talking to Alan, Tom had taken Carrie on a short tour of the place, Amanda was in the kitchen dispensing largesse in leftovers from the feast, and Jim was taking his mother home.

"I think I've made progress with her," Maggie said.

"I kept an eye on you. You were nice."

"She's perked up."

"Keep on being nice, Margaret. Jim's all she has."

"Grrr! I hope I won't lean on my children like that!"

"You won't, but then you don't have to. You have Jim."

"He's worth what I'll have to pay for him. But I'll pay! You know, Aunt Lou, how I swore up and down I'd never, never live anywhere near those people! And you know what I see looming up!" After poor Mr. Ferris died, Jim would go back and help his mother with the burden of his father, and after his father died, his mother would still have to live with him and with Maggie.

"You'll have to face it, Maggie. And put up with it."

Maggie made a face, and Louise laughed. "Not that way, child. Cheer up, I know how you feel, but you'll have enough money to change the house, rebuild it, and you have enough git up and git to make a different sort of life from the way it has been there. You'll make the best of it."

"I wouldn't dare not to, with your eye on me. It's funny the way you've influenced me, Aunt Lou, though we're so different. I suppose I've always dreamed of some wildly dramatic sort of life, when I'd boldly change things and fix things. Of course you've had a dramatic life, you lived through the war——"

Sometimes Louise could hear the sound of marching feet in the thump of the rain, sometimes, in calm, in stillness, the columns seemed to take form, and faces, smiling as they went away from her. "You may live through a war too."

"Oh, no, we're too civilized."

"I hope and pray you're right. But we were civilized."

"Yes," Maggie meditated, "in a different way. Each one of you seems like just you—and you particularly have that quality of being an individual. People now seem masses. I feel myself like part of a mass of other lumpy, struggling women."

Louise said there was no such thing as a mass. Everybody was at least a little different from everyone else.

"All right, but for the sake of argument I have to group us."

Louise said she didn't like lumps.

"That's what I'm trying to say. You don't seem like part of one. Now Miss Medora is a lady——"

Louise said she insisted on being one too. How surprised, and in spite of her vaunted modernity, shocked, Maggie would be if she ever knew Medora's history. Louise had noticed in the books and tracts Maggie read and believed in, the almost militant purity of the "new" woman. They yearned to make men pure too. To Maggie, Medora was the quintessence of finicky, sheltered, delicate spinsterhood. She scored such a life as useless, but it would never occur to her to guess that there was more than she knew.

"I'm not a lady"—Maggie warmed to her subject—"because I try to be honest. And you aren't exactly one either, Aunt Lou. For all the fine talk about them, ladies get mighty trampled on. Nobody tramples on you. You don't need rights and privileges like the rest of us. You get them anyhow."

Louise smiled. "All this sounds very complicated."

310

"Oh, it's too subtle for me, but I know what I mean. I study and try to learn, because I want to do something with knowledge. Use it. You cultivate your mind for the pleasure it gives you. You gather everything up and make a kind of bouquet."

"Full of thorns and brambles."

Maggie's face, bright in the firelight, sobered. She came and kissed Louise. "That's it. The way you've arranged it, the way you fixed that vase on the mantelpiece." The vase held faded leaves and brilliant berries with spiky stems, yet the whole had vividness, grace and symmetry.

"How I hate my brambles!" Maggie said. "I want to chop 'em out of my way. But I'll manage them, just to show you!"

Medora drifted in and asked them what they were talking about. "I'm offering Aunt Lou a birthday tribute."

"I never saw so many presents," Medora murmured. She came over and touched a fold of Louise's dress. Ellen had sent it, and Mary had sent a thick crimson shawl.

"I was thinking over something, Lou. I—we—have money now. We could go to Europe and visit Ellen, and see sights——"

"That would be wonderful!" Maggie started planning their whole trip until little James woke up and started wailing for her, and she had to go to him.

"Maggie has us well on our way. I'd love to go."

"Next summer, let's. It'd be nice to plan——"

Wayne stood in the door and asked them what they were planning. He listened and encouraged them, yet he was frowning. When Medora had wandered out, Louise asked him why he was scowling. He turned to the window and his face was dimly reflected in the glass pane. "Because you ought to go, and I don't want you to go."

Louise sat tense, listening and waiting. She was as still as if she were painted there, all dark and bright. Streaks of brightness darted from the diamonds in her earrings, and a silvery sheen clung to the folds of her black velvet dress. The rose-point lace at the low neckline suited the creamy glow of her skin, and her eyes were like dark velvet too, soft and deep, and the firelight accented the red glow of her shawl.

Wayne turned towards her. "I was a fool, Louise."

She could not speak, then she whispered, "No, it was natural."

"Maybe, but not right. Not right for her either, poor girl. It was Tom she wanted."

"But you chose, and she chose. It's done."

He flung a log on the fire, and the flames crackled up, wild and high, chasing the shadows, enveloping them in the blaze.

"If I could provide well for her, and for Dotty, she would let me go, be glad to——"

Louise shielded her face from the fire and from him. "Don't think about it, don't talk about it. You're used to getting your way, this time you can't."

"But this time, this most important of all times. If Dolly cared, it would be entirely different. She doesn't. A divorce isn't impossible—and we——"

"She cares in a way. And there's Dotty. You've never shirked your responsibilities, Wayne, and you won't this time either. You can't fling aside your greatest ones."

He gave a groan. "I was afraid you'd say this. I wanted to talk to you before, when we were walking back from the little church——"

"I know what you did for us." She told him she had guessed the risk he had run for her sake.

He smiled. "I'd do anything for you."

"Even if we were free," she said gently, "there would still be the difference in our ages."

"That! It doesn't matter a picayune!"

It might not now, as she was. She had the softness of an autumnal bloom, a revivified beauty, more beauty than she had known as a girl, but different. Then her charm had been growing to this zenith, but this was the zenith. It would cling, for a while, shine out at moments like this when she was happy and excited in a blend of flesh and spirit, each lending grace to the other. But the years were there and would show themselves. Let the sight of her face and figure, that aura of elegance, please him now. A time would come when he wouldn't look at her with wild eagerness and love. Not this sort of love.

"It's not the real heart of the matter, Wayne. You aren't free."

"You mean we must go on and on as we are," he sighed. "Louise, remember the night of that—dratted picnic? We were all arguing, and you said if the love story didn't come out right the rest didn't matter?"

"I didn't say exactly that."

"You condemn us to having our lives crisscrossed."

"Your way would only make more tangles. Another thing, you mustn't come to see me so much——"

"Don't say that——"

"Come sometimes. Bring Dolly, or Dotty. But not the way you've been coming." She managed to smile a little. "In another ten years, if you still want to, you can come every day again."

"When we're both old and safe!" His shadow was black on the wall, and his face, in the glow of the fire's leap, startled her with its passion and vehemence. "You throw away what we could have now."

"I don't throw anything away, that's ours. You have to do the best you can with Dolly, and for her and the child. You have to think of Dotty above everything."

"I do, but——"

This was not the only thing, as he would find out. He would find interest in his work, his house, in Dotty, in the wide world. But at this moment let him think his love, if not the only thing, was at least the most important thing.

"What I feel for you, Wayne, matters to me. I'm glad you told me. It's something we know, but nobody else must ever suspect."

"You mean we must each go on, in our ways. Apart——"

"We won't be entirely apart. This is something to hold to——"

"Always." He came over and kissed her. "Happy birthday." He left the room and a few minutes later she heard him galloping off on his way to Avondale.

She left her chair and went to the window. He was out of sight, but she listened until she could no longer hear even the echo of hoofbeats.

Alan came in the room and stood beside her at the window. "Have you enjoyed yourself, Lou?"

"It's been a glorious birthday." But the best gift of all, the one

313

she wanted most, was not hers to take. She drew Alan's hand in hers, thinking of the soft, plump little paw she had taken in her own to steady her baby brother's first steps. It had been a long time ago and everything had changed except the feeling they had for each other. That had grown and flourished and lasted.

"I used to think, when I was a girl, that if I ever reached this advanced and doddering age, I'd be too old to have any interests at all. But I'm not doddery and I do have interests, and I don't feel old." There had been times when the sorrows she had felt and the meagerness she had foreseen for herself and for Tom and Alan had made her bitterly rebellious. Surveying the fabric of her life up to now, she saw it blended together, not sad and not meager. It was like that patchwork quilt she had been making out of bits of silk and velvet stitched together until it made a pattern of dark and bright. Amanda must have packed it away somewhere. Louise thought she would find it and take it with her and finish it someday.

There had been no sunset color to this pallid day, only a dull decline into twilight, but now, at dusk, later than dusk, the sky became fused with rose. In a few minutes the dark would blot it out, but it gave its promise for tomorrow.